David Beveridge

Between the Ochils and Forth

A Description, Topographical and historical, of the country between Stirling bridge

and Aberdour

David Beveridge

Between the Ochils and Forth
A Description, Topographical and historical, of the country between Stirling bridge and Aberdour

ISBN/EAN: 9783337227968

Printed in Europe, USA, Canada, Australia, Japan

Cover: Foto ©Andreas Hilbeck / pixelio.de

More available books at **www.hansebooks.com**

Between the Ochils and Forth

A DESCRIPTION, TOPOGRAPHICAL AND HISTORICAL,

OF THE

COUNTRY BETWEEN STIRLING BRIDGE
AND ABERDOUR

BY

DAVID BEVERIDGE

AUTHOR OF
'CULROSS AND TULLIALLAN'

WITH A MAP

WILLIAM BLACKWOOD AND SONS
EDINBURGH AND LONDON
MDCCCLXXXVIII

PREFACE.

IN the History of Culross and Tulliallan the author endeavoured to present a monograph of two Scottish parishes occupying a somewhat secluded situation on the northern shore of the Firth of Forth. He also sought to exhibit a picture of the domestic life of a bygone day, as elucidated from the kirk-session records of the two parishes, and the minutes of town council of the ancient burgh of Culross. The present undertaking may be characterised as having to a considerable extent a similar object in view, though the illustration of the theme by extracts from the municipal and ecclesiastical archives has not been attempted. A much wider field, however, is included, and at the same time a minute and careful description has been furnished as far as possible of every locality and event of interest belonging to the district under notice. It is a region which, though neither inaccessible nor remote, is still comparatively unknown to, and unvisited by, the majority of Scottish tourists. Yet it is connected with some of the most important events in Scottish history, and as regards natural beauty, it will in many places vie in richness with the finest specimens of English rural scenery.

Whilst the work in question aims rather at a picturesque and historical delineation of that portion of the upper shores of the Forth lying between Stirling Bridge and Aberdour, than at the formal and business-like character of a guide-book, it is nevertheless hoped that in the latter capacity it may not be found wanting in attraction or devoid of practical utility. The distances between the different places have all been set down with special care, as ascertained both by personal investigation and a careful comparison with the maps of the Ordnance Survey. The line and direction also of the various public roads, as well as the principal inns in the different towns and villages, have all been indicated. The author has trodden himself almost every foot of the district, with the most of which he has been familiar from childhood, and he has, moreover, quite recently made a pilgrimage through and investigated the particular localities with great care and minuteness. He would thus fain hope that the completed work, the outcome in great measure of these wanderings, may prove interesting and useful both to travellers and general readers.

Of late years locomotion by means of bicycles and tricycles has come greatly into vogue, and one of the results has been that the old coach-roads, long deserted, have again been largely utilised. For travellers on such vehicles it is also hoped that this work may be found to contain some useful information and directions both as to the line of route and the objects of interest by the way.

Rosehill, Torryburn,
    May 1888.

CONTENTS.

III.

FROM INVERKEITHING TO CROSSGATES, COWDENBEATH, AND LOCHGELLY.

IV.

FROM COWDENBEATH TO BLAIRADAM AND CLEISH.

V.

KINROSS AND LOCHLEVEN.

VI.

ROUND LOCH LEVEN.

VII.

FROM KINROSS TO GLEN FARG.

BETWEEN DUNFERMLINE AND ALLOA.

I.

THE CITY OF DUNFERMLINE.

II.

FROM DUNFERMLINE TO TORRYBURN.

III.

FROM TORRYBURN TO CULROSS AND KINCARDINE.

IV.

FROM KINCARDINE TO CLACKMANNAN AND ALLOA.

V.

ANOTHER WAY FROM DUNFERMLINE TO ALLOA.

VI.

OTHER EXCURSIONS FROM DUNFERMLINE.

THE VALE OF THE DEVON.

I.

FROM LOGIE CHURCH TO ALVA AND TILLICOULTRY.

II.

FROM TILLICOULTRY TO DOLLAR AND YETTS OF MUCKHART.

III.

GLEN DEVON, CROOK OF DEVON, AND RUMBLING BRIDGE.

IV.

ALDIE CASTLE AND SOUTH FOSSOWAY.

V.

FROM THE CAULDRON LINN TO THE FORTH.

CONCLUSION.

BETWEEN THE OCHILS
AND FORTH.

INTRODUCTORY.

General view of the district—Its early history and inhabitants.

IN the ancient nomenclature of Scotland, among districts whose limits may have been perfectly well understood in their day, but are now extremely hazy and undefined, the territory of Fothrik, Fothriff, or Fothreve is frequently mentioned. Thus David I. endows the Abbey of Dunfermline with a tenth part of all the gold which may accrue to the royal treasury from the districts of Fife and Fothrif; the deanery of Fothrik, in the diocese of St Andrews, is referred to; and Fothrik or Fatrig Moor is spoken of as a locality somewhere in the western region of Fife, and extending from Dunfermline to Alloa. The title seems distinct from, at least not convertible with, that of Fortrenn, which adjoined it on the west and north, and denoted a tract of country, afterwards comprised in the districts of Menteith and Strathearn, now belonging chiefly to the southern division of Perthshire, and extending from Callander along the north side of the Ochils to the mouth of the Tay.

Though it is thus not possible to lay down with precision the outlines of the ancient Fothreve, there is a general consensus of opinion as to the territory which it actually comprised. This may be stated generally as the country extending from Loch Leven to Stirling from east to west, and between the Ochil Hills and the Forth from north to south. From the direction taken by the course of the last-named river and its estuary, as well as the contour of the Ochils, the breadth of this tract increases considerably in proceeding from west to east, there being little over a mile at Blair Logie between the hills and the water, whilst a straight line drawn from Glen Farg to North Queensferry would extend to upwards of twenty miles. The shape assumed by this tract is triangular, or perhaps may be described more exactly as that of a cone, of which the apex is at Stirling, the two sides being formed respectively by the Forth and the Ochils, whilst the line from Glen Farg to North Queensferry represents the base.

The Firth of Forth was anciently known as the *Mare Fresicum* or Frisian Sea, whilst its northern coasts received the name of the *Fresicum littus*, or Frisian Shore, having apparently been colonised by Frisians from North Holland and Germany. The monastery of Culross is referred to by early historians as lying between the Ochil Hills and the Sea of Giudi, another primitive designation for this estuary. These Frisian or Teutonic settlers were afterwards dispossessed by the Picts, into whose territory they had intruded, and the Forth for ages subsequently remained the boundary between Celtic Scotland and the Saxon region of Lothian. North of its waters the Picts and Scots, rivals for supremacy, but kindred in blood and language, reigned unchallenged, and their sway was also acknowledged by several tribes of the same race in the central and south-western Lowlands south of the Forth.

The ancient inhabitants of the British Islands are believed to have been of Iberian or Basque origin—that primeval Turanian race which inhabited the countries adjoining the Mediterranean, and is supposed to have formed a large portion of the population of Britain in the early days of the Phœnician traders. They were invaded and overpowered by colonies of Celts, who had gradually forced their way from the east to the west of Europe, and had afterwards in their turn to retreat before the Gothic or Teutonic and Scandinavian races. A marked characteristic in the *physique* of the Iberians was their dark hair and complexion, their comparatively low stature, and the length of their skulls, as exhibited in the remains that have been discovered.

These are of the dolichocephalic or long-headed sort, as distinguished from the brachycephalic (short or broad skulled) type which marks their Celtic conquerors, who were, moreover, a fair-haired ruddy race, of greater stature. Besides these two descriptions of skulls, there is the orthocephalic (straight or oval-headed) type, which seems to form a connecting-link between the races.

By the time of the Roman invasion of Britain the aboriginal Basques had almost disappeared, or retreated to remote regions of the country, where, as in the case of the Silures, they seem, among other localities, to have composed a large part of the population of South Wales. They have left few traces of their presence in local nomenclature, though some names, like the Coquet river and island in Northumberland, and " Urr " and " Ore," as terms for water, are maintained to be derived from their language, which is still spoken in the north of

Spain and south of France, and believed also to be the basis of the ancient Maltese tongue.

The Celtic race comprehends two leading branches—the Gaelic and the Cymric—and it is not yet quite determined which of these two is to be regarded as the elder. In South Britain the latter exhibits itself in the principality of Wales, and also in Cornwall, where a cognate dialect to Welsh, now obsolete, used to be spoken. Ireland, on the other hand, and the Scottish Highlands, belong to the Gaelic stock; whilst the ancient Manx language, not yet extinct in the Isle of Man, may be regarded as an intermediate stage between the Gaelic and Cymric. It has been claimed by the respective advocates of each, that the language of Great Britain has been at one time either wholly Gaelic or wholly Welsh; but there seems a general agreement that the latter tongue was never developed in Ireland, which, as regards the native population, has been exclusively Erse or Gaelic since the days when the Celtic colonists first set foot on its shores, and supplanted the aboriginal Basques.

More than a century elapsed from the first invasion of Britain by Julius Cæsar before the Roman armies penetrated into the northern division of the island, the inhabitants of which are spoken of by classic authors under the appellation of Caledonians—the earliest writer who makes use of the epithet in question being the poet Lucan. They are also referred to as the Picts, a designation which has given rise to an immense amount of controversy, but in all probability signifies nothing more than the *Picti*, or painted people, from the custom of staining their bodies, which attracted the attention of their invaders as a special characteristic. Unlike what took place in England, the Romans established no colonies north of the Tweed, though they occupied in military fashion the country to the south of the Firths of Forth and Clyde, and built a wall across the isthmus between these estuaries, to protect themselves from the inroads of the Caledonians living beyond. Even thither also they carried their arms, erected camps and military stations, and constructed roads to connect these, and furnish themselves with the means of advancing into the country. Thus, from the station at Camelon on the Roman wall near Falkirk, they constructed a direct highway to Stirling, which has always been regarded as the pass or key of communication between the low country and the Highlands. Thence, through the dense forest which then occupied the site of Blair Drummond and Kincardine mosses, they laid down a road which led northwards by the valley of the Allan to the great camp at Ardoch, and so eastwards, on the north side of the Ochils, into Strathearn and the basin of the Tay. Here converged another highway, which seems to have been carried from the neighbourhood of Stirling eastwards through Clackmannan, the west of Fife, and Kinross-shire, across the Ochils to the neighbourhood of Abernethy and Perth. They had probably a station on the north bank of the Forth near Alloa, which may thus have been the " Alauna " of Ptolemy ; and they had certainly a large encampment, called Victoria, at the north-west extremity of Loch Ore, in the parish of Ballingry, in Fife.

At the period of the Roman invasion the peninsula between the Tay and the Forth, as well as a large tract of country to the south of the latter, was occupied by the Damnonii, a tribe which, from the similarity of the name, Mr Skene considers as related to the ancient inhabitants of Devon and Cornwall, and as such to have probably spoken a Celtic dialect akin to the ancient Cornish. They inhabited the whole of the district of

Fife and Fothreve, besides the adjoining territories of Menteith and Strathearn. They must thus have been among the *novæ gentes*, or freshly discovered tribes, which Tacitus represents Agricola as invading on the occasion of his third campaign, in which he advanced as far as the banks of the Tay. Subsequently the Damnonii, with other tribes of North Britain, were merged in two leading nations—the Meatæ,[1] or people of the plains, occupying the low country to the south of the Forth, as distinguished from the Caledonians,[2] or dwellers in the woods and mountains to the north of that estuary. These North Britons were subdued by the Emperor Severus in the beginning of the third century of our era, but shortly afterwards rose in insurrection. To punish this revolt the Roman monarch prepared energetically for a new campaign against them; but before he could make any progress in it, he was attacked by a mortal illness, and expired at York in A.D. 211. To him must be ascribed a large portion of the Roman military roads still existing in Great Britain, including, in the opinion of Mr Skene, the wall between the Firths of Forth and Clyde, which he believes to have been erected by Severus on the lines of that constructed by Lollius Urbicus.

The same district of Fothreve, which was peopled by the Damnonii, included at a later period a portion of the territory of Manau, or Manann, which extended along the shores of both sides of the Forth, and has left traces of its existence in Slamannan, Clackmannan, and probably also Presmennan, in East Lothian, near Dunbar. The etymology of this term appears to be the Gaelic *mu 'n ann*,[3] as denoting a region or locality occupying an

---

[1] From Gaelic *magh*, a plain.

[2] From Gaelic *coille*, a wood, and *dun*, a hill or fortress.

[3] From the preposition *mu*, on or above, the definite article *'n*, and *an*, an obsolete form of *amhain*, water.

elevated position above water. It seems to embody the same philological idea as " Mona," or the Isle of Man, and " Emonia," the ancient name for Inchcolm. There was also comprehended in Fothreve the district of Athran, or Athren, now Airthrey, adjoining Stirling and the Bridge of Allan. The whole of the region known by this designation belonged exclusively to " Pictavia," *Cruithentuath*, or the land of the Picts, and was long the southern border of Alban, or the Scotland of the Gaels. The Lothians and Berwickshire were regarded as belonging to the ancient Saxon kingdom of Northumbria ; whilst the west Lowlands, from the Clyde to the Solway Firth, and across it into Cumberland and Westmoreland, formed the British sovereignty of Strathclyde, which had its capital at Alcluith or Dumbarton.

As already mentioned, the Celtic and Saxon territories were separated by the Firth of Forth, which was anciently known by the various designations of the " Frisian Sea," the " Mirk " or " Dark Fiord," [1] and the " Sea of Giudi." This last epithet refers to a so-called city of Giudi, which, Bede informs us, was situated in the midst of the estuary (*in medio sui*), and a considerable amount of controversy has arisen as to the actual locality. Some have identified it with Inchkeith, some with Camelon, near Falkirk, whilst Mr Skene, in a paper contributed by him to the Proceedings of the Scottish Society of Antiquaries, inclines to the belief that Giudi is Fidra, a small island off the East Lothian coast, not far from the Bass. More recently, however, in his treatise on the ' Four Ancient Books of Wales,' he expresses his opinion that the site of Bede's Giudi and Nennius's Iudeu is to be sought in one of the islands on the south shore of the Forth, between Carriden and the mouth of the Esk. Adopting this view, we have the choice of Inchkeith, of

---

[1] Icelandic *myrka*, dark.

Cramond Island, and of Inchgarvie; and I believe that in the first of these we shall make, as has been pretty generally done, the most likely and best warranted selection. Inchkeith is generally explained as *Innis-cheo*, the Island of Mist; but it may, with as great probability, be rendered *Innis-gaoithe*, the Island of Wind; and here we have in *gaoithe* the genitive of the Gaelic *gaoth* (wind), a word very nearly resembling "Giudi," or "Iudeu."

The Scots who invaded and settled in Argyleshire in the end of the fifth century, and ultimately gave their name to the whole of North Britain, seem for a long period to have confined themselves to their little settlement of Dalriada, in the West Highlands, and to have made no endeavour to enlarge their territory. The Picts governed the remainder of Alban, and had their capital and royal residences at Abernethy and Forteviot in Strathearn. Down to the middle of the eighth century the two dynasties seem to have reigned together over their respective territories (that of the Picts being much the larger) without any serious attempts at dispossession on the part of either. About the period last named, however, the Scots were completely subjugated by the Picts, who for nearly a hundred years remained masters both of Alban and Dalriada. Then a Scottish prince, named Alpin, laid claim to the Pictish throne, but was overthrown and put to death by his rival Drust or Drest. Alpin's son Kenneth resolved to avenge his father's death, and reassert his claim to the crown. He encountered the Pictish monarch near Tullibody, in Clackmannanshire, routed and scattered his forces, and established himself in 844 as sole king of the Picts and Scots. In the seventh year of his reign he is said to have transferred part of the relics of St Columba to a church which he had built—an incident which seems to mark the transference of the ecclesiastical metropolis from Iona to

Abernethy on the south bank of the Tay. The name of the Picts gradually disappears after this from history, and the Scots are the rulers of Alban, or the country to the north of the Forth. It is not till nearly two hundred years afterwards, under Malcolm II., a descendant of Kenneth, that we find Alban, or Albany, coexistent with Scotland, as we now understand the term. This increased extent of sovereignty arose in consequence of the incorporation with the realm of Alban, partly by transfer, partly by conquest, of the British kingdom of Strathclyde, and the portion of the Saxon kingdom of Northumbria lying to the north of the Tweed.

I have considered it advisable to give this prefatory sketch of the early history of Scotland, as an introduction to a more detailed account of the territory which forms the subject of the following work, and with which the district anciently bearing the appellation of Fothreve very nearly coincides. I have only to add now a few remarks on the topography and general character of the district.

In primeval times the territory under consideration must have presented almost entirely the aspect of a dense forest, through which roamed the wild ox, the wild boar, the stag, and the wolf; whilst the few human inhabitants derived their chief subsistence from the chase. Above this portion of the ancient Caledonian forest rose the verdant heights of the Ochils, the Lomonds, and the lower ranges of the Saline and Cleish hills and others, to be crowned frequently in after-days by the circular encampments erected by the Britons as watch-towers of defence, first against the Romans, and subsequently against the Scandinavian invaders. There would be little or no corn-land, and the natives themselves, as regarded civilisation, would probably be much on a par with the North American Indians. Polygamy, or rather community of wives, seems to have been the principle of their social system ; and their religious ideas, like those of other savages, were probably of the most simple and primitive kind. It is very questionable, indeed, if the so-called Druidical system of religion, with its rites and ceremonies, ever existed in North Britain.

In time came a change. Christian missionaries found their way to Britain as early perhaps as the second century, though apparently no systematic scheme of conversion or evangelisation was organised previous to the mission of St Ninian to the Southern Picts in the end of the fourth century of our era. He was, according to tradition, followed by Palladius, who is said to have arrived in North Britain about A.D. 430, visited Culross, and there found a Christian missionary already established —the famous St Serf, the patron saint of a large part of Fothreve, near and about the Ochils and Loch Leven, and the foster-father and master of the still more celebrated St Mungo. Many strange stories and piquant legends are recorded regarding these early pioneers of Christianity, who have left in numerous localities in this district impressions of their life and work. After them an almost total darkness settles down on this part of the country, and with one or two exceptions, such as the battles of Tullibody and Dollar in the ninth century, there is almost no sure resting-place for the historical inquirer till we come to the reign of Malcolm Canmore, in the last half of the eleventh century. Subsequent to this there is, comparatively speaking, a sufficiency of information, both in written records and architectural remains, to enable us to trace the history of the localities down to the present day.

As regards the geological formation of this district, it belongs entirely, with a very slight exception in the north of Kinross-shire, to the basin of the Forth, and

forms also to a large extent a part of the great coal-field
of central Scotland. The coal-measures which extend
through the Devon valley, through Perthshire on Forth,
Kinross-shire, and the western district of Fife, are bordered on the north by the igneous mass of the Ochils,
and permeated frequently by similar upheavals of trap-
rocks, which both interrupt the workings of the coal-field
in particular localities, and break it up into compart-
ments which are frequently quite detached and separate
from each other.

The soil of this district is very varied, the upper shores
of the Forth between Stirling and Alloa consisting of
fertile tracts of rich alluvial ground, or *carse*, as it is
termed, which extends for a considerable distance inland, and at the western extremity seems almost to
approach the foot of the hills. About Kincardine a
good deal of land has been reclaimed from the sea, and
is fairly productive—though below this, throughout the
whole extent almost of the parishes of Tulliallan and
Culross, the sandstone basis on which they exclusively
rest prevents in great measure the development of any
rich soil. In the parish of Torryburn, on the other hand,
where there is a great upheaval of trap-rocks, so effective
in the production of good land, the combination of this
circumstance with the fine sunny slope of the rising
grounds immediately above the sea, renders the whole
of this tract along the Forth, from Newmill Bridge to
Queensferry, as fertile and productive as any in the three
kingdoms.

In further reference to Fifeshire and the northern
shores of the Forth, I may here quote Pennant's remarks on the subject, as given in his ' Tour in Scotland ' in the last century : " As I am nearly arrived at the
extremity, permit me to take a review of the peninsula of
Fife, a country so populous that, excepting the environs

of London, scarce one in South Britain can vie with it; fertile in soil, abundant in cattle, happy in collieries, in iron, stone, lime, and freestone, blest in manufactures; the property remarkably well divided, none insultingly powerful to distress and often depopulate a country, most of the fortunes of a useful mediocrity. The number of towns is perhaps unparalleled in an equal tract of coast, for the whole shore from Crail to Culross, about forty English miles, is one continued chain of towns and villages."

Though long essentially Celtic, and exhibiting in the names of most of its localities unequivocal evidences of its former occupancy by a Gaelic-speaking population, Fife and Kinross have for centuries displayed, as regards religious and social customs, a more decided Saxon tendency than most other parts of Scotland. They have always been noted as the strongholds of Presbytery; and here in the last century was the great Secession from the Established Church inaugurated by the Erskines, and zealously maintained by their followers. From various causes property has been much subdivided in this district, and there are few holders of any large or far-spreading estates. Owing to its peculiar situation, equally removed from English depredators and Highland caterans, it has perhaps been longer and more thoroughly tranquil than the rest of Scotland, and thus been enabled to cultivate from an earlier period the arts of peace. The same characteristics attributed to Fife and Kinross belong likewise, though less markedly, to Perthshire on Forth, Clackmannan, and a portion of Stirlingshire. In manners and customs, in dialect and in race, the ancient Fothreve may be said in its modern component parts to present a homogeneous whole.

ALONG THE GREAT NORTH ROAD.

I.

NORTH QUEENSFERRY AND INVERKEITHING.

The Forth Bridge and its vicinity — Island of Inchgarvie — North Queensferry and its peninsula—Rosyth Castle—The town of Inverkeithing—Its history and objects of interest.

THE passage of the Firth of Forth at Queensferry, already well known, is likely, ere long, to attain a much greater and more diffused celebrity in connection with the wonderful railway bridge now in process of construction at this point across the estuary. It may be premature, as yet, to speculate either on the results of this undertaking when completed, or the general appearance which the structure will present in connecting the shore of the Lothians with that of Fife; but there seems little reason to doubt that it will display one of the most extraordinary and stupendous monuments ever achieved by human ingenuity and industry. Concentrating, as it does, the application of so much skill, energy, and perseverance, there appears little risk in predicting that it is destined to figure as one of the wonders of the world.

In the following work—which is intended to serve as a pictorial and historical delineation of, as well as a practical guide to, the districts lying along the north shore of the Forth between North Queensferry and Stirling, and inland as far as the Ochils—any extended description of an uncompleted structure like the Forth Bridge will doubtless scarcely be expected. Yet, as it is destined to form in future one of the main accesses to this region, and even now looms forth to the eye of the traveller as a gigantic skeleton, it may not be deemed inexpedient that, in conducting my reader to the Fife shore, I should present him with a slight sketch of the history of the vast structure which, in all its interesting though unfinished details, must present itself so markedly to him as he steams across to North Queensferry from Port Edgar.

The adventurous spirit of engineering science which had been called forth so prominently in the achievements of Brindley and Smeaton in the second half of the last, and of Telford in the early part of the present century, had initiated a career of triumphs over natural difficulties and obstructions which exhibited, as the first-fruits of its energy, the Bridgewater Canal, the Eddystone Lighthouse, and the bridge over the Menai Straits. James Watt in developing the powers of the steam-engine, and the elder Stephenson in applying these to locomotives on railways, had effected a still mightier stride in this direction; whilst the younger Stephenson and the two Brunels, father and son, also contributed no less effectual aid. It was an age for mighty schemes—some of them, doubtless, more or less chimerical, but all, in their very extravagance, bearing evidence of the adventurous spirit that was abroad. It was the same spirit of adventure—

now employed in more prosaic and practical undertakings — which in former times had animated British
explorers and navigators in discovering new lands and
forming new settlements in distant regions of the globe.

The breadth of the channel between North and South
Queensferry is, roundly stated, about a mile and a half,
and the island of Inchgarvie is situated nearly midway
between these places. In consequence of the great
narrowing of the Forth at this point—to less than a half
of its breadth between Culross and Borrowstounness—it
is to be expected that the current in the main channel
of the estuary will both be much stronger and flow in a
much deeper bed than is to be found at any point above
or below. There is, accordingly, on the north side of
the island of Inchgarvie, an exceedingly deep channel,
which reaches a depth of at least 210 feet, or 35
fathoms, with a breadth of about 1600 feet. On the
south side of the island there is a depth of 180 feet,
or 30 fathoms, which, however, diminishes considerably
as we proceed to South Queensferry. Between the
island and the North Ferry, the same great depth of
water almost uniformly continues—a depth which is
greater than in almost any other part of the Forth, and
even than in many places of the German Ocean.

With such a vast distance to be spanned between
Inchgarvie and the Fife shore, it will readily be conceived that the idea of connecting the Queensferries
presents, at first sight, the appearance of being too
chimerical to be entertained. In the earlier years of
the present century, however, the project had been
mooted of effecting this purpose by a suspension-bridge
of two spans, the middle support of which should be
on the island of Inchgarvie. It was abandoned as an
impossible scheme; as was also another idea which,
some years previously, had been broached — that of

constructing a tunnel beneath the bed of the Forth. Years passed on, and for a long time Queensferry seemed not only destined to be undistinguished as a theatre of mechanical and scientific ingenuity, but likewise fated to remain less in accord with the spirit of the age than other places in Great Britain. The great railway lines of communication between the north and the south of Scotland, instead of having their traffic carried across the Forth at this point—the natural and most convenient passage—were transferred to the stormy, and occasionally impassable, ferry between Granton and Burntisland; and the direct route to the north, by Dunfermline and Kinross, was abandoned for the circuitous one by Ladybank Junction, through the eastern district of Fife. It is only within the last few years that Dunfermline and Edinburgh have become directly connected by railway.

About twenty years ago the project was again started of constructing a bridge across the Forth; and to obviate the difficulties presented by the depth of the channel and strength of the current between Inchgarvie and North Queensferry, it was resolved to erect it at a point higher up—nearly between the castles of Rosyth and Blackness—where the general breadth of the estuary is certainly much greater, but the depth as well as strength of current of the " fairway," or principal channel, is much less. Monetary rather than physical considerations led to this scheme being abandoned after some eloquent expositions and panegyrics on the subject had been made in the public journals.

The apparently successful completion of the railway bridge across the Tay seems to have revived the idea of a similar one across the Forth; and accordingly, the preparing of a design of this description was intrusted to Sir Thomas Bouch, the engineer of the Tay Bridge. This commission he fulfilled by devising for the passage of the Forth at Queensferry a railway suspension-bridge, of which the middle pier or piers were to reach the height of 596 feet, and those at the extremities 584. To guard against any extraordinary pressure of winds and tempests, a resistance was provided to a pressure of 10 lb. on the square foot, and this was supposed to form a sufficiently ample security for any emergency. The anticipation thus entertained, however, was rudely dissipated by the terrible disaster which befell the Tay Bridge on the evening of Sunday, 28th of December 1879. The overthrow of the structure, and of a railway train passing over it, with an accompanying loss of human life, demonstrated the necessity of a more effectual provision being made against unwonted tempests and cataclysms than had previously been deemed necessary. Sir Thomas himself did not long survive the overthrow of his work, and the whole of the circumstances connected with it led to the conviction that the Forth Bridge, if it were to be proceeded with at all, must be constructed on entirely different lines, and with much more effectual safeguards. Another scheme was accordingly set on foot, and the present structure, which now seems calculated to obviate all chances of a similar catastrophe, is the result.

The designs for this work were prepared by Mr John Fowler and Mr B. Baker, civil engineers, and approved of by the Board of Trade on 9th December 1881. The contractors for the work are Sir Thomas Tancred, C.E., London, and Messrs W. Arrol & Co., Dalmarnock Ironworks, Glasgow. The cost was fixed at £1,600,000, and the work was originally expected to be concluded by the end of 1887.

The present bridge is a girder-bridge, and comprises two long spans of 1700 feet each, over the deep channels lying respectively on the north and south sides of the island of Inchgarvie. There are also two subsidiary spans of 675 feet each—one on the north and the other on the south side of the two great spans; whilst a series of piers, with openings between each of 150 feet, commencing at the Ferry Hill on the north, and ending at the top of the Ha's Brae on the south shore, complete the structure.

In spanning the deep channels on either side of Inchgarvie, a system of " cantilevers " or projecting supports has been employed. These are three in number—one on the island itself, and one on the north and south side respectively. Each cantilever rests on four cylindrical pieces of masonry, which again repose on a bed of concrete, which has been deposited in an excavation made in the solid rock or hard boulder-clay. Each holds forth an arm, 650 feet in length, from the right and left respectively of the centre; and each cantilever rises to a height of 350 feet above its supporting piers. A series of horizontal girders are carried between the cantilevers and the shores of the Forth on the viaduct piers to the north and south. These girders were placed on the top of the viaduct piers, whilst the latter had only an elevation of 20 feet above low-water mark, and have been gradually raised as the stonework beneath is built up to the further height of 130 feet. Each of the viaduct piers will thus have a total height above low-water of 150 feet. Besides a massive abutment at each shore, and the three cantilevers, each resting on its group of four piers, there are sixteen viaduct piers—six on the north and ten on the south side of the island of Inchgarvie. In these sixteen piers are included two great subsidiary cantilever piers—one on the north side on land, and the other on the south side in shallow water—each of which forms the junction respectively of the north and south cantilevers with the viaduct.

Since its commencement the work has been carried on both day and night by the aid of relays of labourers; and to enable this to be accomplished with greater facility, the electric light has been employed for illuminating both the workshops at South Queensferry and the works on the bridge itself. The number of workmen employed is upwards of 1000, and the cost of the plant is roughly estimated at £100,000.

The Forth Bridge is upwards of a mile in length, and as regards that of the two great spans (about a third of a mile for each), is four times the size of any bridge hitherto constructed. There are four classes of materials employed—steel, granite, whinstone, and Portland cement. With regard to the first of them, special considerations of durability and resistance to pressure have led to its employment instead of that of cast-iron, which formed the leading material in Sir Thomas Bouch's design. The superstructure of the bridge, including the girders, cantilevers, and struts, are entirely composed of wrought-steel, which has also been manufactured and adjusted at the workshops on the spot. It is estimated that 50,000 tons of steel will have been used in the course of the operations. The under side of the girders at the cantilever piers is arched, and their depth will amount to 340 feet at the piers, gradually diminishing towards the centre, where it is about 50 feet. This minimum depth of 50 feet is continued for about a length of 500 feet; so that, in the centre of the two great spans, there is a clear elevation of 150 feet above high-water level—thus enabling the loftiest three-master to pass beneath without striking. The resistance of the whole structure, though loaded with a couple of trains weighing 900 tons each, is calculated to withstand a pressure of 56 lb. to the square foot—an enormous amount, and nearly six times greater than that which

Sir Thomas Bouch deemed it necessary to provide against in his design of the Forth Bridge.

The journey by railway from Edinburgh to South Queensferry, by Ratho and Kirkliston, is pleasant enough, but is both much more circuitous and much less beautiful than that by road over the Dean and Cramond Bridges, and down the Ha's Brae. The route between Edinburgh and Cramond Brig has been characterised as about the finest bit of turnpike road in the three kingdoms, whilst the view of the Forth and its shores above and below Queensferry is one of the grandest prospects that can anywhere be obtained. To some extent, indeed, this can still be enjoyed from the train between the stations of South Queensferry and the steamboat pier at Port Edgar; but it falls much short of the *coup d'œil* that presents itself to the traveller by coach, as he descends the hill to the inn at Newhalls—better known by its time-honoured appellation of the "Ha's," as immortalised in the opening chapters of 'The Antiquary.' It is shorn indeed, now, of much of the importance which it enjoyed as the halting-place, in the coaching days, for travellers between the south and north; but it nevertheless continues to remain, both through its proximity to the Forth Bridge and as a pleasant resort of excursionists from Edinburgh, a very comfortable and well-patronised hostelry.

The view in descending the Ha's Brae takes in the whole estuary of the Forth, from Grangemouth and Kincardine to Inchkeith. At the upper extremity to the west the picture is bounded by the Kilsyth and Campsie hills, with the low grounds of the carses of Falkirk and Stirling lying between them and the Forth. Farther round to the north-west appears the mighty Ben Lomond, with his group of attendant hills; whilst the horizon on

the north is bordered from earth to sky by the beautiful
and picturesque chain of the Ochils, extending in varied
and verdant beauty from the neighbourhood of Stirling
to that of Kinross and the lower shores of the Tay. Between them and the Forth, to the north-west of the
spectator, stretches a beautifully undulating country,
which in many places, and more especially adjoining
the water, will vie in richness with the most finely cultivated districts in England. The wooded braes of Culross
Bay are easily discernible in clear weather, and nearer at
hand appears the regal town of Dunfermline, with its
towers and steeples covering the southern side of a
sunny slope. The square grey tower of Rosyth on its
peninsula is seen close to the water's edge; and below
it is the Ferry Hill, projecting into and greatly narrowing the Firth of Forth, with the village of North Queensferry reposing at the foot of the rocky eminence. The
great pool or roadstead above the Ferry, with St Margaret's Hope at its north-east extremity—so well known
as the haven of distressed mariners—widens out placidly
on the left, almost like a landlocked lake, on the southern
shore of which appear in succession the Kinneil Ironworks, the busy and thriving if not particularly attractive town of Borrowstounness, the picturesque village
of Carriden, the castle of Blackness, and the beautifully
wooded grounds of Hopetoun. Then close at hand is the
burgh of South Queensferry, whilst midway between it and
its sister on the north shore is the island of Inchgarvie
—once indeed, with its fortalice, a picturesque-looking
rock, but now almost completely obscured and buried
underneath the works of the Forth Bridge, which form
a prominent object immediately below the spectator, on
the right. Away down in the same direction are, on the
southern shore, the finely wooded grounds of Dalmeny
Park and Barnbougle; and on the north, the entrance

to Inverkeithing harbour, with the picturesque domain of Donibristle extending beyond and eastwards down the Firth. Here, too, directly opposite to the last-mentioned place, and nestling in a nook of the estuary, is the far-famed island of Inchcolm, with its ecclesiastical traditions, and its quaint-looking grey tower rising up from its rocks and old conventual buildings. Beyond extends the ever-expanding bosom of the Firth, with Inchkeith in the middle and the Fife and Lothian shores on either hand. Altogether, from this coign of vantage, the traveller may here contemplate, in a general view, a great part of the district to which he will shortly be introduced in greater detail.

In crossing the Firth from Port Edgar to North Queensferry, the attention of the traveller will naturally be attracted both to the buildings of the Forth Bridge, which he sees on his right, and also to the little rocky islet of Inchgarvie, which is situated in mid-channel, and has been largely utilised, both as a resting-place for the great centre cantilever, and also for a suite of offices and workshops in connection with the structure. So great a change has been effected here as completely to have metamorphosed the island, which, with its little fortress perched on it, seemed in former days to rise like a Patmos in the midst of the waters. It now resounds with the din and turmoil of active labour; whilst the whole place, covered as it is with erections and appliances of various kinds, seems to be consigned to the fate generally meted out to all natural objects that either stand in the way of, or can be utilised for, the requirements of practical science. Hardly now would the *Malva arborea marina*, which, as Sir Robert Sibbald informs us, used formerly to have its special habitat on Inchgarvie, be found in the recesses of its rocks. The plant, in fact, has for a long time disappeared from the island; and it is related that Dr·

Graham, the predecessor of the late Dr Balfour in the Botanical Chair in the Edinburgh University, made an expedition here on one occasion with the express object of securing a specimen. He procured a boat, landed on the island, and, to his utter dismay, discovered a goat in the act of munching the very last plant that still remained!

The earliest notice we have of Inchgarvie is contained in a charter granted by James IV. in 1491 to John Dundas of that Ilk, in which, under consideration of the great damage done to the shores of Scottish estuaries by marauding bands of pirates from England and other countries, his Majesty grants to the Laird of Dundas, in property, the island of Inchgarvie, with the power of erecting thereon such fortifications as might appear necessary for the purpose of defending the coasts of the Forth at the strait of the Queensferry. A fortress of some kind, in consequence of this warrant, seems to have been erected, as, more than half a century afterwards, we find its capture recorded by the Earl of Hertford, during his expedition into Scotland in 1544.

There is, or was till recently, at the west extremity of Inchgarvie, an ancient fort or redoubt, which may have formed part of the buildings erected by the Laird of Dundas in the end of the fifteenth century, and taken by the English fleet during Hertford's expedition in 1544. During the preparations against Cromwell's invasion in 1650—preparations destined to prove so nugatory—the Scottish Parliament issued orders on 21st June for the fortification and victualling of Inchgarvie, "and that 20 musketers and a commander be put therin, that the Provest of Edinburghe furnishe the said garrison with coles out of Duik Hamilton's coleheughe, and he to be payed for them."

I do not know whether it was in connection with the above order of the Scottish Parliament for fortifying Inchgarvie, or its occupation at a subsequent period by the troops of Cromwell, that we find the royal burgh of Culross much exercised by a requisition made on it for a supply of bedding for the use of the garrison. More likely it was on account of the latter's army that it had to make this contribution, as recorded in the Town Council minutes. A similar requisition to apparently a much greater extent was made about the same time on the people of Culross, to furnish feather-beds, blankets, and other appliances to a detachment of the Protector's soldiers who had been sent to occupy the fortress of Castle Campbell at Dollar. The fortification which crowns the summit and eastern extremity of Inchgarvie is probably of ancient origin, but assumed its present appearance and dimensions in consequence of the buildings erected here at the time of Paul Jones's expedition, and also subsequently in the beginning of the present century, when it was fitted up and remodelled as one of the defences of the Forth.

The railway piers on each side of the Forth are situated a little farther up than those which were used in the coaching days, and the passage across is effected by the steamers in little over ten minutes. The whole journey by train from Edinburgh to Dunfermline occupies about an hour and a half, and were the route by the direct line of the old coach-road, the distance might almost be traversed in an hour. The railway from the north pier is carried by tunnel through the Ferry Hill, then turns eastwards by Inverkeithing, where there is a station, and after that in a north-westerly direction, without any stoppage, to Comely Park Station, Dunfermline. Shortly after leaving Inverkeithing it crosses the field of the celebrated battle which bears that name, in the

valley which lies to the north of Castlelandhill, and to
the south of Pitreavie House.   An account will be found
subsequently of the town of Dunfermline and adjoining
district.

North Queensferry (*Hotel:* Albert) is a pleasant and
picturesque-looking village, lying at the foot of the Ferry
Hill, where the latter terminates its long projection into
the Forth, and thus causes a narrowing of the estuary.
It is six miles from Dunfermline by road, and is much
resorted to by visitors in the summer-time.   On the hill
behind, Cromwell's troops were encamped in 1651, when
they were conveyed across the Forth previous to the
battle of Inverkeithing.   The promontory at its north-east
extremity is termed " Cruickness," and forms the south-
west corner of Inverkeithing harbour.   Between this and
North Queensferry is a pleasant walk, leading along the
little lonely recess of Port Laing, whose silver sands and
clear waters afford excellent opportunity for sea-bathing.
The locality at Cruickness is also known by the name
of the " Lazaretto," from its having been at one time a
quarantine station, which, however, ceased to be used
as such nearly sixty years ago, and the buildings in connection with it were sold.   A curious circumstance in
relation to this neighbourhood is, that it used formerly
to be infested with adders, which are still occasionally
to be met with about Port Laing, though their number is
now greatly diminished.   I believe these reptiles are still
to be found in Moss Morran, near Crossgates, to the
east of Dunfermline, and possibly also in one or two
other places of a similar description; but generally speaking, they are quite unknown in the cultivated districts on
the shores of the Forth.

The village of North Queensferry, with the district
lying immediately behind it, belongs civilly to the parish
of Dunfermline; and a former minister of that town, who

used to rusticate every summer for six weeks at the pleasant little watering-place, used to boast that he enjoyed this sojourn within the limits of his own parish. The island of Inchgarvie, however, and the rock called Bimar, are in the parish of Inverkeithing. The superior of the ground at Queensferry is the Marquis of Tweeddale, as representative of the Earls of Dunfermline, the ancient lords of the regality, and from him the village is feued. It must at all times have been, from its situation, a ferry station ; but the earliest historical notice that we have regarding it is in connection with Queen Margaret, sister of Edgar Atheling, and wife of Malcolm Canmore. Along with her mother and sisters and brother, she had been driven by stress of weather into the Firth of Forth, on the occasion of their flight from England and the power of William the Conqueror. Their vessel came to anchor in the little bay at the north-west corner of the Ferry Hill, which has derived, along with the adjoining roadstead, the appellation of St Margaret's Hope, whilst the passage itself has been denominated " the Queen's ferry." Buchanan terms it *Margaritæ Portus*. The Ferry was formerly under the custody of the Abbots of Dunfermline, who were entitled to every fourth penny of passage-money, on the understanding of their maintaining a supply of boats; and over and above this, they were entitled to every fortieth penny, as an impost leviable by them for the erection and repair of the choir of Dunfermline Abbey. After the Reformation the management passed into the hands of the neighbouring proprietors, such as Henderson of Fordel, Stewart of Rosyth, Dundas of Dundas, and others. But it was ultimately, and has been for many years, under the direction of a board of parliamentary trustees. It used to be said that the currents at Queensferry were so peculiar that none but boatmen who had been accustomed to them from boyhood could be intrusted with their navigation. An unpleasant demonstration of this was experienced in the beginning of the present century by the Ferry trustees, when they dismissed the old boatmen, but were obliged to reinstate them in consequence of the impossibility of finding others competent to supply their places.

Besides Inchgarvie, but nearer to the shore, there are in connection with North Queensferry the singular rock of Bimar, on which a stone pillar or beacon is stationed; the rocks known as the Long Craig, opposite Craig Dhu House; and those of Craigmarmor, in St Margaret's Hope. A bank indeed, or reef of rocks, runs the whole way up the north shore of the Firth from Long Craig Island, crossing Culross Bay in the Craigmore and Craigengarth rocks, and terminating at Longannet Point, about a mile below Kincardine-on-Forth. The space between this line and the shore is, for the most part, nearly dry at low water.

The north abutment of the Forth Bridge rests at a point at the south-east extremity of the village, which is generally known as "The Battery," and so called from the fortifications which were erected here at the time when Paul Jones's manœuvres were alarming the denizens of Fife and the Lothians. There is also a pier here, employed in certain states of the tide for the transit of goods and passengers to the opposite shore. Immediately adjoining, and inland, are extensive whinstone quarries, for which the Ferry Hill has long been famous. Pennant, in his tour through Scotland more than a hundred years ago, speaks of the "granite" quarries at Queensferry, and the immense export from them to London and other places of paving-stones. The most important of these quarries, however, is situated on the road to Dunfermline, close to the old Ferry toll-house. The blocks which are wrought and squared here are celebrated over the length and breadth of the United Kingdom for their admirable qualities as paving-stones, and they form an extensive article of export. They have been largely used also in the construction of the Forth Bridge.

The only monument of antiquity of which the village can boast is the gable of an ancient chapel, with its little burying-ground, which is completely surrounded with houses, and almost totally concealed from ordinary observation. Few, indeed, are aware of its existence beyond those living in the immediate neighbourhood. This chapel was originally founded by Robert the Bruce, and attached by him as an appanage to the Abbey of Dunfermline. It was destroyed by Cromwell's troops in 1651.

The old road from North Queensferry to Dunfermline led right over the hill from behind the village, and for those who like a grand view and do not object to a stiff climb, it has many recommendations. But it is quite impracticable for carriages, or at least these would accomplish the journey much faster by taking the ordinary turnpike road round the west shoulder of the Ferry Hill, and then at the old toll-house turning eastwards to Inverkeithing, the distance of which from the Ferry is about two miles. The inner recess of St Margaret's Hope, along which the road passes, seems in ancient times to have served both as a harbour and point of departure for the opposite side; and there is every probability that it was here the unfortunate Queen Mary crossed the Forth, after her escape from Loch Leven, on her way to Lord Seton's castle of Niddry, in West Lothian. Here, too, the vessel containing Edgar Atheling and his sister Margaret, must have anchored when a tempest drove them into the Forth; and here they were visited by King Malcolm Canmore, who shortly afterwards conducted Margaret to Dunfermline as his bride. Probably this recess, so sheltered and convenient, is the original and real *Queensferry*.

Looking westwards from this point up the Firth, the eye rests on the square tower of Rosyth Castle, on its peninsula projecting into the sea, about a mile distant. The early history of this building, like that of many of these old castles, cannot be ascertained; but along with the adjoining lands and barony of Rosyth, it belonged till about the end of the seventeenth century to a family of the name of Stewart, which traced its descent lineally from James Stewart of Durisdeer, in Dumfriesshire, brother of Walter Stewart, son-in-law to King Robert the Bruce, and father of Robert II. It subsequently passed for a time into the hands of the Earl of Rosebery, and afterwards was purchased by the Earl of Hopetoun, in the possession of whose descendant it still remains. The original purchaser of the barony seems to have been Sir David Stewart of Durisdeer, who afterwards took his designation from Rosyth, and was the patron and friend of Walter Bowmaker or Bower, Abbot of Inchcolm in the fifteenth century, and author of the continuation of Fordun's History or 'Scotichronicon.' The Stewarts of Rosyth seem always to have been ardent Royalists, and to have borne no goodwill to the Presbyterian cause. A complaint is recorded in the 'Book of the Universal Kirk of Scotland,' under the year 1577, as made by the Rev. David Ferguson, the well-known minister of Dunfermline, against the young Laird of Rosyth, that, contrary to the law, he had caused his father or other predecessor to be interred within the church of Dunfermline.[1] In the middle of the next

---

[1] Interments in churches were generally prohibited in Scotland at the Reformation, as tending to the fostering of superstitious notions and practices, but in after-times it came to be one of the recognised

century we find the then proprietor suffering severely for his Royalist proclivities by imprisonment, and an order issued to have his woods of " Hairschaw "[1] cut down to repair the habitations in the parishes of Muckhart and Dollar, which had been destroyed by Montrose's soldiers on the march through to Kilysth.

Rosyth Castle is entirely in ruins, and consists of a broad square tower of three storeys and battlements. It contains on the first floor a handsome and ample hall, having on the east and west sides respectively two large windows fitted with elegant cross mullions of much more recent construction than the rest of the building, inasmuch as they have marked on them " F.S." and " M.N.," with the date 1639. On the left-hand side of the entrance to the tower is a stone on which the following inscription might at one time be read :—

"IN DEW TYM DRAW THIS CORD THE BEL TO CLINK,
QVHAIS MERY VOCE VARNIS TO MEAT AND DRINK."

The words are now almost illegible, but I can testify to their having been many years ago more easy to decipher. Outside of the tower to the south and west are the remains of other buildings which have formed part of the castle. Over the gateway entering from the north is a mouldered coat-of-arms surmounted by a crown, with the letters and date "M.R. 1561." It is quite possible that these were put up on the occasion of a visit paid by Queen Mary to the Stewarts of Rosyth, who were members of her own family.

The castle stands on a green knoll projecting into the sea, and almost directly opposite to it on the shore is an

rights of an heritor that he should have a burial-place within the church.

[1] Probably Hartschaw, in Clackmannanshire, a county in which the Rosyth family had property.

ancient pigeon-house, with a vaulted roof evidently co-eval with the castle, and reminding one of what is frequently quoted as a characteristic of a Fife laird: "A wee pickle rent, a gey pickle debt, and a doocot."[1]

The "Loanhead of Rosyth"—that is to say, the junction of the Ferry road with the lane leading down to the castle—is said to have been the scene of the murder in 1530 of Sir James Inglis, Abbot of Culross, by John Blackadder, Laird of Tulliallan. The latter had conceived a grudge against Inglis for granting a lease of some lands over his head to one of the Erskines of Balgownie; and he consequently, with some retainers, lay in wait for the abbot, attacked and slew him. He was condemned and beheaded for the crime in Edinburgh shortly afterwards, as was also one of the monks of Culross, who had been concerned with him in the atrocity.

Turning away now from the prospect of Rosyth Castle, we shall continue along the highroad, and keeping the railway, which has just emerged from the Ferry Hill tunnel, on our right, and also skirting on the same side the shore of Inverkeithing Bay or harbour, we shall arrive after a walk of about a mile at the ancient burgh of that name.

Inverkeithing (*Hotel:* The Royal) is one of that group of little burgh towns which stud the north shore of the Forth from Crail to Culross, and exhibit for the most part unequivocal traces of having decayed from the grandeur and importance which they enjoyed as the emporia of trade and commerce previous to the union of the kingdoms. One or two of them, such as Kirkcaldy and Burntisland, have kept pace with the general prosperity of the country; but with the most of them the days of their glory are gone, never

---

[1] Dovecot or pigeon-house.

to return.   There are still hopes, however, for Inverkeithing, partly from the improvement which the completion of the Forth Bridge may bring about, partly
from the possible revival of one or two trades, such as
shipbuilding and iron-founding, which till recently were
conducted with considerable success in this place.   At
present the only works in full operation are a ropework,
a brickfield, a tannery, and a sawmill.   The Borland
distillery — a depressing - looking ruin — stands on the
banks of the Keithing, and a similar impression is made
by the appearance of the more recently closed foundry
and shipbuilding-yard.

The town of Inverkeithing has rather a quaint and
picturesque aspect when approached from the east; but
on entering it from the direction either of Queensferry or Dunfermline, the traveller is not likely to be
greatly attracted by its appearance.   It occupies a sort
of terrace on a rising ground sloping down to the sea,
and consists mainly of one broad street, having a sort of
parallelogram or square in the centre, with a steep descent at the east or older end of the town, leading down
near the church by the tolbooth and municipal buildings
to the bridge over the Keithing and the road to Aberdour.   The stream just named is of no importance, and,
as the appellation of the town denotes, falls here into
Inverkeithing Bay, which, landlocked as it is, with a
narrow entrance between two projecting points, would
form one of the finest natural harbours in the world had
it a sufficiency of depth of water.   But at ebb-tide it
is left almost entirely dry.

Inverkeithing in the ancient days of the Scottish
monarchy was a place of great importance.   It obtained a charter in the end of the twelfth century from
William the Lion, erecting, or rather confirming a previous charter of erection of the town into a royal burgh.

A subsequent charter of confirmation was granted by James VI. in 1598. The Exchequer Rolls testify to its importance as a commercial emporium, and the customs levied at the port of Inverkeithing formed a valuable item in the revenues of the Scottish Crown. It seems also to have been a favourite port of embarkation and transit, and on one occasion we find the burgh authorities reimbursed by the Exchequer for the expenses to which they had been subjected by the Princess Elizabeth, daughter of James I. of Scotland, landing at and passing through the town in 1429. At another time a charge is entered among the expenses of the Crown for the outlay attending the transmission from Dunfermline to Stirling Castle *via* Inverkeithing of the *chemise* or *sark* of St Margaret, as a guard to Mary of Gueldres, queen of James II., against any dangers which might be impending over her Majesty on the occasion of the birth of the Prince Royal, afterwards James III. The garment in question seems again to have been sent for at the birth of James V. It had evidently enjoyed an exalted reputation as a prophylactic in such emergencies, and was probably one of the most cherished treasures in the reliquary of Dunfermline.

The lands adjoining Inverkeithing, including Spencerfield, the Dales, &c., belonged formerly to the Moubrays of Barnbougle, who were afterwards succeeded in the latter estate by the Primrose or Rosebery family. The Hendersons of Fordel had also great influence in Inverkeithing, and acted as its provosts for several generations. Old houses are still shown in the town as the residences of the Fordel and Dalmeny families.

It is said that Annabella Drummond, queen of Robert III., died in Inverkeithing in 1403, and the mansion which she occupied on the south side of the great square is still pointed out and known as the " Palace " or

"Rotmells Inns." Though within the town of Inverkeithing, it holds of the Crown alone, and is exempted from burgh services. The building is now divided into three tenements, in the westmost of which a room is shown in which Queen Annabella is said to have died. The ceilings of the basement storey are vaulted, and there seems to have been a passage, also vaulted, leading through from the street to the garden. In the latter, beneath a bleaching-green in the south-east corner, are three vaulted chambers, two of them entered by a descending flight of steps; and from one of them, which is entered by a pointed archway, and has a small arched window adjoining, an interior vault opens, though the entrance is almost choked up with rubbish. One of these vaults is said to have been a chapel, but they are all more likely to have been storehouses or cellars beneath either the Dominican or Franciscan monastery, both of which existed at Inverkeithing. The so-called chapel is spoken of as St Mary's Chapel, and above the vaults on the bleaching-green can be traced the remains of buildings, evidently those of the monastery.[1]

The church of Inverkeithing is a modern building, an older edifice having been destroyed by fire in 1825; but the tower, which escaped that fate, is very ancient. At present, and for a long time past, an upper chamber in the tower, opening from the gallery of the church, has been used as a session-house; but this inconvenient arrangement is expected shortly to be remedied by the erection of another building on the south side of the church. Beside the pulpit stands an ancient stone font, one of the few specimens of the

---

[1] It appears from the Exchequer Rolls of 1383-84 that the Franciscans, or *Fratres Minores*, had a house in Inverkeithing, granted them by the king, free from any public burdens or contribution to the revenue.

kind in Scotland which have come down from pre-Reformation times. It stood originally in the porch of the church, but was removed at the instance of the present minister, Mr Robertson, to the position which it now occupies. It is said to have been presented to the church of Inverkeithing by Queen Annabella, whose son, moreover, the unfortunate Duke of Rothesay, is said to have received in it baptism. The Royal and Drummond arms combined are quartered on the font.

Inverkeithing contains several interesting old buildings in addition to those already described. Opposite to the church is a house with a projecting turret, which formerly belonged to the Hendersons of Fordel. In one of the apartments the royal arms are carved above the chimney, and it is alleged that James II. slept there on one occasion. This house and the one adjoining it on the west had at one time been united. The tenement is not held by burgage tenure, but of the Marquis of Tweeddale, there being some similarity in that respect with the " Palace," which does not hold of the burgh but of the Crown. The town hall, situated in the street leading down from the High Street to the railway bridge, bears the date of 1770, but the projecting turret attached is certainly much older. The cross stands in the middle of the street, directly opposite to the town hall. On the right-hand side also of the same street, about half-way down, stands an old mansion known as Rosebery House, from having formerly been the town residence of the Rosebery family.

There is now included in the parish of Inverkeithing that of Rosyth, which was formerly distinct, but was united to the former in 1636, the incumbent of Inverkeithing being taken bound to preach every third Sunday in the church of Rosyth. This last has almost entirely disappeared, though its remains, standing in its little graveyard, may still be seen on the seashore adjoining the village of Limekilns, about two miles to the west of Rosyth Castle.

In the history of the Church of Scotland Inverkeithing has gained an equivocal reputation as the scene in the middle of the last century of the forced induction of Mr Richardson as minister of the parish. For declining to take part in proceedings which they deemed to be wrong and unscriptural, certain clergymen, members of the Dunfermline Presbytery, were summoned to the bar of the General Assembly, and one of their number, Mr Gillespie, the minister of Carnock, who had been specially prominent in his opposition, was made an example of *in terrorem*, and deposed from his charge. The result was the formation of the Dissenting community known as the Relief Church, which about forty years ago formed a coalition with the Burgher and Antiburgher Seceders; and the combination resulting therefrom has since been known as the United Presbyterian Church. I shall have something more to say on this head when I come to speak of Mr Gillespie's parish of Carnock.

Inverkeithing is noteworthy as the birthplace, in 1735, of the celebrated Russian admiral, Samuel Greig, afterwards ennobled as Samuel Carlovich Greig, who not only acted as Commodore of the Russian fleet during the war with Turkey in 1769, and effected much towards the annexation of the Crimea, but was also the designer of the fortifications of Cronstadt, which eighty-five years afterwards proved too hard a nut for Admiral Sir Charles Napier to crack. Greig's father was a merchant captain or skipper, as well as a substantial ship-owner in Inverkeithing; and the son, after going to sea in the merchant service, passed from it into the Royal Navy, in which he rose to the rank of lieutenant. In 1763, in consequence of an application having been made by Russia to Britain for the loan of some officers to help her in the remodelling of her naval armaments, Greig was one of those selected to fulfil this behest. He entered the Russian navy, in which he served with the highest reputation, became an immense favourite with the Empress Catherine, and when he died in 1788, shortly after the battle of Hogeland with the Swedish fleet, he was honoured with a gorgeous State funeral. He is said to have been an admirable man in private life; and when, loaded with honours and at the height of his fame, he paid a visit to his old mother at Inverkeithing, she had the satisfaction of hearing from him that he had neither forgotten a father's instructions nor a mother's prayers. He married a Miss Charteris of Burntisland, and had two sons, one of whom, Sir Alexis Greig, commanded the Russian fleet in the Black Sea for more than twenty years; whilst the other, Samuel Greig, was also connected with the Russian navy, but settled latterly as Russian consul in London: he was the first husband of the celebrated Mrs Mary Somerville (*née* Fairfax), so renowned as a natural philosopher, and who —her mother having been a Charteris—was a kinswoman of Admiral Greig's wife.

Gordon, in his 'Itinerarium Septentrionale,' in referring to battles reported to have been fought between the Scots and the Danes at Culross and at Inverkeithing, says: "At the last of these places there stands an obelisk, 10 feet above the surface of the earth, which, as tradition goes, was erected as a monument of that same defeat of the Danes. On this stone are engraven in low *relievo* several hieroglyphics which I copied on the spot." He accordingly gives, in one of the plates which illustrate his book, a delineation of the stone, on which figures of men and horses seem to be represented. But it is not a little curious that neither is there such a monument in existence now in the parish of Inverkeithing, nor can any information be procured of its having been so at any former time. There can be no reason to charge Gordon with having made any false statement, though it has been surmised that he must have meant St Margaret's Stone in the parish of Dunfermline, and 2½ miles south from that town. But no figures or inscriptions are (now at least) visible on this memorial.

II.

FROM INVERKEITHING TO ABERDOUR.

Victory of Cromwell's army near Inverkeithing—Road to Aberdour—The Moray family and estate—Inchcolm, Donibristle, and Dalgety—Village of Aberdour—Otterston.

PASSING through the east extremity of the town, leaving first on our right the parish church, and then, in descending the hill, the U.P. Church on our left, we find ourselves on the Great North Road, which leads through the Crossgates and Kinross to Perth. It is a quiet and silent highway to what it used to be forty years ago, when it was traversed by the mail-coaches. On our left, trending away to the north-west behind Inverkeithing, is the valley or hollow where the famous battle, which confirmed Cromwell's power in Scotland, was fought between his troops and the Scottish forces on Sunday, 20th July 1651. Cromwell does not seem to have personally taken part in the engagement, nor even to have been present at the transporting of his armament across the Forth, when his troops intrenched themselves on the summit of the Ferry Hill. These, amounting to 10,000, were commanded by General

Lambert, and nearly quadrupled the Scottish forces, which only numbered about 2500, and had moved to this point from Stirling under the direction of General Holburne. The latter did not escape the allegation of treachery and cowardice, though he was afterwards formally acquitted of the charge. The losses on each side are said to have been nearly equal—about 800—but the whole prestige of victory remained with the English, who afterwards marched to Dunfermline and established themselves there for a time.

For some distance after leaving Inverkeithing the road skirts on the right the estate of Spencerfield, belonging to the Hon. R. P. Bruce, M.P., and bounded on the south-east by the ridge of Letham Hill, covered with trees. A beautifully wooded country opens itself directly to the east, with the crater-like summit of Duncarn Hill closing in the far distance; and nearer the spectator the picturesquely rounded and tree-clad knoll overhanging the beautiful loch of Otterston, the scenery enclosing which suggests the idea of a fragment of Italy resting under Scottish skies.

The road from Inverkeithing to Aberdour, a distance of four miles, branches off at the eastern extremity of the town, and passes through the village of Hillend, at the north extremity of Letham Hill. About half a mile beyond this a road to the right leads down to the village and harbour of St David's, to which also a railway is laid through the grounds of Fordel from the coalworks on that estate. A little farther on, on the same side, is the west lodge of Donibristle, the property of the Earl of Moray, whose beautiful domain extends along the shores of the Forth from St David's to Aberdour. It is consequently skirted on the north by the Inverkeithing road during the whole of the intervening distance, the opposite side of the highway being bordered for the greater part by the Fordel and Otterston properties. Lord Moray owns, moreover, a large tract of country extending north from Aberdour over the Cullalo Hills and Moss Morran to Cowdenbeath and Lochgelly, a considerable portion of the coal-field in which neighbourhood belongs to his lordship.

The lands of Donibristle belonged anciently to the Abbey of Inchcolm, the little island in the Firth of Forth opposite Aberdour, which forms so prominent an object in looking down the Firth from Queensferry. It was originally known by the name of Emonia, but had its appellation changed to that of Inchcolm, or the isle of St Columba, in consequence of that saint having for a while made it his residence. It was long tenanted by a succession of anchorites, or solitary ecclesiastics, who occupied a small hermitage here, which is believed to be still represented by the little stone-roofed oratory to the west of the present monastery ruins, and which used to serve the purposes of a cowhouse or byre. The island enjoyed a high reputation as hallowed ground, and on the occasion of the overthrow of the Danes by King Duncan in the eleventh century, as recorded by Boece and referred to by Shakespeare, we find the supplication of the vanquished granted to inter their dead in St Colme's Inch.

The arrival in 1123 of King Alexander I., who had narrowly escaped shipwreck, and with great difficulty gained the friendly shelter of the island and its hermit occupant, changed entirely the fortunes of the place. The grateful monarch vowed to build to the Virgin and St Columba a religious house on Inchcolm, which should serve as a memorial of his preservation. The abbey thus founded was settled with a colony of Augustine friars, became a rich and prosperous community, and numbered among its abbots Walter Bowmaker or Bower, the continuer of Fordun's ' History of Scotland.' Numerous grants of territory on the mainland were made to the monastery, and, among others, a tract of land near Aberdour was bequeathed by Alan Mortimer, then lord of the place, on condition of his body resting within the hallowed precincts of Inchcolm. The remains, so says the story, were conveyed over at night in a stone coffin in an open boat, and either through indifference and treachery on the part of the attendant monks, or to lighten the bark when in peril from the violence of the waves, were cast into the sea. The channel—a very deep one—between Inchcolm and the Fife coast has since borne in consequence the title of " Mortimer's Deep."

Inchcolm may be easily visited from Aberdour, and the traveller, by inquiry at Greig's hotel there, can procure the services of a boatman to ferry him over. The island is long, narrow, and rocky, and the eastern extremity, separated by a low sandy isthmus, is almost cut off at high water. Of the conventual buildings, some of them have disappeared, and a considerable portion built into the house and offices of the tacksman or tenant of the island. The one structure that remains complete is the chapter-house and its surmounting tower, which presents in the distance the special characteristic of Inchcolm. The interior is in good preservation, and the apartment itself, with its encircling row of stone seats, constitutes a very interesting relic. To the south of the conventual buildings is an ancient garden, which has long been famous for its early vegetables. The cell or oratory to the west already referred to is built of and roofed with stone, and has in the interior a length of 16, a breadth of 5, and a height of 8 feet. The island affords pasturage for a few sheep and cows, and though of small extent, is well worthy of a visit. The house is occasionally let for summer quarters.

From its situation the monastery of Inchcolm was readily exposed to the hostile attacks of invaders by sea; and accordingly, in 1547, the year of the battle of Pinkie, we find the Bishop of Dunkeld and other churchmen interponing their authority in the Scottish Privy Council for the payment by the Abbot of Inchcolm to the Scottish Regent of the sum of £500, to be employed in hiring soldiers to recover the island from " our auld ynemeis of Ingland," into whose hands it had fallen. It is also ordered that the abbot and monks who had thus been compelled for a time to abandon their house, should receive meanwhile the hospitality of some other religious house, such as the Abbey of Dunfermline, Lindores, Cambuskenneth, &c.

The temporalities of Inchcolm had, however, already in a manner passed away from the Church and become the spoil of a layman. In 1543, James Stewart, a son of Sir James Stewart of Beath (who was captain of the castle of Doune under James V., and died in 1547), was in the lifetime of his father made commendator of the Abbey of St Colme on a resignation by Abbot Richard in the hands of the Pope. The abbot reserves his liferent of the rents and tithes of the monastery, and engages to pay therefor to the said James Stewart annually the sum of £100 Scots. The considerations stated for this conveyance are the offer of James Stewart to repair the monastery, which had been burned in the month of October by the English, and the promise both of himself and his kindred to defend the island against such attacks for the future.

In January 1563 the same Sir James Stewart was wedded to Lady Margaret Campbell, daughter of Archibald, fourth Earl of Argyll. The marriage was celebrated at Castle Campbell, and Queen Mary made a special journey thither from Edinburgh to attend the

nuptials. In 1581, Sir James was raised to the peerage
by James VI., with the title of Lord Doune, and the
Abbey of St Colme was erected into a temporal lordship
in his favour. He had two sons, the elder of whom,
James, married the daughter and heiress of the celebrated
Regent Moray, and had conferred on him the earldom
held by the latter. He was remarkably handsome in
person, and was consequently known as the " Bonnie
Earl of Moray," an epithet which has come down with
additional interest to posterity on account of his tragical
death at the hands of the Earl of Huntly. His younger
brother Henry had the newly erected lordship of St
Colme bestowed on him by their father, Lord Doune,
who died in 1590.

It was alleged that Anne of Denmark, queen of James
VI., had formed an attachment to the Bonnie Earl, and
thereby excited the jealousy of her husband, who is said,
moreover, to have regarded him otherwise with feelings
of enmity. At all events, on the representation of
Moray's mortal foe, the Earl of Huntly, James seems to
have granted the latter some warrant or authority for
apprehending Moray, which Huntly interpreted in a
more liberal fashion. Accompanied by a retinue of
armed followers, he attacked the Earl's house at Donibristle and set it on fire. Moray endeavoured to make
his escape, but the tassel in his cap caught fire from the
burning mansion as he made his exit. He was recognised, followed to the rocks near the seashore, and there
cruelly shot down and hacked by Huntly, to whom he
exclaimed with the last effort of expiring nature, " You
have spoilt a bonnier face than your own ! " The foul
deed was perpetrated in February 1592, and the place
where it was enacted is still pointed out on the seashore
at a little distance from Donibristle House.

Great popular odium was excited against the king,

who was strongly suspected of complicity in the act. The Earl's mother caused a portrait to be taken of her son as he lay disfigured after death, and presented it to James, with an earnest supplication for justice on her son's murderers. She also caused his body to be conveyed to Leith, where it remained for a long time unburied, with the idea, it is said, of having it exposed at the market-cross of Edinburgh to the gaze of the populace. But to this the king interposed his veto, as he did also to any active prosecution of Huntly, who was arrested and imprisoned for a time, but ultimately liberated without trial. A story is told by Wodrow in his 'Analecta' that "Gordon of Huntly," having been refused admission to the presence of Charles I. after the latter's accession to the throne, on account of his share in the murder of the Earl of Moray, urged his suit with so much pertinacity that the king at last granted his request. Charles reproached him severely for the foul deed, whereupon Huntly drew from his bosom a warrant signed by the king's father for what had taken place. "My lord," said Charles, " this was wrong given and worse executed."

Henry Stewart, younger brother of the Bonnie Earl, was created a peer in 1611, with the title of Lord St Colme. He died the following year, and was succeeded by a son James, on whose death the St Colme peerage became extinct, and the estates attached to it were inherited by the Earl of Moray.

The house of Donibristle, thus set on fire with such disastrous results, has been long since replaced by a modern mansion, which again, in its turn, had about twenty years ago to succumb to a similar fate, and has never been rebuilt. It stands a melancholy ruin in a most beautiful situation by the seashore. The gardens at a little distance used to be regarded as the finest in this part of the country; and though of late years they were somewhat eclipsed by those of Fordel, they are still very beautiful and well kept. As regards the park and grounds generally of Donibristle, nothing can surpass them along the whole shores of the Forth from Stirling to St Abb's. Both nature and art have contributed to adorn the locality, which from St David's to Aberdour presents a charming and ever varied succession of woodland and water, of bays and promontories, of long vistas of trees, and views of the Forth and its opposite shore. In a secluded nook by the seaside stands the old parish church of Dalgety, a most picturesque ruin, and having an interesting history in connection with the monastery of Inchcolm, of which it was a dependency. It was dismantled upwards of fifty years ago, and a new church and manse erected just outside the park of Donibristle, about a mile to the north. The old church is very small, and has at the west end a curious gallery or upper floor, to which access is gained by a turnpike stair on the north side. Attached to the gallery on the south side is a tolerably large chamber, which used to serve as a session-house, and in which it is said that Andrew Donaldson, the well-known Covenanting minister of Dalgety, who had been ejected for nonconformity, was allowed after his expulsion to reside by the connivance of his Episcopal successor. After the Revolution he was restored to his ministerial charge.

It is said that Edward Irving, whilst on a visit in this neighbourhood, was almost the last minister who preached in old Dalgety church. The last incumbent ordained here was the Rev. Mr Watt, who was inducted to the charge in 1830, the Rev. Mr Gilston of Carnock officiating. It was certainly high time for a new church to be built, seeing that the woodwork had become so rotten that the clergyman in getting into the pulpit one Sunday morning suddenly disappeared, to the consternation of his flock, the floor of the *rostrum* having given way !

In a vault adjoining the church are deposited the remains of the Setons, Earls of Dunfermline. They owned the estate of Dalgety, which the first Earl purchased in 1593, and transmitted to his descendants. The mansion which they occupied was situated at a little distance from the church, and a portion of it is still standing, along with the old garden-wall. The property afterwards passed to the Tweeddale family, who succeeded the Setons in their heritable privileges connected with the regality of Dunfermline. It is now all incorporated with the Donibristle estate.

The park of Donibristle abuts on the village of Aberdour, which is charmingly situated in a warm and well-sheltered recess by the seashore, and has long been a favourite summer resort, not only for people in Dunfermline and other Fife towns, but likewise for the inhabitants of Edinburgh and Leith. The place is divided into Easter and Wester Aberdour, the former being the more ancient, and containing the ruins of the old parish church. The feudal superior is the Earl of Morton, whose ancestors have possessed the Aberdour estate since at least the time of David II. Anciently it had belonged to the Viponts, and in the twelfth century passed into the hands of the Mortimers, the benefaction of one of whom to the monks of Inchcolm was so ill requited.

Aberdour House is a mansion of the last century, pleasantly situated in its park immediately adjoining the village, but has not for a long time been occupied by the Morton family, whose chief residence is at Dalmahoy, on the opposite side of the Forth. Not far from it are the ruins of the castle of Aberdour, the ancient abode of the lords of the estate. The Earls of Morton and the Douglases of Loch Leven were of the same family, and so closely connected that the Kinross-shire property came into the possession of the former, who, after holding it for a considerable period, disposed of it in the latter half of the seventeenth century to Sir William Bruce.

A highway runs northward from Aberdour over the west shoulder of the Cullalo Hills and joins the Dunfermline and Kirkcaldy road at Mossgreen, a little to the east of the Crossgates. Reference has already been made to Otterston, which, with the adjoining estate of Cockairny, belonging to the same proprietor (Captain Moubray), borders on the north a considerable part of the road between Aberdour and Inverkeithing. For each of these properties there is a mansion, that of Otterston being charmingly situated on the bank of the beautiful little loch of that name, whilst the house of Cockairny is at a very little distance, on the opposite side of the public road. This branches off the road already mentioned from Aberdour to Mossgreen, and leads down a very steep hill between the two mansions along the shore of Otterston Loch to the highway beween Inverkeithing and Aberdour. Nothing can be more beautiful than a portion of this route, which resembles more nearly a way through romantic pleasure-grounds than a public thoroughfare. The contrast likewise between the cold moorland country about Mossgreen and the soft and Italian scenery at Otterston is exceedingly striking.

III.

FROM INVERKEITHING TO CROSSGATES, COWDENBEATH, AND LOCHGELLY.

The Great North Road—House and grounds of Fordel—Village of Crossgates—The Hill of Beath—Great conventicle held there—Moss Morran and Lochgelly.

RETURNING to the Great North Road, and proceeding along it to about the distance of a mile from Inverkeithing, we cross the Pinkerton Burn at Pinkerton Bridge. This stream comes down from the lands of Duloch, and crossing the eastern extremity of the battle-field of Pitreavie, is said, according to popular tradition, to have run red on that eventful day with the blood of the combatants. To the north-east of us, on a sunny slope, are spread out the lands of Fordel, the property of the Hon. Mrs H. H. Duncan Mercer Henderson, who represents the ancient family which has been in possession of this estate for 350 years.

The Hendersons or Henrysons of Fordel trace their descent from James Henderson, King's Advocate and Justice-Clerk in the reign of James IV., who met his death at the battle of Flodden. He obtained a charter from the king in 1511 of the lands of Fordel, which, previously subdivided among different proprietors, were now united into a barony. His descendants have retained the estate and preserved the name, though within the present century the inheritance has twice devolved on females, and the additional names of Mercer and Duncan have been added to the old family designation.

The grounds of Fordel are very beautiful, and are only surpassed in this neighbourhood by those in the adjoining property of Donibristle. They are traversed by a romantic glen, through which rushes a small stream, on the high bank overhanging which is a small chapel, now only used as a family mausoleum, and adjoining it is a well dedicated to St Theriot, and credited among other virtues with that of the "wishing" order. The house of Fordel, a modern mansion, with a lawn in front, is at a little distance, and on the other side of the glen are the finely laid-out gardens, which, in the hands of the late proprietor, used to be the cynosure of the surrounding country, and attracted numerous visitors in the summer-time, when the grounds were open to strangers every Thursday. The old castle of Fordel adjoining the gardens is interesting as a specimen of an old Scottish baronial mansion. It bears the date of 1567, but a portion of it is evidently much older, and indeed we are informed from Birrell's Diary that in June 1568 "both the old worke and the new" of the "place of Fordell" were consumed "by ane suddaine fyre." It is probable, therefore, that the above date is merely that of the "new work," and that there still remains a considerable portion of the "old work" as restored after the burning, the marks of which can yet be traced. The castle is not inhabited, but the great hall on the first floor has of late years been restored, and used on one or two occasions for meetings. It has a gallery running round it, and is hung with some fine old tapestry which used to adorn the dining-room of Pitreavie House to the south of Dunfermline. In a vault beneath hangs one of those ancient implements of punishment, known as the "branks," or bridle for scolds, so frequently referred to in the minutes of town councils of Scottish burghs.

Robert Henryson, the poet and schoolmaster of Dunfermline, has been claimed as a relative of the Fordel family; but of this no satisfactory evidence has been adduced, and the idea rests wholly on the assumption, from the similarity of name and the vicinity of Dunfermline, that the poet must have belonged to the same stock. Indeed the Henderson family scarcely became connected with Fordel till after the death of the Dunfermline schoolmaster, who flourished in the latter half of the fifteenth century, during the reign of James III. Beyond his poems, which are certainly of a high order, and which fairly rival in merit those of Dunbar and Sir David Lindsay, which they preceded, he has left almost no personal record whatever, and even his pieces are almost wholly destitute of any local colouring.

The prosecutions for witchcraft in the seventeenth century narrate a sad tragedy connected with the Fordel family. The sister of the laird, and the proprietrix of the adjoining lands of Pittadro, was in 1649 arrested on accusation of occult practices, and conveyed to Edinburgh. There she was found dead one morning in prison, under circumstances which led to grave suspicion that she had committed suicide by poisoning or strangling herself. The persecuting times, too, in the reigns of Charles and James II., seem to have been experienced in their fullest extent by the Hendersons, who were mulcted on several occasions in severe fines, both on their own account and that of their tenants, for nonconformity and frequenting conventicles.

The lodge on the Great North Road leading to Fordel House and grounds is about four miles from Queensferry and two from Crossgates, where on the left the road branches off to Dunfermline ($3\frac{1}{2}$ miles), and on the right to Kirkcaldy ($9\frac{1}{2}$ miles). The railway station for Crossgates, on the line from Dunfermline to Thornton, is about a quarter of a mile beyond, on the north side of the village. The surrounding country is by no means of an attractive description, being dotted with numerous collieries, which probably, however, yield their owners harvests much more golden than could be obtained from the most beautiful and fertile districts. The region in which we now are consists partly of moorland, partly of an ungenial sterile soil, and in the winter season the climate is most inclement, the roads becoming frequently quite impassable from snow, which lies longer about Crossgates than almost anywhere between this point and Stirling. Yet the rapid transition that can be made from a cold ungenial upland to a beautiful and picturesque region, will be strikingly manifested in the course of half an hour's drive, by proceeding down the Great North Road for two miles, and then turning off at Fordel lodge in the direction of Donibristle and Aberdour.

To the north-west of Crossgates a round verdant hill presents itself prominently to the eye, and is known as a landmark to the country round under the appellation of the Hill of Beath. It affords good pasture, and as regards reminiscences of the past, is notable as the scene of a large conventicle held there in 1670, at which the celebrated John Blackadder of Troqueer, a cadet of the old family of Tulliallan, and who ultimately died a prisoner in the Bass, was one of the principal officiating ministers. He and his companion had a hard ride to escape capture, after the proceedings of the day were over. First they reached Queensferry, where no boat could be procured to take them across, all having been laid under a strict embargo. They then proceeded upwards along the shore of the Forth, through Limekilns, Torryburn, and Culross to Kincardine, at which last place they calculated on being able to effect a crossing to the other side. But the boats lay on the Stirlingshire shore, and their owners could not or would not bring them over, so that the two ministers had to continue their fatiguing ride for twelve miles farther, by Clackmannan and Alloa to Stirling Bridge, which they crossed a little after midnight. Going through the town with all precaution and despatch, they were fortunate enough to find a postern open in the south gate, through which they managed to lead their horses. Early in the morning they reached the Torwood, where they found shelter in the house of a staunch Presbyterian friend. After resting two hours here, they continued their journey to Edinburgh, from which, after another brief interval of repose of six hours, they had to make their retreat to the south country to avoid pursuit. This was one of the greatest gatherings of the persecuted Nonconformists that had yet taken place in Scotland, and it was followed by numerous others. Great efforts were made by Archbishop Sharp and others to have those who had been present sought out and punished; but though many individuals were in consequence subjected to fine and imprisonment, the clergymen who had been the principal actors there, managed at the time and for a long period subsequently to escape capture.

Proceeding along the Great North Road, we reach Cowdenbeath, which is 2¼ miles from Crossgates and 7¾ from Kinross. Here is the junction of a branch railway to Kinross, passing by Kelty and Blairadam. It is a large and populous place, for the most part of recent erection, and mainly dependent on the adjacent collieries, which have largely increased in this neighbourhood within the last forty years. The discovery and consequent working of blackband ironstone in the coal districts of Fife and Clackmannan, led to a great development here of industrial activity as well as increase of population, though in some places the material itself has been nearly worked out. This latter circumstance led to the discontinuance of the Forth Ironworks at Oakley to the west of Dunfermline; and those at Lochgelly, about a mile to the east of Cowdenbeath, have also been closed.

Away to the south-east of Cowdenbeath stretches a tract of bog and peat, known as Moss Marn or Moss Morran, and extending to the north-east flank of the Cullalo Hills, which separate this dismal country from the rich pastures and smiling region lying between them and the sea. The railway from Dunfermline by Crossgates, Cowdenbeath, and Lochgelly to Thornton Junction, passes through Moss Marn, and in the hot summer of 1868 a spark from the engine ignited the dry peat of the moss, and caused a conflagration that lasted for more than a week, and was not extinguished without considerable difficulty. The smoke and odour of the burning peat were perceptible at least as far as Culross, more than ten miles distant.

The village of Lochgelly crests the ridge of a hill about half a mile to the south of Lochgelly station. On the southern side of the hill is the loch from which the place takes its name. It is a sheet of water of some size, but has no specially picturesque attractions, though Lochgelly House (the Hon. Hugh F. H. Elliot) is rather prettily situated on a wooded slope at the north-west corner. The ground here belongs to the Earl of Minto, who owns the north side of the loch, whilst to Mr Wemyss of Wemyss Castle belongs the south shore. Here is the farm of the Little Raith, memorable in connection with a characteristic prayer said to have been offered up on one occasion by Mr Shirreff, the well-known Secession minister at Kirkcaldy. He was supplicating for more favourable weather for the harvest, and backed his entreaty with the argument, "for they tell me that up at the Little Raith it's a' as green as leeks yet!" The

Raith estate (R. Munro Ferguson, Esq., M.P.) comes up to the east side of Lochgelly, and the Earl of Moray is also a large proprietor in this neighbourhood.

From Lochgelly station a fine view is obtained of the ancient Lochoreshire, or parishes of Ballingry and Auchterderran, with the Blairadam grounds forming the north-west of the landscape amphitheatre. On an eminence behind Blairadam House there is seen a group of trees, which, from the present standpoint, bears a singular resemblance to the figure of a horse. Due north of the spectator, and bounding the horizon, is Benarty Hill with its wooded slope, and away to the east of it appears the south extremity of the Bishop Hill, which borders the eastern shore of Loch Leven. Looking farther east are seen the wooded heights of Balgreggic and Auchterderran, and closing in the extremity of the prospect in this direction is Largo Law with its cleft summit.

———

IV.

FROM COWDENBEATH TO BLAIRADAM AND CLEISH.

The drained site of Loch Ore—Its ancient island castle—Ancient Roman station—Interest attaching to Loch Ore in connection with Sir Walter Scott—Approach to Blairadam—Its classic associations—Benarty Hill and Paranwell—Ballingry church—First view of Loch Leven—Village and barony of Cleish—History of its ancient lords, the Colvilles of Ochiltree—Ruined castle of Dowhill—Gairney Bridge and its associations—The first Secession Synod—Michael Bruce.

Continuing our journey to Kinross by the Great North Road from Cowdenbeath, Lumphinnans Colliery, on the estate of the Earl of Zetland, appears between us and Lochgelly village. About a mile and a half north-north-west from Lochgelly station is the drained site of Loch Ore, formerly a considerable sheet of water, and having an island near its eastern end, on which stood a castle, anciently a seat of the Wardlaws of Torrie who in former days owned the barony of Lochore. The ruins still exist, and in Sir Robert Sibbald's time the words " Robertus Wardlaw " were still to be seen inscribed above the main entrance. This family acquired it by the marriage of Sir Andrew Wardlaw with the heiress of the house of Vallance of Lochore, and the estate (known also as that of Inchgall) was retained by them till the reign of Charles I., when it passed from them, apparently about the same time that they quitted possession of Torrie.

The castle of Lochore must formerly have been very picturesquely situated on its islet, at a little distance from the shore, but completely surrounded by the waters of the loch. It is said to have been built by Duncan Lochore in the time of Malcolm Canmore, and is certainly very old, and of rather rude and cyclopean construction, but has become almost a wreck, having been rent into four portions. The walls are ten feet thick, and there is no appearance of any chimney, except on the first floor on the north side. There are only two storeys remaining, and on the upper one, on the west side, there is a window with lintels, the only opening of the kind that is now to be seen in the building. In the same wall, but separated from it by a rent, and what has probably been a doorway, are the pier and spring of a Gothic arch, which may have led to a central chapel on the first floor, like that in the Tower of London. The ruins are enclosed by a circular wall six feet thick, on the inner side of which, throughout almost its whole extent, has been a series of houses and offices, of which the foundations still remain. At the north-east extremity of the outer wall is the fragment of a semi-circular flanking tower, and the islet, now appearing like a knoll in the meadow-ground, is planted with trees.

Loch Ore was drained in the beginning of the present century, and was anciently known as Inchgall Loch. On the south side of it is a ridge called the Clune, where the remains of two British camps are distinctly visible. At the north-west extremity is Chapel Farm, on the site of the ancient chapel of Inchgall, and close by was the celebrated Roman camp—the Victoria of Ptolemy—referred to by Sibbald and Sandy Gordon, but which has now unfortunately been almost entirely demolished, though faint traces are still perceptible.

Sir Robert Sibbald informs us that in his day the estate of Lochore belonged to Malcolm of Balbedie, who had erected a fine new house, with gardens and enclosures, on an eminence above the loch. Its site is occupied by a more recent mansion, which stands finely amid some good old timber, and is now divided into two dwellings, occupied respectively by the manager and superintendent of the Lochore Mining Company, who are now the owners of the estate. The property possesses some interest from having till recently belonged to Lady Scott (*née* Miss Jobson of Lochore), the daughter-in-law of the great Sir Walter, who, in his visits to the neighbouring proprietor of Blairadam, used frequently to visit the grounds of Lochore, and is said to have directed the laying out of the plantations by which the estate is diversified. There is a fine old avenue leading eastwards from Lochore House, and opening on the public road a little to the south-west of Ballingry church.

The country continues bleak and wild as we proceed on our journey to Kinross; but we are now entering a more attractive region at Benarty, the great verdant hill with the broad summit, on the north side of which lies Loch Leven. Benarty House occupies a pleasant situation on the southern slope, and on the top are the remains of a British camp. The wide plateau here used to be the scene of an annual gathering of the shepherds of Fife and adjoining counties, who bivouacked in the open air for several days, and spent the time in a variety of athletic sports, amid great feasting and merriment. The hill rises to the height of 1167 feet, and its lower slopes are picturesquely clothed with wood, whilst the Great North Road winds round its west flank, in the valley between the hill and the grounds of Blairadam. A little to our left, on a rising ground, is the village of Oakfield, on the old road leading north from the Crossgates and Cowdenbeath by the Kirk of Beath and Cant's Dam. From Oakfield a road leads east across a ridge for about four miles, by Gask and Roscobie to Redcraigs, where it joins the road running north from Dunfermline to the Rumbling Bridge and Glen Devon.

About half a mile north from Oakfield is the village of Kelty, where there is a large colliery, and three-quarters of a mile farther on is the village of Maryburgh, from which the original title of the Blairadam estate, as acquired by the ancestor of the present proprietor, is derived. Midway between Kelty and Maryburgh is the hamlet of Bridge End, where the Kelty Burn from Blairadam grounds crosses the road. Returning again to the Great North Road, we pass on our left Blairadam Lodge, at the distance of 5¾ miles from Crossgates, and 4¼ from Kinross. The mansion of Blairadam (Sir Charles Elphinstone Adam), pleasantly situated amid the trees in its park, appears on the rising ground to our left. About a mile and a quarter due south from it, and within the Blairadam grounds, are the Keiry Craigs, which Sir Walter Scott has rendered classical as the halting-place of John Auchtermuchty, the Kinross carrier, in 'The Abbot.'

Blairadam has many interesting reminiscences. In the early part of last century the estate, then known as that of Blair or Blair-Crambeth, was purchased by William Adam, architect and king's mason, who erected here a mansion and village, to which he gave the name of Maryburgh ; and by the last appellation the property was known both during his time and that of his son and successor. He died in 1748, having previously done much to adorn the property in the way of plantations, which Pennant comments on in his Tour as almost the only appearance of woods that presented itself to him between Queensferry and Kinross. Two of his sons were the celebrated architects, James and Robert Adam, from whom the Adelphi Buildings in London received their designation. A daughter married John Clerk of Eldin, an accomplished draughtsman, as his collection of views of numerous places in Scotland amply testifies, and father of the well-known Lord Eldin of Court of Session celebrity. The grandson of the founder of the family was the Right Honourable William Adam, Chief Commissioner of the Jury Court in Scotland, and though an ardent Whig, the bosom friend of Sir Walter Scott. The latter was for many years in the custom of paying a visit in summer to Blairadam, as it was now designed—the Chief Commissioner having changed its title to this from Maryburgh. Many other eminent persons have been entertained here, and among these, the renowned dramatist and parliamentary leader, Richard Brinsley Sheridan, who on one occasion, when contemplating from Blairadam House, Loch Leven and the adjacent scenery, gave utterance, it is said, to the following impromptu :—

> " How pleasant, away from the turmoil of party,
>   To sit at this window and look at Benarty ! "

On the right-hand side of the way, near Blairadam smithy, a road branches off by the north side of Benarty, and leads to Ballingry church, at a distance of about two and a half miles. It is worth traversing, for more reasons than one. After proceeding along it about half a mile, the traveller arrives at the hamlet of Paranwell, a place which derives its name from a copious spring of excellent water in the neighbourhood. It seems to be a contraction for " Padan-Aram well," and a similar patriarchal appellation has been bestowed on the hill on the east side of Benarty House, which is called " Harran " or " Haran Hill." In a field on the north side of the road at Paranwell stands an arch, erected by a proprietor of Blairadam across a ravine through which anciently the road passed from St Johnston or Perth, through Kelty by the Kirk of Beath to Queensferry. The defile was formerly much deeper than it is now, and was planted on each side with trees. It is exceedingly likely that Queen Mary took this route in escaping from Loch Leven Castle; and we are informed by Lindsay of Pitscottie that she and Lord Darnley in 1564 passed this way in going south from Perth, and were nearly intercepted by the Earl of Rothes and certain confederates, who, it is alleged, were dissatisfied with the marriage, then in prospect, of this celebrated pair, and " thought to have taine my Lord Darnely from the queine." The latter had been warned of the design, and she and Darnley had passed Paranwell on their way to Queensferry ere the conspirators made their appearance. Such is the story, as referred to in an inscription on the arch, which states that it was placed there by William Adam in 1838. About a hundred yards farther on is an old ruined house with another inscription on it—evidently of the same date as that on the arch—"This house in the reign of James V. belonged to Squire Meldrum of Cleish and Binns, celebrated in a poem of Sir David Lindsay of the Mount."

The road from Paranwell to Ballingry (pronounced *Bingry*) church, passes through the woodland on the north slope of Benarty, and commands from its terrace-like elevation of nearly 500 feet a fine view of the country over Loch Ore to the ridge of Lochgelly. The lodge of Benarty House (Thomas Constable, Esq.) is on the right-hand side of the road, about one and a quarter mile east from Paranwell, and Ballingry church is reached in other three-quarters of a mile. The latter is a plain modern building, but the adjoining manse looks very comfortable. A little farther eastward is the hamlet of Shank, where there is a small inn or public-house and a smithy. From this the road continues to Auchmoor Bridge and Leslie, and another highway leads due south from Shank to Lochgelly station, at a distance of about three miles.

Shortly after passing Blairadam Lodge, a beautiful prospect is presented of Loch Leven, expanding itself like a vast mirror, with its girdle of hills on the east and south, those on the former side being the West Lomonds, which comprise from north to south Bishop Hill, rising to the height of 1470, Munduff to 1491, and Greenhead Hill to 1000 feet. They are composed of beds of sandstone, with a surmounting cap of basalt. At their feet, on the slope between them and the loch, nestle the villages of Wester and Easter Balgedie, Kinnesswood, and Scotlandwell; whilst at a place called Levenmouth, at the south-east extremity of the loch, the river Leven debouches itself through the valley between Kinneston

Craigs and Benarty.   From thence it pursues its course down to the Firth of Forth by the town of Leslie, supplying the wants of numerous manufactories on its way, and discharging itself into the sea at Leven.   On the south side of the loch rises Benarty, with the finely wooded gorge on its west flank, through which the Great North Road passes; whilst branching off here from the latter to the right a road skirts the southern shore of Loch Leven by the base of Benarty, and is joined at Auchmoor Bridge by the road leading from Kinross round the head of the loch through Kinnesswood and Scotlandwell.   I shall presently have occasion to delineate in detail Loch Leven and its banks.

At the third milestone from Kinross, on the Great North Road, the latter is joined by the highway which leads from Saline and the western extremity of Fife to Kinross through the broad strath or valley between the Cleish hills and the Ochils.   If we proceed along this for about a mile and a half, we reach the village of Cleish, with its church and manse, and three-quarters of a mile farther west we come to Cleish Castle or the Place of Cleish (Harry Young, Esq.), an ancient mansion, formerly one of the principal seats of the Lords Colville of Ochiltree, and which, after long existing as a stately ruin, was about forty years ago restored and made habitable. Behind it is some fine old timber, including till lately a specially magnificent silver fir, one of the finest of the kind to be found in Scotland.   It rose altogether to the height of about 120 feet, but after presenting a circumference of 15 feet to an elevation of 22 feet from the ground, it branched off into several enormous boughs, each of which would of itself have constituted a large tree.   One of these had a circumference of 10 feet.   It was blown down some years ago, and fell with a tremendous crash, causing to the inmates of Cleish Castle a shock resembling that of an earthquake. The great limb was disposed of for £30. One of its companions, also a mighty tree, still stands, and so does a grand yew-hedge, one of the glories of the old castle.

The barony of Cleish came into the possession of the Colvilles of Ochiltree in the early part of the sixteenth century, and was made over in 1537 by Sir James Colville of Easter Wemyss to his natural son Robert. The same Sir James had exchanged in 1530 his ancestral estate of Ochiltree in Ayrshire for that of East Wemyss in Fife, along with the territory of Lochoreshire in the same county. Robert Colville, thus made Laird of Cleish, became a zealous Reformer, and was killed at the siege of Leith in 1560. A strange story is recorded regarding him in the ' Coronis,' or Supplement to Row's ' History of the Church of Scotland,' by the latter's son, William Row of Ceres. At least we are informed by an annotator on Row's MSS. that the hero of the adventure ascribed to " Esquire Meldrum" was really Robert Colville of Cleish, who has thus been confounded with a William Meldrum of Cleish and Binns, who lived in the reigns of James IV. and V., and whose extraordinary adventures form the subject of Sir David Lindsay's poem of " Squire Meldrum." We have already heard something of this worthy in connection with an old house on his estate of Binns, near Paranwell, which is now incorporated with the Blairadam property.

William Row tells the story with a good deal of lively humour. It would seem that Robert Colville's reforming zeal was not shared by his wife, who, being a devoted adherent of the ancient faith, and at this time in an " interesting condition," had despatched a messenger to the chapel of Our Lady of Loretto at Musselburgh, with a handsome gift to the shrine as a propitiation in expectancy of the coming event. Her husband resolved

to follow the envoy and see what came of his mission.
As it happened, there was then a great excitement at the
chapel of Loretto (also called St Allaret's chapel), in prospect of a great miracle which the priests had stated
would take place there on the following day, when a
man who had been blind from his birth, and been
known to the public as a blind beggar, would receive
his sight through the intercession of the saint. The
ceremony took place as announced, on a scaffold erected
for the occasion ; and the man, apparently stone blind,
opened his eyes, and was cured of his malady in presence
of an immense multitude.   Colville was convinced there
was some trick in the matter, and, to satisfy himself, he
accosted afterwards the subject of the interposition, and
induced him to proceed to Edinburgh, where, on arriving
with St Allaret's *protégé* at his lodgings, the Laird of Cleish
locked the door, and, under threat of immediate death,
extorted from the terrified wight the confession that the
whole affair was an imposture.   He had been, it seems,
in the service of the nuns of the Sciennes convent, near
Edinburgh, as a shepherd, and had a faculty of turning
up at pleasure the whites of his eyes so as to counterfeit
blindness.   The sisters communicated this circumstance
to some ecclesiastical friends of theirs, who thought they
might turn it to account in support of the Church's influence with the populace.   They accordingly kept him
perdu for a long period, and then sent him out to the
roadside to beg as a blind man.   When he had acted
for some time in this capacity, they then advertised the
performance of the miracle, and brought him out to
" play his pavie " on the scaffold at Musselburgh.

The story goes on to say that Colville promised to be-
friend the man and take him into his service, but insisted
that he should first make a retractation and exposure of
the cheat at the market-cross of Edinburgh, immediately

after doing which they would take horse and escape into Fife. This was agreed to; and master and man, after the latter had made his declaration to the lieges, succeeded in making good their flight, crossed the Forth at Queensferry, and arrived safely at Cleish. What Mrs Colville thought of the matter we are not informed; but shortly afterwards, the arrival at Cleish of John Row, the historian's father, who had just returned from Rome on a mission to the Pope, called forth a narrative of the transaction from Colville's servant. It is said that the Roman Catholic emissary was so struck with the story as to be shaken in his belief in the ancient faith, which he shortly afterwards renounced to become an earnest Protestant, and ultimately to die minister of Perth.

Robert Colville was succeeded in the Cleish estate by his son, also named Robert, who in 1569 obtained a grant of the hereditary bailiary of Culross, which had previously, under the abbots of that monastery, been exercised by the Earls of Argyll. He was succeeded by his son, Robert Colville, who died in 1634, and was followed by a son also named Robert—making thus four Robert Colvilles of Cleish in uninterrupted succession. Notwithstanding their severance from the ancient family estate of Ochiltree, this branch of the Colvilles seems always to have taken from it their principal designation. The fourth Robert Colville of Cleish was knighted by Charles I., and raised to the peerage by Charles II. in 1651, with the title of Lord Colville of Ochiltree.

Besides Robert Colville, the first Sir James Colville of Easter Wemyss had another illegitimate son, named James, who in 1560, along with other properties, received from William Colville, commendator of Culross, a grant of the lands of Crombie, then belonging to Culross Abbey, and now included in the parish of Torryburn in Fife. These were afterwards inherited or acquired by his collateral descendants, the Colvilles of Cleish, whom we afterwards find possessors of both estates, and residing alternately at the respective mansions on each.[1] After the death of the third and last Lord Colville of Ochiltree in 1723, the Cleish estate seems to have been sold, and the castle allowed to go to ruin.

By ascending the hill behind Cleish Castle the summit of Dumglow is reached—the highest point (1240 feet) in the Cleish range. A magnificent prospect is commanded from it of Loch Leven and the plain of Kinross, as well as of the lower basin of the Forth, taking in the Bass, North Berwick Law, and the range of Lammermuir. A similar view, though from a lower elevation, is obtained by the traveller in journeying from Dunfermline to Kinross by the old road which leads from the Gask Toll by Lochornie Farm over the heights of Craigencat and Craigencrow down Nivingston Hill. The localities in this upland region are thus combined in the popular rhyme—

> " Craigencat and Craigencrow,
>   Dowhill, King Seat, and Dumglow."

Several lochs exist here, the largest being Loch Glow or the White loch, whilst to the east of it is the Dow loch, and to the west the Black and the Lurg lochs. Loch Glow used to be famous for its perch, and was greatly resorted to by anglers from Dunfermline and the neighbouring country, but the fishing is now strictly preserved.

At Nivingston House the old road across the hill joins the highway leading eastwards from Cleish to the Great North Road. The junction is about half a mile east from Cleish village, and near this, in a stone dyke opposite the mansion of Nivingston, used to be a large rock known as the " Lecture Stane," which is said in

____
[1] See pp. 147-149.

Roman Catholic times to have been used for the support of the coffin during the reading of the burial service.   Several ineffectual attempts had in bygone days been made to blast it—a circumstance which induced the belief that the stone was charmed, and for a long time no further endeavour of the kind was instituted.   But about thirty years ago an irreverent contractor for the repairs of the dyke dispelled all such notions with a strong and effectual charge of powder, by which this interesting relic was blown to fragments.

Returning to the Great North Road by Cleish Mill, and passing on our left a highway which leads by a nearer and more direct route to Kinross, we see on an eminence to the right the ruins of the castle of Dowhill, formerly the property of the Lindsays, who enjoyed baronial rank, and suffered severely during the persecuting times for their Covenanting proclivities.   It is now included in the estate of Blairadam, and must at one time have been a place of great importance and size, but has been much diminished in consequence of having served during the last century as a very convenient quarry.   At present it is a square-looking castellated ruin, with a circular tower at the south-west corner, and the remains of a pepper-box turret on the west side.   At the east end is what may have been a sort of keep, and at the north-east corner, but detached from the rest of the building, is the fragment of a tower.   A range of buildings probably extended from this to the east wall. The remains of the castle consist of a basement storey, with what looks like a large chimney, which had been carried up through the centre of the building, and seems to have served all the floors, as no fireplace appears in the outer walls.   The first floor, with its windows and embrasures, remains entire, and there had probably been above this another storey.   The apartments on the basement are vaulted, and the south wall presents a fine front of dressed stone.

I have before me a print taken from a drawing by John Clerk of Eldin, and giving a view of Dowhill Castle from the south-west as it appeared in 1770. There is not much difference between its aspect then and that at the present day, except that resting on the south wall, but not extending along the whole front, an apparently inhabited building is seen, with a delta-shaped roof, through which two chimneys protrude. The pepper-box turret on the west side, though ruinous, is much more entire than at present, and the circular tower at the corner is provided with a roof. There are a good many trees about the castle, and in the distance appears Loch Leven, with the Castle Island and the Lomond hills.

The Gairney burn, which flows eastwards through the Cleish valley into Loch Leven, crosses the Great North Road at Gairney Bridge, two miles from Kinross. The farm-steading which bears the same name, and is situated close to the road a little to the south of the bridge, is famous in the history of the Secession Church, as occupying the site of the little public-house where the four fathers of the Secession—Ebenezer Erskine of Stirling, Alexander Moncreiff of Abernethy, William Wilson of Perth, and James Fisher of Kinclaven—on being deposed in 1733 by the Commission of the General Assembly, held a few weeks subsequently their first Presbytery or Synod. They received shortly afterwards the accession of four new members — Ralph Erskine of Dunfermline (Ebenezer's brother), Thomas Mair of Orwell, Thomas Nairn of Abbotshall, and James Thomson of Burntisland,—and were thenceforward known as the Associate Presbytery or Associate Synod. To commemorate the event an obelisk has lately been erected near the farm on the roadside.

Another interesting circumstance connected with this locality is that of the amiable and lamented young poet, Michael Bruce, having here for some time taught a school. The schoolhouse was also on the site of the present farm-steading.

V.

KINROSS AND LOCH LEVEN.

Town of Kinross and its environs—Kinross House—Loch Leven and its history—The Castle Island and its memorials of Queen Mary —The Isle of St Serf and its priory.

BETWEEN Gairney Bridge and Kinross there is little to interest the traveller beyond the general view of the town, and of Loch Leven with its islands. The former occupies a slight rising ground near the north-western extremity of the loch, and consists mainly of one long street, traversing the town from south to north, with a number of cross lanes. It contains some good houses at the northern extremity, but can neither be said to be well built nor very attractive in general appearance. Besides smaller inns, it contains two good hotels—Kirkland's and the Green Hotel, within a short distance of each other. The latter, situated at the north entrance of the town, and comprising a great part of what in the coaching days was one of the best-appointed inns in Scotland, is specially to be commended. It is largely patronised during the season by anglers.

Kinross has a population of 1960, and was constituted a burgh of barony by Regent Morton in the reign of James VI. The municipal and county buildings with their clock tower (a modern erection) stand in the centre of the town, and opposite to them is the town cross (also a modern structure), around the upper part of which is suspended the *jougs*, or iron collar, which was used in ancient times as an implement of pillory and punishment for enclosing the necks of malefactors. Kinross was formerly celebrated for its manufacture of cutlery, but this branch of industry has long since completely disappeared, and beyond a factory at Bridge End and a little weaving, no special trade or industry is maintained in the town, which depends mainly on supplying the adjoining district with necessaries. It is also largely supported by the visitors who resort here both as anglers and pilgrims to the loch and castle. The whole of Loch Leven and its islands, with a considerable adjacent territory, including Burleigh Castle and Kinross House, belongs to Sir Graham Montgomery of Stanhope, Bart., as the lineal representative of Sir William Bruce of Kinross, who purchased the estate from the Earl of Morton in the latter half of the seventeenth century. The right of fishing in the loch is rented by the Loch Leven Angling Association, who maintain a supply of boats which may be hired by visitors. The season commences in the month of April, and trout-fishing may be enjoyed at the charge of 2s. 6d. an hour, and 2s. 6d. for the day to one of the two boatmen—the Association paying the other. The charge for perch-fishing is 1s. per hour, including boat, and for visiting the island and castle 5s. In the height of the season there is often a great demand for boats, though twenty are kept for hire.

Kinross-shire comprehended originally only the parishes of Kinross, Orwell, and Portmoak, and these were disjoined from Fife and formed into a separate county in 1426. Two hundred and sixty years afterwards, in 1685, an Act of the Scottish Parliament disjoined from Fife and Perth the parish of Cleish, and portions of those of Fossoway and Arngask, and attached them to the county of Kinross, "to support and maintain the state and rank of a district shire, as it is and anciently has been." After Clackmannanshire, it is the smallest county in Scotland, and the two are incorporated into one sheriffdom.

The monuments of Kinross are of little account, with the exception of the splendid mansion of Kinross House, situated to the east of the town on a long projection of land extending into the loch, and which has at its extremity the remains of the old parish church, with its burial-ground. The house was erected in 1685, by the celebrated architect Sir William Bruce, who had a few years previously purchased the Kinross estate from the Earl of Morton. He was cousin of Alexander, second Earl of Kincardine, and is said to have originally designed the building for the residence of James II., when Duke of York, in the event of the Exclusion Bill being carried to prevent his ascending the throne. The house is of the Renaissance style of architecture, which came greatly into vogue in Britain during the seventeenth century, and of which Inigo Jones was one of the ablest exponents. Sir William Bruce seems to have studied in the same school, and produced, besides Kinross House, Holyrood House, as restored after the conflagration in 1650, and the mansions of Moncreiff and Hopetoun. Presbyterian scandal, as given currency to by Kirkton in his History, has not hesitated to ascribe Sir William's success in money-making to the circumstance of his holding the appointment of Clerk of the Bills, and thus receiving a large portion of the fines levied from the recusant Covenanters. Thus, it asserts, was the estate of Kinross purchased and the foundation of its splendid mansion laid.

Kinross House is approached through an imposing gateway, from which a broad and verdant lawn extends up to the former, with stately rows of trees on each side, but there is—now at least—no proper carriage-way. Though in perfect order and repair, it is unfurnished, and has not been occupied for many years, but is well worthy of a visit as a fine and interesting specimen of a Scottish palatial mansion in the seventeenth century. The entrance-hall and adjoining rooms are all of a sumptuous order, but the grand apartment in the house is the ball-room or large drawing-room up-stairs, which has a length of $54\frac{1}{2}$ feet, by a breadth of 24. The old house previously existing, and which had been for several generations the residence of the Earls of Morton, was situated on the north side of the present garden, and was pulled down about the year 1723. Some traces of its foundations are still visible. In contrast apparently to the old castle in Loch Leven, it used to be known as the New House of Kinross.

Sir Robert Sibbald, in his 'History of Fife and Kinross,' waxes extremely eloquent on the subject of Kinross House, then but recently erected, and characterises it as a mansion "which, for situation, contrivance, prospects, avenues, courts, gravel-walks, and terraces, and all hortulane ornaments, parks, and planting, is surpassed by few in this country." He commends also highly Sir William's ingenuity in draining the ground, and thereby converting a morass into good land, which became thus the site of handsome policies and orchards. But it may well be questioned whether it was judicious to set down a mansion in so level and moist a situation, where, in rainy weather, the basement storey must always necessarily be damp, and even the approach to the house is often wet and uncomfortable.

Loch Leven is 360 feet above the level of the sea, and

throughout the parish of Kinross the elevation above the loch nowhere exceeds 100 feet. A popular saying connects its appellation with the number eleven, inasmuch as it was alleged to have a circuit of eleven miles, to contain eleven islands, be tenanted by eleven kinds of fish, and be surrounded by the estates of eleven lairds. All this, however, is an absurdity. The title "Leven" occurs frequently in local nomenclature in Scotland, denoting the *grey* or possibly the *smooth* water (*liath-am-huinn* or *liomh-amhuinn*), either of which terms, when contracted, is pronounced very like "Leven." As regards extent, it used to have a circuit of 15 miles, but the draining operations of 1830, by which nearly 1400 acres were reclaimed from the loch, chiefly on its eastern side, reduced this amount to 12 miles. The depth at medium height varies from 19 to 14 feet. The surface used to comprise 4638 imperial acres, which the drainage has reduced by nearly a third, leaving the amount at a little over 3000.

The east and southern shores of the loch are, as already mentioned, bordered by hills, whilst the west, and in a lesser degree the north, are level and monotonous. It contains only two islands of any size—the Castle Island at its north-west, and St Serf's Island at its south-east extremity. Its waters have long been famous for their pink-fleshed trout, a characteristic said to be derived from a fresh-water mussel on which they feed. A similar quality belongs to the trout of Lough Neagh in Ireland.

The Castle Island is about half a mile from the shore, and nearly in a line due east from Kinross House and the old churchyard. The water at this point is very shallow, and in dry seasons it is almost possible to wade to the island from the mainland. Traces of an ancient causeway are also to be met with, and there seems little doubt that in primeval times the Castle Island formed the site of a *crannog* or lake-dwelling. In the neighbourhood are two or three small islets, which, having in recent times been planted with wood, add considerably to the beauty of the scenery. Those on the north-west and south-west side are denominated respectively " Lily's Bower " and " Roy's Folly," whilst on the south side is " Reed Bower." There was another islet here called " Paddock Bower," but since the lowering of the water-level of the loch, this has become a peninsula on the mainland. Beyond, and not far from the north shore, are Green Island and Scart Island (both very small). The last-named derives its appellation from the *scarts* or cormorants which frequent Loch Leven, and commit some havoc among the trout. I do not know whether Scart Island is the same that Sir Robert Sibbald mentions as being near to the Castle Island, and bearing the name of " Bittern's Bower." There is no island now in Loch Leven which is so called, and the bittern itself is a bird that occurs but rarely in this neighbourhood.

The castle of Loch Leven, though nothing definite regarding its origin can be ascertained, is said to have been founded by Congal, son of Dongart, king of the Picts ; and, at all events, it seems occasionally in early times to have been a royal residence. Among our Scottish monarchs, Alexander III. is said to have occupied it, and specially on one occasion, after his return from England, where he had been visiting his father-in-law, Henry III., at Wark Castle. In 1301 we hear of Edward I.'s forces besieging the place, and the siege being raised by Sir John Comyn. Thirty-four years later, in the reign of David II., when Edward III. had despatched an expedition to reinstate Baliol, the son of the former pretender to the Crown, Loch Leven Castle, then held by Sir Alan Vypont in the interest of King

David, was invested by the English army under the command of Sir John Strivelyn. An attempt was made by the latter to submerge the island by damming up the river Leven at its exit from the loch, but was frustrated by the enterprise of the Scottish garrison, who, in a sudden and unexpected expedition made during the night to Levenmouth, succeeded in making breaches in the rampart. The water burst through with such violence as to carry everything before it, flooded the English camp, and drove the soldiers to flight in helpless confusion. Baggage and spoils of every kind were left behind, and carried off in triumph by the Scottish army, which thus received an important reinforcement towards resisting the siege. This, too, they had not to sustain long, as a successful sally made by them on the English detachment at Kinross shortly afterwards freed them from the blockade.

In 1429, Archibald, Earl of Douglas, was committed by James I. a State prisoner to Loch Leven Castle, which also, nearly sixty years later, received as a captive Patrick Graham, the Archbishop of St Andrews, who, by a sentence of deposition and imprisonment pronounced in 1484 by Pope Sixtus IV. and the College of Cardinals, had been committed first to a cell in Inchcolm, thence to Dunfermline Abbey, and finally to Loch Leven. Here he died, and his remains were interred in the hallowed ground of the island of St Serf.

Whilst the Castle Island continued an appanage of the Crown, there seems generally to have been resident in it a governor appointed by the sovereign, and known by the title of the captain of Loch Leven. When or how it first came into the hands of the Douglases is not very clear, but in 1540 we find a charter of *novodamus* granted by James V. in favour of Robert Douglas of Loch Leven and his son William, of the lands and barony of Kinross, and of the castle in the loch, along with other lands, of which those of Dalqueich, in the county of Kinross, are said to have been in the possession of the said Robert from time immemorial, though the writs and evidents of ownership had been lost. It was this Robert Douglas who married Lady Margaret Erskine, daughter of the Earl of Mar, who had previously borne to James V. a son, afterwards the celebrated Regent Moray, who was thus brother uterine of William Douglas of Loch Leven, the custodian of Queen Mary.

The main interest in the castle of Loch Leven centres, of course, in its having been the place of detention for a twelvemonth of the unfortunate Queen of Scots, who was conveyed here from Edinburgh in 1567, after her surrender to Moray's army at Carberry Hill. She managed to effect her escape from captivity on the evening of Sunday the 2d of May 1568, mainly by the aid of George Douglas, brother of the laird, whom, it is said, her charms had captivated. A young lad, known as the Little Douglas, doubtless a relation or dependant of the family, and who figures in 'The Abbot' in the character of Roland Græme, managed to steal the keys of the castle whilst the family were at supper, and, with the assistance of George Douglas, conveyed the Queen to a boat which was lying in readiness under the castle walls. She embarked in this, and was safely ferried across to the mainland, where she was met by Lord George Seton and other followers. Then mounting on horseback, she fled across the country with them to St Margaret's Hope, and there crossing the Forth to the opposite shore, proceeded to Lord Seton's castle of Niddry, near Winchburgh, in West Lothian. Here she rested for two hours, and then continued her journey to Hamilton, where she found the army that had assembled on her behalf. A few days more decided her fate at the battle of Langside, which was followed by her flight to the Solway and embarkation for England.

Three places have been assigned as the scene of Mary's landing on the banks of Loch Leven after her escape from the castle. One of these is at the spot known as Mary's Knowe, on the shore of the loch, nearly a mile north from Kinross House. Another is at the north side of "Paddock Bower," nearly 300 yards east from the old churchyard of Kinross, and almost in a line with the castle tower. Not far from this a bunch of keys was picked up by a boy in 1805, and supposed to have been those of the castle, which are stated in one account of Queen Mary's escape to have been thrown by young Douglas into the loch after locking the gates to prevent pursuit on the part of the inmates. A smaller bunch was picked up in the same neighbourhood in 1831, and conjectured to have belonged to one of Queen Mary's wardrobes.

It is more probable, on the whole, that the place of Mary's debarkation was at Coldon, at the south-west extremity of the loch, where she would be less liable to interception than anywhere in the neighbourhood of Kinross, and have at the same time a nearer and more convenient course of flight to the Firth of Forth. Most likely she made her way by the old road leading from Perth, which passed through the villages of Paranwell and Kelty, and thence by the Kirk of Beath and the country east of Dunfermline, across Calais Moor to Queensferry.

In the year following Queen Mary's escape, the Earl of Northumberland was sent a prisoner to Loch Leven Castle, at the request of Queen Elizabeth, to escape whose vengeance he had taken refuge in Scotland. He was detained there for three years, and at the end of that period was removed to England, where he was arraigned and beheaded on the charge of high treason.

The last notice that we have of the castle in Scottish history is the confinement here of Robert Pitcairn, commendator of the Abbey of Dunfermline, and Secretary of State under the regency of Lennox. He had been concerned in the political escapade known as the Raid of Ruthven, under which the youthful monarch, James VI., had for a time been subjected to a species of durance. For his share in this adventure, Pitcairn was arrested and conveyed to Loch Leven, where he died in 1584.

The Castle Island is now, owing to the subsidence of the waters of the loch, considerably larger than it was at the time of the imprisonment of the Queen of Scots, when its extent barely amounted to two acres. The tower or keep rises from it amid some fine old trees, and attached to it is a court, which is surrounded by a rampart wall, and formerly included a garden, besides an extensive range of offices. At the south-east corner of the rampart stands a small circular tower, in which, tradition says, Queen Mary was confined, the principal donjon or keep being inhabited by the Douglas family, with the Dowager Lady Margaret Erskine or Douglas, Sir William Douglas's mother, as resident wielder of authority. Some warrant for the tradition as to the place of Mary's confinement seems to be afforded in the following passage from a letter of Sir Nicholas Throckmorton to Sir William Cecil, dated 2d August 1567 : " The quene of Scotland is straytlier kept at Loughleven than she was yet, for now she ys shut up in a tower, and can have non admitted to speake with her but suche as be shut up with her." It may be fairly inferred, I think, from this, that Mary had at first been a resident in the castle itself, and allowed the liberty of walking about the island, and that having excited the suspicions of her jailers, she had been subjected, with a few attendants, to close confinement in the tower in question.

This small tower of Loch Leven is known as the "Glassin Tower," probably from its windows having been fitted with glass, in contradistinction to the stanchioned openings of the donjon. It consists altogether of four storeys, comprehending a vaulted cellar and three superimposed apartments, each of the latter of which has a diameter of fifteen, with a height of barely ten feet. There are fireplaces in each chamber, but the upper floors have disappeared. On the basement storey, above the vault, is a large projecting window or balcony, and on the first floor there is another large window, but without any projection. It was probably this apartment that the Queen occupied, and it may have been from this window, which commands a view of Benarty and the southern shore, that she was let down into a boat, and thus effected her escape. The waters of the loch must in those days have washed the base of the tower, and with the inmates of the castle locked in, and prevented from pursuing, it would not be difficult to be ferried over to Coldon, which lies nearly directly opposite to this corner of the island. Notwithstanding its pleasant outlook, and the walk from it along the ramparts, which, however, it is questionable that Mary was permitted to enjoy, the Glassin Tower must have been anything but a comfortable abode.

The keep or principal part of the fortress is a square tower of five storeys, the basement consisting of a sort of dungeon or vault, which is approached on the east side by a descending flight of steps. Through an opening in the roof of this chamber a modern stone staircase has been carried, leading to the first floor, the large apartment on which has probably served as a kitchen. From a corner of it a turret staircase leads to the second floor and upper apartments of the castle, the principal entrance to which seems to have been on the north side by a large arched opening in the wall of the second floor, to which access must have been gained by a wooden stair or ladder. There is no trace of any stone staircase, but the opening in the wall in question has all the appearance of a doorway, and the ladder or drawstair could be raised and replaced at pleasure. As regards the upper apartments, the flooring has disappeared. Altogether there is little evidence of good accommodation, although a tradition is preserved in Kinross of the castle being able to furnish fifty beds. Most probably this only meant that fifty persons might there find sleeping-places.

The other important island in Loch Leven is that of St Serf, which lies more than a mile to the south-east of the Castle Island, and presents few attractions to the general observer, exhibiting merely a nearly level expanse of grass, which the drainage of the loch has increased in extent from 32 to 70 acres. It has, however, a more curious history than its more renowned congener, having been the seat of an ancient Culdee priory, said to have been established there by St Serf, who received the island in gift from Brude, king of the Picts, in the seventh century. St Serf, who has thus given his name to his place of settlement, is said to have come originally as a Christian missionary from the East, and after visiting Rome, to have proceeded to Scotland and received the hospitality of St Adamnan, St Columba's biographer, on the island of Inchkeith. He has also been identified with the St Serf of Culross, who brought up St Mungo, the patron saint of Glasgow; but this, as I have elsewhere endeavoured to show,[1] is a mistake, arising from the circumstance of there having been two St Serfs, who lived at two periods—one in the fifth and the other in the seventh century—and the incidents connected with the lives of each having been mixed up together. It is very

---

[1] See 'Culross and Tulliallan.'

likely indeed, however, that both had a connection with Culross, which was certainly the principal scene of the labours of the elder saint.

The Culdee establishment founded by St Serf on the island in Loch Leven, subsisted in great reputation till the reign of David I., who set himself strongly against the maintenance further in Scotland of the ancient clergy *régime*, and converted all the monastic establishments throughout the country, whether with or against their consent, into communities of canons regular. Such was the fate of the monks of St Serf's Island, who were obliged to remodel their discipline and affiliate themselves to the canons regular of the priory of St Andrews. There is little else recorded in history concerning them, unless it be of a benefaction of the lands of Bolgyn and Kirkness,[1] in the vicinity of Loch Leven, made to them by the famous Macbeth and his wife during their sovereignty of Scotland, and also the circumstance of Andrew de Wynton, author of the 'Chronicle' (a metrical history of the world), being in the early part of the fifteenth century prior of the religious community on St Serf's Island.

At the Reformation this community was dispersed, and the property of the island was made over to the Earls of Morton. Scarcely anything now remains of the ancient buildings beyond the walls of a small edifice, which, till comparatively recently, served as a place of shelter for the cattle that grazed on the island. The foundations have, however, been traced and laid open, and the dry hollow which in former days served the monks as a *vivarium*, or fish-pool, has also been rendered manifest. The island lies nearly two miles to the

---

[1] There is still a property named Kirkness belonging to the Marquis of Northampton, and situated in the parish of Ballingry, adjoining the east shoulder of Benarty.

south-east of the castle, and the traveller can easily obtain the services of a boatman to transport him thither. He will thus, too, be enabled to gain a much more complete idea of Loch Leven and its shores than he can obtain by merely crossing over to the Castle Island.

A great part of the east shore of Loch Leven belongs to the parish of Portmoak, which, in ancient phraseology, is denominated Petmook, as signifying the region or district of St Moak, St Moluoc, or possibly St Machutus, for it seems possible to refer it to any of these three names. St Serf's Island has been styled the "island of Petmook"; and on the other hand, the parish of Portmoak used to be anciently known as that of St Servanus, and is so styled in a minute of Presbytery in 1659.

VI.

ROUND LOCH LEVEN.

The loch and its surrounding scenery—Levenmouth and the sluices—Scotlandwell and the Bishop Hill—Portmoak church and village of Kinnesswood—Michael Bruce and his poetry—Hamlets of Easter and Wester Balgedie—The old church of Orwell.

A PLEASANT and interesting excursion may be made from Kinross round Loch Leven, and if the traveller is a tolerable pedestrian, he may easily accomplish it on foot, as the circuit does not exceed fifteen miles. If he prefers to drive or be driven, there are always good horses and carriages to be procured at the Green Hotel. He may either take the north side of the loch first, or return two miles on the road that he has already traversed in coming from Queensferry, and then turn eastwards along the southern shore. This is the course which we shall now follow.

Nearly opposite to Gairney Bridge farm, about a mile to the north of Blairadam station, a road strikes off the Great North Road to the right, and leads along the north base of Benarty by the farms of West and East Brackleigh to Levenmouth, Auchmoor Bridge, and Leslie. The marks of the great landslip which took place here more than half a century ago, are still very visible on the slope of Benarty. The road borders, though at first not very closely, Loch Leven, of which the traveller by this route gets a fine view, and has facing him the Bishop Hill, the south-western extremity of which above Scotlandwell is covered with wood. The river Leven at the present day issues from the loch at a different point from what it used to do when it escaped by its natural channel. This ancient bed of the stream is now partly covered by a plantation of trees, known as the Levenmouth Plantation, and the river quits the loch at the sluices by a canal which has been cut from thence, almost in a straight line to Auchmoor Bridge, a distance of about three miles and a half. The sluice-house is a favourite place for picnics, though all the accommodation that is granted is admission to the grounds, and shelter from the weather should the latter prove inclement. No refreshments of any kind can be obtained, but the situation is rather a pleasant one for enjoyment *al fresco*. The buildings and apparatus here for regulating the outflow from the loch have all been erected since the commencement of the drainage operations subsequent to 1826.

Having arrived within about two miles of Auchmoor Bridge and completely skirted the north base of Benarty, the traveller, if he wishes to make the circuit of Loch Leven, will turn to the left in the direction of the

Bishop Hill and the village of Scotlandwell, which are situated at a distance of about 1¾ mile due north from this point. He will cross the New Gullet Bridge, which spans the new Leven river or canal about a mile from the sluice-house, and a quarter of a mile farther on he will reach the Old Gullet Bridge, near Lochend farm. A little beyond this, on the left hand, at Redhouse, a road leads to the old burying-ground and site of the monastery of Portmoak, which seems to have been connected with and formed essentially a part of the monastic establishment on the island of St Serf. It is situated close to the old shore of the loch, and about a mile south-west from Scotlandwell, to reach which directly from this, it is necessary to cross the boggy tract known as Portmoak Moss.

Following the road north from New Gullet Bridge, the traveller after a mile's walk finds himself at Scotlandwell, a simple, rather ancient, and tumble-down looking village, situated exactly at the south extremity of the Bishop Hill, and overhung by Kilmagad wood. He will find here a small unpretending public-house (Thomas Ritchie's), where he can obtain a modest luncheon of bread and cheese and beer at a very moderate charge. Stepping a few yards to the west of the inn, he will come to the famous spring or well, which, along with one or two others in this neighbourhood, gave the locality of old the name of *Fontes Scotiæ* or Scotlandwells. There is now, however, only one large fountain, which is sheltered by an elegant roof or canopy erected by Mr Bruce of Arnot, a neighbouring proprietor. Beneath this, in the centre, is a large square basin of stone, open at the top, and having a depth of three or four feet. The water, which wells up in great volume through the sand beneath, is both excellent to drink and as clear as crystal. Fortunately there are no villas near at hand to

pollute indirectly with their drainage this pellucid fountain, which, it is satisfactory to understand, is as pure as
it looks, and has no reason to dread the result of any
scientific analysis.

There is an old burying-ground at the south-east extremity of the village, where are also one of the famous
springs, and the site of the old hospital of Scotlandwell.
This was founded by William Malvoisin, Bishop of St
Andrews, and the monks who occupied it were bound
by their original constitution to set apart a third of their
revenues for redeeming Christian slaves from the in-
fidels.   How far they acted up to their obligations I
cannot say, but to judge from the following stanza, introduced into one of the "Gude and godly ballates,"
among other derogatory remarks on the Romish clergy,
the establishment here does not seem to have been in
the highest repute :—

> "Of Scotlandwell the Friars of Faill
> The limmery long has lasted ;
> The monks o' Melrose made gude kail
> On Fridays when they fasted."

The parish church of Moonzie near Cupar, and that
of Carnock near Dunfermline, belonged to Scotlandwell,
and the "parson" of this place, not long after the Reformation had to be called to account for the shameful
state of disrepair in which he allowed Carnock church
to continue.   In an enclosure within the old burying-
ground are the tombs of Alison Turpie, wife of the Rev.
Ebenezer Erskine, and four of their children, as also of
his mother, Margaret Halcro, of an old Orcadian family,
wife of the Rev. Henry Erskine of Chirnside.

Before being translated to Stirling, Ebenezer Erskine
was minister of the parish of Portmoak, to which, as
already mentioned, the greater part of the country on
the east side of Loch Leven belongs.   A story is told

that in announcing to his parishioners his approaching departure from them to another sphere of labour, he spoke of his having received a call from the Lord to go to Stirling. An irreverent "auld wife" in the congregation, meeting her minister shortly afterwards, when he repeated in effect what he had already stated from the pulpit, made the following observation: "Troth, sir, an He had called you to Auchtertool,[1] you wad ne'er hae let on that you heard Him!" Yet in fairness it should be always remembered that Ebenezer Erskine showed by his subsequent conduct that he was ever ready to sacrifice worldly emolument when duty and principle seemed to call on him to do so.

There is no village which bears the name of Portmoak, but the church of that parish stands on a rising ground a little to the north of Scotlandwell, and is passed in going to the village of Kinnesswood. In its churchyard the poet Michael Bruce is buried.

About a mile to the north-west of Scotlandwell, and high up on an acclivity of the Bishop Hill, overlooking Loch Leven, is the village of Kinnesswood popularly pronounced *Kinnaskit*, which possesses some interest as the place where Michael Bruce lived and died. This amiable and lamented youth has for ever associated with his name his native county of Kinross; the little village of Kinnesswood, where he was born; and Loch Leven, which forms the subject of his longest though certainly by no means his best poem. His father was a weaver, and a pious God-fearing Presbyterian of the old Scottish type—a characteristic which was also eminently conspicuous in his mother. As a boy, Michael used to "herd" on the Lomond hills, and he was al-

---

[1] A parish in Kirkcaldy Presbytery, the stipend of which has always been very small. A late incumbent, the Rev. Walter Welsh, was a cousin of Mrs Carlyle.

ways noted as a delicate "auld farrant" child. Having early exhibited an inclination for study, he resolved to devote himself to the ministry of the Secession Church, which had then but recently been called into existence under the leadership of the Erskines. He attended the necessary sessions at Edinburgh University, and there made the acquaintance of the celebrated John Logan, then a student for the ministry of the Church of Scotland. There is no evidence, however, to show that there was any great intimacy between him and Bruce, who, when his college career was completed, set himself to gain a living by acting as schoolmaster at Gairney Bridge. From that he removed to be teacher at Forest Mill, a lonely little hamlet in Clackmannanshire, on the road from Dollar to Kincardine. In fording the Devon on horseback on his way thither, he fell into the water; and the wetting which he thus sustained seems to have developed the consumptive tendency by which his constitution was already marked. The malady was further aggravated by the damp and uncomfortable schoolhouse in which he had to exercise his functions as teacher, and ere many months had passed away, he was compelled to quit Forest Mill and return to Kinnesswood, where he died in 1767, before he had completed his twenty-first year. After his death, Logan called on his father, and obtained from the old man the MSS. of his son's poems, Michael having already achieved a local reputation as a bard, though nothing from his pen had yet appeared in print. Logan published a few of the poems along with some of his own, but included in the latter the celebrated "Ode to the Cuckoo," which in itself was sufficient to make the poetical reputation of any author. The matter is somewhat too intricate to be discussed here, but there can be little doubt, both from the evidence of Bruce's letters and that furnished by contemporaneous testimony, that a base and unworthy fraud was committed by Logan in appropriating the authorship of the ode. His delinquencies, however, in relation to Bruce, did not end here. Among the latter's effusions there were several which were known among his friends and relatives as "Gospel Sonnets," but were really for the most part paraphrases from Scripture, and included the beautiful and pathetic hymn, "The hour of my departure's come." These were all appropriated by Logan, and contributed as his to the collection of metrical translations from the Bible, published by authority of the General Assembly of the Church of Scotland, and appointed to be used in public worship. Many of the best of these, with which Logan was long credited, were really the productions of Michael Bruce, the poet of Kinnesswood. On the appearance of the volume of poems in 1770, Bruce's father paid a visit to Logan in Edinburgh, to learn what had become of the "Gospel Sonnets," of which he had so distinct a recollection as the emanations of his son. He had some difficulty in obtaining an interview, and when he did, could procure no satisfaction, Logan failing, moreover, to produce the volume of Bruce's MSS. which he had received, and alleging that it had been destroyed by mistake, through the servant of the house having used it in the singeing of fowls. Logan long enjoyed his chief reputation as a poet on the strength of this unrighteous spoliation, and it is only comparatively recently that the rights of Michael Bruce have been vindicated.

Kinnesswood is five miles from Kinross, and one of those sleepy "dead alive" places which seem to abound on the eastern side of Loch Leven, but is not devoid of a certain quaint picturesqueness. It consists of one main street, with a long straggling wynd running up from it at right angles towards the hillside. A little

way up this wynd, with its gable facing the entrance,
is a two-storeyed thatched house, of humble appearance,
an inscription on which states that here Michael Bruce
was born in 1746, and here he died in 1767.   The
village was long famous for the manufacture of vellum
and parchment, an industry which is said to have been
originally practised by the monks of St Serf, and continued from their time in the parish of Portmoak.   It used
to be almost the only place in Scotland where this trade
was carried on, and from this quarter the Register Office
in Edinburgh received its supplies of the commodity in
question, at least since the reign of Charles II.   A
family of the name of Birrell was latterly chiefly connected with the manufacture; and one of them—John
Birrell—exercised his vocation in the days of Michael
Bruce, and wrote a biography of the poet.

The hamlet of Easter Balgedie is half a mile north-
west of Kinnesswood, and that of Wester Balgedie is
another half-mile north-west of the former.   They both
partake very much of the characteristics of Kinnesswood
and Scotlandwell, but are smaller in size.   The north-
east corner of Loch Leven has now been reached, and
after walking for a mile or two along the north bank
(there being, however, a broad tract of low ground
between the road and the water), the traveller arrives
at Lothrie's Bridge.   A footpath leads down from this
to the old church and churchyard of Orwell, close to
the shore of the loch.   This was in ancient times merely
a chapel of ease or dependency of the Abbey Church of
Dunfermline, having been bestowed as such on the latter
by Robert the Bruce.   When it was raised to the dignity
of a parish church is not known, and the building itself
has long been a ruin, the present church of Orwell being
situated at Milnathort.

Near Lothrie's Bridge the road bifurcates, one branch

leading on the left to Kinross, and the other on the right to Milnathort, past Burleigh Castle, to be afterwards described. By taking the former, which crosses the North Queich at Burgher Bridge and passes near the mansion of Lethangie, the traveller will, after a pleasant walk of nearly two miles, reach Kinross, and thus complete the circuit of Lochleven.

VII.

FROM KINROSS TO GLEN FARG.

Further progress on Great North Road—Village of Milnathort—Parish of Orwell—Castle of Burleigh and its proprietors—History of the Balfour family—Road from Milnathort to Damhead—Church of Arngask—Glen Farg and the Bein Inn—Old road from Damhead to Perth—the Wicks of Baiglie—Sir Walter Scott's account of distant view of Perth from that neighbourhood—Old drove-road to the Kirk of Dron—The Rocking-stone—Mill and hamlet of Dron.

KINROSS is 16 miles from Queensferry and 17 from Perth. Quitting the town at its north extremity, and continuing along the Great North Road for two miles, we reach Milnathort, a large village, or rather small town, containing several woollen factories, and forming a centre of convergence from several roads, which here join the Great North highway. One of these branches off to the north-east, leading to Cupar, through the opening between the Ochil and Lomond hills; another goes round the head of Loch Leven, and, as already described, skirts its eastern shore, passing through the Balgedies and Kinnesswood to Scotlandwell, Auchmoor Bridge, and Leslie; and a third leads west from Milnathort to Dollar, a distance of 12 miles, through Cambo and the Yetts of Muckhart.

Milnathort (*Hotels:* The Thistle and The Royal), though not particularly attractive in itself, is a thriving manufacturing place, with some good villas in the vicinity. The name seems to be the Gaelic *muilean-a-thairt*, the "cross mill" or "mill on the farther side," the town being divided into two portions by a rivulet from a mill on which the appellation would arise.[1] It is the principal place in the parish of Orwell, the church of which —a plain building—is situated on an eminence immediately behind the town, on the north. Milnathort displays, moreover, a grand recently erected U.P. church, with a spire; a Free church; and a town hall, with a spire and clock; whilst on the road between it and Kinross an Episcopal chapel has recently been erected.

The parish of Orwell comprises the chief part of the north of Kinross-shire, and is separated from Strathearn in Perthshire by the Ochils. These stretch across the north border of the county from west to east, but decline considerably in height from what they attain to in the counties of Stirling and Clackmannan, and have only an elevation of from 1000 to 1500 feet. One of these heights, north-north-west from Milnathort, is termed Cairnavain, from an immense collection of stones which once existed on its summit, but are now greatly reduced in number, in consequence of having been carried away many years ago by the then proprietor, to the amount of hundreds of cart-loads, for the purpose of building field-dykes. A legend clung to the cairn, as embodied in the following popular rhyme :—

> " In the Dryburn well, beneath a stane,
>   You'll find the key of Cairnavain,
>   That'll mak a' Scotland rich ane by ane."

---

[1] There is a place not far distant called " Blairathort," which similarly would denote the "cross field "—*blar-a-thairt.*

When the stones were carted away, as above stated, great expectations were formed by the labourers as to what they might find in the way of treasure-trove. But nothing more valuable was discovered than a stone coffin in the centre of the cairn, containing an urn of bones, partly charred. This affords a demonstration of what is coming now to be pretty generally received among antiquaries as the *raison d'être* of most of these cairns, standing-stones, and so-called druidical circles. It seems to be satisfactorily ascertained that the erection of these has in almost all cases been for sepulchral purposes, and rarely either as stones of commemoration or places of religious worship. Besides that found at Cairnavain, urns filled with burnt bones have been found on the farm of Holeton, and at other places along the sides of the Ochil Hills.

From Milnathort to Damhead by the Great North Road is a distance of four miles. Just after quitting the former there will be seen on the right-hand side of the way, about a quarter of a mile off, the ruins of the castle of Burleigh, situated about a mile from the north shore of Loch Leven. They consist of the square donjon or keep, of which the basement storey is vaulted, and access may be gained to the first floor by a dangerously frail trap or ladder, which I would warn the traveller to be very cautious in ascending. Above this have been three other storeys, but the wooden floors have disappeared. A courtyard extends to the south of the keep, and had evidently formerly been surrounded by buildings, of which nothing now remains but a circular tower at the south-west extremity, connected with the keep by a wall pierced by a fine arched gateway, and surmounted by a sort of rampart or gallery. The round tower consists of three storeys, the two upper of which are occupied by the foreman of the adjoining farm of Burleigh.

The castle has evidently at one time been a place of considerable size and importance. It may be reached also from the road from Kinross to Scotlandwell, by turning aside into a field at Burgher Bridge, which crosses the North Queich a mile to the west of the old kirk of Orwell. From Burgher Bridge by this bypath Burleigh Castle is half a mile due north; and from the former place a long straight road leads west past the mansion of Lethangie to the Great North Road, which it joins a little to the north of the town of Kinross.

The lands of Burleigh were erected into a barony in the fifteenth century by James II. in favour of its proprietors, the Balfours, who in 1606 received a further accession of dignity in being raised to the peerage. Charles II., on the occasion of his expedition to Scotland in 1650, was entertained at the castle, whilst on his way from Perth to Dunfermline, by Lord Balfour of Burleigh. He inspected, Sir James Balfour informs us, his host's "cabinett of varieties, and at his departure my lord presented his majestie with a falcon."

A sad disgrace overtook the Burleigh family in the beginning of the last century. Robert Balfour, only son of the then lord, and heir-apparent to the estate and title, had conceived a violent passion for a young woman in a rank of life beneath himself, and to cure him of the attachment he was sent abroad to travel. Returning after a year or two's absence to his native country, he sought again the object of his affections, and to his rage and dismay found that she had become the wife of Mr Henry Stenhouse, schoolmaster of Inverkeithing. Lying in wait for the unfortunate husband, young Balfour shot him dead at his own door, was arrested subsequently, and sentenced by the High Court of Justiciary to be beheaded. He escaped from prison by changing clothes with his sister, concealed himself for a while in an old tree at Burleigh Castle, and succeeded at last in retreating to the Continent. He returned from thence, and took part in the insurrection of 1715, for which he incurred the doom of forfeiture—though, having previously been outlawed for the crime of murder, it remained a question whether any further attainder attached to the estate and title. Contriving again to escape to the Continent, he died abroad without leaving issue. Of his two sisters, one died unmarried, but the other married Brigadier-General Bruce of Kennet. As the Burleigh peerage is transmissible to females, it was maintained that the right to it remained vested in Mrs Bruce. It was never taken up, however, by her or her family till about twenty years ago, when it was successfully claimed by her lineal descendant, Mr Bruce of Kennet, the present Lord Balfour of Burleigh.

Burleigh Castle and its lands are now the property of Sir Graham Montgomery, having been purchased by his ancestor, Mr Graham of Kinross. There used to be a great deal of fine old timber about the castle, but this has almost all either decayed from old age, or been blown down by storms. Till within the last seventy years the old ash-tree which had furnished concealment within its hollow trunk to young Balfour, the proscribed outlaw, was in existence, about twenty yards westwards of the great tower. It had already received considerable damage, and was completely destroyed by a tempest on Old Handsel Monday in 1822.

At the point where Burleigh Castle comes into view, the old road to Damhead and Perth branches off to the left, keeping first due north, and then proceeding in a direction nearly parallel with the present one, but carried along a sort of rising ground or terrace. In point of distance this is the shorter route to Damhead by nearly a mile, and though somewhat hilly, it is still maintained in excellent order. Near the same point another road proceeds by the mansion of Hattonburn (Henry J. Montgomery, Esq.), across the Ochils by the Path of Condie to Invermay.

The Great North Road between Kinross and Damhead, after leaving Milnathort and losing sight of Loch Leven, is of a very dreary character, being bleak and solitary, without any of those grander features which often impart an interest to a wild and unfrequented country. It cannot indeed be said on the whole that Kinross is an attractive county, and the interest attaching to it may be said to begin and end in Loch Leven. Its greatest length from the western extremity of Cleish parish to the eastern border of Portmoak is about twelve miles, and from Kelty Bridge on the south to Damhead on the north its greatest breadth is about ten. It has an extent of 44,800 imperial acres, or about seventy square miles; and though it contains a large amount of level ground, much of this is very poor soil. Like Fife, it used to be noted for its great number of small proprietors, almost every farm in the county having been at one time a separate lairdship. And the Kinross lairds, like their congeners in Fife, enjoyed an extended reputation in the way of convivial and bibulous proclivities. It should be remembered also, however, that among the people generally the leading characteristics were a deep and fervent devotional feeling, and the Covenanting element was in former days especially strong. During the last century the western district of Fife and the county of Kinross were the cradle in a great measure of the Secession Church, and furnished most of the ministers and people who originally cast in their lot with that movement.

Damhead, four miles from Milnathort, and six from Kinross, is a village in the parish of Arngask, and the meeting-place of three counties—Perth, Kinross, and Fife—to all of which Arngask belongs in nearly equal portions. The parish church is situated in Fife, at the top of the hill, near Arngask House, and about half a mile from the village. It was originally a chapel, belonging to the Abbey of Cambuskenneth, and was erected into a parish church in 1527. The present building is of the plain economical type, which characterises generally the country churches in Scotland erected subsequent to the Reformation.

There is a little inn at Damhead, called the Damhead Hotel, where the hungry and not too fastidious traveller may obtain a good plain meal at small cost. The river Farg, a clear stream, coming down from the Ochils, here turns north-north-east, and flows through Glen Farg, separating the counties of Perth and Fife, and falling into the Earn at Culfargie. The Great North Road skirts the Farg as it descends between the wood-clad sides of the magnificent glen of the same name into Strathearn. This is certainly the finest portion of the journey, and perhaps the only bit of grand scenery that is to be met with on the road between Queensferry and the Bridge of Earn. A railway is in course of construction through this beautiful glen, which will shorten considerably the distance between Perth and Edinburgh. Half-way down Glen Farg, in a romantic situation, about three miles from Damhead, four and a half from Bridge of Earn, and eight miles from Perth, is the small but comfortable Bein Inn, much frequented by excursion parties from the Fair City. In the old coaching days this was the third and last stage on the road from Queensferry to Perth, but the building which then formed the inn is a little farther down the hill than the present caravanserai. The other stopping-places for change of horses were Cowdenbeath and Kinross.

About three-quarters of a mile from the Bein Inn,
on the side of Damhead and a little to the right of the
road, is a large stone, known as the Rocking-stone of
Balvaird, and capable at one time of being moved by
the slightest pressure. The pivot, however, on which it
rests has long been choked up with earth and gravel,
and it is now consequently as firmly set as one of the
Ochils.

The present road through Glen Farg to the Bridge of
Earn was constructed in the years 1808-10, but the
portion from Damhead to Milnathort was not laid down
till 1832. For a little distance beyond Damhead the
old highway has been suppressed as far as the lodge of
the avenue leading to the mansion of Paris, now known
as West Fordel. From this last point a new cut leading
down hill to the east connects the old. Perth road with
the present Great North Road through Glen Farg. The
junction with the latter is effected at the distance of
about a mile from Damhead and two miles from the
Bein Inn. The road from West Fordel then crosses
first the Great North Road, and almost immediately
afterwards the river Farg by the bridge called Paris
Bridge. From this it continues up hill in an easterly
direction, but its further course is beyond the scope of
the present work.

The old road from Damhead to Perth leads over the
pass through the Ochils known as the Wicks of Baiglie.
As Sir Walter Scott has rendered this locality classical
from his reference to it in the introduction to the ‘Fair
Maid of Perth,’ and the splendid prospect which he
states as obtainable from thence of the Fair City, I
shall perhaps be pardoned for treating the subject a
little more at length than might otherwise be deemed
necessary.

Most people who have been induced to visit this spot

in the hope of enjoying the prospect of Perth which Sir Walter has described in such glowing terms, have also concluded naturally enough that it is the present old road to that town to which he refers, in contradistinction to the one made in the beginning of the present century through Glen Farg. Proceeding on this premiss, they have all returned declaring that it is a complete mistake to assert that Perth can be seen either from the Wicks of Baiglie or any other point on the old road from Kinross, and that the Great Magician must have been thinking of the view from Moncrieff Hill on the south bank of the Tay. In one respect they are quite right; the city of Perth is visible from no point of the road, either over the Wicks of Baiglie or through Glen Farg, till the crest is reached of Moncrieff Hill, from which the traveller looks down upon the city.

But may Sir Walter not have been misunderstood? Let it be remembered that the point from which he says Perth can be seen is one on the old road leading from Kinross to the Kirk of Dron, a place which the old road to Perth does not pass through but leaves on its left. And let it also be kept in mind that what is now called the old road is, comparatively speaking, a new one, and was certainly so in Sir Walter's younger days, when he witnessed the prospect with which he represents Chrystal Croftangry as so much delighted.

Now it happens that the old road from Kinross to Perth by the Kirk of Dron is what is known as the "Drove-road," and which, though still perfectly practicable in many places, has yet in others been almost completely effaced. It crosses the old Perth road from Damhead about two miles from the latter place, and one mile from the top of the steep hill or brae which marks the locality of the Wicks of Baiglie. If the traveller has any curiosity

G

in following up such matters, let him turn aside here,[1] through a gate on the left-hand side of the way, and follow the windings of the Drove-road through a field to the top of the rising ground. Here he will see two shepherds' houses, situated nearly in a line with and about two hundred yards from each other. From either of these he will be able to obtain directions for guiding him to the Kirk of Dron, and from either of them he can reach that place, though by different routes. From the western habitation he can follow, through two grass fields, the old, almost obliterated track of the Drove-road; then descending the hill by a third shepherd's house, he will clearly and unmistakably regain the track; and lastly, continuing his journey down a beautiful defile, or "glack," as it is called in that part of the country, he will shortly find himself at the attractive hamlet of the Kirk of Dron. Should he elect to proceed by the easter of the shepherds' houses, he will follow a tolerably well-defined path which leads due north from this, and then trending round to the left by the famous rocking-stone, makes the circuit of the hill, and leads down to the Kirk of Dron by the Mill. The other road just described lies on the hill to the west of this, and there is a valley between.

[1] To mark the spot more exactly, I may state that before coming to the point where the Drove-road crosses the old Perth road, through field-gates on each side of the way, a ramshackle dilapidated farmhouse, with three or four scraggy ash-trees, will be discerned on an eminence to the left; whilst a little past the cross-roads on the right-hand side there is a small semicircular whinstone quarry. About half a mile farther, on the left, there is a road or avenue going up to the house of Blair Struie, and in another half-mile the Wicks themselves are reached, at the top of a steep hill, where the road trends round a corner of the Ochils in a north-westerly direction, and commands a splendid view of Strathearn and the estuary of the Tay as far as Dundee and the German Ocean.

On either of these roads the traveller will at more points than one obtain a glimpse, if the day be clear, of the town of Perth through the gap on the crest of Moncrieff Hill above the railway tunnel. I can testify myself, though the day on which I walked over here was none of the brightest, to having at least seen the high chimneys of public works at Perth through the opening in question, which is just above the city. The point of view to which Sir Walter refers is probably from the Drove-road, a little beyond the third or northmost shepherd's house, and just before descending to the beautiful defile or "glack" above Dron. And as Chrystal Croftangry is represented as obtaining the view whilst seated on a pony, he must have come by the Drove-road—the path over the hill by the rocking-stone being only accessible to pedestrians. At best the view of Perth can never be very magnificent from this point, considering the remoteness of its position, and that the appearance presented by any town at a great distance is generally insignificant. Yet I can conceive that to Sir Walter's youthful imagination this view of the Fair City through the opening in the crest of Moncrieff Hill, with the beautiful foreground of the vale of Strathearn, may have recalled, more especially if witnessed at early morn or dewy eve, when the rising or setting sun was gilding the town with his rays, John Bunyan's description of the Celestial City as seen from the Delectable Mountains. Another way of obtaining this view is by proceeding to the Wicks of Baiglie either from the side of Damhead or the Bridge of Earn, and then ascending the eminence or ridge immediately to the west.

Over this eminence a footpath, already partially described, leads from the old Perth road to the Kirk of Dron, and is occasionally used as a short cut by people travelling in this direction from Damhead. The rocking-stone alone, already alluded to, is well worth the fatigue of a much longer walk. It lies on the hillside, about 200 yards due north of the easter of the two shepherds' houses above mentioned, and about 40 yards from the footpath leading across the hill. It is a large irregular mass of dark whinstone, about 9 feet long by 5 broad, and sloping from east to west. At the very least it must weigh three tons, and yet I could move it quite perceptibly by merely pressing it at the higher end with my finger and thumb. The history of these stones is enveloped in mystery, and the only reasonable conclusion that can be come to is that they were placed there in remote ages in expiation of some crime or fulfilment of some vow. Possibly, also, the aboriginal priesthood found their account in the wonderful properties which the populace would be inclined to ascribe to masses so enormous and yet so easily set in motion. It is extremely unlikely that any such stone could have been placed in such a position from natural causes.

The hamlet of the Kirk of Dron, called also East Dron, is charmingly situated in a recess on the north side of the Ochils, about a mile to the south of the Bridge of Earn, and five miles from Perth. The parish of Dron, however, from its situation, used to suffer considerably in the depth of winter from the want of light and warmth, both natural and artificial. Many of the houses were popularly said never to see the sun from November to February, whilst the distance from any coal-field and the absence of peat caused fuel to be both scarce and expensive. In summer it has the aspect of a veritable Arcadia. The church is a handsome structure in the modern Gothic style, and stands on a knoll overlooking the lower basin of the Tay. The Mill of Dron lies in the hollow to the south-west of the church, and in the plain between the village and the Wicks of Baiglie is Balmanno House, the principal mansion in the parish.

Having now arrived in Strathearn, on the north side of the Ochils and within five miles of Perth, the limits of my course in this direction have been reached. The Great North Road and tracts immediately adjoining have been surveyed from North Queensferry to the Bridge of Earn, and my direction is now "Westward ho!"

I.

THE CITY OF DUNFERMLINE.

Leading features of the "city"—Its ancient history—Malcolm Canmore and Queen Margaret—The monastery and its church—Dunfermline as a royal residence—Remains of the Abbey and Palace—Relations of Edward I. with Dunfermline—King Robert Bruce interred there—Its first Protestant minister, David Ferguson—The Earls of Dunfermline—Visits of Charles I. and II.—Events during insurrection of 1715—Introduction of the damask manufacture—Dunfermline the cradle of the Secession movement—History of the Erskine family—Churches and public buildings.

DUNFERMLINE (*Hotels:* City Arms; Royal) is the principal town in the western district of Fife, and throughout the whole county the only one that can compete with it as a business centre is Kirkcaldy. It stands 300 feet above the sea, on a rising ground sloping to the south, and presents an imposing as well as picturesque aspect when viewed from the latter direction. It is 6 miles nearly due north from Queensferry, 23 from Stirling by Torryburn, and 13 from Kirkcaldy.

For more than 150 years it has been the principal
place in the British Islands for the manufacture of table-
linen, which constitutes it leading industry. It had a
population in 1881 of 17,085, and it is grouped with
South Queensferry, Inverkeithing, Culross, and Stirling
in returning a member to Parliament. About twenty-five
years ago the researches of Dr Ebenezer Henderson, a
native of the place, led him to the conclusion that Dunfermline was entitled to the rank and designation of a
"city" (whatever this denomination may be held to
imply); and having submitted his view to the public
authorities supposed competent to decide the question,
the verdict was given that his contention had in their
opinion been established. It was mainly founded on
the circumstance of the town being designed as a
"civitas" in several royal rescripts and charters, and
Dr Henderson reaped considerable *éclat* with the townspeople from having thus, in their estimation, vindicated
the dignity of the "auld grey toun." It still remains a
moot point, however, as to what meaning our word
"city" really bears, and what special dignity it carries
with it. According to some, "city" denotes a cathedral
town or the seat of a bishop's see ; with others it implies
a royal residence ; and with others it denotes merely a
community of any kind, or an assemblage of streets
and houses which exceeds in extent the dimensions
ordinarily understood by the term "town." However
this may be, the burgesses and townspeople claim for
themselves the privilege of belonging to the "city
of Dunfermline."

Originally Dunfermline lay wholly on the east side of
Pittencrieff Glen, the romantic gorge through which the
Tower burn flows from north to south, and at its termination joins almost at right angles the Lyne or Spittal
burn, flowing from east to west through the level ground

at the foot of the slope on which the town is built. About a hundred years ago, however, a bridge was thrown across the Tower Glen at the head of the Kirkgate, and a large and populous suburb has grown up on its western side. At present the town consists of one broad and leading street, which, crossing the ridge of the hill from east to west, receives at its eastern extremity the designation of East Port Street, which again, in proceeding westwards, merges in the High Street and afterwards passes into Bridge Street. At right angles to the latter, running north and south, is Chalmers Street, which is continued into Woodhead Street, and at the point where this junction takes place, Pittencrieff Street branches off to the west and forms the main entrance to the town from that direction. The High Street proper, or original nucleus of the town, is a steep incline leading upwards from the corporation buildings at the head of the Kirkgate and corner of Bridge Street to the Cross; and the broad level portion lying beyond, between the Cross and East Port Street, used to be known as the Horse Market. On the north and south sides respectively of this line of road from East Port to Bridge Street, a series of cross streets diverge, and these are again crossed by lines running parallel with the High Street, of which the principal are Queen Anne Street on the north, and the Maygate, Canmore Street, and the Netherton on the south. The New Row is a steep street running due south from the east extremity of the Horse Market, and leading out of the town to Queensferry. Canmore Street and Netherton Broad Street open into it, and Douglas Street, a little east of the Cross, passing into Bath and Pilmuir Streets, forms the main outlet to the north. The Kirkgate, now greatly widened from what it used to be, leads down, as its name denotes, from the corporation buildings to the Abbey Church, and the Maygate branches off from it on the left. The road then continues in a south-east direction, through an ancient archway, belonging to the Abbey and known as "The Pends," the Abbey Church and ruins of the monastery being on the left, whilst on the right are the Palace ruins and Pittencrieff Glen. Continuing in an easterly direction along Monastery Street, the latter is joined by Margaret Street, and the roadway then turns to the south down a steep descent and abuts on the wide space which at the foot of the hill extends eastwards to the New Row and Queensferry Road, and bears the name of Netherton Broad Street. At the western extremity of the latter a road turns off to the south by Ladysmill to Limekilns, and at this point also is an old road, now a byway, which joins at the farm of Urquhart the west highway from Pittencrieff Street, leading to Torryburn and Alloa.

Such, generally, are the main features of Dunfermline as displayed in its leading streets. The etymology of the name has been variously explained, though the only question has been regarding the middle syllable "ferm." "Dun" signifies in Gaelic "hill or fortress," and "linne" is a pool, stream, or waterfall. But what does "ferm" stand for? Some make it out to be "faire" (watchtower); others "fiar" (crooked); and others "fearann" (farm or grass land). Dunfermline would thus signify alternately the castle-hill, hill-watch-tower, or hill-fortress by the stream; the hill or castle by the winding stream; or the castle-land by the stream. I am disposed myself to adopt the last of these etymologies. The word "fearann" certainly enters in local nomenclature into Pitfirrane, an estate in the neighbourhood, and there are also a Castleland in the parish of Beath, and a Castlelandhill near North Queensferry. The "dun," tower or castle, as represented in the first syllable, and the Lyne as the name of the stream which bounds Dunfermline on the south, seem, as parts of the appellation, to be beyond all dispute ; whilst " ferm " appears to resemble very closely the Gaelic "fearann," the French "ferme," and the English "farm." The rendering of Dunfermline in medieval Latin by " Fermelodunum " is another testimony of the explanation of the term being, "the castle-land or castle farm beside the stream."

Dunfermline first appears in history as the residence of Malcolm III., King of Scotland, generally known as Malcolm Canmore or "The Great Head." Fordun speaks of it as "a place, naturally very strongly fortified, surrounded by a dense forest, and guarded by steep rocks." He tells us, moreover, that there was in the midst of it a beautiful level tract, likewise guarded by rocks and streams, so that it might well be said of it, that, whilst difficult of access to men, it was almost unapproachable by wild beasts. Here, according to Fordun, Malcolm's marriage with Margaret, sister of Edgar Atheling, took place in 1070, though Mr Skene inclines to the belief that the true date of this event is 1068.

King Malcolm, celebrated as the son of Duncan, and slayer of the usurper Macbeth, seems to have first contracted a marriage with Ingebiorg, widow of Thorfinn, Earl of Orkney, who bore him a son named Duncan, and died after a few years. It was as a widower that, as already mentioned, he received the intelligence of the arrival in St Margaret's Hope of Edgar Atheling, and his mother and sisters, who, as representatives of the ancient Saxon royal family in England, had taken flight after the establishment on the throne of William the Conqueror, but on their voyage to the Continent had been driven by stress of weather into the Firth of Forth. The Scottish monarch hastened to receive these unexpected guests, and was so much struck by the beauty and amiable character of the Princess Margaret, that he forthwith offered her his hand—a proffer which, though accepted by Margaret, seems to have been more in accord with the wishes of her relatives than her own inclinations, which tended all to a life of celibacy and devotion. She was conducted by him to Dunfermline, and on her way thither is traditionally said to have rested on a large stone, which still exists on the Queensferry road, about two miles south from the town, and has had recently an inscription engraved on it to that effect.

Sir James Balfour, in his 'Annals of Scotland,' refers to the wedding of the Princess Margaret with Malcolm III. as having been accomplished "with grate solemnity at his village and castell of Dunfermeling in the Woodes, in the 14 3eire of his rainge, in A° 1070." Malcolm had been crowned at Scone in 1057. Margaret made him an excellent and most devoted wife, and her influence with her husband was employed to the noblest ends— the exercise of charity and benevolence, and the promotion of religion and morality throughout their dominions. She bore him a numerous family of sons, three of.whom —Edgar, Alexander, and David—ascended the throne in succession. A daughter also—Matilda or Maud— became the wife of Henry I. of England.

The *dun* or fortress which Malcolm and Margaret occupied, and which is known as Malcolm Canmore's Tower, is still in existence, on a peninsular eminence on the east side of Pittencrieff Glen, though little more than the foundations can now be traced. It occupies a very strong position, being virtually inaccessible on three sides, as the hill on which it stands is there either exceedingly steep, or descends in a sheer precipice to the stream. The only convenient mode of approach in ancient times could have been from the east. What remains of the walls shows that they must have been of extreme thickness and strength; and to preserve them from further injury, the present proprietor of Pittencrieff has surrounded them with a low wall.

King Malcolm, with two of his sons, was killed in besieging the castle of Alnwick in 1093, and Queen Margaret, who was already on her deathbed in Edinburgh Castle, survived very shortly the intelligence of the event. Not long before, the monastery and church erected mainly at her instigation at Dunfermline by her husband, had been completed and dedicated to the Holy Trinity. The establishment thus founded was in great measure superseded by a later structure, of which the ruins still remain. But the original monastery church, in which Queen Margaret and her husband, their three sons and grandson, were interred, is still in existence, and exhibits a remarkably fine specimen of the Early Norman style towards the end of the eleventh century. The west doorway and north porch are especially admired by connoisseurs in ancient ecclesiastical architecture. Attached to it at its north-west extremity is a tower and spire, from the bartizan of which a magnificent view is commanded, taking in the whole basin of the Forth from Ben Lomond to the Bass. Another tower at the south-west corner is a modern structure, having been erected to supply the place of an older tower which fell down with a terrible crash in 1807, but did no further damage than killing some horses in an adjoining stable.

The interior of the old monastery church is not of great dimensions, but with its ancient rounded pillars and semicircular arches, surmounted by a triforium and clerestory, has an air of great majesty. In recent years the lower windows have been filled in with stained glass—

the memorial benefactions of various individuals—and the great west window has been supplied in like fashion with a national and historical delineation designed by Sir Noel Paton, and presented by Mr Carnegie, a native of Dunfermline. Till 1818 this edifice served as the parish church of Dunfermline, the ancient choir, along with a central tower, though erected subsequently to the nave, having fallen and been reduced to a ruin by the middle of the seventeenth century. In the year just mentioned the foundations of a new church, to which Malcolm Canmore's structure now forms a majestic approach, were laid on the east, on the site of the choir, or what used to be known as the "Psalter Church-yard." In the course of this work the tomb was dis-covered of King Robert the Bruce, who had been buried in front of the high altar. The remains, thus disinterred, and fully ascertained to be those of the victor at Bannockburn, were inspected with great interest by crowds of visitors from all parts of the country. They were reinterred with great ceremony, and the spot is marked by a slab immediately in front of the pulpit.

The New Abbey Church is not without a certain state-liness and grandeur, though it is in many respects a mere sham, the Gothic pillars being only posts of rubble masonry, encrusted with a fluting of Roman cement. There is also an overpowering glare of light, arising from the absence of stained glass, which has been intro-duced with such effect into the windows of the ancient nave. In a side aisle there is a fine sculptured monu-ment by Foley, in memory of General Bruce, uncle of the present Lord Elgin, who accompanied the Prince of Wales on his tour to the Holy Land, and died in return-ing, at Marseilles. There are also here a stained-glass win-dow erected by the Dowager-Countess of Elgin to the memory of her husband, the Governor-General of India ;

a monument to Lady Augusta Stanley, wife of the late Dean of Westminster; and one or two other memorials of the Elgin family. The eastern or new is, like the western or old division of the church, surmounted by a tower, on the bartizan of which there appears in questionable taste the words "King Robert the Bruce" encircling the battlements in great Roman letters.

The monastery founded by Malcolm III. was at first only a priory, and was not raised to the dignity of an abbey till the reign of David I., who altered the terms of the foundation, and in 1130 settled it with a colony of Benedictine monks from Canterbury. This "sair sanct for the Croun," as James I. called him, endowed Dunfermline Abbey " with a tenth of the gold which shall emerge to me from Fife and Fothrif." From this it has been inferred that in those days gold was obtained from the hills and streams in the peninsula lying between the Forth and Tay. The term " Fothrif" has already been discussed. The Abbey of Dunfermline is spoken of as being situated in Fatrick Muir, a designation which is said to have been the ancient one of Calais Muir, lying to the east of Dunfermline, and between that town and the Great North Road.

Before Malcolm Canmore's time the usual burial-place of the Scottish kings seems to have been generally in the island of Iona, but Dunfermline became now for a long period the favourite place of royal sepulture. Among those interred here were, as already mentioned, Malcolm and Margaret; their three sons, Edgar, Alexander I., and David I.; their grandson Malcolm IV.; King Alexander III.; King Robert the Bruce, with his queen Isabella; and his cousin the famous Thomas Randolph, Earl of Moray. The remains of Queen Margaret, however, were in the year 1250 removed from their resting-place in the west church or nave, and by command of Alexander III.

were placed in a magnificent shrine, and deposited in the Lady Chapel at the east end of the recently erected choir. Here the tomb of the canonised queen was visited for hundreds of years by pilgrims, and received the homage of the faithful. About the same time the bodies of her husband, children, and grandson seem also to have been transported from the nave, and deposited within the choir, where most of them still remain. Their place of sepulture is the north transept of the present Abbey Church, where the leaden coffins containing them are still in existence, though the vaults are now covered with planking, and inaccessible to the general public. As regards, however, the tomb of St Margaret herself, a blue slab in the ruins of the Lady Chapel, which forms the enclosure outside and at the east end of the New Abbey Church, is pointed out as covering the remains of the queen. But the fact is indubitable that this is now merely a cenotaph. Previous to the Reformation, the remains of Queen Margaret, who had been canonised after her death, were regarded as holy relics, and her tomb attracted hosts of devotees. But on the overthrow of the old faith some zealous adherents who still clung to it, to obviate the consequences of the probable destruction of the shrine, disinterred secretly the remains, and had them conveyed first to Edinburgh, and then, it is said, to the house of Abbot Durie at Craig Luscar, where they remained for a year. They were then for further safety transported abroad to the Low Countries, and after a series of vicissitudes were taken charge of by Philip II., who deposited them in the church of the newly erected palace of the Escurial. Here, it is said, the greater part of the relics are still preserved; and at all events, two urns alleged to contain them, and bearing the names of Queen Margaret and her husband Malcolm, were till a recent period to be seen.

The head, however, of the sainted queen had been deposited, after having been solemnly authenticated at Antwerp, in the church of the Scots College at Douai in France. Up to the period of the Revolution it was preserved here as an object of veneration; but on the commotion which attended that great outbreak, it disappeared like the holy *ampoule* at Rheims, and all trace of it has been lost. Whilst the late Dr Gillies was Roman Catholic Bishop of Edinburgh, he made an application to the Holy See to use its influence with the Spanish Government to procure the restoration to Scotland of the relics of Queen Margaret and her husband, which were said to be still existing in the Church of the Escurial. The request was so far complied with that an inquiry was alleged to have been instituted by the Spanish authorities, who reported that the remains could not now be identified. Whether a search was really and *bona fide* made is not very clear, but no more satisfactory result could be obtained. Like the body of St Cuthbert, that of St Margaret was destined to sustain a series of migrations, and even yet it is not impossible that they may find their way back to the land where they were originally deposited.

What remains now of the ancient Abbey of Dunfermline, besides the monastery church, consists chiefly of the ruins of the Frater Hall or refectory, with vaults beneath occupying the south-west corner of the Abbey churchyard, with the site of the cloister court, now part of the burying-ground, lying between it and the church. The south wall of the refectory is still almost entire, and exhibits an imposing row of lofty pointed windows in the Early English style, whilst at the west end is a very large and magnificent window belonging to the geometrical decorated period, the mullions of which form themselves at the summit into a crown. All the windows overlook the public road, and the terrace at the east end of the Frater Hall, in front of the churchyard, commands a fine view of the country between Dunfermline and the sea. Adjoining the churchyard on the east, and extending as far as the New Row, is the site of the ancient Abbey Park or monastery enclosure, which contained the pleasure-grounds, fish-ponds, and other amenities for the use and recreation of the monks. It is now all occupied by houses and gardens, but was in former times surrounded by a wall, fragments of which are still in existence. Canmore Street, which bounds it on the north, used to be known as " In aneath the Wa's."

At the angle of the Frater Hall, between the south wall and the great west window, is a tower, consisting of two superimposed apartments, built over the ancient archway, or "pend," through which the public road passes. A connection is thus formed between the monastery buildings and those of the royal Palace—the remains of which, on the other side of the way, occupy the crest of a steep bank overhanging Pittencrieff Glen. Only the south wall is preserved, with some chambers in the angle between it and the monastery ruins—one of which, a vaulted room with pillars supporting the roof, is known as "The Magazine," though it has very much the appearance of a crypt, or underground chapel. It is approached on the east by a descent of steps from the Palace ruins, and at the west end it opens into an apartment called "The King's Kitchen," between which and the monastery there was a communication through the tower over the Pends. The monks are said to have had the *entrée* to the "kitchen," and been in the habit of receiving a contribution, or "mess," from the victuals prepared for the royal table—an intrusion which could not have been very agreeable either to the king's servants or their master. The roof of this apartment and a great portion of the walls have disappeared; but a triangular Gothic recess adjoins it, provided with a shoot or drain—a circumstance which has led to the belief of its having served as a scullery.

Viewed from below, the south wall of the Palace, with its beautiful bay-windows in the Tudor style, presents a very imposing aspect amid its romantic surroundings. When the edifice was erected, or when Malcolm Canmore's Tower, farther up the glen, was abandoned as a royal residence, cannot now be ascertained; but possibly there was an earlier palace on the same site, and, to judge from its style of architecture, the present building could not have been commenced before the reign of James IV. at earliest. It possesses an abiding interest as having been the favourite residence of James VI. and Anne of Denmark, and the birthplace of several of their children—including, more especially, the Princess Elizabeth, afterwards Queen of Bohemia, born here in 1596, and Charles I., born in 1600. The window of the room in which the latter is said, traditionally, to have first seen the light, is still pointed out. It is the second from the west end of the upper storey, has a chimney-place adjoining it on the east side, and has a bush growing from the embrasure. The ceiling of the architrave of a neighbouring window has a fine representation of the Annunciation sculptured on the stone, which was only discovered within the present century. The windows have evidently been converted, in some instances, from pointed Gothic or ecclesiastical arches into Tudor casements with cross mullions — a circumstance which, coupled with the fact that we scarcely hear of the more recent palace of Dunfermline till the reign of James VI., induces me to maintain that the present ruins are the remains of a building which was in the main erected by that monarch himself, or remodelled from the ancient monastery. Had it been the work of any previous sovereign, we should surely have heard of its being at least occasionally occupied by royalty. But no record of any such occupation has been preserved—that is to say, of any structure which succeeded the tower of Malcolm Canmore—till the reign of James VI., who seems to have resided here very constantly.

The Palace ruins and grounds are Crown property, and under the charge of her Majesty's Commissioners of Woods and Forests. Immediately beyond them, to the north, stood formerly what used to be known as the "Queen's House," having, it is said, been originally the dower-mansion secured to Anne of Denmark. Such is the account, at least, commonly given of the "Queen's House," or "Queen Anne's House," and an edifice bearing this designation existed in this locality till within a comparatively recent period. But I have a strong impression that the whole Palace of Dunfermline had been settled as the dower-house of Queen Anne, who also received a grant of the temporalities formerly attached to the Abbey. John Taylor, the Water-poet, who visited Scotland in 1618, informs us in his 'Penniless Pilgrimage' that he travelled from Burntisland to Dunfermline, "where I was entertained and lodged at Master John Gibb his house, one of the grooms of his majesty's bedchamber, and I think the oldest servant the king hath: withal I was well entertained there by Master Crighton at his own house, who went with me and showed me the queen's palace (a delicate and princely mansion); withal I saw the ruins of an ancient and stately built abbey, with fair gardens, orchards, meadows, belonging to the palace: all which, with fair and goodly revenues, by the suppression of the abbey, were annexed to the Crown. There also I saw a very fair church, which, though it be now very large and spacious, yet it hath in former times been much larger." It is evident from this, that in speaking of the "queen's palace," Taylor means ·the royal abode generally at Dunfermline. Had he referred only, in this phrase, to Queen Anne's dower-house, he would certainly have added some account of the "king's palace." But as he has only mentioned one building, I conceive that I am warranted in inferring that the "Queen Anne's House" of later days had, as a portion of or a house formed from the Palace, retained, as a particular designation, what had been originally applied to the whole building.

The southern portion of the Abbey burying-ground was formerly the cloister-court of the monastery. The larger and more ancient part is on the north side of the church, between it and the Maygate; and in the centre, up to the middle of the last century, there stood a very ancient thorn, which was said to have been the trysting-place in Roman Catholic times, when a fair was held on Sunday in the churchyard. It has now disappeared; but in 1807 the graft of the present tree, which occupies the site of the old one, was brought from Culross. Another curiosity in this part of the churchyard is frequently pointed out to visitors. It is a small upright tombstone, erected in memory of a worthy citizen of Dunfermline, who little expected that an amusing *lâche* on the part of his representatives would have procured for him a species of immortality. The inscription runs as follows :—

Here lyes the
corps of Andw.
Robertson, *pre-*
sent deacon convener
of weavers in this
brugh, who died 18
July 1745, aged 62.

An old house in the Maygate, overlooking the church-yard, and now divided into two separate dwellings, is

known as the "Abbot's House," and was the residence
of Robert Pitcairn, who was appointed abbot and commendator of Dunfermline at the Reformation in 1560.
He became afterwards Secretary of State to James VI.,
under the regency of Lennox, and, as has already been
stated, was arrested on the charge of being concerned in
the Raid of Ruthven, conveyed a prisoner to Loch Leven,
and died there in 1584.   Neither politically nor morally
was his course of life to be commended ; and as if to
protest against the voice of censure, he is said to have
carved over the door of his house in the Maygate the
following couplet, which is still legible there :—

> " Sin word is thral and thocht is fre,
>   Keip weil thy tongue I counsel the."

The last Roman Catholic abbot of Dunfermline was
George Durie, a cadet of the family of Durie of that
Ilk, in the east of Fife.   His character was of a more
pronounced kind, as regards personal morality, than even
that of his successor, Commendator Pitcairn, as we find
a royal rescript granting letters of legitimation to two of
his natural children.   He was the ancestor of the Lairds
of Craig Luscar, in the neighbourhood of Dunfermline.
The first abbot of the monastery was Godfrey, formerly
prior of Canterbury, who was nominated to this dignity
in 1128 by David I., when he converted the Benedictine
Priory of the Holy Trinity into an abbey and remodelled
its discipline.   In 1296, "Rauf, abbot of Dunfermelyn,"
appears as one of the subscribers of the Ragman Roll, or
Act of submission to Edward I.

In 1593, after the death of Pitcairn, the temporalities
of the Abbey were formed into a lordship and bestowed
on Anne of Denmark, queen of James VI., and after
remaining in the hands of the Crown for a number of
years, they were granted in a long lease in 1641 by

Charles I. to Charles Seton, second Earl of Dunfermline. The Marquis of Tweeddale acquired right to this lease in satisfaction of an obligation incurred to him by the Earl, and had it afterwards renewed in his own name. It expired in 1780, and a tack of the teinds therein included was then acquired by the heritors of Dunfermline under condition of the yearly payment of £100.

It is in connection with Dunfermline Abbey that we find one of the earliest references to the working of coal in Scotland. In 1291, William de Obervill, then proprietor of the estate of Pittencrieff, grants a charter to the abbot and convent of Dunfermline empowering them to work one coal-pit on any part of his property except arable ground, and when one was exhausted to open another. This was to be, however, exclusively for their own use, and they were on no account to sell or supply coals to others.

In 1296, after Edward I.'s capture of Berwick and reduction for a while of Scotland to an apparent submission, he made a progress through the country, and in course of it visited Dunfermline. This was on Monday, 13th August, the king having journeyed thither from Markinch on his return from Perth by Lindores Abbey and St Andrews. He remained at Dunfermline all night, and proceeded next day to Stirling, from which he travelled to Linlithgow and Edinburgh, and thence by Haddington to Berwick. We hear next of his spending the winter of 1300 at Dunfermline, and the succeeding Lent at St Andrews, from the abbey of which he carried off the lead, to be used at the siege of Stirling, which was surrendered to him three months afterwards. Such is the time assigned to the latter event in one of the 'Cronica Scotiæ,' edited by Mr W. B. D. Turnbull for the Abbotsford Club ; but there is some discrepancy between the dates stated in these Chronicles and those deduced from the letters of Edward I. and other documents preserved in the Record Office, London. From the latter we derive the information that Stirling was besieged by the English king and his forces in the spring and summer of 1304, and that it was surrendered to them on 20th July of that year. We are also informed from the same source that fifty-three waggons of lead were stripped off by Edward from the roof of the church and abbey buildings of Dunfermline at this time for the purpose of being used in the operations of the siege of Stirling, but that compensation was ultimately made to the abbot and convent. A similar recompense for a similar spoliation was made to the prior and convent of St Andrews.

The Prince of Wales (afterwards Edward II.) seems also to have spent the winter of 1303-4 at Dunfermline, or at least was often passing and repassing between that town and Perth. Occasionally he halted at Kinross; and we learn that, while in Scotland, he had frequently nobles and knights to dinner, and entertained them royally from the king's stores.

The Exchequer accounts show that Edward I. was at Dunfermline in January 1304, and received there a New Year's gift, forwarded to him from England by Queen Margaret, daughter of Philip II. of France, whom he had married as his second wife in 1299. This token of affection consisted of a gold cup with stand and cover, and also a golden pitcher. In the same month of January the queen joined the king at Dunfermline, having travelled from England by Tynemouth and Berwick-on-Tweed, and then proceeded by way of Dunbar and Dirleton. At the last-named place she was met by an escort, sent by her dutiful husband, and was conducted into Fife with all proper state.

Edward's career was, however, now fast approaching a close, and his son's mismanagement was soon to destroy the last chance of the English nation making good its claim to supremacy over Scotland.   Little is recorded of Dunfermline in connection with these final struggles, but we do hear something of her in relation to the hero who ultimately achieved Scottish independence. Robert the Bruce, as is well known, was interred in Dunfermline Abbey, and the Rolls of the Scottish Exchequer, as edited by Dr Stuart and Mr Burnett, have been made to educe some interesting details in connection with the obsequies of the great king. We learn from these that the corpse of King Robert, who had died at the castle of Cardross in Dumbartonshire in 1329, was conveyed to Dunfermline by way of Dunipace and Cambuskenneth. A marble monument made in Paris was erected over his grave in front of the high altar of the Abbey Church of Dunfermline.   Part of our information on this subject is derived from the History of Archdeacon Barbour :—

> " With great far and solemnite
> They hef him had to Dunfermelyn,
> And him solemnly erdit syne
> In ane far tumb within the quer."

We are told that £130, 12s. was in all paid for the tomb, the monumental part of which was constructed in Paris, and brought over from thence through Belgium. When the grave was opened in 1819, the body was discovered surrounded with fragments of fine linen cloth interspersed with gold threads, and the breast-bone had evidently been sawn through in order to remove the heart, which, as is well known, had been carried by the Good Sir James Douglas, at the dying request of the king, on his expedition to the Holy Land. The valorous knight, however, fell in Spain in an engagement with the

Moors; and the Bruce's heart, found on his person after death on the field of battle, was reconveyed to Scotland and deposited in the monastery church at Melrose. The Dunfermline monument had consisted of black marble, fragments of which were discovered near the grave. Over the latter, on the occasion of the funeral, a mortuary chapel had been erected of planks of Baltic timber, and a charge is entered in the Exchequer accounts of the day for the expenses of its gilding and decoration. The Abbot of Dunfermline received £66, 13s. 4d., and his servants prepared the candles used for the obsequies, in which upwards of 562 stones of wax were employed. There are charges for vestments for the altar, for horses, and for the gilding of the hearse, also for large quantities of lawn, crape, and black cloth.

We do not hear much of Dunfermline as a royal residence during the reigns of the earlier Stuart kings, who seem generally to have preferred Holyrood or Linlithgow, Stirling or Falkland. Under the abbots the town was only a burgh of regality, having been erected into this in 1363; and it was first created a royal burgh by James VI. in 1588, the same year in which he bestowed that dignity on the monastery town of Culross, seven miles higher up the Forth. James resided very constantly at Dunfermline, and the absence of the Court on his removal to England must have seriously affected the prosperity of the place. It was not till long afterwards that it became noted for its manufacturing industry; and at the beginning of the last century all that Sir Robert Sibbald has to say on the subject in his History of Fife and Kinross is, that "the town has a manufactory of Dornick-cloath."

It is recorded by Lindsay of Pitscottie that in March 1560 "the lords and gentlemen by north Forth having cast down the Abbey of Dunfermling, came to Stirling, but could not enter into it because of the Frenchmen, and therefore returned back to Castle Campbell." Thus, in the year that the Reformation was established in Scotland, we learn that Dunfermline Abbey was subjected to contumelious treatment, and probably seriously damaged, whatever meaning we may attach to the phrase "cast down." There is no doubt that a good deal of mischief was done at this time by furious mobs and over-zealous reformers to the ancient ecclesiastical buildings in Scotland ; but it seems at least equally certain that much of the damage with which our Scottish Protestants have been credited on this account is to be ascribed to other agents and causes. Most of the abbeys in the southern Lowlands, such as Melrose, Kelso, and Jedburgh, were reduced to their present condition during the Earl of Hertford's invasion of Scotland, and at all times the religious houses in this quarter had suffered on the occasion of hostile incursions from England. It was not, however, till the reigns of Henry VIII. and Edward VI. that artillery was brought to bear with such fatal effect on these edifices, which never afterwards recovered from the infliction. And with regard both to them and the religious establishments farther north, little account has been taken of another factor equally potent as English invaders and Protestant zealots—the agency of natural decay, accelerated by the neglect of the custodian parishioners, both lay and clerical. Thus we find an order of the Scottish Privy Council issued at Stirling on 13th September 1563, and directed against Robert Pitcairn, commendator; Alan Coutts, chamberlain; and William Lumsden, sacristan of the Abbey of Dunfermline, by which these are commanded forthwith to put in proper repair the parish church, which had become both ruinous and unsafe

through their neglect and refusal to effect any amelio-
ration. The order proceeds on the application of the
inhabitants of the town and parish, and mention is
specially made of rents in the walls and vaulted roof,
rafters requiring renewal, and windows wanting glass.
All this damage could hardly have been effected by the
Protestant army three years before. From another Act,
too, of the Privy Council, immediately following the
above, and of the same date, it would appear that the
parish churches generally throughout the kingdom had
fallen into a state of dilapidation and ruin. These are
ordered " to be reparit and upbiggit, and quhair thai ar
ruynous and faltie, to be mendit; and eftir that thai be
sufficientlie mendit in windowis, thak, and uther neces-
saris, to be intertenyt and uphaldin upoun the expenssis of the parochinaris and Persone, in maner following : That is to say, the twa part of the expenssis
thairof to be maid be the parochinaris, and thred
part be the Persone." This state of things is said to
be occasioned "partlie be sleuch and negligence of the
parochinaris, and partlie be oursycht of the Personis."

There can be no doubt that immediately previous to
the Reformation many of the religious buildings had
been allowed to fall into a condition of decay and disrepair through the neglect of the abbots, vicars, and
others whose duty it was to see to these being properly
maintained. And no doubt the lay commendators and
impropriators of the tithes and spoils of the Church, after
the overthrow of the ancient faith, would frequently exhibit equal remissness in attending to these requirements.

The first Protestant minister appointed to Dunfermline was David Ferguson, who was nominated to the
charge in 1560, and was a member of the first General
Assembly held at Edinburgh in December of that year.
He continued minister of the parish till his death in

1598; and in a Minute of a Commission of the General Assembly held in the previous year, he is spoken of as "the auldest minister that tyme in Scotland," and is represented as urging his brethren to resist the establishment of bishops in the Church, illustrating his argument by the quotation, "Equo ne credite Teucri." Ferguson was indeed a staunch Presbyterian, and by no means courtly in the exposition of his views. He is said, however, to have been a great favourite with James VI., who relished his conversation, though the monarch received on one occasion from the clergyman a severe rebuke for "banning" (swearing). It is also recorded of him that he "uttered many quicke and wise sentences which were taken much notice of;" and in the year that he died he made a collection of Scottish proverbs, which do not seem, however, to have been published till 1642, when an edition of them was printed at Edinburgh. Some of these are very curious, both for their piquancy and antiquarian interest, and the collection will well repay a perusal.

It is not very clear who held the office of heritable bailie of the regality of Dunfermline under the abbots previous to the Reformation, but in all probability it was exercised by the Seton family, whom we find after that date in possession of the office. One of them, Alexander Seton, who exercised that function, was raised by James VI. in 1605 to the dignity of Earl of Dunfermline. He was the third surviving son of George, seventh Lord Seton, the celebrated champion of Queen Mary, and was born in 1555. He was sent to Rome to study for the Church, but abandoned this pursuit for that of law, and after a residence of several years in France, returned to Scotland, where he seems to have been called to the Bar about 1577. In 1583 he accompanied his father, Lord Seton, on an embassy to Henry III. of France,

and in 1586 he became, with the title of Prior of Plus-
carden, an Extraordinary Lord of Session, as successor
to James Stewart, Lord Doune, father of the "Bonnie
Earl of Moray." In 1588 he was made an ordinary Lord
of Session, with the title of Lord Urquhart; in 1593 was
elected President of the College of Justice; and in 1605,
as already mentioned, was created first Earl of Dunfermline. He seems to have enjoyed great favour at Court,
but was always strongly suspected of tendencies towards
the Roman Catholic faith. In the same year that he
was appointed Lord President, he acquired, as already
stated, the estate of Dalgety, which adjoins and is now
incorporated with that of Donibristle, belonging to the
Earl of Moray, on the shore of the Firth of Forth, between Inverkeithing and Aberdour. He and his family
held this property for several generations, and a portion
of the old mansion which they occupied is still in existence. But their chief residence was Pinkie House, on
the estate of that name near Musselburgh, which also
belonged to this branch of the Seton family.

The first Earl of Dunfermline died at Pinkie in 1622,
and was succeeded by his son Charles, who distinguished
himself for a time as a zealous Covenanter, but on the
death of Charles I. retired to Holland, and returned
from thence to Scotland in 1650 with Charles II.
Thenceforward he is to be identified with the Royalist
party, and at the Restoration became a member of the
Privy Council. Like his contemporary, however, the
Earl of Kincardine, he seems to have exerted his influence at Court in smoothing matters for the Presbyterians
—at least it was through his exertions that a royal warrant was obtained reponing for a time in the incumbency
of Dalgety church the celebrated Andrew Donaldson,
who had been ejected from thence for nonconformity.
The second Lord Dunfermline died in 1672, and his

son Charles, the third Earl, died shortly after him at the early age of thirty-three. James, a younger brother of the latter, succeeded him as fourth and last Earl of Dunfermline. He commanded a troop of horse under Viscount Dundee at the battle of Killiecrankie, incurred forfeiture as a rebel against William III.'s Government, went abroad to James VII., and died at St Germains a few years after the Revolution.

By his first marriage the first Lord Dunfermline had a daughter, Lady Isabella, who married John, first Earl of Lauderdale (only son of Chancellor Maitland, Lord Thirlstane), by whom she was the mother of John, Duke of Lauderdale, the famous or infamous President of the Scottish Privy Council in the reign of Charles II. By his second marriage he had a daughter, Lady Jean, married to John, eighth Lord Yester, and afterwards Earl of Tweeddale. Their son was raised to the dignity of Marquis of Tweeddale, and, in consequence of money advanced by him to his uncle, the second Lord Dunfermline, got transferred to him by the latter the heritable jurisdiction of the bailiary of the regality of Dunfermline, and also the temporalities of Dunfermline Abbey, which, as Crown property, and formerly the dowry of his mother, Queen Anne, Charles I. had made over to Seton in 1641. In consequence of this transfer the Tweeddale family became vested in all those rights and privileges connected with Dunfermline which were formerly held by the Earls bearing that title. To the present day they hold the feudal superiority of the lands of North Queensferry, the patronage of the office of Master of the Song in the Abbey Church of Dunfermline, and also the patronage of St Leonard's Hospital on the south side of the town. Of course the bailiary disappeared with the abolition of heritable jurisdictions; but the appointment of rector of the Grammar School

was, till a comparatively recent period, held by Lord
Tweeddale. The same family, on the forfeiture incurred
by the fourth Earl of Dunfermline in 1690, acquired for
a time the estate of Pinkie, which, however, was, about
1788, disposed of by them to Sir Archibald Hope of
Craighall, grandfather of the present proprietor.

In August 1614, Theophilus Howard, Lord Howard de
Walden, afterwards Earl of Suffolk, visited Scotland, and
an account of his " progress " is printed in the ' Banna-
tyne Miscellany.' He was received at Edinburgh with
great honour by Lord Binning, Secretary of State, was
shown over the castle, " and efter denner, raid from Edinburghe with my Lord Chancelare,[1] who, efter the Secretare
had taken his lieve of thame neir Craumond, convoyed
thame to Dunfermeling, and interteined him thair with all
kyndnes and respect till Monnonday the 16, that he went
towards Culross to sie Sir George Bruce's coill-workes,
whair, having ressaved the best intertainement they could
mak him, my Lord Chancellare tuke lieve of him, and left
him to be convoyed to Stirling be my Lord Erskine, whair
he could not be persuaded to stay above one night."

In 1624 Dunfermline was almost wholly consumed by
fire—a calamity, however, which, though a terrible one,
was not so appalling an occurrence in those days, when
houses were often in great part constructed of wood, and
could be more easily restored than they would be at
the present time. Yet with all the experience of such
disasters there was something very dreadful in the sud-
denness and violence with which this was accomplished.
One hundred and twenty tenements were destroyed and
287 families rendered houseless in the space of four
hours, whilst, in addition, a number of granaries, containing five hundred bolls of grain, were destroyed.
The town-people had the privilege of cutting timber in the

---

[1] Alexander Seton, Earl of Dunfermline.

wood of Garvock, a little to the east of the town, and this they availed themselves of to such an extent in rebuilding their habitations, that the wood itself disappeared, and now exists only in memory. The adjoining lands still bear the name, and such places as " Woodmill " and " Transylvania," or " Transy," attest the existence of the ancient forest.

On the occasion of Charles I.'s visit to Scotland in 1633, he passed through Dunfermline on his way from Edinburgh and Stirling to Falkland and Perth, but seems to have made no lengthened stay. One would have thought he might have given some more attention to the place of his birth, but he does not appear to have remained even for a night there, though he had bestowed this honour both on Linlithgow and Stirling. In journeying from the latter place, he had doubtless passed through Clackmannan, Culross, and Torryburn. After remaining three days at Falkland, he continued his progress to Perth, and was there royally entertained by the Earl of Kinnoull, Lord Chancellor of Scotland. He then returned to Falkland, where he stayed for two nights, and early on the morning of 10th July started for Burntisland, from which he crossed the Forth the same day on his return to Leith and Edinburgh. He incurred no small jeopardy, however, from a violent tempest which suddenly arose, and in less than half an hour as suddenly subsided. The king's vessel weathered the gale, but a boat in which were eight of the royal attendants, besides a quantity of the royal plate and money, was lost. This seems to have been the first and last time that Charles visited Fife after leaving Dunfermline as an infant of three years old in 1603.

Charles II., in his ill-starred expedition to Scotland in 1650, arrived in Dunfermline from Perth on 24th July, remained there for a night, and proceeded next day to

Stirling, taking the same road through Torryburn and Culross by which his father had travelled seventeen years previously in coming from the west. Having gone from Stirling to Leith (probably by water) on 29th July, he remained there till 2d August, and then "sore against his awen mynd he wes moued by his counsell and the generall persons of the armey to reteire himselve to Dunfermlinge." His reluctance to go there is readily explained by the circumstance that a committee of Covenanting leaders and ministers of the Kirk were shortly expected at the town to make terms with their youthful monarch, on which alone they were ready to assist in restoring him to the throne. Thither they came on 9th August, headed by the Earl of Lothian, and pressed his Majesty to subscribe the " declaratione " which had been handed to him a few days before by the Marquis of Argyll. Charles endeavoured to avert the difficulty momentarily, by pleading an engagement to go out hunting,[1] and that they would have their answer when he returned in the evening. But though they again presented themselves then, they received no satisfaction, as the king absolutely refused to subscribe any declaration which might cast reflections on the memory of his father.

A few days afterwards a Council of State was held in the royal bedchamber in Dunfermline Palace, there being present, along with others, the king, the Marquis of Argyll, and the Earls of Eglinton and Tweeddale. Charles now yielded so far to the demands of the Scottish Presbyterians as to agree to transmit a letter to the Commissioners of the Kirk, intimating his readiness to comply with their wishes in all things concerning religion and the peace of the Church, but only begged that they would be as gentle as possible in their ref-

---

[1] So says Sir James Balfour; but considering it was now only the second week of August, we should probably read " hawking."

erences to his father. Such a letter was accordingly sent, and a deputation of Presbyterian ministers waited on his Majesty to help to solve his scruples ; but Charles still hesitated, till the receipt of a peremptory message from the Commissioners of the Kirk and the Commissioners of Estates that they could afford him no support whatever unless he subscribed forthwith the declaration demanded. Thus driven to the wall, Charles had no resource left but compliance ; and accordingly, after a good deal of disputation and a few verbal amendments, he at last, on Friday 16th August, signed the document in question, and immediately afterwards rode off from Dunfermline to Perth. He never seems to have visited the town again, and it never could have possessed afterwards for him any pleasant recollections.

During the Jacobite insurrection of 1715, when Lord Mar with his forces lay encamped near Perth, a detachment of horse and foot was despatched by him under the command of Major Grahame to occupy Dunfermline, and levy supplies of money out of the taxation contributed by the town to the revenue. He proceeded by way of Dunning and Castle Campbell, and reaching Dunfermline, quartered his troops, partly in the Abbey, partly in private houses, but seems to have posted his guards in a very remiss fashion, and to have taken little or no pains to protect himself against any surprise from the Government army. One sentry only was stationed at the bridge leading from the town across the Tower burn to Torryburn and Alloa, whilst Grahame himself and several of his officers were carousing in a private house, and would listen to no remonstrances as to making more effectual the means of defence. The Honourable Charles, afterwards Lord Cathcart, commanding a detachment of Government troops, had meantime been making a rapid and silent advance upon the town, which, in its undefended state, they entered with little difficulty. The unfortunate sentry at the west bridge was slain, and a *mêlée* ensued between the assailants and such scattered parties of the Jacobites as they encountered about the streets. The result was a thorough stampede,—the Pretender's men flying in all directions, and making their way with all despatch out of the town back to the Earl of Mar's headquarters at Perth. Some indeed were slain or badly wounded, but the bulk of them saved themselves thus in an inglorious flight. At least such is the account of the affair given by John, Master of Sinclair, who was then serving under the banner of the Earl of Mar, to whose obstinacy and mismanagement, according to the former, the failure of the expedition and rebellion is mainly to be ascribed.

Just about the time of the first Jacobite insurrection a more prosperous epoch for Dunfermline was inaugurated by the introduction of the damask loom, effected mainly through the enterprise of a native of the town, named James Blake. He went over to Edinburgh, in the neighbourhood of which, at Drumsheugh, the weaving of damask linen was carried on, though the utmost secrecy was maintained regarding the construction and mode of working the loom. Blake assumed the part of an imbecile, wandering through the country and soliciting alms by playing on the flute. He presented himself at the weaver's house, and was allowed to enter the workshop, where he crept like a dog below the loom, and in this position managed to learn thoroughly the whole mystery of its construction and management. Returning home he set up a loom in a chamber of the tower above the Pends, and there worked till he had produced a satisfactory pattern and developed sufficiently the capabilities of his machine. How he acted with regard to the secret he had discovered, we are not informed; but damask weaving soon became, and has ever since remained, a specialty of Dunfermline.

As Dunfermline figures prominently in the history of Scottish Dissent, which may almost be said to have originated there, one of the leading actors in the movement being Ralph Erskine, the minister of the Abbey Church, some history of the Erskine family may not be unacceptable, considering how much they have been "household words" in the town from time immemorial.

Ralph Erskine was a son of the Rev. Henry Erskine of Chirnside, and was born at Monilaws, a village near Cornhill in Northumberland, in 1685. His father was the son of Ralph Erskine of Shielfield, who had, it is said, no less than thirty-three children, whilst his grandchildren were so numerous that they often failed to be recognised by the old man. Henry Erskine was one of the young members of the family. These Erskines of Shielfield were descended from David Erskine, commendator of Dryburgh, who was the son of Robert, Master of Erskine, killed at the battle of Pinkie in 1547. The Master of Erskine was the nephew of Regent Mar, and the leaders of the Secession had thus in their veins the blood of one of the oldest of our Scottish families.

Henry Erskine, Ralph and Ebenezer's father, had his full share in the troubles of the time in which it was his lot to be born. Having completed his studies at Edinburgh University, he was appointed minister of Cornhill in Northumberland, and in 1662 was ejected from his charge for nonconformity. After some wandering to and fro, he settled with his family at Dryburgh, in the neighbourhood of the paternal estate, where his brother, the laird, treated him with great kindness. Such a retreat, however, he was not destined to enjoy unmolested, and having incurred the displeasure of the reigning powers for continuing his Presbyterial ministrations, he was apprehended in 1682, conveyed to Edinburgh, and sentenced to the payment of a fine of 5000 merks, and imprisonment in the fortress of the Bass. The latter part of the sentence was remitted on his nephew pledging himself under a bond for other 5000 merks that his uncle should quit the kingdom within fourteen days. Henry Erskine accordingly betook himself to a village in Cumberland, ten miles from Carlisle, and afterwards to Monilaws, in the parish of Brankston, two miles from his old living of Cornhill. Here his son Ralph was born in 1685, but he himself was shortly afterwards arrested, carried off, and committed to prison in Newcastle. From this detention he was liberated under the Act of Indemnity, by which James II. sought to secure the help of the hitherto persecuted nonconformists in the restoration of the Roman Catholic religion. He returned to Monilaws, and after remaining there for two years, he crossed the Border, and after exercising his ministry for a season in the parish of Whitsome, he was shortly after the Revolution appointed minister of Chirnside, a charge which he held till his death in 1696, in his seventy-second year. He was survived by his wife, Margaret Halcro, a lady of an old Orcadian family, who lived to see her two sons, Ralph and Ebenezer Erskine, distinguished pillars of the Church, and ultimately found a resting-place herself in the little burial-ground attached to the old hospital of Scotlandwell, in her son Ebenezer's parish of Portmoak. Ebenezer Erskine's history has already been traced in the account of the parish of Portmoak.

Ralph Erskine was longer than his brother in severing his connection with the Established Church, but his abilities as a leader and organiser seem to have been greater, and the movement in which they both took so prominent a part is chiefly identified, in popular estimation at all events, with the minister of the first charge of Dunfermline, who, notwithstanding his deposition by the General Assembly in 1740, continued to officiate in the Abbey Church for nearly two years subsequently. He had commenced his ministerial career about 1705, by entering as chaplain and tutor the household of Colonel John Erskine of Carnock, commonly known as the Black Colonel, and then residing at Culross. To him, as a descendant of the Earls of Mar, Ralph Erskine was distantly related. His first sermon was delivered at Culross on a week-day (Tuesday), 14th June 1709. A call was given him from Tulliallan, but, as in the case of his brother Ebenezer, it proved ineffective, and Dunfermline became the scene of his ministrations. To the second charge in its Abbey Church he was admitted on 7th August 1711, and in 1716 he was promoted to the first charge. The influence which he exercised in the town was deservedly great, and when he seceded from the Church he carried along with him almost the whole of the congregation. So strong and persistent was this feeling, that for more than half a century after his death the adherents of the Church which he founded comprised all the principal townspeople, whilst only an insignificant remnant lingered in the Abbey. He died in 1752, and the house where he lived and died still exists in the High Street of Dunfermline, and has formed the object of many a pilgrimage. In the end of the last century it was occupied by my grandfather, and my father used to tell me, as an interesting circumstance, that he himself had been born in the same room where Ralph Erskine had breathed his last.

With the exception of the Abbey and its surroundings, almost all the public edifices in Dunfermline are of modern erection. The corporation buildings or town hall, erected in 1878 on the site of the old town-house and jail, at the head of the Kirkgate and corner of Bridge Street, is a handsome structure in the medieval Gothic or Florentine style, and is surmounted by a massive projecting tower, which forms a conspicuous object in descending the High Street, and harmonises admirably with the Abbey Church and monastic and palatial remains in the neighbourhood.   The peaked clock-house which rises above the tower contains a large bell, of great vigour and mellowness of tone.   In Margaret Street, near the principal entrance to the Abbey churchyard, is St Margaret's Hall, also erected in 1878, and used for public meetings, concerts, and occasionally theatrical performances.   It contains a fine organ, and there is also within the building a smaller hall and a reading - room.   Adjoining St Margaret's Hall, in the Maygate, is the Public Library, a handsome public building, and the result in great measure of a munificent gift of £13,000 by Mr Carnegie, a native of Dunfermline, who has amassed a colossal fortune as an ironmaster in the United States.   The same gentleman has provided the town with public baths, which are situated in the northern quarter in School End Street.   A grand new school for secondary or higher instruction has recently been erected, mainly by subscription, on the slope between Canmore Street and Priory Lane, and with its lofty projecting pavilion or belfry, which surmounts the structure, stands out conspicuous in approaching the town from the south.   Another prominent object is the high spire which rises above the county buildings and post-office, now formed out of the hotel and assembly rooms which used to be known collectively as the " Spire Inn."

Dunfermline has long been noted for the number of its churches and religious sects. Besides the Abbey, which was at one time its only place of worship, it has in connection with the Establishment the district or *quoad sacra* churches of St Andrew's, at the head of Randolph (formerly Chapel) Street, and the North Church, situated at Golfdrum, at the north-west extremity of the town. The "Muckle Kirk," or old Burgher church, a huge barn-like edifice, occupies the most elevated and prominent position in Dunfermline, and would be considerably improved in appearance by the addition of a steeple. In the United Presbyterian body, to which it now belongs, are amalgamated the Burgher, the Antiburgher, and the Relief denominations, and of these the town contains four congregations, accommodated in as many churches. There are three Free churches: the Free Abbey Church, for which a large new circular building has recently been erected in Canmore Street; Free St Andrew's in Margaret Street; and the Free North Church in Bruce Street. The Congregationalists or Independents have a church in Canmore Street, adjoining the Free Abbey Church; the Baptist denomination have lately built for themselves a handsome church in East Port Street; the Episcopalians have a church in School End Street; and the Roman Catholics a church at the east end of the town, near the cattle-market and railway station. There is also a variety of smaller religious bodies, including the Catholic Apostolic Church, the Universalists, and other sects.

As might be expected, the factories of Dunfermline bulk greatly in a general survey of the public buildings. The largest of these is St Leonard's factory (Erskine Beveridge & Co.), situated at the Spital Bridge, at the southern extremity of the town. It is both a handsome and spacious building, and from its proximity to the Queensferry road, was the first large edifice that met the traveller's eye in entering Dunfermline by the coach. It employs about 1000 power-looms. The Bothwell factory (Messrs Matthewson) is situated at a little distance in Broad Street, Netherton, alongside of the railway, and is the most extensive next to that of Messrs Beveridge. Besides these, there are in the north quarter of the town the establishments of Messrs Alexander, of Messrs Donald, of Messrs Walker & Co., and of Messrs Hay & Robertson — all doing an extensive trade. Notwithstanding the lamentable depression which has long affected the commercial world, and in which Dunfermline has participated, this has nevertheless been less felt here than elsewhere among the working classes. The mills have always been kept going, and it has scarcely ever been found necessary on any occasion to have recourse to " short time."

II.

FROM DUNFERMLINE TO TORRYBURN.

Old and new roads from Dunfermline to the west—Urquhart Cut —Berrylaw Top—Villages of Crossford and Cairneyhill—Conscience Bridge — Village of Torryburn — The Colville family and the estate of Crombie—Torryburn witches.

IN journeying from Dunfermline to Alloa, three different ways may be taken—one by Torryburn and Kincardine, a second by Carnock and Comrie village, and a third by rail. We shall commence with the first of these routes, which involves a distance of 16 miles, and which, though two miles longer than the more northern route by Carnock, is, on the whole, the most frequented.

Till within the last hundred years, the access to Dunfermline from the west lay through the domains of Pittencreiff, passing close to the mansion, crossing the Tower burn near Malcolm Canmore's fortress, and

entering the town nearly opposite the great west door of
the Abbey Church.   Here it joined a lane, known as St
Catharine's Wynd, which connected the Kirkgate with
the road leading through the Pends.   The old bridge
by which it crossed the Tower burn, close to Malcolm
Canmore's castle, still exists in the same form of two
superimposed arches, though the structure of both has
been to a great extent remodelled.   It was here, doubtless, that the unfortunate solitary sentry placed to guard
it on the occupation of the town by the Jacobites in
1715, met his death at the hands of the Government
troops, as we are informed by the Master of Sinclair in
his narrative already quoted.   There was also another
road farther south, which entered the town from the west
by the Netherton Bridge, and which is still used.   The
old road through the Pittencreiff grounds seems to have
joined this one at what used to be known as the Bridge
of Urquhart (from the adjoining farm), and the united
road appears then to have proceeded westwards along
the hollow by the now drained loch of Keavil, and then,
entering the Pitfirrane grounds and passing near the
mansion-house of the last - named property, to have
abutted on the present road to Torryburn, about half a
mile to the east of the village of Cairneyhill.

After the new bridge over the Tower burn was constructed about 120 years ago, and the suburb of Pittencreiff erected on the western side of the glen, a new
road was formed by a cut through the hill above Urquhart farm, and this is now the chief access to the town
from Torryburn and the west.   We shall now proceed
along it towards the latter place (4½ miles distant),
leaving Dunfermline by Bridge Street, Chalmers Street,
and Pittencreiff Street, and descending the road over the
hill, generally known as " Urquhart Cut."   As we go
down, a beautiful view presents itself of the basin of
the Forth from Queensferry to Stirling, taking in both

sides of the estuary, whilst· the Kilsyth hills, Ben Lomond, Ben Ledi, and the Perthshire mountains close in the distance on the west. A finely wooded and fertile country, rivalling in beauty the best cultivated districts in England, appears beneath us, stretching away in the direction of Torryburn, Kincardine, and Alloa. It attracted the admiration of William Cobbett when he made his tour through Scotland in the autumn of 1832 and paid a special visit to the farm of Urquhart, a mile from Dunfermline, which we are now passing.

On the crest of a rising ground to the right will be observed a circular plantation, which from its conspicuous position serves as a landmark to the country round, and is known by the name of Berrylaw Top, or vernacularly, " Berrylaw Tap." The name, which is of Gothic origin (*burh*, Anglo-Saxon for town or fortress, or modern Swedish *berj*, a town, combined with *hlæuw*, a hill), seems to point to some ancient fortress or city having existed here in former days. Nothing of the kind, however, is visible at the clump of wood itself or its neighbourhood, though I have heard of an ancient village at Berrylaw which was standing till near the end of the last century. I have also heard a strange story repeated, which connects this remote hill-slope with the orgies of the Medmenham Club. Lord Sandwich, a member of this infamous fraternity, had a *chère amie* who came from Berrylaw, near Dunfermline. How she made his lordship's acquaintance I cannot say, but she is said, as his favourite sultana, to have remembered, like a second Esther, her own people in the far north, however questionable and dubious the position which she herself occupied. Many Dunfermline people, it is reported, received appointments and places under Government through her influence with Lord Sandwich, who was one of the Lords of the Admiralty.

About half a mile farther on we reach the prettily

situated village of Crossford, with its numerous market-gardens, and then immediately beyond it the mansion and grounds of Keavil (Lawrence Dalgleish, Esq.) and those of Pitfirrane (Sir Arthur Halkett, Bart.) After the Wardlaws the Halketts are the oldest family in this part of the country, having been connected with Pitfirrane at least since 1399. Between this and Cairneyhill the road is very shady and beautiful, though without affording any distant view. On our right a singular-looking stone of blue limestone appears in a field, and is known as the Witch's Stone, the popular legend being that a notable witch in this neighbourhood found it on the seashore, and that after she carried it some distance in her apron, the string of the latter broke, and the stone has since continued to lie in the place where it fell. Science proclaims it to be a boulder, brought by ice from the upper basin of the Forth, the nearest mountain formation to which it could have belonged and from which it could have been severed being that of Menteith, in the neighbourhood of Callander. Another theory put forward by Sir James Simpson is that it is of meteoric origin. But there seems little reason to doubt of its having found its way to this place as an ice-borne boulder.

Nearly opposite the Witch's Stone, in a field on the south side of the road, is another smaller boulder, of the description known as conglomerate. It is called the Cadger's Stone, from the circumstance of its having formed a landmark for the "cadgers" or itinerant merchants, who were wont to rest themselves and their ponies whilst they deposited for a short while their burdens on the stone. It is close to the old road, which can still be traced through the Pitfirrane grounds to Dunfermline.

The village of Cairneyhill, which we are now approaching, consists of a long street running over a ridge ; and having mainly arisen within the last century and a half, with the development of the manufacturing industry in Dunfermline and the west of Fife, it presents little that is attractive to the lover of the picturesque. Formerly it was almost entirely occupied by weavers, who plied their occupation with great success, and became the owners of little pendicles of land in addition to their houses and gardens on the estate of Pitfirrane. The passing of the Reform Bill in 1832 gave many of them votes in the county, and induced a strong interest in politics, with an accompanying intense feeling of independence and self-importance. They were almost all Dissenters, and supported their own meeting-house, a building which stands at the eastern extremity of the village, and has the honour of being the first "Antiburgher" church erected in Scotland on the split taking place in the Secession body as to the lawfulness of taking the burgess oath, which the stricter members deemed contrary to their conscience to take, as involving a recognition of the Established Church. Those who held this view were denominated "Antiburghers," whilst those who believed there was nothing in the oath in question inconsistent with their principles received the appellation of "Burghers." The latter were by far the more numerous body, whilst the Antiburghers were generally credited with being the straiter and more austere sect. So strict were they with regard to terms of communion, that it was no uncommon thing for them to exercise discipline on any member who had been so far left to himself as to worship even with a Burgher congregation. These distinctive appellations are now forgotten, being merged for the most part in the union of various Secession bodies under the comprehensive title of the United Presbyterian Church. But there are still a few outlying congregations which refused to coalesce in the union, first of the Burghers and Antiburghers, and the subsequent junction of these with the Relief Church, and have formed themselves into a body known as the Original Associate Synod, which may thus be said still to preserve the rigour of the " Antiburgher " or " Old Light " element.

Cairneyhill is in the parish of Carnock, though situated a considerable distance from the latter village and its church, and affords another instance of the remissness of the Church of Scotland in failing to make provision for the spiritual wants of outlying parishioners, and thus handing them over to Dissenting influences. Up to the middle of last century, however, it is said only to have contained two or three houses. At the west end of the village, where a stream separates the parish of Carnock from that of Torryburn, there is a bridge which has borne from time immemorial the epithet of " Conscience Bridge," from a murderer having, as is alleged, been here overcome with the pangs of remorse and induced to confess his crime. It also bears the reputation of a " wishing " bridge. In the minutes of the town council of Dunfermline, under the year 1610, a bond of caution is entered by the schoolmaster, Mr James Douglas, before the bailies of the burgh, for David Boswell, brother of the Laird of Balmuto, that he shall within a year from the date thereof restore a silver bell now placed in his keeping, " Be resson of the said Davids blak hors wyning the custody and keiping therof be rining frae conscience brig to the brig of urquhat in companie with uther twa hors—viz., ane dapil gray hors belonging to Sr Wm. Monteth of Kers, Knyt, and the uther ane broun hors belongg to Lues Monteth his brother-german—and wan frae thame the race." The bell was the property of Alexander, Earl of Dunfermline, Chancellor of Scotland, who seems to have taken good care that it should be safely returned, as the cautioner binds himself "that the said David Bosewell sall delyver and produce the said bell in the lyke and als gud state as he now ressaves the same, under the pains of fyve hundret merks mony scots to be payit be said caur. to the said noble erle in case of failyer." The "heat" must have been rather a long one, extending over a distance of fully two miles. Probably enough it was a cross-country ride, like our modern steeplechase, though likely of a much less arduous description than the latter, from the absence in these days of enclosures. In our own time the magistrates of a royal burgh, even in their judicial capacity, would hardly be called on to interpone authority to any transaction connected with racing matters.

From Cairneyhill a pleasant road of little over a mile conducts us to Torryburn church, on a knoll at the eastern extremity of the village. The lands of Craigflower (Eden Colville, Esq.) are on our left, and those of Torrie (R. G. Erskine Wemyss, Esq.) on our right. A field on the latter estate, coming down to the public road near the church, bears the name of the "tuilzie" or "battle" park, and contains a great standing-stone. Around this are several barrow-like eminences or tumuli, which have been supposed to mark the burial-place of combatants slain in some great engagement here in ancient times—possibly in a conflict between the Scots and an invading army of Northmen.

Just before coming to the church, a declivity known as the Crosshill Brae is descended, with a picturesque hollow on the left through which the Torrie burn flows. This last is crossed at Craigflower Lodge by a bridge leading to the mansion and grounds of Craigflower. An older bridge, situated a little lower down the stream, near the eastern extremity of the garden of Torryburn Manse, has now disappeared. It was built, as Sir Robert

Sibbald informs us, by the Rev. Mr Aird, minister of the parish in the latter half of the seventeenth century, and who is recorded by him to have been "a man eminent for his piety and charity to the poor."

Torryburn was formerly a place of some importance, and in the end of the last century there were thirteen vessels belonging to the locality, with an aggregate tonnage of upwards of 1000, and giving employment to about seventy seamen. At Crombie Point, about a mile below the village, two ferry-boats used to be maintained for the transport of passengers and goods to the port of Borrowstounness on the other side of the Forth, with which a great traffic was carried on, more especially by the merchants and manufacturers of Dunfermline. These both built the pier at Crombie Point, and owned the larger of the passage-boats by which their manufactures, after being brought down here in carts, were conveyed to Borrowstounness, and thence were shipped to London in vessels from that port. And large quantities of coal, ironstone, and salt used to be exported here in the last century, when the then proprietor of Craigflower was largely engaged in mining and kindred operations, which for a time seemed almost to emulate those of the great Sir George Bruce at Culross nearly two centuries before. But they were not conducted with the same ability or good fortune. The unfortunate speculator became bankrupt, and with his disaster the prosperity of Torryburn came to an end, and has never since been regained. There is now no trade of any kind whatever carried on here, and the diminution in size of the village, within living memory even, is very perceptible. Many of the old houses and feus have been bought up and enclosed within the grounds of Craigflower.

The village itself has no special attraction, but its

situation is extremely agreeable when viewed either from the water or the town of Culross at the opposite side of the bay. The view, on emerging from Torryburn or its "Ness," or projection of greensward, which forms its western extremity, is such as must strike every traveller, and all the more forcibly that the prospect which there meets his gaze is generally unexpected. After entering the village from the east, he traverses rather a squalid-looking street, at the end of which he suddenly finds himself fronting a noble expanse of land and water, such as charmed the heart of William Cobbett on his Scottish tour, and will call forth admiration from any spectator. If the tide should be full at the time, the prospect is very much enhanced. The beautiful bay of Culross is seen in all its extent, with its sloping braes crested with woods, and the ancient royal burgh rising on a tongue of land by the water's edge. Away in the distance, on the opposite shore of the Forth, appears the fertile carse of Stirling, behind which rise the Kilsyth hills, whilst farther round to the north-east are the mountains round Ben Lomond and Ben Ledi. Near at hand, in the middle of Culross Bay, rises Preston Island, with its grey buildings, looking like the ruins of an old cathedral or monastery, though in reality these are merely the remains of coal-pits and salt-works. On the shore to the right, and separated from Torryburn by a level tract of greensward, through which the public road passes, is the village of Newmills, picturesquely straggling over a ridge, with a gap in the background through which the heights of the Ochils are visible. The view, too, down the Forth from Torryburn Ness towards Crombie Point by the wooded slopes of Craigflower, with the prospect on the opposite shore of the castle of Blackness and the fine sylvan region about Hopetoun, is extremely beautiful.

K

Torryburn church is a plain building, erected in 1800 on the site of an older edifice which dated from 1616. It is said that when the estimates of its cost were given in by the competing contractors, the economical heritors chose that which was not only the lowest, but considerably beneath that of any of the other offerers. The individual so selected had no cause to plume himself on his good fortune, as it turned out that in making up his calculation of the various items, he had quite forgotten to take into account the roof! Whether he wriggled out of the scrape as easily as contractors have sometimes done under less justifiable circumstances, I am really unable to say. In the churchyard there used to be a tombstone with an inscription which has gained some celebrity, though both have now disappeared. It is thus given by Mr Balfour in the 'Old Statistical Account of Scotland':—

> "At anchor now in Death's dark road
>   Rides honest Captain Hill,
> Who served his king and feared his God
>   With upright heart and will.
>
> In social life sincere and just,
>   To vice of no kind given ;
> So that his better part, we trust,
>   Hath made the port of Heaven."

Dr Rogers in his 'Scottish Monuments and Tombstones' quotes two inscriptions from Torryburn churchyard ; but I must say that I never heard of them myself, though I have known the locality for more than half a century. They are :—

> "In this churchyard lies Eppie Coutts,
>   Either here or hereabouts ;
> But whaur it is there's nane can tell,
> Till Eppie rise and tell hersell."

" Here lieth one below this stone
   Who loved to gather gear ;
Yet all his life did want a wife,
   Of him to take the care.

He won his meat both ear and late
   Betwixt Cleish and Craigflower,
And craved this stone might lie upon
   Him at his latter hour."

The names of Cleish and Craigflower in the above would seem to 'point to some member of the Colville family, to whom in former times both of these properties belonged, and in whose hands that of Crombie, including Craigflower, is still vested. They are the representatives through females of the Lords Colville of Ochiltree, a peerage which is now extinct, though that of the Lords Colville of Culross, another branch of the same family, still subsists. Both of these branches derive their origin from Sir James Colville of Ochiltree in Ayrshire, who about 1530 exchanged that estate with Sir James Hamilton of Fynnart for the barony of Easter Wemyss and Lochoreshire in Fife. With other offspring he had one legitimate son James, and an illegitimate son Robert.[1] The former, who like his father bore the title of Sir James Colville of Easter Wemyss, had two sons, James and Alexander, the elder of whom became the third Sir James Colville of Easter Wemyss, and having served with great reputation in France under Henry of Navarre against the Catholic League, was ultimately in the beginning of the seventeenth century raised to the peerage by James VI. with the title of Lord Colville of Culross. His younger brother, Alexander, became at the Reformation commendator of Culross Abbey, and to the family of his son John the Culross peerage in

---

[1] For some further particulars regarding the Colville family, see pp. 62-65.

process of time reverted, and is still enjoyed by a descendant.

Robert Colville, natural son of the first Sir James Colville of Easter Wemyss, had a grant from his father in 1537 of the barony of Cleish in Kinross-shire, and having joined the Reformation party, was killed at the siege of Leith in 1560. His only son Robert succeeded to the estate of Cleish, and in 1568 obtained from his uncle Alexander, the commendator, a grant of the bailiary of Culross Abbey, an office which, previous to the Reformation, had been enjoyed by the Earls of Argyll. This conveyance was ratified by a royal charter in the following year.

Another illegitimate son of the first Sir James Colville of Easter Wemyss, who, like his legitimate brother, bore also the name of James, seems to have adhered to the ancient faith; at least we find in April 1560 a charter granted to him by a William Colville, joint " commendator and usufructuar of Culross," with John Colville, its last abbot, of the lands of Crombie, in the county of Fife, belonging to the convent, on the narrative of a sum of money having been paid to Culross monastery by the said James Colville, "for the preservation of the liberty of the Church in those dangerous days of Lutheranism." This charter was confirmed by Queen Mary in 1565.

How those lands of Crombie passed to the descendants of James Colville's brother Robert, ancestor of the Lords Colville of Ochiltree, we are not informed, but they certainly were so transferred; and in after-times we find the Place or Castle of Cleish and the mansion-house at Crombie equally occupied by the family as their residence. Thus we find the death of Lady Colville, wife of the first Lord of Ochiltree, who had been raised to the peerage by Charles II. in 1651, taking place at Cleish in 1655, whilst in 1658 his niece is married at his house of Crombie to the Laird of Skeddoway, and he himself shuffles off this mortal coil also at Crombie in 1662. A curious circumstance recorded in connection with this last event is, that the first Lord Colville was buried at his own request by torchlight on the evening of the same day that he died. A gravestone still marks his memory within the precincts of the old ruined church of Crombie. He was succeeded by his nephew Robert, who died at Cleish in 1671, and the peerage and estates then fell to the latter's son, who died without issue in 1723. One of his sisters married a Sir John Ayton, whose son succeeded to the Crombie and Craigflower estates as Robert Ayton Colville, and from him the present proprietor of these estates is descended. The Cleish estate has long since passed out of the hands of the family.

Another sister of the last Lord Colville of Ochiltree married the Rev. Alan Logan, minister of Torryburn, so famous as an energetic prosecutor of witches, and who ultimately, after being transferred to Culross, succeeded as heir to the estate of Logan in Ayrshire, belonging to his family. In connection with him and Lord Ochiltree, Wodrow tells in his 'Analecta' the following curious ghost-story, which he says was communicated to him by Lord Grange :—

"My Lord Colvil dyed in March last [1723], and about Culros it is very currently believed that he has appeared more than once, and has been seen by severalls. Some say that he appeared to Mr Logan, his brother-in-law, but he does not own it; but two of his servants wer coming to the house, and saw him walking near them, and, if I remember, he called to them just in the same voice and garb he used to be in; but they fled from him, and came in in a great fright. They are persons of credibility and gravity, as I am told."

Crombie formed at one time a separate parish, but was united with Torryburn in the early part of the seventeenth century.　Apparently, however, the idea prevailed for some time afterwards of still keeping up the kirk of Crombie, as we find in a minute of the Torryburn kirk-session, dated June 21, 1629, that "the session convened at the kirk of Crombie, appointed ane stent for repairing the kirk of Crombie, extending to 30 lib., to be paid by parishioners."　No such project, however, was ever carried out, and the little church was allowed to continue to decay.　The churchyard which surrounds it occupies a picturesque eminence overlooking the sea on the shore-road from Torryburn to Crombie Point.

The other principal estate in the parish of Torryburn is that of Torrie, which in days long gone by belonged to the family of Wardlaw, who appear to have originally come to and settled in the western district of Fife from Dumfriesshire, from an eminence in which they probably derived their name.　They are believed, moreover, to have been originally Anglo-Saxon refugees from England, who at the time of the Conquest escaped into Scotland, and received kindness and benefactions from Malcolm Canmore.　They rose to great wealth and influence, and at one period seem to have owned almost the whole region from the Cullalo hills and Lochgelly to the western limit of Fifeshire.　What was known as Lochoreshire, in the parishes of Ballingry and Auchterderran, belonged to them; and the castle of Lochore, already described, was one of their principal seats.　A junior branch also held the lands of Pitreavie to the south of Dunfermline, which at a later period gave its name to a baronetcy conferred on the family by Charles I.　The Wardlaws were likewise proprietors of Logie, of Balmule, and of Luscar; and they are unquestionably the very oldest family belonging to the neighbourhood of Dunfermline. Not an acre of these ancestral domains does any member of the house now retain, though the baronetcy still exists, and is enjoyed by Sir Henry Wardlaw, residing in Tillicoultry. The famous Cardinal Henry Wardlaw, founder of St Andrews University, the earliest in Scotland, was a cadet of the Wardlaws of Torrie, whom we find taking part in all the prominent incidents of the time in which they lived. Thus the 'Cronica Scotiæ' informs us that among the train of nobles and ladies who accompanied Princess Margaret, daughter of James I., to France in 1435, to be wedded to the Dauphin Louis, son of Charles VII., was "Henricus Wardelau de Torry." And in another record, a "Sir Henry Wardlaw, Lord of Terry, Knight," is mentioned as one of the witnesses to an act of homage by Sir John Kennedy and his son on 2d July 1444.

The Wardlaws continued Lairds of Torrie at least down to 1619, but not long after that period they ceased to hold that estate, which passed into the hands of the Bruces, Earls of Kincardine, and in the end of the seventeenth century was purchased from them or their creditors by Colonel William Erskine, son of Lord Cardross, and brother of Colonel John Erskine of Carnock, who about the same time acquired the Culross estate and other possessions of the Kincardine family. Colonel William Erskine was succeeded in Torrie by his son and grandson, the latter of whom became a baronet under the title of Sir William Erskine, and died in the end of the last century. His three sons who successively succeeded him having all died without issue, the estate went to his grandson, Admiral Wemyss, whose mother was the eldest daughter of Sir William Erskine. The present proprietor is the Admiral's grandson.

Adjoining the Torrie estate on the north is the property of Inzievar (A. V. Smith Sligo, Esq.), with which the estate of Oakley (formerly Annefield) is now incorporated. The original Inzievar forms a beautiful expanse of undulating ground, with a fine southern exposure, and contains some of the best land in the western district of Fife. In old times it belonged to the Blackadders, cadets of the Tulliallan family, and afterwards came into the possession of the Earls of Kincardine.

The earliest reference to Torryburn is the signature at Berwick-on-Tweed of " Richard, persone eglise de Torry del counte de Fyfe, " to the Ragman Roll, or Act of submission of the Scottish clergy and laity, along with John Balliol, to Edward I., in August 1296. The village enjoyed anciently an extended reputation for its witches, a circumstance probably attributable to the more energetic prosecutions which seem to have obtained here of those suspected to be members of the sisterhood. Many poor creatures doubtless suffered death on this charge; and in ' Satan's Invisible World Displayed ' notice is taken of wizards at Torryburn, and of an anacreontic ditty which one of these taught to a novice, who himself afterwards was burned to death at the stake. But the fame of Torryburn as regards witchcraft and *diablerie* rests chiefly on the history of Lilias or Lily Adie, who in 1704 was arrested by the baron bailie of Torryburn, committed to prison, and examined with all solemnity by Mr Logan and his kirk-session. The poor woman, who was evidently the victim of insanity, delusion, and failing health, confessed in the most minute and categorical fashion to a series of interviews which she had had on various occasions with the Prince of Darkness,—one notably in the " Darn [1] Road," a lonely hollow way leading down to Torryburn from the farm of Cauldmailin on the Torrie estate; and another at " The Gollet," between Torryburn and Newmills. These are

---

[1] Dismal, generally written "dern."

all carefully minuted by the session-clerk; but it is satisfactory to observe that there is no evidence of any torture or other cruelty having been practised to extort a confession. Indeed by this time the claws of inquisitors, clerical or lay, were—in Britain at all events—getting pretty well pared, and the civil power was becoming very chary in recognising or countenancing any prosecution for the crime of witchcraft.

Poor Lily did not long survive her committal to prison, but died there, having a short time before her death reasserted solemnly, in the presence of Mr Logan and his elders, the truth of her former statements. As an excommunicated person, she was buried on the sea-shore within high-water mark; and a large stone still marks the place of sepulture. Lily's bones, however, no longer rest in this spot. About thirty years ago an irreverent curiosity prompted an examination and dis-interment. The result has been the dispersion of the remains, which appear to have been as eagerly coveted as the relics of any canonised saint. My friend Dr Dow of Dunfermline has now the skull, which shows a re-markably receding forehead, like that of an idiot. And a relative of mine owns two of Mrs Adie's ribs. The minutes of the kirk-session regarding this extraordinary case were long ago given to the world by that enthu-siastic antiquary, John Graham Dalzell. Mr Logan's zeal in these prosecutions does not seem to have been altogether reciprocated by his parishioners, since in 1709 a disrespectful member of the flock, named Helen Kay, is summoned before the kirk-session, and rebuked for saying that the minister was "daft" in stirring up such commotions in the parish about witches. Mrs Kay was probably not very far wrong in her estimate of Mr Logan. On being translated, rather against his will, in 1717 to Culross, he endeavoured to exercise the same watchful care that he had used in Torryburn in suppressing all sorcery and dealing with evil spirits; but as far as we can learn from the kirk-session records of that parish, he never succeeded in ferreting out anything more alarming than the consulting of a " dumbie" for obtaining the restoration of stolen property, and the employment by a farmer's wife of a charm to ensure a successful churning of butter.

III.

FROM TORRYBURN TO CULROSS AND KINCARDINE.

Village of Newmills—Newmill Bridge and its vicinity—Western limit of Fife—Detached district of Perthshire—Approach to Culross —Valleyfield House and the Preston family—Upper road to Kincardine—Tulliallan woods—Bordie and the Standard Stone—Town of Culross—Its early history in connection with St Serf and St Mungo —Sir George Bruce and his descendants, the Earls of Kincardine— Ancient monastery and church of Culross—Mansion of Culross Abbey—The "Colonel's Close" and Sir George Bruce's "Moat" —Lower road to Kincardine—Dunimarle and Blair Castle— Blair and Longannet quarries and their traditions—Phenomena of the "lakies"—Town of Kincardine-on-Forth.

IN proceeding from Torryburn to Newmills, a house will be noticed on the right-hand side of the road, pleasantly situated in the midst of a park with old trees, and sheltered behind by a rising ground. This is Tinian, a name which has something of a Gaelic ring about it, but in reality is derived from the well-known and beautiful island of that designation in the South Sea. It was built by a native of Torryburn who had accompanied as a seaman Lord Anson's expedition round the globe in the years 1740-1743, and on his return with a considerable amount of prize-money, purchased the field and built on it the house to which he gave the appellation of Tinian, in remembrance of the friendly shelter which the island in question had afforded to himself and his companions. I have also heard it alleged that the individual in question had found it prudent to quit his native country on account of his having been implicated in the Porteous Mob, that mysterious affair in which it is said many persons of superior condition were involved, and in which scarcely any discovery was ever made regarding the ringleaders. Tinian now forms part of the estate of Torrie.

At the foot of Newmill Brae we are five miles from Dunfermline, five from Kincardine-on-Forth, and six from Alloa. Looking back from the top of the hill at the smithy, a fine view is obtained of Torryburn and road beyond along the seashore to Crombie Point. A little beyond on our right we pass the main entrance to Torrie, the mansion-house of which is a handsome though somewhat irregularly constructed building in the Italian style, finely situated on an eminence overlooking the village of Newmills and the Firth of Forth. The grounds were beautifully laid out by Sir James Erskine more than sixty years ago, with shady walks, gardens, and ponds, after the manner of those at Virginia Water; but till very recently they had been greatly neglected and allowed to run into a wilderness. At one time they were resorted to by visitors from all parts of the country.

Having got clear of Newmills, the traveller will come to a handsome stone bridge, spanning the Bluther burn, which here divides the parish of Torryburn from that of Culross, and the county of Fife from a detached portion of Perthshire. Looking up the stream, he will see a picturesque old bridge, wanting a parapet, and behind it a finely wooded rising ground, with a precipitous whinstone quarry descending to the bank of the stream. The view has already engaged the attention of more than one artist. Beside the old bridge used to be a mill, the "New Mill," which gave its name to the adjoining village, but has recently been converted into a bleach-work. It originally belonged to the monastery of Culross, and in 1540 was made over by William and John Colville, joint commendator and abbot of that convent, along with the lands of Blairhall, to Edward Bruce, ancestor of the present Lord Elgin. The burgh of Culross and lands in the vicinity were *thirled* to it—that is to say, were obliged to carry all their grain to be ground at this the monastery mill. When it was first erected there is no means of determining, but it must have been prior to 1540, and was at that time known as the "Novum Molendinum" or New Mill. In 1596 it seems to have been taken down, and a new building erected in its stead, which was demolished and replaced about seventy years ago by the structure which, in its turn, has recently been removed to make way for Mr Marshall's bleach-work. As already stated, the New Mill was long the property of the Lairds of Blairhall, about two miles higher up the stream; but in the early part of the last century General Preston purchased the property from them, and incorporated it in a new entail of the estate of Valleyfield, to which indeed, from its proximity, it would seem naturally to belong.

It will probably be a matter of surprise to find a portion of Perthshire lying along the shores of the Firth of Forth, but for nearly seven miles from Newmill Bridge the road to Alloa through Kincardine passes through this county, to which the parishes of Culross and Tulli-allan both belong. They are quite cut off from the greater Perthshire by the intervection of the parish of Saline in Fife and that of Clackmannan in the county of the same name; and part of them, at all events, was formerly included in the Stewartry of Strathearn. As regards civil jurisdiction, they wholly belong to Perthshire; but for parliamentary representation they are combined with the counties of Kinross and Clackmannan.

There are two ways of proceeding from Newmill Bridge to Culross and Kincardine—one along the shore, the other by a terrace-road along the side of a rising ground or brae. Both have their attractions, and as regards time and distance, the results are pretty nearly the same, whether the journey be accomplished on foot or in a carriage. The shore - road is certainly more level, but is counterbalanced by being somewhat more circuitous. Whichever route the traveller elects to take, I will engage that he shall have no cause for dissatisfaction. He has already traversed a tolerably agreeable country in his route from Dunfermline to Torryburn and Newmills, and the same amenities will attend him through almost the whole of his journey beyond to Alloa and Stirling. A striking contrast in the aspect of the country, to the cold and bleak region lying to the north and east of Dunfermline, has become manifest ever since we descended Urquhart Hill.

The shore-road to Culross (about a mile and a half distant) leads through the straggling village of Low Valleyfield, if indeed village it can be called, seeing it is rather a succession of detached cottages bordering the concavity of Culross Bay, with large gardens stretching up the sunny slope of the braes, the tops of which are crested with wood, through which the upper road passes. A considerable quantity of fruit used to be grown here and sent to market, but foreign competition has tended much to render this unprofitable, except with regard to some of the earlier kinds, such as gooseberries and strawberries. The Forth is more than three miles wide at this point, and on a fine day nothing can be more delightful than a sail either across to Borrowstounness and Kinneil, or upwards past the town of Culross towards Longannet Point and Kincardine. The view of Culross Bay from the water is the most charming that can be imagined, and will vie with many of the most beautiful reaches on the Rhine or Seine. A visit to Preston Island is also a very pleasant outing; but let strangers be cautious, in straying over it, to avoid falling into the open and unguarded coal-pit, which is generally nearly full of water.

Till the end of the last century Preston Island was merely an expanse of green turf at the eastern extremity of the reef known as the Craigmore Rocks, which, being within low-water mark, all belong to the estate of Valleyfield. On Sir Robert Preston succeeding to the property in the beginning of the present century, he conceived the idea of converting this lonely spot into a great centre of trade, as well as source of pecuniary profit to himself. The seams of coal which underlie the basin of the Forth were here cropping out at the surface, and it seemed quite feasible to undertake the revival of the coal and salt industries, which in former days, under the auspices of Sir George Bruce, had made the fortune of Culross and its neighbourhood. Sir Robert had attained to great wealth, partly obtained in trade as the captain of an East Indiaman, partly accumulated by successful speculations in the Funds, and partly derived by marriage with the daughter of a wealthy London citizen. He accordingly set to work in erecting a large range of buildings on the island, including engine-houses, salt-pans, and habitations for colliers and salters. Pits were sunk, fresh water brought from the mainland, and for a period a vast industry was carried on, the Forth resounding with the working of the engines, and sloops lying constantly alongside for loading with coals. But whether the preparations had been made, like all Sir Robert's undertakings, on too magnificent a scale, or whether, as is extremely likely, there was gross mismanagement in the conduct of the business, the affair was not long in showing itself to be a losing concern, and ere long completely collapsed, leaving the baronet out of pocket to the extent at least of £30,000. Fortunately his means were such, that after so great a loss he still remained a man of immense wealth. After the colliery was stopped the salt-pans were let, and worked to a period within my own recollection. The last tenant of them added to his legitimate occupation that of an unlicensed distiller of whisky, and having received a hint that the Revenue officers were upon his track, he decamped, and Preston Island has ever since remained a deserted but still singularly picturesque object, bisecting, as it does, the chord that connects the two extremities of the beautiful Bay of Culross.

The Prestons of Valleyfield belonged to the same family as the Prestons of Craigmillar, in Mid-Lothian, and the estate in Culross parish was first acquired in 1543 by James Preston, grandson of William Preston of Craigmillar, and son of Henry Preston, burgess of Edinburgh. It was conveyed to him by Patrick Bruce, son of Sir David Bruce of Clackmannan, to whom it had been transferred by the commendator and abbot of Culross in the same year that they made over, as already mentioned, the estate of Blairhall to his brother Edward Bruce. The grandson of James Preston received the honour of knighthood from James VI., and his son George was in 1637 made a baronet by Charles

I. The title still exists, though no longer connected with the estate of Valleyfield since the death of Sir Robert Preston, from whose sister the present proprietor (R. Clarke Campbell Preston, Esq.) is descended.

The highroad to Culross, leading through woods along a terrace behind the gardens of Low Valleyfield, is of great beauty, and has suggested to more than one observer a comparison on a reduced scale with the famous Cornice road between Nice and Genoa. The east approach to Valleyfield branches off from it immediately after leaving Newmill Bridge, and in an opening through the trees, about a quarter of a mile farther on, is seen Valleyfield House, a square building with wings, but presenting, nevertheless, rather an imposing appearance across a wide expanse of sward, with a background of .wood. Another quarter of a mile up a wooded incline brings us to a finger-post opposite the west lodge of Valleyfield, where two roads branch off,—one going downhill to Culross, and meeting at the foot the shore-road which we have already traversed, and to which we shall shortly return ; the other going on to Kincardine by the old turnpike and coach road. We shall for the present follow the latter.

At the lodge on our left hand, about four miles from Kincardine, is the main entrance to Culross Abbey, which we shall afterwards have occasion to discuss more in detail. The road we are now travelling on was laid out in the beginning of the present century, and leads almost in a straight line to Kincardine, over what used to be known as Culross Muir, but which is now nearly all either cultivated ground or woodland. It commands a beautiful view of the Ochils, with their wavy line of rounded eminences covered with rich verdure, and divided from each other by deep wooded gorges, in one of which, on a projecting platform, the grey tower and buildings of Castle Campbell may be discerned on a clear day. Between us and them is a series of parallel valleys running east and west. At the house of Gowerfield, three miles from Kincardine, a cross-road intersects the highway, the north branch leading to the upper Dunfermline and Alloa road by Balgownie Mains and West Grange, the southern passing to Culross by what is called the Gallows Loan. From the eminence which crests the latter about a quarter of a mile south from Gowerfield, the finest view in the neighbourhood is obtained of the surrounding country, taking in the whole region between the Ochils and the sea, with the Wallace Monument and Stirling Castle in the middle distance, and Ben Lomond, Ben Ledi, and the hills about Callander in the background. In clear weather, too, the valley of the Allan between Ben Ledi and Dunmyat, at the western termination of the Ochils, comes into view, with its encircling fringe of mountains, including the Ben Voirlich and Uam Var of the 'Lady of the Lake.'

Proceeding onwards to Kincardine, we pass on our left the gateway of the avenue leading to Dunimarle, and then a little farther on we enter the Tulliallan woods, which extend on both sides of the road for more than a mile. We emerge from them about a mile from Kincardine, near the ruined tower of Bordie, which, however, is said to be nothing more than an abortive work which was never completed. Here another magnificent view presents itself of the distant mountains, similar to what may be seen from the Gallows Loan, with the silver Forth winding its way downwards from Stirling through a rich alluvial tract of carse-land.

A little to the north of the road on our right, within a tract of unreclaimed moorland, is the so-called Standard Stone, a rectangular block, flush with the ground, and indented with two square sockets, in which the Scottish Standard is traditionally said to have been fixed on the occasion of the battle of Culross with the Danes. The engagement is recorded by Boece to have taken place in 1038, during the reign of King Duncan, who himself, with his general, the celebrated Macbeth, commanded the Scottish forces. The Danes had landed in Fife, and advanced farther under the leadership of Sweyn, King of Norway, and brother of Canute the Great. They are said to have been victorious in the engagement, but were unable to follow up their advantage in pursuing Duncan, who retreated with his army to Perth, and there shut himself up in the fortress. Sweyn followed and besieged him closely there, and a negotiation is then said to have been entered into with the Scots. The latter had made indications of being ready to surrender, and now undertook to send a supply of provisions to the Danes, who were reduced to great straits on that account. The Northmen readily accepted the insidious proffer, whereupon a large quantity of bread and ale was sent by the Scots to the Danish camp; but these provisions had been previously drugged by the former with the juice of the deadly nightshade, or "mekilwort berries," as they are called by Boece.

The Danes eagerly ate and drank of the poisoned victuals, and Duncan having meantime sent for Macbeth, who had been employed in gathering reinforcements, the combined Scottish force fell upon the enemy in their sickened and intoxicated condition with such deadly onslaught that only a mere handful (including Sweyn himself) succeeded in making their escape to their ships in the Tay.

It is the fashion now to discredit everything related by Boece, who has certainly incorporated many fables with his History; but it may be well, I think, to pause before rejecting superciliously any special incident which he may record. It is not very likely that he would invent such a narrative as a Danish expedition against Scotland—an undertaking of which there were numerous examples. However much he might embellish the narrative, it is not probable that he would deem it worth his while to invent the whole groundwork of such a story. Much more likely is it, when fabulous incidents are introduced into a history, that they are connected with a basis of fact, than that the whole story should be absolutely fictitious. It is true that we have only the authority of Boece for the Danish expedition and battle of Culross in the reign of King Duncan, and that it is this authority that has been followed by Major, Buchanan, and subsequent historians who have recorded the same events. But it is, to say the least, quite conceivable that Boece has availed himself of a real and authentic incident, though no other writer has given it currency. That the story of the drugging of the provisions, and consequent overthrow of the Danes, may be altogether a romance, I am quite ready to admit; but it by no means follows that Sweyn's incursion and his victory at Culross belong to the same category. At all events, no positive evidence has been adduced to demonstrate their falsity, and it would be unpardonable to overlook them in treating of the locality in which they are said to have taken place.

Having thus advanced to within a short distance of Kincardine, which lies in front of us at a bend which the Forth has taken in passing from the condition of an estuary to that of a river, we shall exercise the power which travellers like ourselves have always at command, and transport ourselves forthwith back to the finger-post at the west Valleyfield lodge, and take the road to our left, which leads downhill to Culross. A singularly

attractive route it is—though, being now much less travelled by carriages than formerly, when it was the only
highway, and the shore-road by Lower Valleyfield was
almost impassable, it is not kept quite in such good
condition as I think it might be. Bicyclists had better be cautious in descending through this beautifully
winding bit of woodland, as there are both a few
holes and a good many loose stones scattered about.
At the foot we join the Low Valleyfield road, about
a quarter of a mile from the ancient royal burgh of
Culross.

There are one or two interesting objects, however, to
be noticed before we get there. First on our right is the
" Endowment," a handsome cottage-like building, at the
foot of a steep bank, which was erected by Sir Robert
Preston, mainly at the instance of his wife and in fur-
therance of a provision made for the inhabitants of the
parish of Culross. Under the last, Sir Robert bur-
dened the lands of Spencerfield, belonging to him, and
subsequently bequeathed to the Elgin family, with an
annual rent to supply the cost of maintaining twelve pensioners in this institution (six men and six women).
These all receive a weekly dole of two shillings in money
and a peck of meal, besides a pound at each term of
Whitsunday and Martinmas, and in the winter months a
supply of soup and coals. The whole annual value of
the benefaction to each recipient may be estimated at
about £12, and it will thus be readily understood that
whenever any one of the pensioners dies there is an
active competition to obtain the vacant place. A lady
custodian resides in the " Endowment," and has the
charge of the distribution of the weekly dole, as also of
the soup-kitchen which is maintained here during the
winter months.

Opposite to the " Endowment" is a grassy plot known

as the Pow,[1] from the adjoining creek or canal which existed here in former times, and was originally constructed, it is believed, by Sir George Bruce in the end of the sixteenth century, for the purpose of shipping his coals and salt. A solitary post for the mooring of vessels remains still to tell the tale of former glories. Closely adjoining is a large enclosure surrounded by a wall, and washed by the sea at high water on the south and east. This is what is known as Pond or Preston Cottage, and appears to have been constructed by Sir Robert Preston as a reproduction or memorial of a fishing cottage which he formerly possessed at Dagenham Reach, Essex, when he was member of Parliament for Dover. He was a great friend of George Rose, William Pitt's secretary, and both of these were in the habit of partaking annually of Sir Robert's hospitality at Dagenham Reach. The time occupied, however, in going there was in these days considerable, and the suggestion was made, and readily acceded to, that the three friends should have their yearly " outing " at Greenwich. They were joined here by various Cabinet Ministers, and in process of time the gathering assumed a political form, and became a regular recognised institution. So was inaugurated the well-known entertainment of the " Ministerial Fish Dinner." At first the entertainment was entirely defrayed by Sir Robert, who acted as host; but in process of time it was suggested that the tavern bill should no longer be exclusively defrayed by him. He continued, notwithstanding, to issue the invitations, and to the end of his life furnished a buck and champagne as his yearly and special contribution.

Passing on towards Culross, we see opposite the Pond

---

[1] From the Gaelic *poll* (pronounced liquid), a pool. The name is applied both to creeks and to sluggish streams which run in pools, and occurs very frequently in the upper reaches of the Forth.

Cottage a weird-like ruin, with a long frontage of win-dows, of which those in the lower storey have been built up, to prevent access thereby to the wood, which closely adjoins the building. This used to be what was known as Lord Bruce's Hospital, an institution for the residence and maintenance of six poor men and as many women, which was founded by the first Lord Elgin in 1637, though the building which was originally erected in connection with it stood farther east, near the foot of the Newgate of Culross. The present structure has been a ruin for more than half a century, since the removal of the bene-fits of the charity from Culross by the grandfather of the present Lord Elgin to the village of Charleston, adjoin-ing his lordship's seat of Broomhall. The patronage or right of presentation to the hospital was vested, by the original deed of foundation, in the first Lord Elgin and his descendants, who were also empowered to nominate beneficiaries who might not belong to Culross. Found-ing on this permission, the whole benefits of the charity were withdrawn from the town and parish of Culross.

Going on a little farther, the house and garden of St Mungo's are passed on the right-hand side of the road. This is the ancient designation of a portion of the burgh territory at this spot, which derives its name from a chapel dedicated to St Mungo, which was founded here in 1503 by Archbishop Blackadder of Glasgow, on the spot assigned by tradition as the birthplace of the pa-tron saint of his cathedral city. It probably occupies the site of an older building which had existed in commemoration of this event. The legend asserts that Thenew, a Lothian princess, having formed an illicit connection with Eugenius, prince of Strathclyde, was banished in disgrace from her father's Court, and placed on board an old rotten boat at the port of Aberlady, from which she was wafted, at the mercy of the winds and waves, up the Forth to Culross, where St Serf, as one of the earliest Christian missionaries, had established a settlement. Having landed here, she was in a short space of time delivered by the seashore of a son, who was brought up by St Serf and baptised under the name of Kentigern, though he is better known to his countrymen by the designation of Mungo, which seems to be a corruption of the Gaelic *Mo ghaol*, or " My love." On coming to man's estate he was informed in a divine vision that a great work was destined to be accomplished by him in the west country. Thither, accordingly, he proceeded, till he arrived at the Molendinar Burn at Glasgow, where the Cathedral now stands, and there he founded a church and established a religious community, which grew up ultimately into a great episcopal see. I have already, in a larger work,[1] given a number of details regarding the history of St Mungo and his patron St Serf, and to this I would refer my readers. From the same I shall quote here the description of St Mungo's kirk or chapel :—

" The chapel is a complete ruin, almost level with the ground, with the exception of the north wall, which resembles a sunk fence in the bank above, and leaves it a matter of uncertainty whether it was originally built in this form or from the first stood detached, the intervening space between the wall and declivity having been subsequently filled up by the gradual descent of earth and rubbish. Two large beech-trees, certainly not of remote antiquity, flourish on the summit of this space. There is also the decayed trunk of an ancient elder-tree which grows near the north-western extremity, where some remains of the west wall and entrance are still visible. Of the south wall only the foundations are traceable, and these project into the public road beyond

[1] See 'Culross and Tulliallan.'

the present enclosing wall, which was built by Sir Robert
Preston.   The eastern extremity of the building formed
a three-sided apse—a construction differing from the
ordinary shape of the apse, which is generally semicircular.   The lower part of its east and north-east side
is still entire, the latter exhibiting on the outside a fine
front of hewn stone.   Traces of windows are also to be
seen here.   The length of the chapel from east to west
is 54 feet, and the breadth 20 feet.   A wall, still partly
remaining, separated the outer compartment or nave from
the interior or chancel, and the raised floor of flagstones
with their rounded edges is still very plainly marked here
in front of the site of the high altar and east window.
Traces of *sedilia* or seats appear along the north wall,
which has a height of from 10 to 12 feet."

A sunny walk of about two hundred yards farther
along the wall of the Abbey orchard brings us to the
town of Culross, a royal burgh, though of small dimensions, and the only one in the county of Perth besides
the Fair City herself.   First a burgh of barony under the
abbots of Culross monastery, and then in 1588 advanced
by James VI. to the dignity of a royal burgh, Culross
rose at the same time into a condition of great commercial prosperity under the auspices of the celebrated Sir
George Bruce, who engaged with such ability and success in the working of coal and manufacture of salt in
this neighbourhood that he was soon enabled to acquire
a princely estate, which he bequeathed to his descendants.   His father, Edward Bruce, became laird, in the
middle of the sixteenth century, of Blairhall, and was
the father of four sons, of whom at least the second and
third were men of distinguished ability.   The eldest inherited the family property, and married a natural
daughter of John Hamilton, the celebrated Archbishop
of St Andrews ; the second son, Edward, became an

eminent lawyer and statesman, and having been created by the king commendator and lord of Kinloss, was employed in some delicate and important negotiations with Secretary Cecil previous to the death of Elizabeth, in securing the Scottish monarch's accession to the English throne.   Further honours and lucrative offices were bestowed on him by the king, with whom he was a great favourite, and whom he accompanied to England. Here he died in 1610, having some years before his death enjoyed the office of Master of the Rolls.   He was interred in the Rolls Chapel in Chancery Lane, and had erected to his memory a splendid monument which still exists.   He had evidently determined, however, to maintain his connection with his native place, and for this purpose seems to have engaged the celebrated architect Inigo Jones to design for him the splendid mansion of Culross Abbey, the foundation of which was laid in 1608, two years before his death.   At least I think there is every reason to conclude that Edward Lord Bruce of Kinloss availed himself, on this occasion, of the services of Inigo Jones, who was then residing at the English Court, and was employed in planning mansions for the nobility, and notably among others for the Earl of Salisbury.   The architecture of Culross Abbey, in the Renaissance style, certainly resembles that of Inigo Jones, and it is difficult to conceive that any Scottish architects of the day were capable of devising such a structure.   It immediately adjoins the church of Culross and ruins of the old monastery; and the latter is traditionally said to have been the quarry from which the materials for the more modern abbey were obtained.   It seems to have been transferred by Lord Kinloss's grandson, second Earl of Elgin, to his kinsman Alexander, second Earl of Kincardine, and grandson of the great Sir George Bruce, Lord Kinloss's younger brother. Lord Kincardine added in 1670 a third storey to Culross Abbey, the original design of which (a quadrangle with flanking towers) was never completed.

Lord Kincardine was succeeded by his son Alexander, third Earl of Kincardine, and he again by his sister, Lady Mary Bruce or Cochrane, wife of William Cochrane of Ochiltree. Her son, Thomas Cochrane, who inherited the abbey estate, succeeded also in 1758 to the earldom of Dundonald. His son Archibald, ninth Earl of Dundonald, and father of the celebrated Admiral, the hero of Basque Roads, involved himself in difficulties with mining and other speculations, and the abbey estate was in consequence sold for behoof of his creditors, and purchased in the beginning of the present century by Sir Robert Preston of Valleyfield. The latter bequeathed it, with a large amount of the property, to the Elgin family, and it is now the property of the Hon. R. Preston Bruce, M.P. for the western district of Fifeshire.

In the work already referred to,[1] I have detailed the various ramifications of the Bruce and Cochrane families as occupants of Culross Abbey, and those of the Prestons of Valleyfield, into whose hands it ultimately passed. For present purposes these are too long to be here reproduced, but I shall have occasion shortly to abridge some of the descriptions of the localities.

Culross (*Hotel:* the Dundonald Arms, small, but admirably conducted) may not inaptly be described as a sort of fossilised town, a monument of days gone by, and, with its old-world look and belongings, almost an anachronism in the present age. It has a beautiful appearance from the water, stretching like a big Y along the seashore in the recess of its bay, and along the acclivity which rises behind, and is crowned at the sum-

[1] See 'Culross and Tulliallan.'

mit by the venerable Abbey Church, the ruins of the monastery, and the mansion of Culross Abbey.   In passing through it, the stranger is struck with the general sleepiness with which the place seems to be characterised; but he will also be impressed by the quaint picturesqueness and variety of its streets, whether in the Laigh Causeway or principal thoroughfare, or in the Middle and Back Causeways, which lead up from thence to the open space at the Cross.   From the latter a steep lane leads upwards to the church—an ascent which, though somewhat fatiguing, will amply reward the traveller for his trouble.

Culross used to be famous throughout Scotland for its manufacture of "girdles" or iron plates for baking cakes, of which its smiths or "hammermen" held a monopoly. The original charter or deed of gift, of which the date is uncertain, was lost, it is said, during the great civil war at the storming of Dundee, in which many of the Scottish burghs had deposited their titles for security.   The privilege had, however, been ratified by a royal letter from James VI. in 1599.   After subsisting for more than a hundred years, it was set aside as unconstitutional by a decree of the Court of Session in 1725.   Another pre-eminence enjoyed by Culross was her extensive coal and salt works, an industry chiefly developed by the enterprising genius of Sir George Bruce.   For a long period they were the largest of the kind in Scotland, and in 1663, by an Act of Charles II., the Culross chalder was made the standard measure for coals.

The Monastery of Culross was founded by Malcolm, Earl of Fife, in 1217, but nothing whatever is known either as to its progress or completion.   A "Gilbert, Abbot of Kylros," subscribes the Ragman Roll in 1296. Our information in regard to the buildings is derived entirely from their present condition, and the very imperfect accounts which have come down to us from the period of the Reformation.   They are noteworthy as the scene in 1402 of the meeting between Albany and Douglas, when the murder, by starvation, of the Duke of Rothesay, eldest son of Robert III., was arranged.   So we are informed on the authority of the chronicle known as the 'Liber Pluscardiensis.'   In 1434 we find a Robert Wedale, who afterwards became Abbot of Culross, employed as master of works at the erection of the Palace of Linlithgow by James I.   He is spoken of on one occasion in the Exchequer Rolls as "Robert de Weddale, *monachus*," and on another as "Abbas de Culros, dominus Robertus de Weddale."

In the middle of the sixteenth century, immediately preceding the suppression of the religious houses, Culross Abbey must, like other conventual establishments, have consisted of a congeries of buildings—square, massive, and imposing—enclosing a yard or cloister court, with the church forming one side of the square, whilst the other three were devoted chiefly to the secular requirements of the monks.   Following the general rule, the Monastery Church occupied the north side of the square, whilst it is probable the chapter-house or council-chamber of the abbey filled the north-east corner, and the refectory or great dining-hall extended along the south side in a parallel direction with the church.

As at present standing, the buildings consist of the Monastery or Abbey Church, of which now only remain the choir and central tower, with some fragments of aisles or chapels.   The choir serves as the present parish church, and is entered through the tower, from which formerly the nave extended in a westerly direction as far as the present churchyard gate.   The nave has completely disappeared, with the exception of the lower part of the south wall, which forms the south side of the churchyard, and separates it from the old cloister court, now used as the upper manse garden. A doorway near the south-west extremity of this wall had evidently given access to the nave from the cloister court, and at the very end is a small fragment which marks the corner, and formed a part of the west front of the church. From this point the western range of the conventual buildings extended southwards to a considerable distance down the hill—as far at least, it would seem, as the southern boundary of the lower manse garden. They are now restricted to the present manse, which, originally constructed out of the old convent buildings, abuts on the south-west extremity of the churchyard, and, with its offices, adjoins the only part of the monastic ruins that still preserves the appearance of their original condition. These consist of a grand vaulted chamber, which, with its imposing groined roof and arches, may possibly have been the entrance or great hall of the monastery. Behind it, and perhaps originally forming part of it, is a vaulted passage of a similar description, which leads through a beautiful Norman doorway into the cloister court. At the entrance of the hall is a staircase leading to an upper storey, which now presents nothing but a bare flat roof, unprotected by any parapet, but which had doubtless anciently contained the cells or dormitories of the monks. The southern end of the great chamber or hall has been completely demolished, and standing on an elevated position, it takes the aspect, to a spectator ascending the hill, of a vast yawning cavern, terminating in front in a precipice. Beneath it, and stretching to an unknown distance, is a series of vaults, which were formerly very extensive, but are now in great measure demolished, and the remaining portion choked up with rubbish.

The Monastery or Abbey Church, at least the tower

and nave, belongs to the same period as the convent—
that is to say, the beginning of the thirteenth century.
The tower is a very marked specimen of Norman architecture, having two fine doorways of that style; one
giving access to the porch, which forms its basement
storey—and the other, directly opposite to it, leading
from the porch to the choir, which since the Reformation has been used as the parish church. Previous to
that event the parish church was that now known as the
West Kirk, to be described shortly, and situated about
half a mile to the west, on the old road leading from
Culross through the moor to Kincardine.

The lower storey of the tower, which serves as a porch
to the present church, is on three sides, and was possibly
also at one time on the fourth, pierced with arches. On
the west is the fine outer doorway opening into the
porch, and flanked by two pointed openings now closed
up. Adjoining the arch on the south side of the door
is an ancient *piscina* or recess attached to an altar,
where the chalice was washed, and its rinsings emptied
through a conduit in the stonework. On the north side
of the porch is an arched opening, now filled in with
glass and serving as a window, but which formerly
opened into an aisle or chapel on the north side of the
tower, which had been lighted on the west by a large
window, of which part of the arch still exists. At the
same point are still to be seen the remains of an arch
which had contained the window at the north-east corner
of the nave. The place where the roof of the latter had
rested on the tower is still distinctly visible; and a little
below, in the south corner, is seen a closed-up doorway,
which had probably served as a communication between
the upper part of the nave and the choir by a passage or
ledge in the south wall of the porch. To the north of
this opening, and right over the outer door of the tower,

is a semicircular opening, likewise closed up, which, it is surmised, may, in the days when the church was entire and the nave served as the place of assembly for the laity, have contained the rood or cross with its attendant images.

The roof of the porch on which the first floor of the tower rests is a fine groined vault with an opening in the centre. A staircase attached to the south wall leads to the gallery of the church. On the inner west wall above the outer doorway is sculptured what appears to be the Angel of the Annunciation. On one side is the letter 𝔄, and on the other what seems to be the letter 𝔐, in the Old English character. They probably stand for *Ave Maria*, the Abbey Church of Culross having been dedicated to St Serf and the Virgin.

The fact of the tower of Culross church rising direct from the ground, and not springing, at a considerable elevation, from the summit of lofty supporting arches, is said to be unique, or, at least, rarely paralleled in other central towers. It consists of three storeys, each of which is very lofty. The basement has already been described. Immediately above it is a vast void apartment, in which it would appear that those accused of witchcraft were formerly detained. It must have been a weird-like dreary abode, indeed, for the poor creatures. Above this, again, is the clock-room and belfry; and over all, the roof with its bartizan. Access to all these stages is gained by a narrow spiral staircase on the north side of the tower, opening from the churchyard. From the bartizan a magnificent prospect is commanded— taking in the basin of the Forth from Ben Lomond to the Bass, and extending over nearly thirteen counties. Culross church-tower, with its pinnacles, is indeed a landmark for the country round, being visible from a great distance, and forming a most picturesque object as it rises amid woods on the crest of the hill. This very picturesqueness, however, is not altogether a matter for unqualified approbation, as, to produce this effect, the old Norman character of the tower was sacrificed, and the building, as far as its summit is concerned, converted into a structure of the perpendicular order. Previous to 1824, it was surmounted by a curious ark-like roof, not unfrequent in old church towers, and popularly known as the "kae-house,"—from its being the favourite haunt of the "kaes," or jackdaws. This was surrounded by a walk or ledge, which was unprotected by any parapet; and to run round the kae-house was a favourite deed of daring on the part of the Culross boys.

The old choir of the Abbey Church, now fitted up as the parochial place of worship, has been so much metamorphosed in the course of the alterations which, at different times, it has undergone, that it is difficult now to understand the original condition of the building. Entering it by the inner doorway of the tower, we find ourselves in a very neat and comfortable-looking church, with galleries at the east and west ends, and a north and south transept, which, as nearly as possible, bisect the north and south walls of the edifice. Two very fine Gothic arches, with corresponding pillars, form the entrances respectively of the north and south transepts, and are almost the only objects of antiquity that meet the eye in the interior of the church. There is, indeed, a fine east window of an Early English or semi-Norman character; but this is almost entirely blocked up by the gallery and adjoining staircase. The pulpit is placed within the arch at the entrance of the north transept, whilst facing it is a gallery that spans the south transept and its corresponding arch.

The exterior of the church now requires our attention. Beginning on the north side of the tower, where, as already mentioned, there seems to have been an aisle or chapel, we pass along the outer wall of the church till we reach the aisle or north transept of the choir, erected by the younger George Bruce.   There is nothing in the external aspect of the church here calling for special remark, as the original windows or arches of the choir have been built up, though the Bruce aisle has rather a handsome one at its north extremity.   Proceeding still farther east, we come to the vault of the Bruce family—including the great Sir George and his descendants, the Earls of Kincardine.   Latterly, it was converted into his own mausoleum by Sir Robert Preston, on becoming proprietor of the Culross estate; and here both he and his wife, Lady Preston, repose.   Against the east wall, just opposite the door, is a very fine monument, in alabaster, to the memory of Sir George Bruce.   The knight and captain of the industry of old Culross is represented in a reclining position, while in front of him are kneeling figures, also in alabaster, of his children.   The diminutive scale on which the latter are represented has procured for the group the popular appellation of "the babies." The monument itself, which reaches nearly to the summit of the vault, is a close imitation of the monument of Edward Lord Kinloss, Sir George's elder brother, erected in the Rolls Chapel, Chancery Lane, London.

On the south wall of this vault is, perhaps, the most interesting memorial connected with Culross.   A brass plate, fixed in the wall above a projection resembling an altar, has the following inscription :—

"FUIMUS.[1]

"Near this spot is deposited the heart of Edward Lord Bruce of Kinloss, who was slain in a bloody duel, fought in 1613, with Sir Edward Sackville, afterwards Earl of Dorset, near Bergen-op-

---

[1] The motto of the Bruces.

M

Zoom in Holland, to which country the combatants repaired, the one from England, the other from Paris, for the determined purpose of deciding their quarrel. The body of Lord Bruce was interred in the great church of Bergen-op-Zoom, where, among the ruins caused by the siege in 1747, are still to be seen the remains of a monument erected to his memory. A tradition, however, existing, that his heart had been sent over to his native land, and was buried near that place, a search was made by Sir Robert Preston of Valleyfield in the year 1808, when it was found embalmed in a silver case of foreign workmanship, secured between two flat and excavated stones, clasped with iron, and was again carefully replaced and securely deposited in the spot where it was discovered.

"For the particulars of the challenge and fatal duel, in which the Lord Bruce was killed on the spot, disdaining to accept his life from his antagonist, who was also dangerously wounded, see Lord Clarendon's 'History of the Rebellion,' B. i., and the narrative published in Nos. 129 and 133 of the 'Guardian.'"

The Lord Bruce of Kinloss above mentioned was the eldest son of the first Lord Kinloss, elder brother of Sir George Bruce. A tradition of the encounter in which he fell is still preserved in the neighbourhood of Bergen-op-Zoom, where a field near the village of Halsteren, about two miles to the north-west of the former town, is still known by the grim appellation of the "Bloedakker"—the "Champ de Sang," or the "Field of Blood." In consequence of the destruction of a large portion of the great church during the siege operations of 1747, no trace now remains of a very beautiful marble monument erected shortly after the fatal occurrence by Lady Magdalen Bruce of Kinloss, Lord Edward's mother, in memory of her unfortunate son. She is said to have employed two famous artists of Antwerp in the execution of this work, which was, moreover, distinguished by a long Latin inscription. It has been supposed, indeed, that Lord Bruce was interred, not in the great church of Bergen-op-Zoom, but on the rampart "William," in a corner of the fortifications which are all now levelled. But this is disproved by the positive statement of a contemporary Dutch author, who, a few years after the duel, gives a detailed description of the monument in the church. He does not, indeed, mention the bronze mirror with a death's-head of white marble in the centre, in connection with which a curious supernatural incident is recorded by the Rev. Mr Macleod of Stamer, in Skye, in his ' Treatise on Second Sight,' published at Edinburgh in 1763, under the pseudonym of Theophilus Insulanus. The latter's account is as follows :—

" The unfortunate Lord Bruce saw distinctly the figure or impression of a mort-head on the looking-glass in his chamber that very morning he set out for the fatal place of rendezvous, where he lost his life in a duel, and asked of some that stood by him if they observed that strange appearance, which they answered in the negative. His remains were interred at Bergen-op-Zoom, over which a monument was erected, with the emblem of a looking-glass impressed with a mort-head, to perpetuate the surprising representation which seemed to indicate his approaching untimely end. I had this narrative from a field - officer, whose honour and candour are beyond suspicion, as he had it from General Stuart in the Dutch service. The monument stood entire for a long time, until it was partly defaced when that strong place was reduced by the weakness or treachery of Cronstrom, the governor."

As Lord Bruce died without issue, he was succeeded in his title and estates by his younger brother Thomas, who, in 1633, was created by Charles I. Earl of Elgin, and in 1637 founded the almshouse at Culross already referred to, known as Lord Bruce's Hospital. The circumstances attending the duel have been woven into a story by Dr Robert Chambers, which appeared in one of the early numbers of 'Chambers's Journal' under the title of the "Tale of the Silver Heart." An account of the discovery of the heart is contained in two communications by Mr Begbie, Sir Robert Preston's factor, made in 1808 and 1815, to the treasurer of the Society of Antiquaries, Edinburgh. Previous to being redeposited with great ceremony in its original resting-place, the silver box containing it was exhibited to the public in a room in Culross Abbey.

Quitting the Bruce aisle, we find, immediately to the east of it, behind the north wall of the church, the ruins of what used to be denominated the Old or Little Aisle. Nothing remains of it now but a very fine fragment of a window of the decorated order, and belonging apparently to a later period than any other part of the ancient architecture of the church. It is said traditionally to have been the burial-place of the Argyll family, who acted as hereditary bailies of the Abbey in Roman Catholic times, and occupied the Castle of Gloom, afterwards Castle Campbell, at Dollar. Several bodies, enclosed in leathern shrouds, were a good many years ago dug up here, and are considered to have been those of members of the house of Argyll.

The monks of Culross belonged to the order of Cistercians, who were first established as a religious community in the year 1098 by Robert, Abbot of Molesme, in the diocese of Langres in France. The name is derived from their chief house Cistertium or Citeaux in Burgundy; and they were also called Bernardines, on account of St Bernard having, fifteen years after the foundation of the monastery of Citeaux, betaken himself thither with thirty of his companions. Here he conducted himself with such reputation that he was elected abbot of Clairvaux, from which he generally takes his designation. The dress of the Cistercians was white, with the exception of a black cowl and scapular; whereas that of the Benedictines was entirely black. They owned thirteen monasteries in Scotland. The Culross monks enjoyed a great reputation for their caligraphic skill, and several beautifully executed MSS., missals, and other religious works, are still in existence from the *scriptorium* of the convent.

It is well known that ancient monastic buildings had generally round them an enclosure more or less extensive, which contained, besides the gardens and pleasure-grounds, a small extent of pasture-land, and also various domestic offices—all being surrounded with a protecting wall. It is not possible to determine now the limits of the wall of defence which thus enclosed the sacred territory of Culross, but there can be little doubt of the north lodge or portal having been at the spot now known as the Chapel Barn, close to the west Abbey Lodge, and opposite to the entrance of the road leading to the West Kirk. There is here to be seen an ancient wall of great thickness, having its inner side turned to the road, and pierced by a doorway and a small window or *bole*. Fixed in the upper part of the wall is the spring or foundation-stone of an arch. The locality has long been known as the Chapel Barn; and in ancient Scottish Acts of Parliament and other old documents relating to Culross, the place is spoken of as the Bar Chapel, or the Chapel of Bar, probably from the rising ground immediately above called Barhill. A daughter of the proprietor of the estate of that name became in after-days the wife of the celebrated Thomas Boston of Ettrick, author of the 'Crook in the Lot.' There had certainly been a chapel here, and it must also have been in this neighbourhood that there stood the gateway which is spoken of as "the upper port," leading to the town of Culross, near which was the " Auld Tolbuith" or prison, afterwards pulled down and re-erected in the Sand Haven.

Opposite to the Chapel Barn a road branches off to the west, and leads, after a walk of about three-quarters of a mile, to the West Kirk or old parish church of Culross. Much speculation has prevailed regarding this building, of which little more now exists than a portion of the walls, enclosing what must have been an edifice of very small dimensions. With the quaint little church-yard in which it stands, it is a lonely and sequestered but not unromantic locality—a veritable "God's acre," such as might have inspired Gray to the composition of his "Elegy." Scarcely any authentic record of it has been preserved beyond what is contained in an Act of the Scottish Parliament passed in 1633. This ordains that in future the Abbey Church shall be regarded as the parish church, and enjoy as such all the emoluments, immunities, and privileges which legally appertained to the West Church. The reason assigned for this transfer is, "that the abbay kirk of Culrois hes beine the kirk quhairine the cure hes beine servit, be preatching of the Word of God, celebrating the holy comwnion, and exercising and vsing of vther ecclesiastical discipline sen the Reformatione, and that the kirk callit the paroche kirk of Culrois is ane old kirk quhairine service is not, nor hes not beine vsit since memorie of man, and is altogether ruinous, decayit, and falline down in divers pairts, swa that the said abbay kirk of Culrois is the most apt and fitt kirk for serving of the cure thairat in tyme coming, and be reputt and haldine the ordinar paroche kirk for that effect in all tyme heireftir."

It appears from the above that so far back as 1633 no remembrance existed of the West Kirk having been used as a place of worship—that no Protestant service had ever been held in it, and that probably even at the Reformation it had become ruined and dilapidated. It probably dates its origin from the first division of Scotland into parishes, which is supposed to have taken place in the twelfth century, in the reign of David I. The primitive rudeness of its architecture warrants us in referring its erection to a very remote period, the style of building approximating closely to those ancient edifices, few in number, which are still to be found in England, and have been classed under the denomination of Early Saxon. It has a length from east to west of about 68 feet, and a breadth of 18 feet, the only part of the walls that remains tolerably entire being on the east and south sides. The latter contains a low and primitive doorway, with jambs and lintel, unprovided with any ornament; and immediately adjoining it, on its west side, is a narrow aperture or window, once surmounted by a plain pointed arch. This last is the only remaining object in the architecture of the West Kirk that preserves a distinct ecclesiastical character, if we except two large stones sculptured with crosses. These have been built into the walls, one of them serving as a lintel for the doorway just mentioned, and the other as that of a plain window, 3 feet square, on the north side. It seems difficult to account for their situation in their present position, unless we suppose them to have been originally tombstones, and that in Protestant times the ruined church may have been used as a burial-place, and the decaying walls patched up with those relics of a past age. By some the sculptures in question have been held to represent swords, to which, indeed, they bear some resemblance, and a theory was in consequence maintained that the West Kirk had formerly belonged to the Knights Templars. But there is no evidence whatever to support this, and there can be little question

that the delineations on the stones are crosses, and
possibly of the kind known as "pre-Christian."

What may originally have been a projection or transept on the south side of the church, is now used as the
burying-vault of the Johnstons of Sands. It was purchased in the middle of the last century by the ancestor
of the present proprietor from the Browns of Barhill.
The churchyard is still occasionally used for interments,
though, for the most part, these are confined to the
Abbey churchyard. A handsome mausoleum has of
recent years been erected on the west side, though not
actually within the precinct, as the burial-place of Mr
Dalgleish of West Grange.

In a field to the north of the West Kirk, on the farm
of the Ashes, is a spring of excellent water, which bears
the name of the Monks' Well. The name seems to have
come down from Roman Catholic times, as the designation of the fountain-head from which the monastery
was supplied. At least there was then some kind of
reservoir here, as, in an Act of the Scottish Parliament
in 1594, confirming to Alexander Gaw of Maw his possession of certain lands conveyed to him and his prede-
cessors by the commendator and convent of Culross,
the field in question is designated "The Cisterns."

The mansion of Culross Abbey, which closely adjoins
the eastern side of the Abbey churchyard, and has succeeded to the title of the old monastery, is an oblong
building of three storeys, flanked by turrets at the east
and west extremities of its south front, which, standing
on the crest of the hill, both commands a magnificent
prospect, and when viewed from below or the water,
forms, with the church and monastery ruins, a most
imposing and picturesque group, overshadowing the
town of Culross. It had originally only been an edifice
of two storeys, with a tower at each end, and the inten-

tion doubtless was to have it completed in the form of a quadrangle, with a court and grand entrance, most probably on the eastern side. A portion of the west side of the quadrangle, at right angles to the front or south side, was actually erected, and now remains to show the plan of the founder.

The architraves of the windows on the first floor, as well as those on the upper storeys of the turrets, are marked with the initials L. E. B., D. M. B.—these denoting respectively Lord Edward Bruce of Kinloss, and his wife, Dame Magdalen Bruce, a daughter of Sir Alexander Clerk of Balbirnie. On the east gable are two superimposed dates, 1608 and 1670. The first refers to the edifice as originally erected by Lord Kinloss, the second to the third storey, added in the year last mentioned by Alexander, second Earl of Kincardine, whose architect was probably his kinsman, the celebrated Sir William Bruce of Kinross.

The entrance to Culross Abbey is on the north side, but all the principal apartments face the south, and command splendid views of the Forth and opposite shores. The first floor is almost entirely occupied by a grand suite of rooms, consisting of dining and drawing rooms, connected by a noble gallery. One of these used in Lord Dundonald's time to be hung with fine Gobelins tapestry, and was known as the *King's Room*, from the tradition of King James having been entertained here on his visit to Scotland in 1617. Notwithstanding the imposing appearance of the structure, the number of apartments that it contains is, owing to the narrowness of the building and the space taken up with corridors and state-rooms, not so great as might be imagined. Sir Walter Scott, indeed, on the occasion of his visit to Valleyfield, when Sir Robert Preston was repairing the Abbey as a dower-house for his wife, after having many years before ruthlessly converted it into a ruin, expressed his opinion that it could never be much more serviceable than as a banqueting-house.

By his will, Sir Robert's trustees were directed to maintain the Abbey in a habitable condition, and he moreover directed, in somewhat whimsical fashion, that the old designation should be exchanged for the appellation of the Abbey Elizabeth, in compliment to his deceased wife, Lady Preston, *née* Miss Elizabeth Brown. This new nomenclature, however, was never adopted except in one or two legal documents, and is now quite abandoned. After remaining untenanted, except by a housekeeper in charge, and almost wholly unfurnished, during a period of more than thirty years, Culross Abbey was, on the accession of the Elgin family, held in lease for eight years by Henry Liddell, Esq., of the Bombay Civil Service, who died here in 1873. It was afterwards occupied by Major Johnston of the Madras Service, who died in 1888.

The Abbey garden and orchard, comprising for the most part those belonging to the old convent, stretch down the slope of the hill towards the public road, and from their productiveness and fine exposure, still testify to the horticultural skill and judgment of the monks. They seem to have been laid out in their present terrace form by Alexander, second Earl of Kincardine, who at least must have built the pavilion or arbour which occupies the eastern extremity of the fine upper terrace, and bears the date of 1674. An ancient oak settle placed within this summer-house has carved upon it, among other indentations, the words "Jo. Cochrane, 1767," which were probably cut there in his boyhood by the Hon. John Cochrane, Deputy Commissary to the Forces in North Britain, and younger brother of Archibald, ninth Earl of Dundonald, the unfortunate projector and speculator. It is probable, however, that the seat is as old as the pavilion itself.

Next to the Abbey there are no houses more interesting about Culross than the two old mansions enclosed within a court at the north-west corner of the Sand Haven, as the open space in front of the town-house is termed. Their old and proper name is "The Colonel's Close," from one of them, at least, having been occupied in the first half of the last century by Colonel John Erskine of Carnock, generally known from his dark features as the "Black Colonel." A kinsman of his, also a Colonel John Erskine, but a man of fair complexion, is said to have inhabited the other of these houses, and, to distinguish him from his swarthy relative, was known as the "White Colonel." It may here be stated in passing that these epithets were no nicknames, but given and received as most honourable appellations, and as such we find them used in a list of the Culross elders, presiding at a communion occasion in 1722, as recorded in the kirk-session minutes. Of the two houses, one bears the date 1597, and the initials G. B., from the great George Bruce, its founder; the other has the date 1611, and the initials S. G. B., having been erected after Bruce had been raised to the rank of a knight. Though respectable and substantial in appearance, such as befitted the residence of a wealthy burgess of the day, they are by no means remarkable for splendour or beauty of architecture, and certainly were not designed by Inigo Jones.

It is the interior of these houses which possesses the chief interest, from the curious painted ceiling with which the principal apartment in each is adorned. The ceilings are coved, and the material on which the paintings are executed consists of thin planking, now very much decayed. The colours are still wonderfully vivid, though in many places time and damp have obliterated the pictures. In the older house these consist of a series of allegorical designs, well drawn, and having attached to each a sentence in black-letter as a text for the pictorial sermon, which is either some moral lesson or a representation of the general instability and uncertainty of human affairs.

These pictures in the old house, though they cannot lay claim to a high artistic excellence, are nevertheless of very respectable execution. Among the designs are "Ulysses and the Sirens," "Fortune with her Wheel," &c. They are most valuable as specimens of house decoration of the period, and King James has doubtless frequently sat under and contemplated them on occasion of his expeditions from Dunfermline and partaking of the hospitality of Sir George Bruce. The same house contains a muniment or strong room, with a vaulted roof and a massive iron door.

The painted room in the mansion of 1611 is of a less pretentious character than that in the older house, the ornaments consisting mainly of geometrical delineations. Each house is quite distinct from the other, and both are in a woful state of dilapidation. No one has occupied either for many years, and the havoc caused by wind, weather, and general neglect has been very great. It is possible enough that the second house may have been erected by Sir George to accommodate his son, the younger George Bruce of Carnock. It is clear that, being both situated within the same court, they could only have been intended as residences for members of the same family, or at least very intimate friends. And there seems to have been only one garden, common to both mansions.

From references in the burgh and kirk-session records there can be little doubt of at least the first Earl of

Kincardine, Sir George Bruce's grandson, having resided in the tenement in the Sand Haven, though in which of the houses is quite uncertain. His brother Alexander, second Earl, may also have resided here for a time, though shortly after 1670, at latest, he had removed to the Abbey, which had passed from the representatives of the first Lord Kinloss to those of his younger brother, Sir George Bruce. The Kincardine family continued to possess the property in the Sand Haven till about 1700, when it was transferred, with the bulk of their estates, by judicial sale, to the Black Colonel.

Colonel John Erskine of Carnock having found himself prevented from including in his purchase the mansion and grounds of Culross Abbey, which he had to resign to Lady Mary Cochrane, took up his abode in the Sand Haven, and from him the tenement derives its old and most fitting designation of the Colonel's Close. Tradition has constantly asserted, though I have been unable to find direct confirmation of the fact, that the Black Colonel occupied one of the houses in the court, whilst the other was tenanted by his kinsman the White Colonel. There was thus a double propriety in the bestowal of the appellation. Latterly the Colonel's Close became the property of the Halkerston family, two members of which, father and son, were successively town-clerks of Culross. It passed by inheritance from Miss Halkerston, last resident of the name in Culross, to her relative, the late Captain James Kerr of East Grange. After his death it was sold by his representatives to Mr Luke, in the possession of whose family it still remains.

When Captain Kerr succeeded to the Colonel's Close, he found it designated in the title-deeds as the Palace or Great Lodging in the Sand Haven of Culross. Not well versed in ancient legal phraseology, he at once leapt to the conclusion that the tenement of which he was now proprietor had in ancient times been a royal residence. He consequently dubbed it "The Palace," and its surrounding court "Palace Yard." The title was captivating, and to the present hour not merely do people speak of the building as "The Palace," but assertions have even found their way into print of its having been an ancient residence of one or more of the Scottish kings.

Now the whole of this nomenclature is an absurd blunder, originating in Captain Kerr's mistake of identifying with a royal residence the "palatium" or "palace" in the title-deeds of the Colonel's Close. This is nothing more than the appellation which, in law Latin and phraseology, is used to denote any large or imposing building, more especially any building which is occupied by a nobleman. Culross Abbey is also designed the Palace or Great Lodging, and many similar instances from other places in Scotland might be produced. The term "Colonel's Close" ought still to be retained, both from having been so long employed, and from its preserving the memory of an important local if not historical personage. But when the public has once laid hold of a name, it is almost impossible to get it altered ; and I fear, therefore, that the misnomer of "The Palace" will continue to mislead and perplex as long as the building itself exists.

The town-house of Culross deserves some notice, were it for nothing more than the elegant bell-tower which imparts so picturesque an appearance to the lower part of the town, and is, in its way, as characteristic a feature of Culross as her church and abbey. The building itself dates from the year 1626; but the tower was only erected in 1783, and provided then with a clock and bell. The town-hall, or "tolbooth," as it used to be called, faces the Sand Haven, and is approached by a double flight of steps leading to the first floor, which contains the council-chamber, and a room formerly known as the "debtors' room," on the wall of which a stone is fixed with an inscription in gold letters, by a grateful municipality, to Sir George Preston of Valleyfield, for his benefaction of 2000 marks to the town of Culross. The ground storey is what used to be called the "Laigh Tolbooth," or the "Iron House," and, as this last grim title imports, was frequently used as a prison. Another place of confinement was in the so-called "High Tolbooth," or garret of the town-house, a dreary fireless place, contained within the lofty roof of the building, and lighted through the slates. Here the unfortunate women accused of witchcraft used to be confined and "watched." In front of the town-hall stands a stone platform, well known in Scottish burghs as the "Tron," or "Trone," which in Edinburgh and Glasgow gave a designation to the churches immediately adjoining. It was the place where commodities were weighed, and the term belongs properly to the weighing-machine itself, which consisted of a wooden post supporting two cross horizontal bars with beaked extremities. From the latter circumstance the word is derived—*i.e.*, from the old Norse *trana*, a beak or crane. It is probably also connected radically with *tree* and *throne*.

Just where a narrow passage, like the neck of a bottle, connects the Back Causeway with the open space about the Cross, stands a tower-like building containing a fine spiral staircase, which gives access to two large apartments in the adjoining tenement, used as workshops by Mr John Harrower, the proprietor. The lower one of these is a fine, well-proportioned room, lined with oak-panelling beautifully carved, of which that on the east wall is still in good preservation, and is moreover adorned with some fine inlaid work of a different material. It bears the date 1633, which, however, is probably only that of the panelling itself, as indicating the period when, in church-warden phrase, the apartment was " beautified " by its owner, some wealthy burgess of the seventeenth century.

The tenement in question looks to the south, facing the Cross, and has other apartments besides those to which access is gained from the turret stair. One of these is on the same floor, was originally fitted up in the same style, and communicated probably with the lower wainscoted room. The wall which forms the north boundary of both is provided with a range of curious arched recesses of hewn stone, which some have imagined served the purpose of containing book-shelves. Following out this conjecture, it has been surmised that the two apartments formed a library, and had possibly belonged as such to the abbots of the monastery. Others have connected them with Bishop Leighton, to whose diocese Culross belonged. And the appellation of "The Study," which the tenement has borne from time immemorial, has been explained as expressing the purpose for which it was originally employed.

As no positive evidence whatever exists on the subject, I venture to put forward my own opinion, that the recesses were nothing more nor less than cupboards or buffets, which served to contain plate and other articles, as a fitting appendage and set-off to the general splendour of the apartments. And as regards " The Study," I think the term has been derived not from these rooms, but from a very curious apartment at the top of the turret stair. This forms externally a prominent object, projecting, as it does, slightly from the lower walls of the tower, on which it rests. It is entered from the summit of the spiral staircase, by a tiny corkscrew stair of its own, which is both of the narrowest dimensions and closed at the foot by a door. Ascending it, we find ourselves in a small chamber of about 9 feet square, and a little over

7 feet in height. It contains a fireplace, and three small windows or apertures, looking respectively east, west, and south, commanding views of the whole town of Culross, and taking in the Forth and its shores as far as Queensferry on one side, and the Carse of Falkirk on the other. It is exactly such an apartment as formed the habitation of the sage Herr Teufelsdröckh and overlooked the whole city of Weissnichtwo. Certainly no place could embody more completely the idea of a philosopher or wizard's chamber, cut off, as it is, so completely from the outer world, and yet affording such scope for the study both of nature and mankind, in the distant view of sea and land, and the near one of the surging tide of humanity which on market-days gathered round the Cross of Culross.

I conclude, therefore, that this little chamber, from having been used at one time as a study or observatory, has given its name to the whole tenement, the walls of which, it may be remarked, are of an extraordinary thickness—the gable-end having a breadth of nearly four feet. Adjoining the house, as we ascend the hill, is another tenement, occupied by Mr Harrower himself, which has a remarkable semicircular projection that may at one time have served as part of a staircase. What may also have been the doorway at the foot is now converted into a window, and over it appears the following Greek inscription :—

Ὁ ΘΕΟΣ ΠΡΟΝΟΕΙ ΚΑΙ ΠΡΟΝΟΗΣΕΙ—

"GOD PROVIDETH AND WILL PROVIDE"—

one of those pious and pithy sayings which our forefathers were so fond of engraving on their dwellings. The date and author of the inscription are unknown, and the house to which it belongs, though old, has no other characteristic deserving of special notice.

N

The Cross of Culross is an ancient structure as regards its basement; but the upper part is modern, having been re-erected in 1819. Four streets converge on the little space fronting the Cross. A little down from the latter is the Dundonald Arms Inn, an exceedingly snug and comfortable as well as admirably conducted little hostelry. On the opposite side of the street, still farther down, as we descend to the Laigh Causeway, stands a fine old house, which tradition has connected with Robert Leighton, who as Bishop of Dunblane, the diocese to which Culross belonged, is said to have resided here during his official visitations. The house is old enough to have existed in the days of "the saintly Leighton," and it contains at least one large and handsome apartment, finely panelled. But the tradition has been as little verified as the conjectures regarding the Study.

Culross used to pride herself on her wells and copious supply of excellent water. Bessie Bar's Well beside the Colonel's Close, Baby's Well on the Laigh Causeway, and the Lockit Well at the head of the Tanhouse Brae, were each, and more especially the first, regarded as veritable Bandusias, clear and sparkling as the heart of any poet could wish. Alas for specious appearances and the stern verdict of analytical science! Bessie Bar was pronounced by the latter to be no better than she should be; and as for Baby, her condition was "past praying for." A new water-supply has quite recently been introduced from Glen Sherup in the Ochils, a source which now supplies not only the town of Dunfermline, but a large portion of the western district of Fife.

Facing the town of Culross, and running parallel to the shore at the distance of about a hundred yards, is a ridge of rocks, known as the Ailie Rocks, behind which the votaries of Neptune may indulge in the luxury of a bath, without the least risk of being overlooked by profane gazers.   At the western extremity of these rocks is what is referred to occasionally in the burgh records as the Oxcraig.   This derived its name from the existence there of a species of rude staircase, up which cattle were driven to be shipped on the farther side for Borrowstounness.   Near this point is a large blue boulder-stone, which, according to popular tradition, marks the place of sepulture of those who died of the plague in 1645, and were buried here to prevent the dissemination of infection by their being interred in the churchyard.   Here also were deposited, it is said, the bodies of any persons who, by suicide or other offences, had rendered themselves unworthy of Christian burial. Bones and fragments of coffins have frequently been exhumed and floated ashore from this spot, as I am credibly assured by persons on whose averments I can place unhesitating reliance.   The Blue Rock has now been somewhat diminished, from portions of it having been broken down and carried away to make road-metal.   At a little distance on the west side of the harbour is the pier of Culross, which originally was disconnected with the shore, and could only be reached at low water or by wading.   A new pier, constructed of stones taken from the Oxcraig, was erected a good many years ago, and joined to the outer pier by a wooden jetty.

About two hundred yards up the Forth, and nearly due west from the extremity of the outer pier, is the celebrated moat of Sir George Bruce, now merely visible at low water like a heap or *rickle* of stones.   It was here that formerly a massive circular building towered above the surface of the water, as described, along with its adjacent submarine workings, by John Taylor, in his

'Pennilesse Pilgrimage,' already quoted.   He gives there a very graphic picture of the moat and mine as they appeared in 1618, though he says nothing of the renowned adventure which is reported to have befallen James I. there in the preceding year, on the occasion of the latter's visit to Scotland.   My own impression is, that the adventure in question occurred before James's accession to the English throne, and whilst he was as yet only James VI. of Scotland.   The incident is well known, but it may nevertheless be as well to recapitulate that the king had been paying a visit to his friend and favourite Sir George Bruce, whose commercial genius and enterprising activity were raising Culross to a sudden and exalted degree of prosperity in connection with the working of coals and manufacture of salt.   The great mine, whose workings extended beneath the Forth, and had two entrances, one on land and another from the sea, was visited by his Majesty, who descended it from the shore, and after being conducted through a long dark passage underground, was conveyed upwards to the summit of the moat.   Arriving here, and seeing himself surrounded on all sides by water, the affrighted monarch, who had already had a pretty extensive experience in plots and conspiracies against the royal person, thought, not unnaturally perhaps, that another of these schemes was now in preparation, and bawled out lustily, " Treason ! treason ! "   But he was soon reassured by the tranquil urbanity of his host, who explained the situation to him, and showed him an elegantly fitted-up pinnace which was to convey him ashore.   The story further goes on to say that the day concluded with a sumptuous banquet, probably served to his Majesty in the Painted Chamber in Sir George's house in the Sand Haven of Culross.

By a singular coincidence, the same year that witnessed the deaths of King James and Sir George Bruce, chronicled also, within three days of the royal demise, the destruction of the monument of industrial enterprise with which both their names are connected. In the great tempest of 30th March 1625, which was long remembered, in reference to a popular appellation, as the storm of the " Borrowing Days," the moat and its workings were completely destroyed, and never again rebuilt or resumed. At present the three concentric walls of hewn stone of which the building consisted are still distinctly visible, though almost level with the ground. The tops of piles are also to be seen, and the spaces between the three walls are firmly packed with blue clay. The distance between the two outer walls is 3 feet, and between the second and third walls fully 15. The diameter of the inner wall, which enclosed the shaft of the pit, is 18 feet, while that of the outer wall from edge to edge is about 60. The landing-place is supposed to have been on the eastern side, and there are also remains on the south-west side of what seems to have been a breakwater. The moat communicated, as already mentioned, by workings under the sea, with a pit on the shore, which is supposed to have been sunk in the hollow below the house of Castlehill or Dunimarle. The projection on the seashore, formerly an old "bucket-pat," has also some claims to be regarded as the site of the pit which the king descended on his memorable visit, to emerge subsequently by the moat. Remains of masonry which belonged to this pit, and the draining apparatus connected with it described by Taylor, are said to have been in existence in this neighbourhood up to the beginning of the present century. At the present time nothing regarding its site can be affirmed with certainty.

Culross by the shore-road is about four miles from

Kincardine.   A very pretty route it is for the most part, winding among plantations, overhung by the slopes of Dunimarle and Blair, and affording fine glimpses of the Forth and the opposite shores of West Lothian and Stirlingshire.   Dunimarle (the original name of which has recently been restored) was long under the appellation of Castlehill, the property of the ancient family of Blaw, which intermarried with the ancestors both of the Elgin and Rosebery families.   About fifty years ago it was acquired by Mrs Sharpe Erskine, grand-aunt of the present Earl of Rosslyn ; and its revenues were bequeathed by her as an endowment of the Episcopal chapel of St Serf's-next-Culross, which she erected on the slope adjoining the hamlet of Blair-Burn.   The house of Dunimarle, with its tower and castellated surroundings, she appointed to be the residence of the incumbent, the Rev. William Bruce.   It contains a fine collection of pictures and other curiosities, which, in terms of Mrs Erskine's will, are open on Wednesdays and Saturdays to the public during the summer months.

Immediately to the west of Dunimarle is Blair Castle (Robert Miller, Esq.), formerly the patrimony of the Dundases, and at an early period the property of the Hamiltons, the illegitimate progeny of the celebrated Archbishop of St Andrews of that name.   He appears in his younger days to have been Abbot of Culross ; and it is at all events tolerably well authenticated that he gave great scandal by an intrigue with a lady of quality, who was then living separate from her husband, and proprietrix of Blair.   They had several children, one of whom, John Hamilton, succeeded to the estate ; and another, a daughter named Margaret, married Robert Bruce of Blairhall, elder brother of the celebrated Sir George.   The Archbishop built, it is alleged, at Blair, the substantial mansion which Mr Dundas, many years ago, had the greatest difficulty in demolishing, owing to the thickness of the walls. It stood a little in front of the present house.

The Blair quarries, though at present disused, are well known for their excellent building-stone, from which large portions of the New Town of Edinburgh have been erected, besides Drury Lane Theatre and other distant structures. From an older quarry at Longannet Point, a little farther up, it is said that the town-hall of Amsterdam was erected in the seventeenth century, when the lands in the neighbourhood were in the possession of the Earl of Kincardine. An interesting confirmation of this tradition is furnished by the great Dutch poet Vondel. In his poem on the rebuilding of the town-hall of Amsterdam in 1655, he speaks of the stone material as brought from the " Marble Cliff in the West," and in a footnote the locality referred to is explained as denoting Scotland. The fine white freestone of Blair quarry may well be regarded as warranting its description by poetical licence as marble. At that period the commercial intercourse of Holland with Scotland was very great, and more especially with the towns on the shores of the Firth of Forth. Alexander Bruce, afterwards second Earl of Kincardine, was then residing in Holland as a sharer of the fortunes of Charles II. He married a Dutch lady, Veronica Van Arsens, daughter of Cornelius Van Arsens, Baron of Sommelsdyk, and a descendant of the celebrated Francis Van Arsens, the first holder of the title and estate. The last-mentioned is famous as the ambassador of the States-General of Holland to the Court of Henry IV., and also not so creditably known as the enemy of the unfortunate John of Barneveldt. In further reference to the Blair and Longannet quarries, we are distinctly informed, in a case reported in Morison's ' Decisions of the Court of Session,' that the Jews of Amsterdam in the seventeenth century entered into negotiations with the Earl of Kincardine for a supply of building-stone from a celebrated quarry on his estate, to be employed in the erection of a synagogue. The transaction, however, was never completed.

Before coming to Longannet Point (about a mile below Kincardine), the mansion-house of Sands (Laurence Johnston, Esq.) will have been noticed on the right-hand side of the road, pleasantly situated on a verdant slope bordered with trees. The district here formerly belonged to Culross parish, but in the middle of the seventeenth century was annexed to that of Tulliallan.

Kincardine-on-Forth (*Hotel:* The Commercial) is a burgh of barony belonging to or connected with the estate of Tulliallan (Lady W. G. Osborne Elphinston), which comprises all the ground in the immediate neighbourhood. It was formerly noted, like Culross, for its coal and salt works; but this industry has long since entirely disappeared, to be succeeded by the shipbuilding trade, which in its turn has also become extinct. With the exception of a rope-work, a woollen factory, and a paper-mill, constructed out of the famous distillery of Kilbagie about a mile to the north of the town, there is little commercial activity about Kincardine, though it covers a considerable space of ground, and was once the grand *entrepôt* of communication in the coaching days by means of its ferry between Fife and the west country. An air of depression now hangs over it, and altogether it possesses few attractions, though the view from the pier, looking up the Forth towards Alloa and Stirling, with the Ochils in the background, is uncommonly fine.

A singular natural phenomenon connected with the

tides is to be observed in the neighbourhood of Kincardine and adjacent places in the upper reach of the Forth from Culross to Alloa. This is the so-called *lakies* or double tides, which have long been a subject of remark, but to account for which hitherto no explanation has been devised. When the tide is flowing, and has done so for three hours, it recedes for the space of two feet, or a little more, and then returns on its regular course till it has reached the limit of high water. Similarly, in ebbing it begins to flow again, and then recedes to the limit of low water, thus causing four tides in twelve hours, or eight in the twenty-four. The space over which it thus flows and recedes varies a little, and sometimes the *lakie* only shows itself by the tide coming to a standstill for about an hour and a half. The legendary account of the matter is, that on one occasion when St Mungo with some of his ecclesiastics was sailing up the Forth to Stirling, the vessel went aground in ebb-tide, and could not be floated. The saint exercised his miraculous powers, and the tide in consequence returned, so as to enable him and his companions to proceed on their journey; and there has ever since been a double tide in this region of the Forth. It is believed that these lakie or leakie tides are peculiar to this locality, though a somewhat similar phenomenon is said to occur at Southampton and Portsmouth.

Kincardine church is a modern building of a little over half a century old; and on the rising ground behind stands, in a picturesque situation in its churchyard, the dismantled old church, erected in 1675, on the occasion of the annexation to Tulliallan of a large portion of the parish of Culross having rendered a still older church quite inadequate to accommodate the new influx of worshippers. This last, now converted into the mausoleum of the Keith family, stands about a mile farther north in its little churchyard, in a corner of the park of Tulliallan. The present castle of Tulliallan was erected about 1820 by Admiral Lord Keith, who purchased the estate from Mr Erskine of Cardross in Monteith. It is a handsome building in the Italian style, closely adjoining the town of Kincardine at the western extremity of the extensive woodland which now covers a great part of the old moor of Culross. Lord Keith was succeeded in the property by his eldest daughter, the late Baroness Keith, and she again by her half-sister, the present proprietrix, Lady W. G. Osborne Elphinston, whose husband, Lord William Godolphin Osborne, is uncle of the Duke of Leeds.

IV.

FROM KINCARDINE TO CLACKMANNAN AND ALLOA.

The old castle and estate of Tulliallan—The Blackadder family —Kilbagie and its distillery—Kennet village—Town of Clack-mannan—Clackmannan Tower and the Bruce family—Approach to Alloa—Alloa and the Earls of Mar.

A BROAD road, finely shaded with trees, leads northward from Kincardine to old Garterry Toll, where it is crossed by the upper road from Dunfermline, leading westwards to Clackmannan and Alloa. Just before quitting the town a road branches off to the left, which, passing through the West Carse, will conduct the traveller, pleasantly enough, by a shorter route, to both of these places. At present, however, we shall follow the main highway.

About a mile from Kincardine is the entrance, on the

right-hand side of the road, to the home-farm of Tulliallan, and on the opposite side a road through a wood which leads to the old castle of Tulliallan, a picturesque ruin, pleasantly situated among some fine old trees. Formerly the waters of the Forth almost washed its walls; but these, through the reclamations of ground which have taken place, are now at least half a mile distant. It must in its day have been a stately building, as befitted the residence of the family of Blackadder from the Merse, one of whose members in the fifteenth century married Elizabeth Edmiston, the heiress of Tulliallan. The castle is spoken of as a stronghold held by the English in the time of Edward I., who, when wintering at Dunfermline in 1304, addresses a letter from thence regarding the occupancy of the castle of "Tolly-alwyn." It had subsequently, probably, received considerable additions, so as to bring its accommodations within the palatial order. The basement storey has a fine groined roof, and one or two of the apartments on the first floor have been very magnificent.

A brother of the Laird of Tulliallan in the end of the fifteenth century was the celebrated Robert Blackadder, Archbishop of Glasgow, who both built the south transept of the cathedral in that city, and founded at Culross in 1503 the little chapel already described as occupying the supposed scene of the landing of St Thenew and birth of St Mungo. The end of the Archbishop was a singular one. Having gone on a pilgrimage to the Holy Land, he visited Venice on his way, and, as we are informed from a record preserved in the library of St Mark, was received with the greatest respect and honour by the Doge and his ministers. He accompanied them in the Bucentaur on the occasion of the famous annual ceremony of the wedding of Venice and the Adriatic. Shortly after this he embarked for Jaffa on board one of the vessels belonging to the Republic; but a deadly sickness having broken out among the pilgrims who were fellow-passengers with him, the "great Scotch archbishop," as he is called, also succumbed, and met his death on the waters of the Levant. A more tragical occurrence was destined to overtake his family in the next generation, when John Blackadder, the Laird of Tulliallan, was beheaded in 1530 for the murder of Sir John Inglis, Abbot of Culross, who had offended him by letting in tack some lands over his head to Erskine of Balgownie.

The Blackadders seem indeed to have been a hot-headed, fierce race, as we find in 1603 the then Laird of Tulliallan fined in 500 merks for striking in the church the Rev. Henry Forrester, minister of the parish, "with his gluiffis upon the face." On 24th May 1568 an order is made by the Scottish Privy Council denouncing certain persons as rebels against the king and Regent Murray, and ordering their strongholds to be searched. Among these are "Robert Bruce of Clakmannane, the tour place of Clakmannane," and "Johne Blacater of Tulliallan, the castell, tour, and fortalice of Tulliallan." Subsequent to this we find various references in royal charters and the registers of the Privy Council to the Blackadders of Tulliallan, who seem to have continued to hold the estate till well on in the seventeenth century, when the extravagance and mismanagement of the last laird brought the family fortunes to ruin. The barony of Tulliallan then passed into the hands of the Earls of Kincardine, and when they too yielded to pecuniary misfortunes, it was purchased with their other domains by the Black Colonel Erskine of Carnock, in the end of the seventeenth century. From a descendant of his it passed, as already mentioned, to

Admiral Lord Keith. John Blackadder of Troqueer, the celebrated Covenanting minister, was a cadet of this family, and latterly its representative. Most probably he belonged to the Blackadders of Inzievar,[1] in the parish of Torryburn, an estate which afterwards became the property, as in the case of Tulliallan, first of the Earls of Kincardine, and then of Colonel Erskine. They occupied the old castle of Inzievar, which was described to me many years ago as a "grand gentleman's house," and in existence till within the last hundred and ten years. It stood on the site of the present garden of Fernwoodlee, as the house of Old or Nether Inzievar is now called, and was demolished about 1782 to supply stones for the erection of the present mansion.

I have already described one of John Blackadder's adventures as holder of a conventicle in 1670 at the Hill of Beath. In 1674 he held another one near Dunfermline, which was attended by 3000 persons. In 1678 he presided at one near Culross, and with this object crossed the water from Borrowstounness in the early morning of a beautiful Sabbath-day in July. After landing he rode, we are informed, two miles to the place of meeting, which is described as being situated beside a burn, two miles below Culross and one mile beyond Blairhall. Most probably some sequestered spot on the Bluther Burn, near Shiresmill—perhaps Comrie Dean—is meant.

Blackadder was at last apprehended and brought before the Privy Council in 1681. He was condemned to imprisonment in the Bass, and in the course of his examination was asked by General Dalziel if he belonged to the house of Tulliallan. "Yes, General," he replied, "I do, and am the nearest alive to represent that family, though it is now brought low and ruined." He was con-

---

[1] Blackadder's father was probably John Blackadder of Inzievar.

fined for four years in the Bass prison, and after two applications to the Privy Council, was ordered to be liberated on coming under recognisances for 5000 merks to confine himself to the town of Edinburgh. But the order came too late; he died on the Bass in December 1685, and was buried in the churchyard of North Berwick. A son of his entered the army and achieved some distinction as Colonel Blackadder.

Passing the ancient hamlet of Dalquhamy, we arrive, near the second milestone from Kincardine, at the entrance to the paper-works of Kilbagie (J. A. Weir, Esq.) These have been formed out of the once famous distillery of Kilbagie, which many people will think has been thus *reformed* in more senses than one. A hundred years ago it was the most extensive distillery in Scotland, producing more than 3000 tuns of whisky annually, for which upwards of 30,000 imperial quarters of grain were used up, supplying with food about 7000 cattle in its outhouses, and keeping in cultivation in the neighbourhood for its exclusive use about 850 acres. The buildings covered about 7 acres of ground, and there was both a canal and tramway leading down from the distillery to the creek of Kennet Pans on the Forth. Burns has spoken of the "dear Kilbagie," an appellation which, however, is only to be understood as one of affection, seeing that in those days the whisky produced here was retailed at a penny a gill, so that it was an inestimable boon to his own "Jolly Beggars," who could thus enjoy at Poosie Nancy's hostelry the happiness of getting "blind fou" for fourpence. Long after that Kilbagie continued to flourish, but, as with other institutions, hard times came and the distillery went down. One of the last incidents that I remember hearing connected with it was about thirty years ago, when a great vat of imprisoned spirit burst its bonds, and flowing down the Kincardine road, proved like Falstaff to be not merely frolicsome itself, but the cause of a variety of gambols on the part of others, who rushed to partake of its exhilarating influences.

A little beyond Kilbagie, and about a quarter of a mile south from Garterry Toll, a road to the left joins the Dunfermline and Alloa road at the village of Kennet. This is a clean and substantial-looking village, inhabited chiefly by the miners employed in the coal-works of Lord Balfour of Burleigh, who owns the Kennet estate in this neighbourhood. The Kennet woods lie on the left-hand side of the road, and the lodge of the avenue leading to his lordship's mansion is passed at a little distance after getting through the village. The family of the Bruces of Kennet dispute with that of Elgin the honour of being the head of the family since the Bruces of Clackmannan, to whom the position undoubtedly belonged, became extinct on the death of Henry Bruce, the last Laird of Clackmannan, in 1772. The present Lord Balfour of Burleigh succeeded, as Bruce of Kennet, about twenty years ago, in making good his right to the peerage of Balfour of Burleigh, which had been in abeyance for nearly a hundred and fifty years. The romantic story in connection with the ancient holder of this title has already been detailed in treating of Burleigh Castle in Kinross-shire.

About three miles from Kincardine, and two from Alloa, a road turns aside on the left to the ancient county town of Clackmannan, a place which the hero in one of Professor Aytoun's stories declares he had often heard of, but had never met any person by whom it had actually been seen. The traveller will now have the opportunity for himself of making its acquaintance. In some respects, as far as a deserted appearance is concerned, it may remind him of Culross, but it wants the quaint picturesqueness of the latter as regards streets and houses, which in Clackmannan have a decidedly mean and uninteresting appearance. The town, however, occupies a fine salubrious position, straggling up the ridge of a hill, with the old Tower and park, of which I shall have something to say presently, forming the termination of the principal street. The church is a handsome building, in the modern Gothic style, with an elegant tower, and forms a prominent landmark in sailing up the Forth from Kincardine to Stirling. The manse adjoining is a snug, comfortable-looking building, and both command a fine view, and have a warm, sunny exposure.

There are several inns or public-houses in Clackmannan. Opposite the principal one, in the centre of the main street, stands a huge shapeless mass of basalt, from which the town derives, it is believed, its name; and there can be little doubt that this denotes the *Clach* (Gaelic for "stone") of Mannan. I have already[1] ventured a conjecture as to the etymology of the last term. Mr Skene tells us that the name was applied anciently to the district on both sides of the Forth, extending on the south from the mouth of the Esk at Musselburgh to that of the Carron at Grangemouth, and on the north shore comprising the greater part of the modern county of Clackmannan. He does not offer, however, any explanation of the term, of which there are two notable instances—Clackmannan on the north and Slamannan on the south bank of the Forth, the former denoting the Stone or Stones and the latter the Hill or Moor of Mannan. A foolish story is told of King Robert the Bruce having left his glove (*manan*) on the stone, and thus given rise to the name, as signifying "the stone of the glove." Whatever opinion we may entertain regard-

[1] See p. 6.

ing the appellation, it is certain that the stone is of great and mysterious antiquity. Beside it stands a sort of bell-tower with a clock. Clackmannan is the old county town, and till a comparatively recent period the county courts used to be held here, though they and all the offices connected with them have now been transferred to Alloa. Clackmannan fair, though greatly diminished in importance, is still an annual gathering in the end of August. It was formally established by James V. in his minority, " with advise and consent of our derrest cousing and tutoure Johne, duke of Albanye, &c. ;" and this warrant was ratified by a royal charter in 1542. It proceeds on the preamble that there had been for some time a yearly concourse of merchants at Clackmannan, and the fair is appointed to be held on the Feast of St Bartholomew (24th August).

The old Tower of Clackmannan, in its park or chase at the top of the hill, forms a landmark for many miles · round, and is well deserving of a visit. There is ready access to the park by a gate at the head of the main street of the town, and entrance to the building itself may be obtained by applying to the custodian, who resides in one of the cottages near the gate. The Tower and adjoining estate are now the property of the Earl of Zetland, who has been at considerable expense in repairing and keeping in order this interesting relic of antiquity. It is a sort of double tower, is 79 feet high, and contains a number of apartments which are almost all accessible. Formerly there adjoined it a mansion, occupied by the later Lairds of Clackmannan, in which Mrs Catherine Bruce, widow of the last proprietor, Henry Bruce, received Robert Burns and his friend Dr Adair, on the occasion of a visit made by them here from Harviestoun, at the foot of the Ochils. The old lady died shortly afterwards in consequence of a fall, at the great age of ninety-five, and bequeathed to Lord Elgin, whom she considered as the proper head of the family, the great sword and helmet of King Robert the Bruce, which had been possessed by the members of her house as an heir-loom.

The precise relationship of the Lairds of Clackmannan to King Robert the Bruce is a matter of dubiety, though it has been surmised with some degree of probability that the first of them was the descendant of an illegitimate son of Edward Bruce, King Robert's brother. It is certain that a charter was granted by David II. (King Robert's son) to a Robert Bruce, of the lands of Clackmannan, in which he styles the recipient his "consanguineus," or cousin, whatever propinquity this may be supposed to denote. Old Mrs Bruce, indeed, had a much more exalted idea of the belongings of her progenitors. When asked whether her ancestors were descended from Robert the Bruce, she would reply, "No; the Bruces were descended from my family."

It is commonly stated that Clackmannan Tower was built by King Robert Bruce; and there can be little doubt of its having been erected at that period, and of both the king and his son having occasionally made it their residence. The surrounding lands were royal property, and the platform on which the castle stands is termed the King's Seat or King's Seat Hill. An extensive forest, known as the Forest of Clackmannan, stretched around, and many royal grants are in existence bestowing on Churchmen and others rights of pasturage of cattle and swine within its boundaries. In 1305, Edward I., then apparently master of Scotland, orders twenty oaks fit for timber to be given to the monastery of St Andrews from the forest of Clackmannan, to repair the priory houses. A large portion of the natural wood of which the ancient forest consisted was preserved till near the end of the last century, and a very small portion of it still subsists within the grounds of the Earl of Mar and Kellie at Alloa. The hamlet of Forest Mill, too, on the road to Dollar, with its adjoining tract of woodland, preserves the memory of the old forest of Clackmannan.

To visit Clackmannan we have diverged from the modern highway, and will therefore return to it, passing down the lane on the north side of the principal street near the clock tower and great stone. Having joined the road to Alloa at a distance from the latter of two miles, we continue downhill, and cross the Black Devon, which is here spanned by Mary Bridge, an older structure on the same site having been known as Queen Mary's Bridge. Ascending then a little in a northerly direction, we turn westwards at the new cemetery, and continuing for upwards of a mile close to and parallel with the Stirling and Dunfermline railway, we enter the east suburbs of Alloa. A little before coming to the town, on our left, within Alloa Park, on the summit of the rising ground called the Hawkhill, is a large standing-stone, having carved on it, on both sides, a simple cross. Near it a cist or stone coffin containing human bones was found.

Alloa (*Hotels:* The Crown and The Royal Oak—also The Victoria, near the railway station) is a pleasantly situated town on the north shore of the Forth, which here commences that singular course of windings· that render the passage by water to Stirling a voyage of nearly twenty miles, whilst by road the distance is only seven. The alluvial soil and carse-land included within those reaches is extremely fertile and valuable, giving rise to the old rhyme—

> "A crook o' the Forth
> Is worth an earldom o' the north."

The rocky ridge on which Clackmannan is built descends gradually in passing upwards from thence to Alloa, and at last comes to a termination near the harbour of that town, where it meets the alluvial ground of the Carse. On the termination of this rock the old tower of the Earls of Mar, and the old portion of Alloa, are built. The principal street of Alloa passes through the town nearly from east to west, sending forth numerous branch streets, of which those on the north side conduct to the neighbourhood of the railway station and the road to Tillicoultry and Dollar, whilst those on the south lead to the river, the ferry, and the harbour.

The town has a population of nearly 9000, and carries on an extensive trade in shipping, in woollen and worsted manufactures, and in the making of glass and brewing of ale. The Alloa breweries especially have long been famous, though the sweet ale for which they enjoyed a reputation throughout Scotland, is no longer made here, the public taste having come to evince a decided preference for "bitter beer." A railway bridge has recently been completed across the Forth, and a direct communication has thus been established by way of Larbert with Glasgow, without entailing on travellers the necessity of going round by Stirling. A ferry gives access to South Alloa, which is a busy and thriving, though not particularly attractive place. The Forth forms two islands or "inches" here—one opposite the town, called Alloa Inch, and the other a little farther up, entitled Tullibody Inch. Within the port of Alloa are included, on the north side of the river, the town itself, and the creeks of Kincardine, Kennet Pans, Clackmannan, Cambus, and Manor; and on the south, Airth, Dunmore or Elphinston, and Fallin, together with the shore of Stirling. New docks were formed a few years ago.

Round the old Tower of Alloa, erected previous to
1300, the town gradually grew up under the protection
and sovereignty of the lords of the territory. This seems
originally, like Clackmannan, to have been a royal
demesne, and in 1365 it was bestowed by David II. on
Lord Erskine, in exchange for the estate of Strathgartney
in Perthshire. A descendant of his claimed right to
the earldom of Mar, and was served heir to the title
in 1438. Robert Erskine, fourth Earl of Mar, of this
family, fell at the battle of Flodden; and his successor,
John, fifth Earl, became Regent of Scotland during the
minority of Queen Mary, and had the custody of the
person of his infant sovereign previous to her being
sent away to France. The son and successor of the last-
named Earl has attained still greater renown as Regent
Mar, and governor of James VI., who occasionally, while
a boy, it is said, resided in Alloa Tower, under the strict
discipline of George Buchanan, who spared not the rod,
and treated with scorn the remonstrances of the Regent's
wife, the Countess of Mar, on behalf of his royal pupil.

On 27th July 1566, shortly after the birth of James,
his mother, Queen Mary, whilst temporarily reconciled
to her husband, Lord Darnley, paid a visit to the Earl
of Mar at Alloa Tower, and remained there for two days.
Darnley was also there, but he made the journey to
Alloa by Stirling Bridge, whilst the Queen sailed up the
Forth under the conduct of Bothwell, as Lord High
Admiral of Scotland. On the 29th she returned to
Edinburgh, and on 1st August again made the voyage
to Alloa, and was joined there as before by her husband.
They spent other two days with Lord Mar, and on 4th
August the Queen again returned to Edinburgh. It
might also seem to have been as a souvenir of this visit
that the Mar family had long in their possession a por-
trait of the unfortunate Queen on copper, and believed,

on good grounds, to be a genuine likeness. In reality, however, it is said to have been given by Mary to one of her attendants at Fotheringay before her execution. It would appear that the elder brother of Charles I., who died prematurely — the gallant Prince Henry — spent several years of his childhood at Alloa Tower.

In 1670 a notice is recorded of the marriage, at her father's seat at Alloa, of Lady Barbara Erskine, daughter of the Earl of Mar, to the Marquis of Douglas, who proved in every respect a bad husband. The unfortunate lady had, in consequence of his irregularities and harsh treatment, to obtain from him a judicial separation or divorce.   She is the heroine of the well-known plaintive ballad, " Waly, waly."

Alloa Tower has a height of 89 feet, and its walls are 11 feet in thickness. It stands within the grounds of Alloa Park, on the east side of the town, and had formerly connected with it a more recent building, which was destroyed by fire in 1800. In this conflagration the portrait of Queen Mary perished. At a little distance is the modern mansion of Alloa Park, the residence of the Earl of Mar and Kellie, which was erected in 1838. The gardens adjoining were laid out by the celebrated John, Earl of Mar, who took the principal share in the Jacobite insurrection of 1715, and incurred thereby forfeiture of his title, which was only rescinded in 1824. He formed the gardens at Alloa House under the direction of Le Notre, the celebrated landscape-gardener of Louis XIV., and they were long the admiration of the country round for their beauty, though they had a rival in those of Culross Abbey, belonging to the Earl of Kincardine.

This Jacobite Earl of Mar had not only a turn for landscape-gardening, but a very decided talent for mechanics and engineering, which might have been much more profitably cultivated than the military proclivities which led their owner into so much trouble. He built John Street in Alloa, with its fine " Walk " and rows of lime-trees. He also constructed at the east end of the parish, and about two miles north from the town of Alloa, the reservoir known as Gartmorn Dam, which covers a space of 162 imperial acres. This was with the object of providing a supply of water for the collieries on his lordship's estate, and to effect this he caused a dam to be thrown across the Black Devon at the hamlet of Forest Mill, four miles north from Kincardine. From the river thus raised in level 16 feet, he conducted, by an aqueduct of four miles, in a westerly direction, the water into the great reservoir which he had prepared for its reception. It is perhaps the largest artificial lake in Scotland, and being bordered by the fine woodlands of Shaw Park, is by no means the least picturesque.

Lord Mar had also a share in the planning of the North and South Bridges, and laying out of the New Town of Edinburgh, and he is also said to have been the original projector of the Forth and Clyde Canal. He was twice married: first to Lady Mary Hay, daughter of the Earl of Kinnoull; and secondly, to Lady Frances Pierrepoint, sister of the celebrated Lady Mary Wortley Montagu, and daughter of Evelyn, Duke of Kingston. He followed the Pretender to Rome, and afterwards to Paris and Aix-la-Chapelle, where he died in 1732. He left a son, Thomas, Lord Erskine, who died without issue; and also a daughter, Lady Frances Erskine, who married her cousin, John Francis Erskine, eldest son of James Erskine, Lord Grange, younger brother of the attainted Earl. Most of the forfeited Mar estates had meanwhile been purchased by Lord Grange and another member of the family, and settled successively on Thomas, Lord Erskine, his sister Lady Frances, and their heirs. In consequence of this arrangement, the Alloa property remained vested in the Erskines, but the lands of Mar in Aberdeenshire had to be sold after the Rebellion.

John Francis Erskine, grandson of Lord Grange, became the representative of the Erskine family on the death of his father in 1785, and in 1824 he was restored by Act of Parliament to the dignity of Earl of Mar. He died in 1826, and was succeeded by his eldest son, John Thomas, who survived only for a short period, and died in 1828. His son and successor, John Francis, established in 1835 his right to the earldom of Kellie, in addition to that of Mar, and died in 1866 without issue. A younger brother of the last, Henry David Erskine, inherited as heir-male the Kellie peerage, and claimed that of Mar also, on the ground of the peerage having been reconstituted by Queen Mary in 1565, and made transmissible only to heirs-male. This position, however, was disputed by Mr John Francis Goodeve, son of Lady Frances Goodeve, sister of the late Earl, on the ground that the ancient earldom of Mar, which admitted of female succession, had never been abrogated, and remained unaffected by the subsequent creation of Queen Mary. A long and tedious lawsuit ensued, and the matter was ultimately referred to the Committee of Privileges of the House of Lords, who gave as their verdict that the peerage created by Queen Mary must be regarded as a new one; and as it only recognised heirs-male, the Earl of Kellie was the person to whom it rightfully belonged. Still Mr Goodeve was not satisfied, and persistently brought forward, at the election of Scottish peers to serve in the imperial Parliament, his claim to be admitted to vote as Earl of Mar under the original and ancient peerage. The matter has now been settled by a royal rescript and Act of Parliament, under which Mr Goodeve's claim to the earldom of Mar has been declared, under the ancient peerage, equally good with that of the Earl of Kellie under the patent of 1565. The former accordingly takes rank in the Scottish Peerage as Earl of Mar, whilst the latter bears the combined title of Earl of Mar and Kellie.   The present holder of the last is Walter Coningsby Erskine, whose father, Henry David Erskine, Earl of Kellie, died in 1872 during the progress of the lawsuit.

The parish church of Alloa is a handsome Gothic building erected in 1819, and the tower of an older church still stands in the churchyard.   There are also Free and U.P. churches.   An Episcopal chapel was built by the Earl of Mar and Kellie in 1869.   Among the public edifices may be mentioned the Municipal and County Buildings, the new Post-office adjoining the Crown Hotel, and the Museum of Natural History and Antiquities.   Around and in the suburbs of the town are many handsome villas—more especially the splendid mansion of J. T. Paton, Esq., at the western extremity of the town, on the Stirling road.

V.

ANOTHER WAY FROM DUNFERMLINE
TO ALLOA.

Road from Dunfermline to Carnock—Baldridge—Luscar—Village and church of Carnock—Their associations with Scottish ecclesiastical history—John Row and Thomas Gillespie—Sacramental occasions at Carnock—Road from Carnock to Clackmannan and Alloa.

IN proceeding from Dunfermline to Alloa by way of Carnock and Comrie village, we have to pursue some intricate windings through not very attractive suburbs; but having once got clear of the town, the road, though somewhat bleak and exposed, becomes sufficiently interesting. Dunfermline, as already explained, is built on both sides of a very picturesque and romantic glen, which the builders of Bridge and Chalmers Streets seem to have exercised all their powers to exclude from general knowledge and observation. Had such a laying-out of building-ground to be made at the present day, there is no doubt that a different procedure would be followed. Instead of constructing the houses so that only the back windows command a view of the glen, whilst from the street itself no general observer would ever divine that any such gorge existed, there would be a series of elegant terraces, " cliffs," " drives," and " views," which would have seized every picturesque " coign of vantage," and been eagerly bought up as feuing-ground by the well-to-do inhabitants of the place. As it is, it is for the most part only citizens of the humbler class who can contemplate from their dwellings the romantic braes and precipices of the Tower or Pittencrieff Glen. We shall get a few glimpses of it as we wend our way out of the town to Carnock.

There is a nook in the glen just behind the houses in Bruce Street—formerly known as the Collier Row—which deserves a visit, from the association which it is reported to bear with the sainted Queen Margaret, wife of Malcolm Canmore. At the bottom of a steep winding path which leads down from the hill above, and close to the water's edge, is a niche or cavern scooped out of the rock, which is said to have been an oratory to which the good queen was in the habit of retiring for secret prayer. Her husband Malcolm, it is added, had entertained some unworthy suspicions as to the real object of his wife's visits to this spot, but had them completely dispelled on following her thither and finding no companion with her in the shape either of angel or devil. This so-called oratory of Queen Margaret is reached through rather a tortuous series of narrow passages which lead from Bruce Street to the steep path just mentioned, and may remind one of the labyrinth of lanes in London leading from Smithfield by Half Moon Passage to Aldersgate Street. It is necessary to obtain the key of the door leading to the glen, and this may be procured from Mr George Robertson in Bridge Street, the Government custodian of Dunfermline Abbey.

Proceeding on our journey, we pass the entrance to Wooers Alley Cottage, romantically situated on the edge of the glen, and which deserves notice as the place where Sir Noel Paton, the distinguished artist, spent his youth. His father, Mr Joseph Paton, was a zealous antiquary, and had formed a most unique and interesting museum of antiquities, which, it is to be regretted, were dispersed after his death. The museum comprised relics of all kinds from different parts of Scotland, and used to be one of the leading objects of interest in the town.

About this same neighbourhood we are probably near the place where Sir Robert Sibbald, the historian of Fife, tells us that he had a narrow escape. He was journeying from the Duke of Perth's mansion of Drummond Castle to Dunfermline, and had, without knowing it, approached in the dark what he calls the precipice at the north-west extremity of the town. His horse, however, had been more observant, and by coming to a standstill saved his master's life. Passing " Buffie's Brae," and winding round by Provost Walls's grain and flour mills, we find ourselves first in the suburb of Baldridge Burn, and then in that of Rumbling Well, after which we reach that of Milesmark, where we are a mile from "the Cannon,"[1] and two and a half from Carnock. To the north of us, on our right, is the estate of Baldridge, now the property of the Wellwoods of Pitliver, but which in former days belonged to the Gedds, a zealous Jacobite family who took active part in the rebellions both of 1715 and 1745. Besides Baldridge they owned an estate near Burntisland. A boarding-school of high repute for young ladies used to be kept in Edinburgh by the Misses Gedd, members of this family. Another Miss Gedd, who married a Mr Buntine, a brewer in Dunfermline, died in 1820 at the age of ninety-five, and was well known to my mother, whom I have often heard speak of the old lady and her reminiscences of Prince Charlie and his times. One of these, I remember, regarded a relation of hers who had led down a dance with the Chevalier at Holyrood.

After passing through the village of Milesmark, and proceeding westwards about a mile, we see in front of us the steeple of Carnock church, an interesting object in the landscape, and on our right, within a mile of the village, the mansion and grounds of Luscar (Mrs Hastie). This formerly comprised East and West or Stobie's Luscar, so called from an Adam Stobie or Stobow, a zealous Covenanter, who owned it in the days of Charles II., and was captured here in a malt-kiln by Captain Creichton, as related in his Memoirs edited by Dean Swift. Stobow was conveyed to Edinburgh, brought before the Privy Council, and sentenced to the payment of a heavy fine and transportation beyond sea. He contrived, however, to be landed in England, and ultimately re-

---

[1] The distances from Dunfermline are reckoned from the corporation buildings at the head of the Kirkgate; and from a cannon being fixed in the pavement beside the old town-house, the popular expression regarding the distance of any place was that it was so many miles from "the Cannon." The phrase is still in common use.

turned to his native country, where he survived the Revolution, and died peacefully on his patrimonial estate
of Luscar in 1711 at the advanced age of ninety-one.
He lies buried in Carnock churchyard beside Row, the
historian of the Church, whose granddaughter he married. A daughter of Stobow married Andrew Rolland
of Gask, a descendant of whom became proprietor of the
whole estate of Luscar; and another descendant from
the same ancestor is now the wife of Principal Rainy,
one of the leaders of the Free Church.

Carnock is a small village, not unpicturesquely situated on the banks of the burn of the same name, which,
coming down from Luscar Dean, after a course of several
miles is joined first by the Comrie and then by the
Grange burns, and ultimately falls into the sea at Newmill Bridge under the designation of the Newmill or
Bluther burn. The country round, however, is rather
bleak and exposed, though in the southern portion of
the parish, about the village of Cairneyhill, which belongs
to Carnock, there is some good land. The present
church stands in the centre, and the old ruined church
with its churchyard at the north-west extremity, of the
village. I can remember the latter being used for public worship, and of the foundation-stone being laid of
the former, my father, if I mistake not, as an heritor in
an adjoining parish, performing the ceremony on that
occasion. I well remember the dinner which followed
in the schoolhouse, and though not admitted myself
to the feast, standing with the minister's son and other
boys outside and listening to the cheers and rattling
of glasses which followed the toasts. It was high time
that a new church should be built for Carnock, as the
old one was both one of the smallest and most uncomfortable in Scotland. It had existed from Roman
Catholic times, and been an appanage of the hospital of

Scotlandwell in Kinross-shire, and for some time after the Reformation it remained under the charge of the " parson " of that place, who seems to have allowed the little church of Carnock to go almost to ruin. On Sir George Bruce, the merchant prince of Culross, however, purchasing in 1602 the estate of Carnock from Lord Lindsay of the Byres, he " skleated " and otherwise repaired the church, which hitherto had only been covered with heather. The pulpit bears the date 1674, and the old church bell bore 1638, as does also the bridge over Carnock burn. There used to be, at a little distance from the church, an ancient cross, supported by six rounds of stone steps, and from these last, the cross itself having been apparently removed, at some distant epoch there sprang a venerable thorn-tree, which till at least the end of the last century continued to flourish vigorously, and was a favourite trysting-place for the inhabitants. Indeed the kirk-session seem to have deemed it necessary to interpose their authority to prevent the place in question being used as a Sunday lounge. The whole fabric was removed many years ago for the purpose of widening the road.

John Row, the historian of the Church, was appointed minister of Carnock in 1592, and continued in that capacity till his death in 1646. He was the son of John Row, minister successively of Kennoway and Perth, and Margaret Bethune, daughter of the Laird of Balfour, and was remarkable from childhood for his scholarly proclivities, having at a very early age been instructed in Hebrew by his father, who was a man of great learning. The elder Row seems to have been bred a lawyer, and was sent on the eve of the Reformation on a mission to Rome, from which in 1558 he returned by way of Eyemouth with important powers conferred on him by the Pope for the purpose of averting the threatened changes in the Church. But he proved, to use the expression of his grandson, "corbie messenger" to his Holiness, and was ere long led to renounce the ancient faith. One of the main causes of his conversion was, it is alleged, an interview with the Laird of Cleish, who had been the chief instrument in detecting the fraud of the priests of the chapel of Loretto at Musselburgh, regarding a man whose eyesight was said to have been miraculously restored.[1] He became a zealous and active Reformer, and died in 1580.

John Row, the younger, when his father died, was only twelve years old, and he was indebted for his upbringing to the care of his uncle, the Laird of Balfour, to whose children he acted for a while as tutor. He studied for the ministry at the recently erected University of Edinburgh, and in 1592, on the application of Lord Lindsay of the Byres, then proprietor of Carnock, he was presented to that parish by the Presbytery of Dunfermline. The parish church, as already mentioned, was at that time in a state of great dilapidation through the supine neglect of the minister of Scotlandwell, who owned the tithes. The year after Row's admission to the living, the roof fell in one Sunday at eleven o'clock in the forenoon, a time when in ordinary circumstances the congregation would all have been assembled inside. It happened providentially on this occasion that there had been a surcease of ordinances, in consequence of the minister suffering from a tertian fever which detained him at Aberdour for some months on a bed of sickness. In consequence of this disaster the parson of Scotlandwell had to renew the roof, and the whole building was thoroughly repaired nine years afterwards by Sir George Bruce. It had another new roof placed on it by Sir George's son in 1641.

[1] See p. 62.

The stipend of Carnock, which to this day is very small, was in Row's time so miserably inadequate that it was a constant wonder to his friends how he managed to subsist at all. He was, however, a man not only of the most ardent piety, but of the most unselfish and philosophical disposition regarding worldly matters. Though he received various offers for bettering himself by removal to another charge, he steadily resisted all inducements to withdraw himself from the little flock whose spiritual oversight he had undertaken. Mr Colville, the minister of Culross, offered to exchange charges with him, on the ground of the number of communicants in that parish being so great, though the stipend was much better than that of Carnock. Row declined this as he had done other offers of translation.

He was not destined, however, to pass a life of obscurity or quiet, for such were the fervour and activity of his ministrations, that under his superintendence the communion occasions at Carnock acquired a celebrity which they retained for more than 200 years afterwards. Persons flocked to them from all parts of the country, and we are told that these included many of the nobility and gentry. Row did not himself, it seems, take a prominent part in the services, but he endeavoured to assemble all the most famous preachers that could be procured. And after the establishment of Episcopacy in the first years of the seventeenth century, when many ministers who refused to comply with the new order of things were suspended from their charges or otherwise incapacitated, such recusants were heartily welcome to and heard with eagerness at the Carnock communions.

Row was indeed a strenuous opponent of Episcopacy, and had his lot been cast in other places, his resistance might have involved him in severe penalties, if they had not brought about actual deposition. But he was a great favourite with Sir George Bruce, who used his influence on Row's behalf with the then Archbishop of St Andrews, and thereby prevented any strong measures being taken against the minister of Carnock, though for two years during the predominance of Episcopacy his ministrations were interdicted except within his own parish. It is even said the Archbishop was bribed by Sir George, with the annual despatch to St Andrews of a shipload of coals from Culross, to wink at Row's shortcomings.

After Jenny Geddes had thrown her stool, and the uproar thus inaugurated in the High Church of Edinburgh had spread over the kingdom, leading to the dethronement of the bishops and re-establishment of Presbytery, a sort of Indian summer gilded the last days of John Row. He was summoned to Edinburgh to preach in the Greyfriars' Church, and he took a prominent part in the famous Glasgow Assembly of 1638. During the years that immediately followed he seems to have worked with unabated zeal; but he was now an old man, and in January 1646 he died after a few days' illness. Shortly after being placed in Carnock he had married Grizel Ferguson, daughter of the celebrated minister of Dunfermline of that name, and who is said to have made him an excellent wife. They had four sons, all of whom studied for the ministry—the eldest, John, becoming in 1652 Principal of King's College, though shortly after the Restoration he was deposed. Another, Robert, became minister of Abercorn; a third, James, was minister of Monzievaird and Strowan; and a fourth, William, became minister of Ceres, and added a "Coronis" or continuation to the 'History of the Church' which his father left in MSS., and which was published along with it by the Wodrow Society.

Row lies buried at the east end of the old church of

Carnock, and beside him lie his granddaughter and her husband Adam Stobow of Luscar, the celebrated Covenanter already mentioned. After his death, George Belfrage was appointed to the church of Carnock, but was deposed after the Restoration by Archbishop Sharp. Carnock, though an insignificant place in itself, figures prominently in the history of the Church of Scotland. There is first her association with John Row. Then in 1699 the ministry in her pulpit fell to James Hogg, so famous for his vindication of the principles laid down in 'The Marrow of Modern Divinity,' and the part taken by him in the "Marrow" controversy. He was minister of Carnock from 1699 to 1736.

But the most noteworthy association connected with Carnock is that of the ministry of the Rev. Thomas Gillespie, who was deposed by the General Assembly of the Church of Scotland, and became in consequence the founder of the Relief Church, long an influential body, which about forty years ago united with the majority of the Burghers and Antiburghers to form the United Presbyterian denomination. Mr Gillespie was presented to the church of Carnock by Colonel Erskine in 1741. He had long been a zealous member of the Evangelical party in the Church, having in early life known intimately Boston of Ettrick, and afterwards attending the academy at Northampton, presided over by Dr Doddridge, with whom he became a great favourite. In after-days he was a frequent correspondent with Dr Doddridge, and also with President Edwards of New England.

After having officiated in Carnock for about eleven years, a great commotion arose in the Dunfermline Presbytery, to which Carnock belongs, regarding the settlement of Mr Richardson as minister of Inverkeithing. Mr Richardson had been nominated by the patron, and found satisfactory by the Presbytery as far as morals and competency were concerned, but a strong aversion was displayed towards him by the majority of the parishioners over whom it was proposed that he should minister in spiritual things. So strong was this feeling that the Presbytery refused at first to give effect to the presentation of Mr Richardson ; but the matter having been brought before the General Assembly, the subordinate judicature was peremptorily ordered to proceed forthwith with the induction and ordination of the patron's nominee. Six members of the Presbytery, including Mr Gillespie, gave in a memorial or representation to the Assembly, stating their conviction of the impropriety of forcing Mr Richardson on a recusant congregation, and that it was not merely contrary to their consciences, but, as they deemed it, contrary to the fundamental laws of the Church to proceed with the induction in such circumstances. The Moderate party were now in the majority in the Church, and high-handed measures had come to be regarded by them as necessary for maintaining the position which they had taken up, of the supreme authority of the Church courts, as distinguished from lay opinion and control. It is much to be regretted by every lover of the Church of Scotland that they were ever tempted to assert such an authority in the way which they followed on the present occasion. By a majority of forty-six it was carried in the Assembly that to punish the contumacy of the Dunfermline Presbytery in delaying to obey the orders of the supreme ecclesiastical court one of them should be deposed. The six members were each called successively to the bar of the Assembly and asked if he adhered to the memorial which he had presented. Five of them simply declared their adherence to it ; but Mr Gillespie, besides doing so, presented an additional paper which he read as reaffirming his views on the subject. The vote was then taken as to whether he should be made the scapegoat. Only fifty-six members voted, and of these fifty-two voted for deposition. The whole affair seems to have been carried through with scandalous haste. The sentence of deposition was pronounced on a Saturday, and the same day Gillespie returned to Carnock. It is said that it was late at night when he returned, and his wife not expecting him had retired to bed. When he knocked at the door for admittance she rose, went to the window, and desired to know who it was that was seeking entrance at so unseasonable an hour. "THE DEPOSED MINISTER OF CARNOCK," was the reply.

Next morning Mr Gillespie would not allow the church bell to be rung ; but assembling the people in the church-yard, he explained to them briefly, without any censorious comment, what had happened, and then proceeded to the ordinary Sunday services. He continued through-out the ensuing summer to hold these meetings in the churchyard, which were resorted to by crowds of people, more especially from Dunfermline ; but he had at last to cease holding them there, and take up his position on the public highway. Ultimately a church was built for him in Dunfermline, and in it he continued to minister till his death to a large congregation. Such was the origin of the Relief Church. Gillespie, notwithstanding the treatment he had received from the highest ecclesiastical judicature, seems nevertheless to have remained an ardent lover of the Church of Scotland, and is said to have expressed on his deathbed a wish that his con-gregation should return to the fold of the Establishment. Dr Erskine, the Evangelical leader in the Church, repeats this statement in his preface to Gillespie's 'Treatise on Temptation'; and although Dr Lindsay, in his 'Life of Gillespie,' disputes its correctness, there seems no reason to doubt its substantial truth. Gillespie died on 19th

January 1774, and was buried in the Old Abbey Church of Dunfermline—in the north wall of which, a few years ago, a slab of marble was fixed in memory of him, though its admission was objected to for some time by the officers of State, on account of its containing a reference to Gillespie's deposition for "refusing to take part in a forced presentation to Inverkeithing."

The old house of Newbigging, situated on the rising ground to the right a little before entering the village of Carnock, used to be the summer residence for many years of John Erskine of Carnock, son of Colonel Erskine, and Professor of Scots Law in the University of Edinburgh. Here it is said that his celebrated ' Institutes of the Law of Scotland,' long a text-book for students of Scots law, were compiled. His son, Dr Erskine, minister of the Greyfriars', succeeded him in the Carnock estate ; and Robert Gillespie, Thomas's brother, was his factor. A daughter of Dr Erskine married Mr Steuart of Dunearn, and the property thus passed to her son, by whom, about thirty years ago, it was sold to Mr Hutchison of Kirkcaldy. It was afterwards disposed of by the latter to Mr Hastie, M.P., and it is now the property of his widow, Mrs Hastie.

The sacramental occasions at Carnock, the celebrity of which seems to have commenced under the ministry of John Row, continued long afterwards to attract crowds of people from all parts of the country. The *tent*, a sort of covered pulpit or platform, was erected in the glen or hollow below the bridge, and the audience stood or reclined on the adjoining grassy slopes in the open air. Here a succession of preachers held forth ; whilst the church was reserved for the rites of the Holy Communion, which was administered to the recipients in a series of services or tables, which were protracted to a late hour in the afternoon. Viewed merely from an æsthetic standpoint, these gatherings must have been very picturesque; but attracting as they did a host of idlers and excursionists from Dunfermline and the country round, who came merely for an outing, they were inevitably accompanied with a large amount of licence and disorder—such as Burns has very graphically described in his "Holy Fair." The story, often repeated, is, I believe, quite authentic, that when servants took employment in a household in this part of the country, they were accustomed to stipulate that they should have liberty to attend *either* Torryburn Fair *or* Carnock Sacrament—each of these occasions presenting apparently an equal amount of attraction. The Carnock gatherings had at last become such a scandal that, on the appointment of the Rev. William Gilston to the ministry of the parish in 1827, he resolved to have these village saturnalia abolished; and this, with the concurrence of the heritors and kirk-session, he effected. The tent preachings were given up, and a great and lasting improvement took place as regards order and propriety. It is said that on the first Communion which took place under the new arrangement, the receipts of the principal inn or public-house in Carnock, which on such occasions had generally averaged five pounds, now barely amounted to half-a-crown.

About a mile and a half to the west of Carnock, the traveller arrives at Comrie village, which has in great measure been created by the establishment in this neighbourhood of the Forth Ironworks, which, after promising for a time to change the whole aspect of the country as regards industrial activity, at last collapsed into desolation. Several mining villages which were erected in connection with them, are now either wholly obliterated, or present a still drearier appearance in the form of unroofed and dismantled cottages. Comrie village still remains, but all its bustle and activity have vanished.

The remainder of the road to Garterry Toll is a very lonely one, and it is quite possible that the wayfarer may traverse it without meeting a single person—though the road is both wide and kept in excellent order. It belongs wholly to the detached portion of Perthshire which comprises the parishes of Culross and Tulliallan, and is separated from the larger division of the county by Saline and Clackmannan. Most of the present road from Comrie village belongs to Culross parish, the greater part of which, from its northern boundary, lies extended to the right and left of the spectator after he has emerged from the Comrie woods, a little beyond the road which leads down to the town of Culross, about three miles distant, by East Grange station and the hamlet of Shiresmill. The last-named place, though only consisting of a mill, a smithy, and two or three houses, deserves some notice as the birthplace of Robert Pont, a celebrated minister of the Church of Scotland immediately subsequent to the Reformation. He became "commissioner of Moray," an office which seems to have resembled that of an ecclesiastical superintendent or bishop; and he also acted for a time as one of the senators of the College of Justice. He officiated latterly as minister of St Cuthbert's Church, Edinburgh. An interesting circumstance recorded of him is his appointment as reviser of the new metrical version of the Psalms, and he also compiled the first Presbyterian catechism. He married Catherine Masterton of East Grange, in Culross parish; and a daughter of theirs became the wife of Adam Blackadder, grandfather of the celebrated John Blackadder of Troqueer, the Covenanting minister. In 1599 he published at Edinburgh a curious little volume entitled 'A Newe Treatise of the righte reckoning of Yeares and Ages of the World,' and dedicated to Alexander Seton, then President of the Court of Session, and afterwards first Earl of Dunfermline. Pont was the first to congratulate James VI. on his accession to the English throne. He died in 1606, at the age of eighty-one. He had a son, Timothy, a distinguished mathematician and geographer, who became minister of Dunnet.

There is now a fine open country before the traveller, with the rising ground on the right crested by the Dow Craig and the pine-woods of Brankston Grange —standing out from which, on its platform of green-sward, is the mansion of that designation on the estate of West Grange (John J. Dalgleish, Esq.). Proceeding downhill, through a pretty bit of woodland, Bogside station, on the Stirling and Dunfermline railway, is passed. Enclosed within a wood at a little distance from the road, on the south side, is a tolerably complete British camp. On the opposite side to the north, at the western extremity of the pine-woods, will be seen the Hartshaw Mill, now the property of Lord Abercromby, and formerly that of the Stewarts of Rosyth, who were saddled, during the civil wars of the seventeenth century, for their Royalist proclivities, with the burden of supplying timber from their lands of Hartshaw for the rebuilding of the houses in Dollar and Muckhart parishes which had been destroyed by Montrose's army. An ancient tower, similar to those at Clackmannan and Sauchie, existed here at one time, but in the beginning of the last century was demolished, like " Arthur's Oon," to build the mill and its dam-dyke. On the rising ground a little farther to the west is seen the mansion of Brucefield—once a stately house, and the residence for a long time of the gallant Sir Ralph Abercromby, the hero of Alexandria, but now very much dilapidated and almost unoccupied. There are some fine old trees about it, and the grounds form occasionally the resort of a picnic party from Kincardine or Alloa.

From Bogside station (8 miles from Dunfermline and 6 from Alloa) there is a long hill to climb, but after reaching the top there is a very pleasant bit of breezy upland, with almost a mountain flavour about it, and at one point a magnificent view of the Forth and its banks up to Stirling Castle and Ben Lomond. Clackmannan with its tower and church appear in the middle distance, whilst on the right hand the Ochils, with their verdant sides and rounded summits, bound the northern prospect from earth to sky. Descending afterwards a long hill, we reach the old turnpike of Garterry, with the cross-roads to Kincardine and Dollar; and nearly half a mile farther the village of Kennet, from which, as already detailed, the distance to Alloa by the north outskirt of Clackmannan is about 3½ miles. By taking the route that we have just traversed, the distance of Alloa from Dunfermline is shortened by 2 miles, the amount being only 14 miles in all.

The railway between Dunfermline and Alloa is sufficiently direct, but passes through the bleakest and most uninteresting part of the country, having been originally laid down thus in the expectation of receiving an immense amount of traffic from the then newly started Forth Ironworks on the Oakley and Blair estates. It does not pass by a single village or even hamlet between Dunfermline and Alloa, for the town of Kincardine is more than three miles distant from the so-called Kincardine station, and that of Clackmannan is at least a mile from the foot of the ridge on which the town stands. Nor is there any large population scattered through the country adjoining the line, which, on the contrary, rarely presents to the passenger the view even of a farmhouse, and between Bogside and Clackmannan passes through a tract of peat-moss and desolate woodland. To complete the *fiasco*, the Forth Ironworks, for the accommodation of which the convenience of the inhabitants of the villages and populous district on the shores of the Forth was set aside, have long since not merely been closed, but the buildings themselves, which with their furnaces used to form so prominent an object at Oakley station, have now been almost entirely demolished, and nothing but heaps of rubbish remains to tell of their site. Altogether, though the route is certainly the most direct that could have been taken, there are few lines of railway in Scotland on which the traveller will find so little either to attract or interest him as on this route. Speed is, of course, a matter of paramount importance in these days; but the traveller who wishes to receive some pleasure, and retain some remembrance of what he has seen, will be infinitely more gratified in both of these respects by walking or driving along the road, either by the north or south, from Dunfermline to Alloa.

VI.

OTHER EXCURSIONS FROM DUNFERMLINE.

Road from Dunfermline to Rumbling Bridge—Village and parish of Saline—Road from Dunfermline to Queensferry—St Leonard's Hospital — Pitreavie and the Wardlaw family—Broomhall and Pitliver.

THE country between Dunfermline and Alloa has now been surveyed in so far as it borders the principal lines of communication between these places. I shall here take occasion to describe several localities which could not conveniently have been introduced there, and require to be noticed in completing the picture of the district.

A favourite excursion for Dunfermline people is to the Rumbling Bridge—a distance of 10½ miles. Indeed it is the great excursion to which every " citizen " deems it incumbent on him to treat any friend who may be paying him a visit. In themselves, the place and its surroundings lie for the present beyond my scope, but will be detailed in a succeeding chapter, when I come to notice the vale of the Devon. The road leading to them, however, belongs, for the greater part, to the region of Dunfermline, and as such may be here detailed. The direct way is to the north of the town, by the Wellwood colliery, to Dunduff and Red Craigs, thence by the Outh, Hillside, and Meadowhead, to Powmill, and so to the Rumbling Bridge. Occasionally the jaunt will be continued along the highway to Crieff through the Yetts of Muckhart to Glen Devon, a farther journey of five miles.

The road from Dunfermline is almost throughout of a wild and mountain character, being all uphill, till it reaches a point behind the house of Hillside (Alexander Colville, Esq.), which is situated at an elevation of nearly 800 feet, and is almost the highest residence in Fife. About two miles from the town, at Colton (John Brown, Esq.), a road branches off to the left, leading by Craigluscar and the back of Luscar House to Carnock and Saline ; whilst a mile farther on, another to the right conducts by Balmule and Gask to Oakfield and the Great North Road. At Gask also, the old road to Kinross, already referred to, branches off to the north across the hill by Loch Glow. The mansion of Balmule (James Alexander, Esq.) deserves notice as the ancient residence of the Wardlaws, who seem to have retired here after disposing of Pitreavie to the first Earl of Rosebery. It was here that Lady Wardlaw (*née* Miss Halkett of Pitfirrane) lived, and here probably she composed the famous ballad of " Hardyknute."

At Red Craigs the highway to the Rumbling Bridge and Crieff is crossed by the road leading from the border of Clackmannanshire through Saline to Oakfield. We here skirt the eastern shoulder of the Saline hills, and continuing to ascend by the Outh farm, reach our highest point behind Hillside, from which we descend by a long winding road to the valley, which extends along the north side of the Cleish hills for about six miles, from Blairadam to Powmill. The highway leading through it from the Great North Road joins the road from Dunfermline to the Rumbling Bridge at the farm of Meadowhead, at a point where the county of Kinross meets that of Fife. It is the readiest way of reaching the town of Kinross from Carnock and Saline, passing the mansions of Morland and Hardiston, with their hazel copses on the hillsides behind, and then proceeding by Cleish Castle through the village of Cleish, a little beyond which a road turns off to the north to Kinross. On the north side of the valley are the heights of Aldie, extending eastwards to Powmill, which will be more properly treated of in connection with the Rumbling Bridge. Retracing our steps now up the hill, we shall turn off at the old toll-house at Hillend into the road, which will conduct us, after a journey of nearly three miles, to the village of Saline, crossing the Black Devon, and passing the mansions of Grey Craigs and Balgonar.

Saline (6 miles from Dunfermline, and $2\frac{1}{4}$ from Oakley station on the Stirling and Dunfermline railway) is a very clean and prettily situated village lying in a hollow at the western extremity of the Saline hills. It has been termed "the Paradise of Fife"; but though a very nice-looking place, it can scarcely be entitled to this epithet, seeing that it lies at a considerable height above sea-level, that during winter it is a cold and remote locality, and that the harvest here is generally a fortnight or three weeks behind that of the districts on the shores of the Forth. There are, however, many pleasant walks about it, and the views of the Ochils and the country extending westwards to Stirling and Ben Lomond are very fine. The land in the parish is subdivided among a number of proprietors, the chief of which in ancient times were the Earls of Mar, who had their seat at Alloa, and the Earls of Argyll, who had theirs at Castle Campbell. Neither of these own any property here at the present day.

The Saline hills extend from west to east, as a short detached range, fronting and parallel with the Ochils. They attain their highest point in Knockhill (1189) at their eastern extremity, whilst Saline Hill has an elevation of 1176. The latter commands a beautiful and extensive view of the valley of the Forth from Ben Lomond to the German Ocean, and on a clear day the summit of Goatfell, in Arran, can be discerned across the isthmus that separates the estuaries of the Forth and Clyde. The hills are covered to their summit with verdant turf, and are separated from the parallel Cleish range to the north by a valley through which flows the Black or South Devon. This has its source here, and maintains an east-south-east course through the parish of Saline, then enters Clackmannanshire, passes the hamlet of Forest Mill, and then flowing through a romantic dell, enters the domain of Alloa Park at Mary Bridge, near the town of Clackmannan, and falls into the Forth a little below Alloa.

As regards antiquities, Saline has not much to present.

Into the march fence which crests the ridge of the hill behind Bandrum House, there are built two standing-stones, but nothing whatever can be averred regarding their history. On the eminence above the picturesque gorge of Saline Dean, at the south-west extremity of Saline Hill, are the ruins of Killernie Castle, which belongs, with the neighbouring property, to Mr Aytoun of Inchdairnie. In former days, it seems to have been possessed by the Scotts of Balwearie, one of whom was Sir Michael Scott, the renowned knight and wizard. Indeed Killernie Castle used to be known also as the Castle of Balwearie. The ruins now consist only of the fragments of two towers, of which the southern is said to be the more recent, and to have borne the date of 1592. There used to be connected with it a large vaulted apart-ment, which has now disappeared. A strange legend is recorded of this part of the building regarding Lady Scott having commissioned a mason to erect it for her as a summer-house. She refused to pay the stipulated cost, and the disappointed artist revenged himself by murdering her and her child. He was punished for the crime by being shut up in the tower, where he starved to death, having previously been reduced to feed on his own flesh, like another Count Ugolino and his sons. This is one of the many places where the famous ballad of "Lamikin," which treats of this episode, has been local-ised, and a version of it used to be current in the parish.

The first minister appointed to Saline after the Refor-mation seems to have been Peter Blackwood, inducted in 1567. He had also under his charge the parishes of Auchtertool, Dalgety, and Aberdour. A James Black-wood, "Reader in Saline," is also mentioned as incur-ring the censure and prosecution of the ecclesiastical authorities for celebrating the marriage of the commen-dator of Dunfermline, residing outside of the parish, without requiring a certificate from the minister of the place to which he belonged.

Saline is 7 ¼ miles from Oakfield on the Great North Road, and about 3½ from the old Redcraigs Toll on the road from Dunfermline to the Rumbling Bridge. The highway from Oakfield, which crosses the latter road at Redcraigs, is the great artery of communication of this part of the country from east to west, and after passing through Saline and approaching the Black Devon, it takes a bend to the north-west, and joins at the old Ramshorn Inn the road which leads from Powmill to Alloa through the village of Blairingone. Another continuation of the west road from Saline, though hardly passable in the latter part of its course for carriages, leads to the hamlet of Forest Mill on the Black Devon, through which the main highway passes from Kincardine to Dollar. With the south, Saline communicates by two roads, one passing Upper Kinnedder, at the east extremity of the village, and going over Bandrum Hill towards Carnock and Dunfermline — the other branching off at the west end, near the church, and joining at Comrie village the north road from Dunfermline to Alloa.

A walk or drive of manageable compass from Dunfermline is to go south as far as the old toll-house at St Margaret's Hope, on the Queensferry road, then turning westwards along the shore and leaving Rosyth Castle on the left, to proceed to the entrance-lodge to Broomhall, and taking the road there on the right, to return to town by Leckerston, Ladysmill, and Broad Street, Netherton. In taking this way the traveller will cross, at the lower extremity of the town, the Spital or Lyne burn, which forms its southern boundary. It derives the former appellation for this part of its course from the fact of an hospital having formerly existed in this neighbourhood, dedicated to St Leonard, and which still exists as a charity, though the building connected with it has long since disappeared. The name of the original founder is not known, but the account-books date from. 1594. The revenues are derived from sixty-four acres of land, lying in the immediate vicinity, and they are employed in the maintenance of eight widows, the selection of whom rests with the Marquis of Tweeddale, who still retains certain privileges connected with Dunfermline, in virtue of his representing the ancient lords of the regality. According to the original terms of the foundation, each widow was to have a chamber in the hospital, with a small garden; four bolls of meal, four bolls of malt, eight loads of coal, fourteen loads of turf, eight lippies of fine wheat, and eight lippies of groats yearly, whilst some were to receive in addition two shillings annually for pin-money.

The ascent from the bridge on the farther side of the Spital burn is called Hospital or St Leonard's Hill. On the left hand, after crossing it, are the St Leonard's Works (Erskine Beveridge & Co.), for the manufacture of damask and table-linen, and the largest factory of the kind in Dunfermline. On the summit of the rising ground are, on the right, the house and grounds of St Leonard's Hill (Erskine Beveridge, Esq.), both commanding a wide and extensive view, and forming a conspicuous object from all parts of the neighbourhood.

About 2½ miles from Dunfermline, a short distance after passing St Margaret's Stone, already referred to, is on the left-hand side of the road the lodge of the avenue leading to the house of Pitreavie, the residence of Henry Beveridge, Esq., who has recently become the proprietor of the ancient domain of the Wardlaws. As stated previously, this family owned at one time nearly the whole country between Dunfermline and Torryburn. In the 14th century Pitreavie appears to have belonged to Lady Christian Bruce, sister of King Robert, and it also seems at one time to have been incorporated with the barony of Rosyth. It also became attached to a chaplainry in the church of St Giles of Edinburgh, the incumbent of which, with the consent of the magistrates, made it over to a relation. The first Wardlaw mentioned in connection with it is a Sir Cuthbert Wardlaw, knight, who was the second son of Sir Andrew Wardlaw of Torrie, and besides Pitreavie was proprietor of Balmule, to the north of Dunfermline. His eldest son Henry, who inherited both of these properties, became in the reign of James VI. chamberlain to his queen, Anne of Denmark, and was made a knight by her husband. His eldest son Henry inherited Pitreavie, and had conferred on him by Charles I. the dignity of baronet in 1631, whilst his second son William succeeded to Balmule. Sir Henry, the first baronet, died in 1653—according to Lamont's account, "suddenlie, and, as it was said by some, the last word he spake was ane oath." It was popularly said of him that he had brought down a judgment on his family by authorising a truculent act against the Highlanders who fought for the royal cause at the battle of Inverkeithing. The engagement took place in the valley fronting Pitreavie House, and was at its hottest almost below the walls of the mansion. The Highlanders ensconced themselves there, but received no support from the inmates, who destroyed many of them by hurling down great stones from the battlements. It was remarked that after this the Wardlaw family declined and disappeared " like snaw aff a dyke."

Notwithstanding this ill-omened procedure, the Wardlaws still held Pitreavie for two generations, a second

Sir Henry succeeded his father in 1653, and he again was followed by a third Sir Henry Wardlaw, Baronet, of Pitreavie, who married in 1696 Elizabeth, second daughter of Sir Charles Halkett, first baronet of Pitfirrane. As already mentioned, she was the discoverer or author (for the matter has never been very satisfactorily cleared up) of the ballad of "Hardyknute," and as she is generally spoken of as Lady Wardlaw of Balmule, it would seem that she and her husband had retired thither shortly after their marriage. Sir Henry had inherited Balmule along with Pitreavie, but the latter was sold by him in the beginning of the last century to the first Earl of Rosebery, who retained it only for a short time, and then disposed of it to Sir Peter Blackwood, Lord Provost of Edinburgh. In the hands of the Blackwood family it remained for upwards of 150 years, till it was recently purchased by Mr Beveridge from Miss Madox Blackwood.

The old house of Pitreavie seems to have been built in the early part of the seventeenth century, but had been subjected at different times to various alterations. There now only remain of it the north and west walls, which have been retained in the new mansion erected on the site of the old one. The ancient style, however, has been preserved throughout, and the additions made harmonise very satisfactorily with the reminiscences of the older building. The latter was honoured by the attendance of a ghost, whose special habitat was a small weird-looking chamber in the uppermost storey on the north side of the house. I never could learn what appearance the spirit was supposed to assume; but so fixed and persistent was the belief in it, that not many years ago, when the house was empty, and a number of harvest labourers were bivouacked there, nothing could induce them to do otherwise than congregate together in one large room. A similar visitant was believed formerly to haunt Otterston, but in this case it took the form of a lady with a child in her arms—the victim of misplaced affection.

On the high ground to the east of Pitreavie, and included in the estate, is the village of Masterton, which is said to have been so called originally from the circumstance of an ancient proprietor of the lands here having been the master-architect of Dunfermline Abbey. In the year 1675, Sir Henry Wardlaw, the second baronet, founded an hospital here of a similar character to that of St Leonard's, near Dunfermline, but making provision only for four widows. The charity still subsists, and the patronage, which was originally vested in the proprietor of the Pitreavie estate, was retained by Miss Blackwood when she sold the property to Mr Beveridge.

Continuing along the Queensferry road for about a mile, we reach the very steep ascent of Castlelandhill, at the summit of which a road branches off to Inverkeithing. The descent on the other side is almost equally steep, and after crossing the level ground at the bottom, we reach the old Ferry toll, where a highway branches off to the west and traverses the district lying on the sea-coast between North Queensferry and Torryburn. It is the same point at which, in coming from the former place, we turned round towards Inverkeithing and had the distant view of Rosyth Castle. Proceeding now in an opposite direction, we pass on the slope of the hill to our right the house of Castlelandhill occupied by Mr Sheriff Gillespie ; and then, skirting the seashore and ascending a hill, the farm of Orchardhead and the road leading down to Rosyth Castle are reached. There is now a fertile but very open and treeless country to be crossed before reaching the well-wooded park of Broomhall, the residence of the Earl of Elgin, beneath which, on the seashore, are the villages of Limekilns and Charlestown, both of them built on his lordship's estate. The former, as its name imports, has long been noted in connection with the limeworks in the vicinity, but the latter dates only from the middle of the last century, when new lime-quarries were opened on the estate of Broomhall, and an immense industry developed under the auspices of Charles, Earl of Elgin, father of the celebrated ambassador to Turkey, and grandfather of the late Governor-General of India. The village, situated on a sort of plateau above the harbour, is a model for neatness and general amenity, and the port of Charlestown is both a large emporium of merchandise, and supports an extensive export traffic of coal, lime, and ironstone. Formerly, when the Stirling steamers touched at the pier, there used to be a tramway for passengers to Dunfermline, but this has long been converted into a mineral railway. No fewer than three coaches, however, run every week-day between Limekilns and Dunfermline.

The present house of Broomhall is a comparatively modern mansion, of the early part of the present century. The estate originally belonged to the great Sir George Bruce of Carnock, and was bequeathed by him to his second son Robert, who became afterwards one of the judges of the Court of Session, under the title of Lord Broomhall. He was succeeded by his son Alexander, who was first made a knight, and afterwards successfully contested with his kinswoman, Lady Mary Cochrane, the claim to the Kincardine peerage. His grandson Charles, the originator of the village of Charlestown and its limeworks, succeeded, in addition, in 1747, to the title of Earl of Elgin on the death of his kinsman, the great-grandson of the first Earl, who was the younger son of the first Lord Kinloss, elder brother of Sir George Bruce.

Nearly opposite to Broomhall Lodge, a road leads northward to Dunfermline, by Leckerston farm and Ladysmill. Near the latter place, just before turning round into the Netherton, there stands on the right-hand side of the road a singular-looking detached mound on which one or two Scotch firs are growing. The legend regarding this is, that it is composed of sand brought from the seashore in former days by individuals who had this fatigue imposed on them by their confessors as a penance. Hence it goes by the name of " Perdieu," or " Penance Mount."

Continuing westwards along the Queensferry road from Broomhall, the traveller will pass on his right first a road leading to the village of Crossford (through which he has already journeyed on his way from Dunfermline to Torryburn), and afterwards another which conducts by Mid-Mill up the Lyne burn to the mansion of Pitliver, a fine specimen of an old Scottish manor-house. In former days it belonged successively to the families of the Dempsters and the Lindsays, and in the last century was acquired by the Wellwoods of Garvock, a family that had long been settled in the neighbourhood of Dunfermline. It has been asserted that they are descended from a Danish gentleman named Velvod, who came over to Scotland in the train of Queen Anne, wife of James VI. But no evidence can be produced in support of this averment, and there can be no doubt whatever that the lands of Touch, near Dunfermline, belonged to the Wellwoods at a period anterior to the arrival of Anne of Denmark, whilst various other instances of the name as a local one might be adduced. Among others, the burgh records show that in 1499 there was a certain John de Walwode, who held the office of sergeant of the regality of Dunfermline. The estate of Pitliver is now possessed by Mr Maconochie

Wellwood, a grandson of the second Lord Meadowbank, whose mother was a Miss Wellwood of Garvock.

A little beyond the entrance of the road leading up to Pitliver, the ancient hamlet of Fiddy's or Feddy's Mill is reached, and the parish of Torryburn entered. From this point it is about four miles to the village, which may be reached either by way of Gillanderston Toll, or by the road which branches off near Crombie farm, and leads down to the seashore by the old church and churchyard of Crombie.

THE VALE OF THE DEVON.

I.

FROM LOGIE CHURCH TO ALVA AND TILLICOULTRY.

The Ochil Hills—Road along their base from Bridge of Allan—Logie church and Blair Logie—Ascent of Dunmyat—Menstrie and its glen—Alva and its silver-mines—Ascent of Ben Cleuch—Tillicoultry and its glen.

THE Ochils are a range of hills wholly unconnected with any other, which extend from the extremity of Stirlingshire, near the Bridge of Allan, in a direction almost due east, and parallel with the Firth of Forth. They form the northern boundary of Clackmannan and Kinross shires, which they separate from Strathearn, or the southern division of Perth, and then entering Fife, and trending east-north-east, almost approach the German Ocean at the mouth of the Tay. They commence in this order with a gentle ridge, which at Blair Logie rises suddenly into the twin peaks of Dunmyat, the higher and easter of which has an elevation of 1375 feet; next comes a succession of hills, all increasing in height as we proceed from west to east, and culminating in Ben Cleuch—the loftiest of the Ochils—which closes the upper extremity of the glen of Tillicoultry, and rises to the height of 2341 feet. Proceeding towards Dollar, we meet with a series of summits not greatly inferior to Ben Cleuch—such as the Law, the King Seat, and the White Wisp. From this last point they gradually decrease in height, though in a small portion of Perthshire, which here projects like a wedge to the south of the range, Sea Mab, in the parish of Muckhart, attains an elevation of 1441 feet. The diminution, however, becomes very manifest as they skirt the northern edge of Kinross-shire, and by the time they reach Glen Farg, the average elevation is little over 800. It is something lower even than that when we follow the range into Fife, as it proceeds in an east-north-east direction, forming the southern border of the estuary of the Tay. With this latter portion of the Ochils I have, in the present work, nothing to do, as I am only concerned with the range from the Bridge of Allan to Glen Farg, where the Great North Road enters Strathearn.

The formation of the Ochils may be described as porphyritic trap, which, at their southern base in the valley of the Devon, meets the great coal-field of the middle Lowlands of Scotland, which extends on both sides of the Forth from Alloa down to Aberlady, and takes in the Carse of Stirling, the greater part of the counties of Clackmannan, Fife, and the three Lothians. The Ochils are its barrier on the north, and nowhere almost in Scotland, with the exception of a small district in Sutherland, does any coal exist to the north of the range. They abound in minerals of various kinds, and silver, copper, lead, and cobalt have at different times been wrought in them with various degrees of success.

In an æsthetic point of view there is no more beautiful range of hills. They have been familiar to me from my childhood as a distant barrier that rose from earth to sky, shutting out the world beyond like the ridge that enclosed Rasselas and his companions in the Happy Valley. Certainly the world contains far loftier peaks and sublimer adjuncts of scenery, but nowhere can it show mountains with a more beautiful contour of outline, or such a charming succession of those wavy and rounded curves—those lines of beauty and grace—which delight the eye of an artist. The sides of the hills are covered with the richest and most luxuriant herbage, which afford admirable pasture to numerous flocks of sheep, and the tints on the Ochils are ever of the loveliest kind, whether it be at early morn, mid-day, or dewy eve—in misty weather when the rainbow spreads its hues over some particular spot, or in winter when they are white with snow. This beauty of light and shade on the Ochils has been attributed to the peculiar slope of the hills, which lie nearly at an angle of 45°, so that every cloud passing over the sun has its shadow reflected on their surface. There is no long, unbroken ridge, but a succession of rounded, detached hills, the sides of which are sometimes clothed with wood, and the intervening glens, gorges, and ravines are of the kind that Salvator Rosa loved to paint.

The country at the foot of these hills has been termed the Arcadia or Tempe of Scotland. It is certainly a beautiful strath, sheltered by the hills behind from the north, and watered by the " clear winding Devon," on the opposite side of which rises a long ridge or eminence which forms the other side of the valley. The fine pasturage on the mountain-sides naturally rendered wool plentiful in this neighbourhood ; and this circumstance, along with the abundant water-supply furnished by the streams from the glens and gorges of the hills, gave rise to numerous mills and factories, around which several large villages, or rather small towns, have gradually grown up. The whole valley has long been an important seat of the worsted and woollen manufacture, the chief places where it is carried on being Menstrie, Alva, and Tillicoultry. Here, too, it strikes a visitor as being divested of the prosaic and monotonous surroundings which are often the characteristics of factory life in our great towns; and certainly the picturesque and romantic nature of the surroundings—where rocky glens and cascades abut on the factories, and beautiful mountain scenery is within five minutes' walk of the whir of the spindles and clack of the power-looms—must tend, one would think, to alleviate in some degree the sombre monotony of daily toil. And yet, after all, work is work wherever carried on, and brings this blessing with it, that it makes, for those who are actively employed, all places alike.

In taking a survey of the Ochils and the "hillfoots" or towns at their base, I shall proceed from west to east, starting from the Bridge of Allan, to which and its neighbourhood reference has already been made. The point which naturally commends itself, in the first instance, is the hill of Dunmyat, to which Hector Macneill thus refers in his "Will and Jean":—

> " Saft her smile like sweet May morning
> Glintin' o'er Dunmyat's brow,
> Sweet wi' openin' charms adorning
> Strevlin's lovely plains below."

In proceeding thither from the Bridge of Allan, the traveller may take two or three different routes. If he turns off at the south-west extremity by the road which leads by the home farm of Airthrey Castle to Logie church, he will shortly come to the old road leading uphill through a finely wooded defile to the Sheriffmuir. From this he will easily make his way to the summit of the ridge of low-wooded hills which extend between Logie church and Blair Logie. This ridge, again, gradually rises into that of Dunmyat, whose summit he will thus be able to reach without great trouble or fatigue in about two hours. Instead of following the Sheriffmuir road, the path may be taken up the hill at the back of the old church of Logie. To reach the latter, the traveller must continue the beautifully wooded road at the back of the Airthrey home farm, which will bring him out at the old church of Logie, situated in one of the most picturesque nooks in the world. The Ochils, in a recess of which it stands, are here, though of no great height, beautifully clothed with wood, and the little old church standing in its ancient burying-ground is covered with ivy. One of its early Protestant ministers was Alexander Hume, who has achieved some reputation as a religious poet, and deserves to be better known in the present day. He was a great friend of the celebrated Lady Culross, to whom he dedicates his poems. He died in 1609. The house of Lord Abercromby's factor immediately adjoins the old church in a charming situation.

I have mentioned the two foregoing routes as the easiest for the ascent of Dunmyat, but it may also be climbed from Blair Logie glen, to which we shall now proceed. Leaving old Logie church and going downhill for a quarter of a mile, we come to the new parish church of Logie, a neat though plain building, surmounted by a spire; and here we join, near Airthrey East Lodge, the public road which leads from the Bridge of Allan and Causewayhead, between the Abbey Craig and Lord Abercromby's grounds, to Blair Logie and Menstrie. It is, in fact, part of the great road leading from Stirling by the hillfoots to Dollar and Kinross.

Our distances are here — Stirling 2¾, Dollar 9¼, Kinross 22¼ miles. On our right, a long straight road called the Pows Loan, a mile in length, but finely shaded with trees, leads down to the main highway running from Alloa to Stirling by the south side of the Abbey Craig. Passing this, the traveller will keep due east, and following a pleasantly shaded though very uniform road for about three-quarters of a mile, will arrive at the village of Blair Logie, which nestles under the west shoulder of Dunmyat at the outlet of its own glen or gorge.

Blair Logie is what in gushing language would be described as a " sweetly pretty " place, consisting of a small hamlet of houses, a U.P. church, and (behind the village) the old Castle or Place of Logie, the property of Lord Balfour of Burleigh, who owns a good deal of the land in this neighbourhood. It used to be famous as a " goats-whey quarter," in the days when the drinking of this beverage was prescribed by physicians as a sovereign remedy in consumption and kindred disorders. Many people used to resort thither for this purpose ; and in the time of our grandfathers it enjoyed a great reputation as a specially beautiful and salubrious spot. In these days people were less exacting than they are now in the matter of accommodation, when they seem to expect not merely "to carry the comforts of the Sautmarket with them," but to find luxuries and conveniences to which in their Sautmarket homes they are strangers. As far as can be judged from outward appearance, the prestige of Blair Logie is gone, and the tide of fashion has set in to other quarters. But it is still an attractive place, though it does not even own a hotel.

The old Place of Logie is an interesting specimen of an old Scottish mansion-house in the end of the sixteenth century, though it is now only the residence of a hill-farmer.   Let us ascend the glen, or rather gorge, which rises above it, and takes up to the hillside below the western peak of Dunmyat.   This, though not the higher of the two, is noteworthy as the site of an ancient Pictish fort and castle, part of which may still be traced, though both natural causes and human agencies have made the greater part of it disappear.   A description of the locality has been contributed by Miss C. Maclagan to the 'Proceedings of the Scottish Antiquarian Society.'

Keeping up the glen, we enjoy, as we turn round from time to time, beautiful views of the windings of the Forth and the rich country extending up between it and the foot of the hills.   After rather a stiff climb, we turn to the right, descend into the valley between the two summits, and then ascending again, soon find ourselves on the ridge which leads to the higher eminence, on which the cairn of the Ordnance Survey stands.   It is soon reached, and the ascent of Dunmyat has been accomplished, as I can testify personally, in an hour and a quarter from Blair Logie.   The view well recompenses any trouble or fatigue that may have been incurred.   It is certainly not so extensive as that from Ben Cleuch, of which more anon; but it presents a most magnificent prospect of alpine and champaign country combined, taking in all the country between Stirling Castle and Ben Lomond in the upper basin of the Forth, and all the windings of the river with its shores and estuary from Stirling to the Bass.   The panorama of mountains to the north and west is also singularly magnificent, including even, it is said, Ben Nevis.   The whole of the Sheriffmuir, with its battle-field, lies at our feet on one side; and on the other we can look on the Abbey Craig and the Wallace Monument to the plain of Stirling; while a little farther off, away to the south, is the field of Bannockburn.

There is a very easy descent from the top of Dunmyat through the beautiful glen of Menstrie, to the thriving manufacturing village of that name, and the distance may be accomplished in little over half an hour. The upper part of the glen is very broad and spacious, and a cart-track passes through it, by which Strathallan and the opposite side of the Ochils may be reached. Several glens open into Menstrie Glen, and the dwelling-house belonging to a large sheep-farm forms a prominent object. As in every part of the Ochils, the turf is delightfully elastic and "velvety" to the tread, and the only care that we have to take is in the first descent from the summit, which requires to be made with some caution. As we approach the village the glen narrows to a most romantic and picturesque gorge, the precipitous sides of which are bordered by a profusion of natural wood, including the mountain-ash or rowan, the alder, hazel, elm, &c., whilst the clear stream at the bottom foams over its rocky bed. At every turn, as we descend the mountain-path, some new feature in the scenery presents itself. Having reached the village of Menstrie, which is about a mile from Blair Logie, we may turn back for a little along the road in order to look up to Dunmyat, from which we have just descended. The two peaks have here a singularly imposing aspect, more especially the western or lower one, which shoots up like a mighty cone. They almost project over the public road, and look as if they were ready to topple over and overwhelm the passer-by.

Part of the slope or descent of Dunmyat, to the west of Menstrie, is traversed by a country road leading to a hill-farm, and is seen to considerable advantage from the Stirling and Dunfermline railway between Cambus and Causewayhead stations. It is probably this which is referred to in the popular local song :—

> "Oh ! Alva's woods are bonnie,
>   Tillicoultry's hills are fair ;
>   But when I think o' the bonnie braes o' Menstrie,
>   It makes my heart aye sair."

The legend regarding the above is that the miller of Menstrie had a beautiful wife, whose charms captivated the king of the fairies, and induced him to carry her off, greatly to the sorrow of her bereaved husband. She did not appear, however, to be contented with her fate, and was frequently heard by her former partner warbling the verse just quoted, though he could not see the singer. At last one day, whilst he was winnowing some corn at his mill-door, he accidentally made a magical gesture which broke the spell, and the Eurydice of Menstrie dropped from the air at the feet of her Orpheus.

Another local rhyme is :—

> "There's Dollar, and Alva, and Tillicoultry,
>   But the bonnie braes o' Menstrie they bear the gree."

The barony of Menstrie belonged formerly to the Alexander family, the last representative of which has transmitted a reputation to posterity both as a poet of considerable merit, and as the author of the ' Paraenesis,' or Exhortation on Government, dedicated to Prince Henry, the short-lived son of James VI. He received from Charles I. a grant of territory in North America, which, under the name of Nova Scotia, might be disposed of in lots, not exceeding 150 in number, each of which should confer on the holder the rank of baronet. Many of our baronets derive their title from this source, and hence are sometimes spoken of as "Nova Scotia baronets." Subsequently to this Sir William Alexander received a higher mark of royal favour, in being made Earl of Stirling—a peerage which was only enjoyed by him for a few years, and became extinct at his death, which took place in 1640.   No one has ever established a right to it since, though the surname of Alexander is very common in Scotland.   About forty years ago a pretender to the title and honours came forward, but the grounds of his claims proved to be only fraud and imposture.

Menstrie is 3½ miles from the Bridge of Allan, 5 miles from Stirling, and 2 from Alva.   Though occupying a beautiful position, it is not in itself a particularly attractive place, but it carries on a thriving industry in the manufacture of tartans and woollen goods.   It is said to be the birthplace of Sir Ralph Abercromby, whose baptism in 1734 is certainly recorded in the register of Logie parish, to which Menstrie belongs; but another account states that he was born at the house of Tullibody on the Forth, a little above Alloa.   A junction railway connects Alva and Menstrie with the Stirling and Dunfermline line at Cambus.

The road from Menstrie to Alva lies close to the base of the hills, and while very level and straight, is almost unsheltered.   Taking the elevations in succession as we proceed eastwards from Dunmyat, the names and altitudes are Myreton Hill (1240), a farm on the slope of which was long occupied by Mrs Thomson, sister of Mungo Park ; West Hill of Alva (1682), the precipitous crag on the front of which is known as Craigleith ; the Middle Hill of Alva (1437) ; and the Wood Hill of Alva (1723), so called from its being clothed with timber almost to the summit.   The town of Alva lies at the foot of the West and the Middle Hills, and the glen between them is called Alva Glen.   The whole of the parish belongs to J. Johnston, Esq. of Alva, whose mansion is beautifully situated among trees on a projection in front of the Wood Hill, about midway between Alva and Tillicoultry.

Alva (*Hotel:* The Johnstone Arms) is a manufacturing town of some size, and much more pleasantly situated than such places generally are.   Immediately behind it, between the West and the Middle Hill, is Alva Glen, traversed by the Alva burn, which supplies many of the woollen factories with water, and is in itself a fine mountain-gorge, gradually widening out as the explorer makes his way through its romantic recesses.   The precipice of Craigleith, which rises on the west side of it, and presents its rocky front to the Devon valley, used to be famous for its breed of falcons, one pair only of which are said to build their nest in the most inaccessible part of the crag.   They long retained a great reputation for purity of breed amongst hawking connoisseurs, and in the last century an English gentleman in Yorkshire sent a special messenger to Alva to procure him a specimen. The request was readily acceded to ; but the envoy, in order to obtain the bird, had to be let down to the nest in the face of the rock by a rope fastened round his waist, and held by a company of people on the edge of the precipice.

The parish of Alva belongs to Stirlingshire, but is completely detached from that county, being bounded on the north by Perth, and on the other three sides by Clackmannan.

The ancient history of Alva is connected with St Serf, who seems, as one of the early Christian missionaries, to have evangelised the greater part of the country lying between the Ochils and the sea, from Culross to Loch Leven.   The church of Alva was dedicated to him, and there is still a well in the slope below the present church which bears the name of St Serf's Well.   The parish was in the diocese of Dunkeld, and in 1260 the church of Alva, with its revenues, was made over as a "mensal church" to the Abbey of Cambuskenneth.   Down to

1632 it seems to have been united with that of Tilli-coultry, the minister of Alva officiating in both places. The disjunction is said to have been effected by Alexander Bruce, second son of the celebrated Sir George Bruce of Culross, who had become proprietor of the Alva estate.   The latter subsequently passed into the hands of the Erskines, cadets of the Mar family, and after being held by them for nearly a hundred and fifty years, it was sold to the ancestor of the present proprietor, a son of Sir James Johnstone of Westerhall in Dumfries-shire.   The baronetcy vested in their family has merged in that of the Rosslyn peerage, which descended, in terms of the original patent, to Sir James Erskine of Alva, whose mother was a sister of Lord Chancellor Wedderburn, first Earl of Rosslyn.

As with all the " hillfoots," the staple manufactures of Alva are woollen, and these have been carried on here for nearly two hundred and fifty years.   Originally they consisted, as at Tillicoultry, chiefly of serges, but plaid-ings and blankets were in process of time added, and more recently tartans.

In the beginning of the last century an industry was started in the neighbourhood of Alva, which promised at first to lead to important results, but after a short while entirely collapsed. This was the working of silver-mines in the glen between the Middle and Wood Hills, and which to this day is known by the appellation of the Silver Glen.   Here exist the disused mines which were opened by Sir John Erskine of Alva in the early years of the last century, and with such success that they are said at one time to have furnished a yield of £4000 a-week. This is probably an exaggeration ; but certain it is that the attention of Government was attracted to those valu-able veins of ore, two of which were especially rich, and produced in a few weeks 134 ounces of the richest silver, as assayed and tested by no less a personage than Sir Isaac Newton, then Master of the Mint.   Sir John Erskine, shortly after he had commenced the working of these mines, engaged in the Jacobite insurrection of 1715, leaving to his wife, Lady Erskine, the oversight in his absence of the operations, which were carried on to some purpose, as no less than forty tons of silver ore were dug out of the mountain-side and buried in the ground near the gate of Alva House.   With the view apparently of procuring a remission of the sentence of outlawry incurred by him in consequence of his participation in the Rebellion, it would seem that Sir John communicated to the Government some information regarding these mines, and succeeded in his purpose. A German expert connected with the Mint, named Dr Justus Brandshagen, was sent down to Scotland to investigate and report—a behest which he accomplished in the winter of 1716-17.   A copy of the report furnished by him is preserved in the Earl of Portsmouth's papers as recently examined by the Royal Historical Commission.   It states, *inter alia*, as follows : " I found it (the ore) of an extraordinary nature, such as to my knowledge few or none like have ever been seen in Europe. It consists of sulphur, arsenic, copper, iron, some lead, and good silver.   Of all these the silver is only to be regarded, for the other minerals and metals contained in the ore are of little value, and not worth the charges to separate and keep them."   The report has a plan attached to it of the mining works, a " Description of the Mine," and an " Account of Ore assayed at Alva."   There are several documents among these papers in the handwriting of Sir Isaac Newton regarding these mines of Sir John Erskine.   It had been proposed at first to send the great philosopher himself down to Alva to examine the workings, but he pleaded to be excused on the ground that it was not a matter in which he had much skill, and that it would be better to send some one of experience from King George's silver-mines in the Harz. Dr Brandshagen, and an assistant named James Hamilton, were accordingly sent in his stead, but Sir Isaac both assayed some of the ore and furnished a lengthy report on it in a letter addressed to Lord Townshend. One of the passages in it is as follows : " By two assays which I caused to be made of clean pieces cut off from the silver, it proved xvii. dwt. better than standard. Now, fifteen pennyweight of such fine silver is worth four shillings and twopence. And, therefore, the ore is exceedingly rich, a pound weight avoirdupois holding 4s. 2d. in silver.   This silver holds no gold."

Notwithstanding all this splendid treasure-trove, which is said to have produced to Sir John Erskine from £40,000 to £50,000, his fortunes do not appear to have been materially benefited ; and ere long, the precious ore becoming " small by degrees and beautifully less," the yield did not compensate for the outlay, and the workings came to an end. They were resumed about forty years afterwards by Charles Erskine, Lord Tinwald, who had purchased the estate of Alva from his nephew, Sir Henry Erskine, a successor of Sir John ; but though prosecuted with considerable industry, they produced no adequate return beyond occasionally some small strings of silver ore, and they had finally to be abandoned.   There was found, however, and wrought, a considerable quantity of cobalt, which was used largely in a china manufactory erected about this time at Prestonpans, in East Lothian. A pair of communion cups made from some remains in his possession of the silver ore obtained from Sir John Erskine's mines, was presented by James Erskine, Lord Alva, son of Lord Tinwald, to the church of Alva in the year 1767. The whole history of this extraordinary discovery of silver in the Ochils is as curious a chapter in the chronicles of metallurgy as that of the gold-workings in the Lead Hills in the reign of James V.

The ascent of Ben Cleuch, the highest of the Ochil range, though the distance is somewhat less from Tillicoultry, may yet be very satisfactorily accomplished from Alva in three and a half hours by following the horsepath which leads through the hills to Blackford. The traveller who wishes to follow this route will take the track along the lower slope of the Middle Hill of Alva, which he will reach by going up to the church [1] and following the road to the left, which conducts to the hillside. The track is very easy to follow, but I have tried another, and what I deem fully "a more excellent way." This is to descend from the slope of the Middle Hill into the Silver Glen, which lies between the Middle and the Wood Hill, and then ascend the latter through the woodland, from which it derives its name, to the summit. Arrived at this point (1723 feet of elevation), the traveller has gained a lofty ridge, which forms the crest of the western side of the glen of Tillicoultry. From where he now stands he will see the top of Ben Cleuch on the opposite side of the glen, to the north-east of him, and to the south of this, and more nearly in a direct line opposite his present station, the peak called " The Law."

The ascent of the Wood Hill, though it is made among

---

[1] The wayfarer may sometimes be a little perplexed in this region, when he makes inquiry regarding some old ruined church, and is directed to one which evidently has not existed for half a century. The reason of this is that the parish church has, since the Disruption in 1843, been popularly known as "the Auld Kirk," and consequently, when a countryman is interrogated about any "old church," he only thinks of the Church of Scotland, as distinguished from the recent offshoot known as the Free Church.

trees, is a very stiff one, and a feeling of considerable satisfaction is experienced when the climber has got fairly clear of them, and finds himself in a more open and bracing atmosphere on the hillside above. In a hollow here, just above Alva House, is the spreading-ground of the well-known Lady Alva's Web, or Lady Alva's Veil, which is regarded with a good deal of interest by those who view the Ochils from a distance. From the sheltered position of the locality, screened from the rays of the sun on all sides by a projecting rock, snow frequently remains here far on in the summer, when it has melted on every other part of the range, and it then assumes the appearance of a fine linen web or lace veil—hence its appellation. I remember noticing it on two special occasions—one on 1st June from the the highroad above Culross, and the other on 29th May from the road between Kincardine and Kilbagie. On the first of these it appeared in the distance no larger than a pocket-handkerchief; on the other it assumed the size of a tolerably large tablecloth.

However steep may be the climb up the Wood Hill, the view which is enjoyed from the summit of the rich country spreading out between the Ochils and the sea, and extending to the mouth of the Forth, is such as would be an ample recompense for any amount of fatigue. The remainder of the route to the summit of Ben Cleuch is now comparatively easy, and there the traveller will be greeted by a still more magnificent prospect. All that he has to do now is to turn his face northwards and follow the great west ridge of Tillicoultry Glen by the wire-fence which separates the Alva and Tillicoultry estates. Let him follow this till he comes to the head of the valley, where the same boundary fence makes first a descent to the east, and then runs up the hill to the ridge on the opposite side of the glen. He will leave the rounded eminence of Craighorn (1904 feet) on his left, and then taking the wire-fence as his guide, follow its course, which will bring him to the top of the slope. Here he is now on the ridge which crests Tillicoultry Glen on the east side, and within a very short distance indeed of the summit of Ben Cleuch, the goal of his exertions. Turning southwards and ascending an easy incline of a few hundred yards, he arrives at his destination and the Ordnance Survey cairn.

Ben Cleuch has a height of 2341 feet above the level of the sea, and though the highest point of the Ochils, makes no great appearance from a distance, there being several other eminences in the neighbourhood of little inferior elevation. The view which it commands is, on a clear day, something extraordinary—a panorama which, like Justice Shallow's pippins, leaves one something to talk about afterwards for the rest of one's life. The mere height is, of course, of no account, but the position, situated as it is midway between the basins of the Tay and Forth, and in sight of the rich champaign countries which each of these comprises, gives this hill an advantage over many others of much greater altitude. In the case of many mountain-ranges it frequently happens that the prospect from the higher summits consists for the most part of a vast ocean of hills, very grand and striking no doubt, but withal somewhat monotonous. From Ben Cleuch and Dunmyat, on the other hand, there is the most attractive variety and contrast, from the grand and majestic to the soft and beautiful. The story has often been repeated of a Scottish laird travelling in Italy, and being informed by a fellow-wanderer that to all the fine prospects which he had witnessed on the Continent, he preferred the view which he had obtained from the top of Ben Cleuch, in the

Scottish Ochils. His interlocutor experienced not only surprise, but a slight shock, as he himself was the proprietor of Ben Cleuch, and had never in his life made its ascent. Sometimes Dunmyat is the hill assigned in the story, which generally concludes with the circumstance that the "Scot abroad" resolved at once to return to his own country and climb the hill on his own estate, which he had hitherto neglected for prospects in foreign lands.

The view from Dunmyat, as already mentioned, is very fine, but that from Ben Cleuch is much more extensive. It takes in at the same time the estuary of the Tay as far as Dundee, the fertile district of Strathearn, with the town of Crieff projected on a sunny slope to the north; Loch Leven, with the Lomond Hills; and the plain of Kinross, only slightly elevated above the valley of the Devon, which makes its chief descent at the Cauldron Linn, and flows in its turn through a region very little elevated above the level of the Forth. The whole basin of the last-named stream, it is needless to add, is spread out at the feet of the spectator, and its whole course may be followed from Ben Lomond by Stirling, Alloa, Kincardine, and Queensferry, down to Leith, North Berwick Law, and St Abb's. The mountain ranges and peaks that can be seen are also very numerous and well defined. Away to the north-east may be observed the Grampians in the north of Forfar, and adjoining corners of Aberdeen and Inverness shires. Those chieftains among Scottish mountains— Ben Macdhui, Cairngorm, and Loch-na-gar—can all be seen, with their sides, even at midsummer, flecked with snow; whilst nearer at hand every famous peak in Perthshire is visible, including, in a line from east to west, Schiehallion, Ben Lawers, and Ben Voirlich. The distant Ben Alder, which rises above Loch Ericht, on the

confines of Inverness-shire, and even the mighty monarch
Ben Nevis, beside Fort William, come in within the ken
of the gazer from Ben Cleuch—so do Ben Cruachan in
Argyleshire, Ben Ledi and Ben Lomond in Stirlingshire,
and Goatfell in Arran, across the lower elevations of the
Campsie and Kilsyth hills, in the district between the
Forth and Clyde.   Altogether, from our present "coign
of vantage" no less than seventeen counties can be
seen.

It will scarcely be credited that a few years ago a
project was started of carrying a railway from Tillicoultry to the summit of Ben Cleuch!   The ground, however, was actually surveyed for this purpose, and possibly, in consideration of the circumstance that such
a feat has been accomplished on mountains of much
greater elevation, such as the Righi in Switzerland, the
scheme is not so chimerical as might at first sight be
supposed.   But no such influx of visitors as yearly
throng to the Lake of Lucerne could ever be expected
to betake itself to the Ochils, whatever attractions they
may possess.   The idea could never be realised in the
only form which could recommend itself to our practical
age as an excuse for such undertakings—that of proving
a commercial success.   Meanwhile no admirer of Nature, simple and unadorned, will regret that the hoof of
the iron horse has hitherto been only allowed to tread
the base of the Ochils.

Having done full justice to this glorious panorama,
the traveller may wend his way southwards along the
ridge, which will conduct him first to the top of the Law
(2093 feet), and then downwards into Tillicoultry Glen
by a projecting incline or wedge, at the extremity of
which, two streams—the Daiglen from the north-north-
west, and the Gannel from the north-north-east—unite to
form Tillicoultry burn.   There is a beautiful waterfall

here on the former; and all down the valley after the junction of the streams the scenery is exceedingly picturesque, both in point of cascades and the precipitous wooded sides of the gorge which overhang the water. A narrow and somewhat "risky" sheep-path leads from the "meeting of the waters" along the hillside to a broader and well-trodden track, which ultimately lands us on the summit of the so-called Castle Craig, right above the town of Tillicoultry, to which there is a descent by a "Jacob's ladder" or succession of wooden steps. The locality in which we now find ourselves is said to have been at one time a well-defined and strongly constructed Pictish fort, which was roofed over with stone, and used to serve the children in Tillicoultry as a grand playground for hide-and-seek. The foundations of a circular structure were certainly visible here in the end of the last century; and tradition averred that it had been a mighty fortress of the Picts, and that the stones had been carried away to build the castle of Stirling. It bore the name of "Johnie Mool's" house; but whatever it may have been in past times, there is no artificial erection that can be traced on the crag now— the remaining stones having been all, it is said, utilised in the erection of sheepfolds. On the opposite side of the glen to the Castle Craig are the Western and Eastern Kirk Craigs.

Tillicoultry (*Hotel:* The Crown) stands at the foot of the hills at the entrance of its glen or gorge, with its burn running through the middle of the town. We descend thither from the Castle Craig by the factory of Mr William Gibson, who has contributed a good deal in his History of Dollar and Tillicoultry' to invest his native district with interest. The stream whose course we follow comes down occasionally, like its congeners in the Ochils, with terrific force, and though strongly embanked, has at times committed great havoc. The last time that such an event took place was in 1877, when both Tillicoultry and Dollar suffered severely. In 1785 there was a tremendous cataclysm, when the Devon rose in four or five hours 13 feet above its usual level at Tillicoultry Bridge. It carried away an immense quantity of grain, and a narrow escape is recorded of a woman who was assisting a farmer on the south side of the stream to save his crop, and was carried off by the flood, but was borne up by her clothes, and landed in safety on the opposite bank.

The name of Tillicoultry seems to be derived from the Gaelic *tulach-cul-traigh*—the knoll or hillock at the back of or behind the slope—a designation which seems applicable to the slope of the Kirk-hill and its continuation, the so-called Cuninghar, which extend from the old church of Tillicoultry downwards to the highroad. As with other places, an absurd story has been invented to explain the etymology. According to this veracious legend, a Highlander was driving a herd of cattle along the foot of the Ochils, and fully expected that when they were passing through the Tillicoultry burn the animals would stop and slake their thirst. To his surprise, not one of them did so—an omission that made the astonished Celt exclaim with his peculiar enunciation, "There's teil a coo try!"[1] Such an etymon will rank with the alleged origin of the name of Alloa, which is only a few miles distant. It is alleged that shortly after a beginning had been made of the building of the town, a meeting was held to determine the name. A long discussion arose, and nothing satisfactory having been proposed or agreed on, one of the company rose in high dudgeon, exclaiming, "A'll awa' then"—*i.e.*, Alloa. To such derivations the hackneyed saying,

---

[1] There's deil a cow dry—*i.e.*, "There's Tillicoultry."

se non è vero, è ben trovato, can certainly not be applied, as they are the veriest drivel; but it is noteworthy how much blundering is current regarding the names of places from attempts to explain the terms of Celtic nomenclature by fancied resemblances to words in either the Teutonic or Latin languages. Such *nugæ* may sometimes be amusing enough when they are given forth as mere *jeux d'esprit* by professed wits like Dean Swift and Thomas Hood, but they become unendurable when such miserable inventions as those just referred to are gravely recorded as historical facts.

Tillicoultry was raised to the dignity of a burgh, with commissioners and a chief magistrate, in 1871. It was anciently famous for its manufacture of a coarse woollen cloth—a species of shalloon—which used to be known as early as the sixteenth century by the name of "Tillicoultry serge." It has in more recent times carried on an extensive industry in the production of blankets, shawls, and tartans. The territory round the town seems to have originally belonged to the Earls of Mar, but the church, like that of Alva, belonged to the Abbey of Cambuskenneth. At the Reformation, the church and glebe of Tillicoultry became vested in the Mar family; but as the abbot and convent of Cambuskenneth had meantime granted a tack or lease of the teinds to the Colvilles of Ochiltree, who were now proprietors of the Tillicoultry estate, this conveyance was in 1628 ratified by John, Earl of Mar, and infeftment granted them in the Church lands. These Colvilles acquired the Tillicoultry estate in 1483, and retained it till 1634, when they sold it to William Alexander of Menstrie, afterwards the first and only Earl of Stirling.

After the death of the Earl of Stirling in 1640, the Tillicoultry estate passed into the hands of Sir Alexander Rollo of Duncrub, and subsequently it has belonged to many different proprietors.   Since 1814 it has been the property of the Wardlaw Ramsays, a branch but not the leading representatives of the ancient family of the Wardlaws of Pitreavie, Torrie, and other properties in the western district of Fife.   The head of the family, however, Sir Henry Wardlaw, Bart., has long been connected with Tillicoultry, where he carries on business as sole partner in the old-established firm of James Wardlaw & Sons, millwrights and machine-makers.   He succeeded to the baronetcy in 1877 on the death of Sir Archibald, cousin to his (Sir Henry Wardlaw's) father.   There is also a branch of the family in Dollar.

II.

FROM TILLICOULTRY TO DOLLAR AND YETTS OF MUCKHART.

The Colville family as Lords of Tillicoultry—Harvieston and its associations with Burns—Town of Dollar—Castle Campbell and its surroundings—Road from Dollar to the Yetts of Muckhart.

THE present house of Tillicoultry is a modern square mansion, situated on the slope of the Kirk-hill, about a quarter of a mile to the east of the town, and near it is the old churchyard, though the old church is almost obliterated.   On a terrace at the north end of the Kirk-hill there remained till the end of the seventeenth century a venerable thorn, beneath which the Laird of Tillicoultry, the first Lord Colville of Culross, was wont to repose.   He had served with great distinction in the wars of Henry of Navarre against the Catholic League, and continued a great favourite with that prince throughout the remainder of his life.   He was sent afterwards on various missions to France from the English Court, and was always received there with the utmost honour and respect.   During his latter days he resided almost constantly at his house of Tillicoultry. Standing on the terrace one day, and looking up to his favourite thorn, whilst he was recounting his military adventures to some friends, his foot slipped, and the old man fell down the bank, never to rise again.   His son, the Master of Colville, had predeceased him, and his grandson, Lord James Colville of Culross, sold the Tillicoultry estate, as already mentioned, to Sir William Alexander of Menstrie.

Going due south from the Kirk-hill, we arrive at its continuation " the Cuninghar," at the extremity of which, where it abuts on the public road, may still be seen the fragment of a circular rampart.   There were some standing-stones here at one time, and the locality was regarded as the site of a Druidical circle ; but with the exception just mentioned, almost every vestige of antiquity has disappeared, in consequence of the excavations that have been made in the bank for the digging of sand.   A number of bones have been found at this place.

The present church and manse of Tillicoultry is situated at the east end of the town, close to the road leading to Tullibody and Alloa.   Proceeding eastwards towards Dollar, and passing the new cemetery on the south side of the road opposite to the extremity of the Cuninghar, a long descent is made, at the foot of which, one mile from Tillicoultry and two from Dollar, is the west entrance to Harvieston, now the property of James Orr, Esq., who succeeded his brother Sir Andrew Orr in 1874.   Sir Andrew purchased in 1859 the Harvieston estate, which for many years previous had been in the hands of the Globe Insurance Company.   It used to belong to the family of the late Archbishop of Canterbury—Mr Tait, the Archbishop's father, having been the last proprietor of that name. It had come into their hands in the beginning of the last century, having previous to that time formed part, of the lordship of Campbell, which in its turn was, in the end of the last century, incorporated with and now forms part of Harvieston. The Archbishop was, with his brothers, brought up here, and his family still retain in their possession the mausoleum or walled enclosure known as " Tait's Tomb," on the banks of the Devon, between Tillicoultry and Dollar. His paternal grandmother, Mrs Tait of Harvieston, was sister of Mrs Hamilton, stepmother of Burns's great crony, Gavin Hamilton of Mauchline. On Mrs Tait's death, Mrs Hamilton came with her family to reside at Harvieston and keep house for her brother-in-law, Mr Tait. Burns, who visited Harvieston more than once, has celebrated the charms both of Charlotte Hamilton—Gavin's step-sister—and of the stream by whose banks she dwelt :—

> " How pleasant the banks of the clear winding Devon,
>   With green spreading bushes, and flowers blooming fair !
>   But the bonniest flower on the banks of the Devon
>   Was once a sweet bud on the braes of the Ayr."

And it is not a little interesting to find that the poet's very last song, written at Brow on the Solway Firth, from which he only returned to Dumfries to die, has also reference to Charlotte Hamilton and the Devon :—

> " Fairest maid on Devon banks,
>   Crystal Devon, winding Devon—
>   Wilt thou lay that frown aside,
>   And smile as thou wert wont to do ?"

Harvieston is most beautifully situated amidst the woods and declivities which here, as generally in the

Dollar valley, constitute the great charm of the lower slopes of the Ochil range. Above rise the verdant hills, and seem to overhang the road, to the portion of which extending from Tillicoultry to Dollar must perhaps be assigned the palm, in point of picturesque attraction, in the whole route by the hillfoots. The present house of Harvieston is a large and imposing mansion in the Italian style, and the grounds attached to it form an important feature in the landscape. The estate includes Castle Campbell and its glen, with which we shall soon make acquaintance.

Continuing along a finely shaded road, we pass on our right the mausoleum of the Tait family, and at a little distance afterwards on our left the east entrance to Harvieston. Shortly after this we enter the town of Dollar (*Hotel:* Castle Campbell), which, originally a small village lying on the side of a mountain-gorge, has now spread out into a large town with handsome streets, villas, and all the appliances and luxuries of modern civilisation. Much of this development has doubtless been owing to the erection here of Dollar Academy, an extensive educational establishment, founded through the munificence of a Mr John M'Nab, a native of Dollar, who, leaving the place a poor boy, with barely enough in his pocket to defray his fare for crossing at Queensferry, found his way to Leith and thence to London. There he settled, and in the course of a long life, spent in seafaring and shipowning, he contrived to amass an immense fortune. This he left to the minister and kirk-session of Dollar, to be employed in the erection of an institution for the purposes of education, he himself having apparently experienced in his young days the desirability of such a provision being made for poor scholars. Through some ambiguity in the wording of his will, executed in England, it was questioned whether, in accordance with the testator's directions regarding the foundation of a " charity," its conditions might not be fulfilled by the establishment at Dollar of a large hospital or poorhouse. There was also a difficulty caused by the bequest to the minister and parish of Dollar, a circumstance which for a time left practically the application of the funds and management of the trust in the hands of one man—the clergyman. A keen and protracted contest ensued, in which were invoked the authority of the Court of Session, the English Court of Chancery, and the Imperial Parliament. Ultimately the matter was arranged by the creation of a body of trustees, by whom the affairs of the institution were managed for a number of years, and recently there has been a fresh organisation at the hands of the Educational Endowments Commission. The idea of a vast poorhouse or hospital had long been abandoned, and a large and handsome academy had been built at an expense of £10,000. It was opened in 1820, and has enjoyed a great and ever extending reputation. All householders residing within the parish of Dollar have a right to partake of its benefits, and hence multitudes of families, chiefly of the middle classes, have been induced to settle in the place in consideration of the educational advantages which it affords. Dollar Academy provides higher or secondary education for both sexes, and the capital fund of its endowment amounts to about £90,000.

The street leading up to the Academy is termed Cairnpark Street, and so named because it occupies the site of a field in which stood an immense cairn of stones, 30 feet in height, with a base of 30 feet square. It was removed in the beginning of this century, and the stones of which it was composed, to the amount of about a thousand cart-loads, were broken up and used as metal for forming the new road by the foot of the Ochils. At the bottom of the cairn a number of clay urns were found, and these, in a similar spirit to that which prompted the whole procedure, were allowed to go to destruction.

The original nucleus of Dollar consisted of what is now known as " Old Dollar," situated at the north-east extremity of the present town, on the rising ground at the entrance of the gorge of Castle Campbell. The Dollar burn, formed by the union of two streams from the hills, flows past it in a southerly direction to the Devon, and the modern town of Dollar spreads itself out on the acclivity on either side of the stream (though chiefly on the western bank) which ascends from the Devon to the Ochils. The main street crosses it from west to east, along the great road from Stirling to Kinross, from both of which places, as also from Dunfermline, Dollar is equally distant (12 miles).

A fine view of Dollar is obtained from the train as it passes from Alloa to Kinross, along the elevated bank or terrace on the south side of the Devon. A road from Alloa leads along the crest of this to the Rumbling Bridge and Kinross, through Blairingone, parallel with that which we have just been traversing by the foot of the Ochils, and commands throughout a complete prospect of the Dollar valley. At a point where the roads from Forest Mill and Saline converge, a steep and winding descent leads down to the Devon, which is now crossed here by a wooden bridge, though till within the last forty years there was only a ford, which frequently was impassable when the water was high. It was not an uncommon practice in those days for the Devon to be forded on stilts. The only access to the northern bank which could then be obtained in all weathers was by the Vicar's Bridge, three quarters of a mile farther up, and approached on the south side by a steep descent leading down from the village of Blairingone.

Unlike the other "hillfoots," Dollar has no factories or large works, with the exception of the bleachworks near the wooden bridge, established by Mr Hay of Dollarfield about a hundred years ago. In some respects the place may be regarded as a miniature of Edinburgh, its mainstay being its educational advantages, and the attractions presented by the mountain scenery and salubrious climate. In the latter respect Dollar has always enjoyed a pre-eminence. The minister of the parish, speaking of it in the end of the last century, says that in the course of a parochial visitation in the month of December he did not find a single sick person. The only disease which used to be considered as peculiar to the locality was what is known as bronchocele or a glandular swelling of the neck, attributable, it is said, to the drinking of the water of Dollar burn, which is mingled during a large portion of the year with the melted snow coming down from the Ochils. A similar cause has been assigned for the prevalence of goitre in the Swiss valleys. A new water-supply, however, and altered conditions of life, have rendered this characteristic one of the reminiscences of the past.

A great deal of fanciful absurdity has been expended in connection with the origin of the names of Dollar and the surrounding localities, which are all supposed to have had their source in some depressing or melancholy characteristic. Thus the parish itself is said to be that of "Doulour" or "Grief"; Castle Campbell, which overshadows it, was formerly called the Castle of Gloom, and the two streams which surround it and unite in the gorge at the southern extremity of the castle hill, had the appellations respectively of the Waters of Sorrow and Care. The idea was not an unattractive one, and received some support from the fact that Castle Campbell was really in ancient times known as the Castle of

Gloom, and had this designation changed to its present one by the authority of an Act of the Scottish Parliament, passed in 1489. But Dollar is merely the Gaelic *doilleir*, or the dark place, an epithet very applicable to the situation of the castle in the centre of a wooded gorge, and the position of Old Dollar at the entrance of the ravine. The Castle of Gloom and the Gloom Hill, immediately adjoining, on the east, are a natural Saxon rendering of the Gaelic term, and appear still more applicable when, as not unfrequently happens, the locality is shrouded in a dense mist. As for the Waters of Sorrow and Care, their peculiar appellations must be dismissed as the emanations of a poetic fancy, and they are now in great measure discarded for the more prosaic epithets of the Bank and Turnpike burns.

Little can be stated regarding the early history of Dollar; but an engagement is said to have taken place here in 877 between the Danes and the Scots, in which the latter were worsted, and pursued with great slaughter to the north-east extremity of Fife. The occasion for the battle arose in consequence of the expulsion from Ireland of the Danes by the Norwegians, a kindred nation of Scandinavian settlers. The former then passed over to Scotland, and crossing the isthmus between the Firths of Clyde and Forth, made their way into Stirling and Clackmannanshire. A legend, too, is recorded in the Scottish Chronicles of a company of English pirates landing in Fife, and plundering the whole country as far as the Ochils, without encountering any resistance. They arrived at Dollar, and carried off from the church the recently fitted and beautifully carved woodwork of its choir. This they transported to their ships, and sailed off in great glee, till they approached Inchcolm, when the vessel containing the sacred timber disappeared suddenly beneath the water. The rest of the expedition, warned by the punishment which had thus followed their sacrilegious act, desisted from prosecuting further their hostile intentions against the monastery on the island.

It is in the middle of the fifteenth century that the Campbell family first appear on the scene, the lands of Dollar having become vested in coheiresses, one of whom married the first Earl of Argyll. The date of 1465 is commonly assigned for this event; and subsequently to this period we find them, as evinced by numerous royal charters, confirmatory and otherwise, proprietors of large tracts of territory, not only in the neighbourhood of Dollar, but through the whole adjacent country, ranging from Menstrie on the west, to the Yetts of Muckhart on the east, and extending as far south as the parish of Saline in Fife. They were, in fact, the governing family in the district—one specially important office that they held being the hereditary bailiary of Culross Abbey, which they exercised till 1569, when the jurisdiction was made over to Robert Colville of Cleish, ancestor of the Lords Colville of Ochiltree.

Dollar belonged to the diocese of Dunkeld, and in the earlier half of the sixteenth century it had the fortune to be under the spiritual oversight of Thomas Forrest, or Forret, who has come down to posterity as the "Good Vicar of Dollar," and one of the early martyrs in the cause of the Reformation. He is said to have belonged to the family of Forret, landed proprietors in Fife, and his father is styled by Calderwood "master stabler to James IV." He himself was a canon of the monastery of Inchcolm, and was early noted both as a pious youth and earnest student. After his appointment to Dollar, he soon became renowned through the whole country for the zeal and activity of his ministrations, which were principally directed to the exposition of the Holy Scrip-

tures.   Nor in the inculcation of good works did he omit
to practise what he preached.   He was both extremely
charitable to the poor, and refrained from oppressing
them by those exactions which had become so intoler- .
able on the part of the clergy.   In particular, he never
availed himself of the ecclesiastical privilege which
claimed as a perquisite on the occasion of the death of
the head of a family, the best cow and the coverlet or
uppermost cloth of the best bed.   He is also traditionally said to have erected for the public convenience the
bridge across the Devon, known as the Vicar's Bridge,
which has thus served to perpetuate his name.

All this zeal and unselfishness, however, proved eminently distasteful to his ecclesiastical superiors, who per-
ceived in the former a tendency towards justification by
faith and cognate Protestant doctrines, whilst in the
latter they foresaw an encouragement to the laity to
resist the temporal claims put forward by the Church.
Forrest was cited before the Bishop of Dunkeld, and
examined as to the practices alleged against him : his
answers proved, as might have been expected, unsatis-
factory; and he was sent for trial to Edinburgh, where
he was convicted of heresy, and, with four other fellow-
sufferers, burned to death at the stake on the Castle Hill
in 1538.

The Earls of Argyll, who seem then to have occupied
Castle Campbell as their chief residence, adopted zealously the cause of the Reformation during the last years
of the regency of Mary of Guise; and we find the "old
Erle of Argyle," as John Knox terms him, extending his
hospitality and protection to the Reformer, who spent
some days at Castle Campbell previous to his departure
for Geneva in 1556.   Here he "taught certane dayes;"
and the place is yet pointed out on the castle eminence
where he is traditionally said to have preached.   A few

years afterwards Castle Campbell was honoured by a visit from Queen Mary, who travelled thither from Edinburgh in January 1563, to be present at the marriage of Sir James Stewart of Doune (afterwards Lord Doune) with Lady Margaret Campbell, daughter of Archibald, fourth Earl of Argyll. They were the parents of the "bonnie Earl of Moray," whose tragic fate has already been recorded.

In 1605 the greater part of the possessions of the Argyll family in the parish of Dollar were feued out by Archibald, Earl of Argyll, the father of the celebrated Covenanting leader, with the reservation only of Castle Campbell and two farms in the neighbourhood. The rights of lordship or superiority, however, were retained both here and over the adjoining district of Muckhart. During the great civil war, the Marquis of Argyll, in command of an expedition against the Ogilvies in the Braes of Angus, had burned in 1640 their mansion of the "bonnie house o' Airlie," an act for which summary vengeance was taken by Montrose's army in 1644 on their march through the Dollar valley to the field of Kilsyth. Not only was Castle Campbell burned and wrecked, but almost every house in the parishes of Dollar and Muckhart was committed to the flames. The case of the unfortunate inhabitants of this district was brought subsequently before the Covenanting Government, and active measures taken for relieving the sufferers, on whose behalf several Royalists were severely mulcted in the way of compensation. The castle never recovered from the onslaught to which it had been subjected, but in Cromwell's time it was garrisoned by a detachment of his troops, who sent out in 1652 a requisition to the town of Culross for a supply of bedding—a demand the enforcement of which occasioned a vast amount of trouble and annoyance to that little burgh.

The building itself was allowed to go to ruin, and the Argyll family living at a great distance at their seat at Inverary Castle, seem to have gradually lost .interest in Castle Campbell and its territory. Their connection with it finally ceased in 1805, when they disposed of it to Mr Tait. It is now the property of Mr Orr of Harvieston.

Castle Campbell is, of course, the principal object of interest connected with Dollar; and from the elevated knoll on which it stands, in the midst of a densely wooded gorge, it looms forth like the presiding genius of the place. Always attractive with its surroundings, its appearance is perhaps most striking in winter or early spring, when the trees are bare of foliage, and clouds of mist are partially shrouding its grey walls and battlements. Before the use of cannon in sieges, it must have been a very strong fortress indeed, seeing that before the present walk up the glen was constructed along the precipitous banks where scarcely any natural footing exists, the only approach was from the north side by the narrow road which leads up from Old Dollar on the western flank of the Gloom Hill. The castle knoll is a wedge-shaped eminence, washed on the east side by the Turnpike burn or Water of Care, and on the west by the Bank burn or Water of Sorrow, which unite at the point of the wedge near that singular rift or cleft in the rock known as " Kemp's Score."

The opening up of the pathway through the glen has been an immense boon both to the inhabitants of Dollar and the general public, who have thus been spared the fatigues of a circuitous route, and been enabled to contemplate in comfort and safety a scene of mingled grandeur and beauty that resembles a miniature Switzerland, and may call up to the traveller reminiscences of that country. The work was accomplished mainly through the exertions of the late Dr Strachan of Dollar and Mr Peter Stalker, who, having obtained the permission of Sir Andrew Orr, the then proprietor, managed to collect a sum of £300, which was expended in the formation of the roadway. This was no easy undertaking, as the rock required in many places to be blasted, and bridges had to be constructed at the junction of the streams. To maintain the road in good order a toll of sixpence is charged at the entrance of the glen, and as this procures also admission to the castle, the impost must in the circumstances be regarded as a very reasonable one.

Dollar or Castle Campbell Glen, is certainly on the whole the finest in the Ochils; though doubtless the natives of Menstrie, Alva, and Tillicoultry will each claim the superiority for his own valley. It is flanked on the west side by Dollar Hill, which rises to the height of 1129 feet; and on the east by Gloom Hill, which is lower, and has only an elevation of 728. Above Dollar Hill rises the pyramidal King Seat (2110 feet), which commands a magnificent view of the Dollar valley; whilst to the north of the castle is the Saddle Hill (1633 feet), behind which is the White Wisp or Craiginnan Hill (2111 feet), one of the highest in the Ochils. All these hills look down on the castle, which is seen to special advantage from a point at the crest of the ravine, where the slope of Dollar Hill abuts on the latter. The grey tower there stands forth on its green knoll amid the border of bright foliage which clothes the sides of the gorge, the depths of which the eye strives to penetrate, whilst the ear meets the sound of the clear rushing waters as they descend in cascades or ripple gently over the smooth shining pebbles.

Castle Campbell bears no date, but seems to have been built at three different periods. There is the keep or tower at the north extremity, constructed much after the orthodox model of such buildings—that is to say, of a basement storey for stores, or possibly occasionally cattle; a kitchen above, with a vaulted roof; then a great hall, with a modern roof of wood, the old one having been destroyed; then a grand vaulted apartment at the very top, and above that the battlements or flat roof, now surrounded by a low parapet, though it used to be merely an expanse of green turf without any protection.   Yet here parties used to picnic, and even have dances !

Attached to the keep on the south side is a species of supplementary tower with mullioned windows, and a porch with a flat stone roof resting on two handsomely carved pillars.   To the south of this had been a group of apartments ranged in storeys, part of which are still inhabited by the custodian of the castle.   The lower rooms are vaulted, but the upper ones have been repaired and modernised.   What seems to have been a long corridor or gallery extends south of the porch from east to west, with towers at each end; and south again of this are the remains of a large hall, which forms the south front of the castle, and commands a grand prospect of the gorge down to the Dollar valley.   The courtyard of the castle is entered from the north beside the keep by an arched gateway and porch, and there are still some fine old trees on the grassy slope beyond towards the stream.   A small piece of garden-ground extends before the south front of the castle, and beyond this are the remains of some kind of outwork in the form of an archway.   Going through this, we reach a small expanse or grassy projection, which forms the southern extremity of the castle knoll.   It is almost precipitous on three sides, but at the very extremity a rude footpath, still passable for a short distance, seems to have wound along the face of the cliff down to the stream.   On this grassy plot John Knox is said to have preached; but if so, it could not have been to a very large audience, seeing that the space is not merely small, but bordered by precipices. Just before passing through the archway the traveller will observe a narrow chasm or cleft in the rock leading away down to the water's-edge. This rift is called " Kemp's Score," and a story is told of a gigantic robber of former days named Kemp who made himself notorious by his depredations, and at last was so daring as to enter the king's palace at Dunfermline and carry off the royal dinner. He was pursued by a young nobleman who had got into disgrace at Court, and determined if possible now to regain favour. Overtaking Kemp after a long chase, he attacked him, cut off his head, and hastening back with it to Dunfermline, received pardon and reinstatement at Court. The body was thrown by him into the Devon at a place which subsequently bore in remembrance of him the appellation of " Willie's Pool." Such is the history of Kemp, who is said to have scooped out the great cleft at Castle Campbell, which was called after him Kemp's " score " or " cut." But it is scarcely necessary to observe that all this is mere fable. The real explanation of the term is the Gaelic *Ceum scoir*, the step or staircase in the rock. The cleft is probably natural; but there can be little doubt of a sort of rude staircase or series of steps having been made here to enable the garrison in the castle, when besieged, to have access to the stream either for water or as a means of egress. A similar purpose had doubtless been served by the narrow path leading down from the grass plot already mentioned. It only remains to be stated that Kemp's Score, though an ugly, awkward-looking place, has been not unfrequently both ascended and descended in modern times. There is indeed no extraordinary difficulty in doing so in dry weather, if a reasonable amount of care and precaution be taken ; but after rain, the earth which has accumulated in the bottom and sides of the chasm becomes very unctuous and slippery, so that it is extremely difficult for the climber to steady himself or keep a firm grip.

Like Alva, Dollar has also had her mines. Both lead and copper were wrought for several years in the Ochils a little above the town, and silver, it is also said, was discovered in considerable quantities beside the Burn of Care, in Dollar Glen. But in none of these cases did the yield compensate for the expense of working. Valuable pebbles have been found on the summit of the White Wisp Hill. How far it may be worth the traveller's while to climb the hill for this purpose I cannot take on me to say, but there can be little doubt that he will receive ample compensation for his trouble in the splendid prospect which he will obtain from this point if the day be fine. The hill is directly north from the castle, and the proper line of ascent is by the old ruined steading of Craiginnan, which stands out prominently on the green slope. The valley between the Gloom Hill and the White Wisp or Craiginnan Hill is called Glen Quey, and by continuing in an easterly direction along the cart-track which leads up from Old Dollar to Castle Campbell, the traveller will, after a walk of three or four miles, emerge on Glen Devon.

The ascent of the grassy slope above the ruined steading is tolerably steep, but the top of the White Wisp is very level, resembling a wild upland moor, and the cairn or highest point is very far back. With regard to the prospect, it may be generally described as closely resembling that obtained from the summit of Ben Cleuch, which will be seen away to the north-west, and may be reached in this way without much difficulty. Almost directly west from the White Wisp across the ridge is

Tormengie (2091 feet), from which the traveller will look down on Glen Sherup with its reservoir, from which recently not only the town of Dunfermline, but a great part of the country lying between the Devon and the Firth of Forth, have derived their water-supply.   If he descend from this point into the valley to the south-west, he may climb the King Seat, and then descend to Dollar by Dollar Hill and the Castle Glen.

One of the derivations assigned for the old name of the castle is that one of the Scottish princesses, having misconducted herself, was shut up there as a prisoner, and said very naturally that it was a " gloomy " place. At the foot of the Gloom Hill, to the east, an unfortunate individual was burnt as a wizard in the end of the seventeenth century; and a more cheerful reminiscence is called up by a locality at the east end of Old Dollar, which bears the appellation of Fiddlefield.   The popular account of this etymology is tolerably authentic.   Dollar used to be rather famous for its fiddlers, and in the last century there lived here a noted performer of the name of Johnnie Cook.   Johnnie had repaired to Edinburgh to take part in a fiddling competition got up by the Duke of Argyll at his town mansion of Argyll House.   He won the prize, and a considerable sum of money besides, which was subscribed for him as the successful competitor.   With this he returned to his native place, and bought the field to which Scottish sarcasm affixed the title just mentioned.[1]

[1] The Scotch are very fond of affixing satirical designations of this kind.   A piece of land near Edinburgh, which had belonged to a tailor, received the epithet of "Cabbage Ha'"; and another that of the "Castle o' Clouts," for a similar reason ; whilst a house built by a milliner, who had retired from business with a fortune, was dubbed "Lappet Ha'."   At Hogganfield, near Glasgow, is, or used to be, a house known as the " Roly-Poly House," from the circumstance of its having been erected by a dealer in ginger-bread, who

From Dollar to the so-called Yetts of Muckhart, on the great north road from Dunfermline and the Rumbling Bridge to Crieff, through Glen Devon and Glen Eagles, is a distance of four miles. The hamlets of Pitgober, Bauldie's Burn, and the Pool of Muckhart, are passed, as is also the domain of Castleton or Cowden (J. Christie, Esq.), noteworthy as in former times the property of the Archbishops of St Andrews, who made it over to the Argyll family in the end of the fifteenth century. Some remains, including an ancient doorway and tower, are still to be seen of a castle said to have been built in the thirteenth century by Bishop Lamberton. The gardens and grounds of Cowden are very agreeable and interesting. At Bauldie's Burn, towering upwards on the left, is Sea Mab, rising to the height of 1441 feet, the highest of the Ochils in this neighbourhood, and presenting the appearance of a lofty cone of beautiful greensward. The term "Pool" of Muckhart seems a singular designation, and possibly the correct rendering may be the "Peel" or Castle of Muckhart. The Yetts of Muckhart receives its designation from being situated on the great highway leading from Strathearn to the south through Glen Eagles and Glen Devon. The place where the road through the latter entered Muckhart parish used to be called the "Mantrose (Montrose) Yetts," in reference to the frequent descents this way of the Grahams, whose chieftains, the Earls of Montrose, had their stronghold at Kincardine Castle, on the north side of the Ochils, near the northern outlet of Glen Eagles. This is only twelve miles from Castle Campbell, and they were therefore in close proximity to the lands of the Argyll family, who suffered dreadfully in 1644 from the ravages of Montrose and his

had made his fortune by retailing at fairs a particular kind of it known by this epithet.

clan, when Castle Campbell was burned, and the parishes
of Dollar and Muckhart laid waste.

The Yetts of Muckhart may be regarded as a sort of
centre from which numerous distances in all quarters of
the compass are measured. It is eighteen miles from
Crieff, eighteen from North Queensferry, nine from Kinross, eight from Milnathort, four from Dollar, three and
a half from Glen Devon, and one and a half from Rumbling Bridge. In itself it is only an insignificant hamlet,
but there used to be a large and important inn here
which did an extensive business before the days of railways. An immense number of carts, especially, used to
pass this way going to Strathearn with coal and lime
from Blairingone and Fife.

III.

GLEN DEVON, CROOK OF DEVON, AND RUMBLING BRIDGE.

*General Account of the Devon and its vale—Glen Devon and
Glen Eagles—Parish of Fossoway—The Crook of Devon and Tulliebole—The Devil's Mill, Rumbling Bridge, and Cauldron Linn.*

THE whole of the region which we have been traversing
from Logie church eastwards belongs to the vale of the
Devon, which has its source in the parish of Blackford,
in the western range of the Ochils, behind Ben Cleuch.
It flows first east and then south-east through Glen
Devon, separates the parishes of Muckhart and Fossoway,
and maintains a south-easterly course till it reaches the
village of the Crook of Devon, where it makes a singular
bend to the west. It flows in this direction till it reaches
the extremity of Dollar valley in the neighbourhood of

Menstrie and Tullibody, where it turns to the south-west and falls into the sea at Cambus, about two miles to the west of Alloa. Here it is only six miles due south from its source, though including its windings the whole of its course has a length of forty miles. At the Rumbling Bridge, about a mile below the Crook of Devon, it forces its way through a tremendous rift or chasm, and then emerging from this, it pursues a gentle and placid course till it reaches the Cauldron Linn, over which it precipitates itself in a singular and terrific fashion, making a descent of 88 feet. Having thus arrived at a lower level, it resumes its former placidity of current, and preserves it to the end. Indeed the vale of the Devon below the Cauldron Linn is so little raised above the level of the sea, that projects used to be entertained of connecting Alloa and Dollar by means of a canal. In the latter part of its course, the "clear winding Devon" becomes polluted by the discharges from the factories and villages at the foot of the Ochils ; and when it enters the sea at Cambus, it has become a very unsightly stream.

The upper vale of the Devon is known specially as "Glen Devon," which is also the name of the parish in which it is situated. The stream at first is simply a mountain-brook flowing through a lonely and remote valley, which gradually opening out, becomes cultivated, and joins at the hamlet of Glen Devon, at its entrance, the sunny slopes on the southern side of the Ochils. This region is a favourite place for making excursions to, not only from Dollar and the "hillfoots," but from places as remote as Alloa or Stirling, Dunfermline or Kinross. The hamlet is very prettily situated, and at a short distance up the glen there is a very comfortable inn, at which any traveller proceeding northwards to Crieff will do well to refresh himself, seeing that for fully twelve miles between Glen Devon and the village of Muthil there is not merely an absence of inns and hotels, but absolutely not one place where even a biscuit can be procured. The road in this direction proceeds first up Glen Devon, then passes into Glen Eagles, and so into Strathearn. A most beautiful road it is, and equally suited to the requirements of the pedestrian, the bicyclist, or the guider of a four-in-hand team; indeed a four-in-hand coach, conducted by the Messrs Goodwin, used to run some years ago between Auchterarder and the Rumbling Bridge *viâ* Glen Eagles and Glen Devon. But it is one of the loneliest routes in the three kingdoms, and, though much softer as regards the character of the scenery, reminds one strongly in point of solitariness of the famous pass of Drumouchter, between Dalwhinnie and Dalnacardoch.

The distances from Glen Devon are—Rumbling Bridge five, and Crieff fourteen and a half miles. It has a very pretty little church, which, in its sequestered nook by the roadside, is sure to arrest the attention of the traveller. Glen Devon Castle, an old mansion still inhabited, appears on an eminence on the right-hand side of the road about half a mile beyond the church in going to Crieff. At the distance of another half-mile Glen Sherup abuts on Glen Devon, and merits notice as the locality from which Dunfermline and a large portion of the western district of Fife, along with the burgh of Culross, derive their water-supply. Having made the ascent from Glen Devon into Glen Eagles, and passed the twelfth milestone from Crieff, the traveller will find on the left-hand side of the road, a little to the south-west of the old toll-house, a spring which bears the name of St Mungo's Well. The whole district between the Ochils and the Firth of Forth seems to have been the special patrimony of St Mungo and his master St Serf.

An additional interest attaches to the spring in question from the circumstance of its being the source of the Ruthven, which flows through the romantic glen of the same name into the Earn.   Kincardine Castle, the ancient residence of the Montrose family, and now a ruin, stands on an eminence overlooking Ruthven Glen. The Glen Eagles estate was the patrimony of Mr Haldane and his brother, the celebrated evangelist, in the beginning of the present century.   It is now the property of the Earl of Camperdown.   In bygone days Glen Eagles Castle enjoyed an equivocal reputation as the scene of the intrigue of its mistress with Squire Meldrum of Cleish, whose adventures have been recorded by Sir David Lindsay.

On emerging from Glen Eagles the traveller will find himself near a railway station, and also within a few miles of Muthil; but as my present journeying is limited by the Ochils, the north side of which we have now reached, as we did previously at the Kirk of Dron, I can proceed no farther in this direction, and must return to Glen Devon.

In going southwards from Glen Devon towards the Yetts of Muckhart and the Rumbling Bridge, the traveller may notice in the month of June, in a field on his left hand, sloping down to the Devon, a collection of beautiful yellow flowers, which possibly he may be ready to pass without further notice than that they seem to be a lot of very large buttercups.   In reality they are globe-flowers—the " bonnie lucken gowan " of Hogg, which was formerly in great repute as a charm, and which has its habitat in mountainous shady places.   It is rarely, however, that these flowers are found growing together in such quantity as in this meadow, at the entrance of Glen Devon.

Near this place will be observed an ancient narrow bridge over the Devon, which bears the name of St Serf.

An old road crossed here and led through the Ochils to the village of Dunning, in Strathearn, which is now reached by a more convenient highway across a bridge a little lower down the stream, and which branches off from the Glen Devon road immediately to the north of the Yetts of Muckhart. Near the same place the great road from Dollar and Stirling crosses the road to Glen Devon and Crieff, and continues in an easterly direction downhill. Crossing the Devon at Old Fossoway Bridge, it skirts the base of the Ochils through Carnbo to Milnathort, a distance of eight miles; whilst at a point three and a half miles to the west of the latter place it sends off a branch to Kinross, which is thus nine miles from the Yetts and thirteen from Dollar. It leads through the finest and most attractive part of Kinross-shire, the soil being good and the country well wooded, whilst the ridge that here forms the south front of the Ochils is cultivated almost to its very summit.

The parish of Fossoway, which is entered after crossing the Devon at Old Fossoway Bridge, is rather singularly placed, having its north and south districts in the county of Perth ; whilst an intervening portion, originally forming the old parish of Tulliebole, belongs to Kinross-shire, and is inserted like a wedge between the divisions belonging to Perth. To distinguish these two last, the northern is generally known by the appellation of Old Fossoway; and it also contains the old parish church, manse, and burying-ground, which are situated on the rising ground on the north side of the road, about half a mile to the east of Old Fossoway Bridge. The high hill that rises behind to the north is called Lendrick Hill, and has a height of 1496 feet.

The old manse of Fossoway has been refitted as a private residence, and is very pleasantly situated, being approached by an avenue from the Milnathort road.

The churchyard immediately adjoins it on the east, and is still occasionally used for interments; but as regards the church, little more than the foundations can now be discerned.   An ancient tomb or *through-stane* will be observed in memory of the Rev. Laurence Mercer, minister of Fossoway in the seventeenth century, and a member of the family of Meikleour, who owned Aldie Castle in the southern division of Fossoway.

Fossoway is said to be a form of the Gaelic *Fasach fheidh*—the desert of deer—just as the adjoining parish of Muckhart is said to be *Muic-ard*, or the height of the wild boar,—derivations which are not without some degree of probability.   It seems to have been incorporated about 1614 with Tulliebole, where a "reader" used to officiate, and had a stipend assigned out of the third of the revenues of the Abbey of Culross.   The ancient lords of the parish were the Murrays of Tullibardine, ancestors of the Dukes of Athole, who are or were till recently the feudal superiors of the greater portion of the lands in Fossoway and Tulliebole, though they no longer hold any actual property.

The village of the Crook of Devon lies about a mile to the south of Old Fossoway church, and belongs to Kinross-shire and the old parish of Tulliebole.   It may be reached from Old Fossoway by a by-way which runs south from the Milnathort road and abuts on its eastern extremity.   The great artery of communication to and from it is the highway from Kinross, which, issuing from the middle of the town, keeps first north-east towards the railway station at Kinross Junction, and then proceeds nearly due east, crossing the South Queich at Balado Bridge, and skirting on the north side the grounds of Tulliebole Castle.   The distance of the Crook of Devon from Kinross is about six miles, and the road, though somewhat tame and monotonous, is an excellent one, and admirably kept, like all the others in the county. A stranger cannot fail to remark the multiplicity of roads, all good, which intersect in every direction this portion of Kinross-shire.

Tulliebole lies about a mile to the east of the Crook of Devon, with the hamlet of Drum between the places. Among the documents relating to Scotland preserved in the Record Office in London, there are, of 20th April 1304, "letters patent" from "Tulliebotheville," declaring that the King (Edward I.) has granted to Gilbert Malherbe all the goods and chattels of William Oliphant, knight, and others, and of the garrison of Stirling Castle, then in arms against him, wherever they may be found in Scotland. The identity of this term with the modern Tulliebole is rendered more than probable from a memorandum of a writ to be sent in King Edward's name in the year last mentioned to John, Earl of Athole, who was lord of the domain of Fossoway, and Edward's warden between Forth and Orkney. He and the chamberlain of Scotland, John, are ordered to buy or procure in exchange a castle in a good place beyond Forth, inasmuch as his Majesty had decided to build one at "Tulliebotheville," but could find no proper site.

The castle communicates by a north avenue with the road from the Crook of Devon to Kinross, and by a south one with that to Cleish. The Tulliebole estate belongs to Lord Moncreiff, and the castle is a fine specimen of an old Scottish baronial mansion. It bears the date of 1608, is in good repair, and is let to an Edinburgh gentleman for summer quarters. Lord Moncreiff's grandfather, Sir Henry Wellwood Moncreiff, the well-known leader in the Church, and minister of St Cuthbert's, Edinburgh, used to retire here regularly in the summer months, and dispense for a time the dignified hospitality of an old Scottish baron.

The castle is surrounded by some fine old timber, and at the north-east extremity of the policy, on the outside, are the old churchyard and church of Tulliebole. As in the case of Old Fossoway, however, there is nothing to be seen of the latter beyond the foundations. A small obelisk is erected to the memory of the late Lord Moncreiff, and forms a conspicuous object on the road from Crook of Devon to Kinross. At about two miles from the former place, and a little beyond where the Moncreiff monument comes into view, the highway is crossed by a rivulet known as the "Trooper's Dub," and connected with which there is a tale. It is said that a King of Scotland in former days, whilst passing in this direction between Stirling and Falkland, was hospitably entertained at Tulliebole Castle, whilst his retinue were feasted in a meadow by a burnside at a little distance. A drinking-match ensued between one of the royal guards and a retainer of the Laird of Tulliebole named Keltie. The latter came off victorious, but the unfortunate trooper succumbed to the evil effects of the protracted potation, and died on the scene of the debauch. He was buried there, and to this day the rivulet or pool bears the name of the "Trooper's Dub," and the field that of the "Trooper's Park." The ghost of the unfortunate trooper was believed to haunt the spot, and up to a recent period few country-people cared to pass the "Trooper's Dub" at night. Another strange story, not suitable to be related here, has long been current in Fossoway regarding the vengeance taken by an infuriated blacksmith on a priest who had seduced his wife. The smith's anvil, which figures prominently in the legend, is or used to be preserved in the parish under the epithet of "the Reformation Clog."

The Crook of Devon is a straggling village, and contains one little inn at which refreshments may be obtained

and horses put up.   It used to be famous for its cattle
fairs, and certain inhabitants of the village connected
with these, who were in the habit of occasionally visiting
the burgh of Culross, are dealt with severely by the kirk-
session of that parish as "outlandish drunkards" and
disturbers of the quiet of the town on the Sabbath-day.
This was in 1634; and about the same period it is recorded that a murder took place at one of these markets,
in consequence of a vassel of the Laird of Tulliebole
having stabbed another in a quarrel.   The guilty party
took to flight, but was pursued, captured, and brought
before his superior as lord of regality.   He was condemned, and executed the same evening on a rising
ground at the east end of the village, where the road
to Old Fossoway branches off, and the place still bears
the name of the "Gallows Knowe."

The present church of Fossoway is situated at the
west end of the Crook of Devon, on the left-hand side of
the main highway proceeding from that village to the
west.   The Devon here takes its curious turn in the
same direction, and in about a mile reaches the chasm
at the Rumbling Bridge.   Before arriving there it passes
through a rugged and precipitous defile, and about 450
yards above the bridge occurs the singular phenomenon
known as the "Devil's Mill."   This is a peculiar movement resembling in sound the clack of a mill, which,
being heard both Sunday and Saturday, has given rise to
the epithet.   It is only heard to perfection in certain
conditions of the water, and is caused by the latter striking and rebounding from a particular point in the rock.
This sound is often very clear and distinct, and the surroundings are sufficiently picturesque, partaking, indeed,
somewhat of the terrific.   The Devil's Mill is situated
within the grounds of the Rumbling Bridge Hotel, the
proprietor of which is the lessee also of the path leading

down from the bridge to the Cauldron Linn. Strangers desirous of visiting these places obtain at the hotel passes which admit them to the grounds.

The highway from Kinross, after passing through the Crook of Devon, continues in a south-west direction for nearly a mile, till it meets the north road from Dunfermline to Glen Devon and Crieff, close to the Rumbling Bridge station on the Alloa and Kinross railway. A very fine view is obtained here of the lower Devon valley, which stretches away in the distance to the west; whilst nearer to the spectator the stream is bordered on the north by a finely wooded steep bank on the estate of Blairhill (James R. Haig, Esq.), whose grounds extend from the Rumbling Bridge down to the Cauldron Linn. Here the traveller may either turn to the right and visit the Rumbling Bridge, or he may proceed south for about a mile to the village of Powmill, from which a road leads almost due west through Blairingone to Alloa.

The shorter road from the Crook of Devon to the Rumbling Bridge is by turning to the right, near the west end of the village, and crossing the bridge which here spans the Devon. Proceeding onwards for about half a mile in a north-west direction, with the mansion and grounds of Naemoors (John Mowbray, Esq.) on the right, the north road is reached within 200 yards of the Rumbling Bridge Hotel. This establishment long enjoyed deservedly a great reputation under the management of the late Mr M'Ara, and its prestige is still maintained by his son. The locality has from time immemorial been an object of attraction, as recited in the following couplet:—

> "The Rumblin' Brigg and the Cauldron Linn,
>   And the Links o' Devon water."

The Devil's Mill, a few hundred yards higher up, has

already been described. As regards the bridge and the
tremendous rift which it spans, it is one of those
wondrous and appalling places of which the traveller
receives no warning from any appearances in the adjoining scenery. Every adjunct is of the calm and peaceful
order, whether he approach the bridge from the Yetts of
Muckhart or from the south. It is not till he is actually
crossing the structure and has looked over the parapet
that he becomes sensible of the terrific as well as romantically picturesque character of the place. Down he
gazes into the stupendous defile with its precipitous
walls of rock, at the bottom of which the tortured and
imprisoned stream struggles to force its way, but at last
emerges between a range of lofty and beautifully wooded
banks. The height of the parapet of the bridge above
the bottom of the chasm is about 120 feet.

The present bridge is a modern structure erected
about seventy years ago. Beneath it, and completely
overshadowed by the modern erection, but quite visible
from the banks above or below, is an older bridge, 86
feet above the stream, having only a breadth of 12 feet,
and wholly unprovided with any parapet. It superseded
an old wooden bridge, and was erected in 1713 by a
mason named William Gray, a native of the parish of
Saline, though Burns in his account of his visit to this
place speaks of the popular belief of the architect being
no other than the Devil, whose name is connected with
so many of the grander features in natural scenery.
How a bridge could have been erected at such a spot
without any protecting ledge, and have been allowed to
continue so long in that condition, seems strange at the
present day; but so it was, and there is no record of any
accident whatever having ever taken place whilst it
formed the medium of transit. It had doubtless been
constructed at first with the view only of accommo-

dating passengers on foot and on horseback; but vehicles certainly crossed it also, though in such a case it was customary for travellers to descend, and the driver to go to his horse's head and lead him over. Till within the last few years the old Rumbling Bridge was accessible from the bank at the south-west corner, but a fatal accident which took place here on one occasion led to the approach being rendered quite impracticable.

From the Rumbling Bridge is a pleasant walk of nearly two miles along the left bank of the Devon to the Cauldron Linn. The river, after emerging from the rocky defile, flows in a very mild and peaceful fashion, its clear rippling waters sometimes settling into limpid pools of no great depth. The pathway lies close to the stream, the bank of which on this side is very low. At last a low growl is heard, increasing speedily into a loud roar. The river-bank rises suddenly in front of the traveller, and, advancing a few steps, he finds himself on the side of a terrific abyss, into which the hitherto placid stream precipitates itself through a succession of cauldrons or excavations in the rock, and then, after passing through these, takes a final and single leap over a precipice into a pool below. The whole height of the fall is 88 feet, which is divided into two nearly equal descents of 44 feet each, the upper one comprising the passage of the stream from the summit of the cascade to its issue from the last of the cauldrons, and the lower one consisting of a sheer and unbroken descent.

The whole aspect of this celebrated cascade leaves a decided impression of the horrible as well as the sublime; and I can testify from my own experience that I never approached the scene without a shudder. This may partly be due to a terrific story, which, however, is perfectly authentic, in connection with the Cauldron Linn.

About seventy years ago, or a little more, Mr Harrower of Inzievar, in the parish of Torryburn, happened with some friends to make an excursion to this place. It ought to be mentioned, in passing, that at the very brink of the cascade it is possible for an adventurous person to make a spring across from one side to the other of the Devon, the breadth at this point barely amounting to 12 feet, whilst an intervening rock may be used as a stepping-stone. Mr Harrower made the attempt, but having spurs attached to his boots, one of these caught the rock. He stumbled, fell, and was swept at once over the fall into one of the cauldrons. Fortunately there was no great depth of water in it, and instead of being carried through it with the stream, he was retained within its narrow enclosure, and managed to gain an upright position and support himself on a bed of sand. How to get out of the fearful abyss, however, was the question, as the sides were quite precipitous, and it was utterly impossible to do so unaided. A friend rushed off to the nearest farm—a distance of at least half a mile—procured a rope, and hurried with it to the spot, when, dreadful to relate, it proved too short to reach the unfortunate man, who in the meantime was slowly and gradually sinking into the sand on which he was standing. Another race had to be made, and a longer rope procured. It was adjusted into a noose, thrown over his head and round his waist, and the process of pulling up commenced. A new danger here presented itself. The rope twisted itself round his neck, and he was in imminent danger of being strangled. He had fortunately, however, the presence of mind to interpose his hand between the cord and his neck, and thus escaped such a catastrophe. At last, after having been nearly half an hour in the cauldron, he was extricated, and safely landed on *terra firma*. A relative of mine met him at the same spot a year or two afterwards, and received an account of the adventure from his own lips.

Another story of a fall into the Cauldron Linn is recorded of a fox. On the occasion of several runs in this neighbourhood, Reynard had always managed here to elude his pursuers, and even cause the destruction of several dogs, whose blind ardour made them tumble headlong into the abyss. How he managed himself to escape such a fate remained a mystery, till it was discovered that he contrived to lay hold of a projecting twig above the linn, and there lie safe till danger of pursuit was over. The huntsman, however, one evening cut off the branch. Poor Reynard made his customary leap next day to his place of refuge, and of course went headlong into the whirlpool below.

The garden at Blairhill comes close to the edge of the Cauldron Linn on its right bank, and from an arbour in an elevated corner the whole course of the cascade is overlooked. The view of it is equally good from either side of the stream, but it is generally witnessed from the south or Fossoway side. It is worth while to descend the hill to the pool at the bottom of the fall and witness the effect from below. In winter or in time of floods this is very striking.

When visiting at Harvieston, Robert Burns took part in an excursion to the Rumbling Bridge and Cauldron Linn, and, it would appear, rather disappointed his host and friends by remaining silent and unimpressed by the grandeur of the scenery. Various accounts and explanations have been given of the matter, but the simple truth is, probably, that the bard, like other men, had from some cause or other been out of humour, and indisposed to make himself agreeable or act the part of a lion.

IV.

ALDIE CASTLE AND SOUTH FOSSOWAY.

Road from Powmill to Cleish—Aldie Castle and its traditions—Ancient connection of the Athole family with Fossoway—Blairingone—The "Monk's Grave."

IN a previous chapter, the traveller, after journeying from Dunfermline and coming, at the farm of Meadowhead, within sight of Aldie Castle and the entrance to the valley of Cleish, was made somewhat unceremoniously to retrace his steps and proceed by a branch road from Hill End to Saline. We shall now resume again the journey to the Rumbling Bridge at the point then abandoned, and thus link together the different scenes through which we have passed.

Leaving Meadowhead on our right, we continue to descend the hill past Pow Lodge; and then at the bottom, after crossing a flat tract of marsh-land, we ascend again to the hamlet of Pow Mill, where a road on the left branches off to Blairingone and Alloa. We now proceed downhill to the bridge which crosses here the Pow, as the lower course of the West Gairney is called, and then again ascending a steep acclivity, we find a road on the right leading along the Aldie ridge to Cleish. Here we are within a mile of the Rumbling Bridge, and not much farther from the Crook of Devon, the road to which, as already mentioned, branches off from the present one near the railway station.

Let us now follow the upper road to Cleish. Having travelled along it about a mile and a half, we pass on our left the rising ground of Carleith, on which used to be the ruins of a circular building, about 24 feet in diam-

eter. In the end of the last century the ground where
it stands was planted, and the stones of the ancient
edifice were employed in the construction of the enclosing
fence. In the course of the excavations two stone coffins
containing human bones were found near the centre of
the structure. It had evidently formed one of those
burial-places of the primeval inhabitants of the district,
of which so many have been discovered in all parts of
the British Islands.

Proceeding a little farther east from Carleith, a road
on the right leads down to the parks of Aldie and Aldie
Castle, the ancient patrimony of the Mercers, and now
the inheritance of the Dowager-Marchioness of Lans-
downe, whose maternal grandmother, Miss Mercer, as
heiress of Aldie, conveyed the estate to the Elphinstone
family by her marriage with Lord Keith of Tulliallan.
The old castle, though not absolutely a ruin, is still in a
very dilapidated state, and has not been inhabited for a
long period. It stands on an eminence overlooking the
Cleish valley, and consists of a keep flanked at the upper
corners with turrets, whilst attached to it in front is a
house of more recent construction. A little to the east,
on the castle green, is a holly-tree, regarding which an
old legend states that a groom was hanged on it for the
comparatively venial offence of "stealing a caup [meas-
ure] of corn." Before being turned off he invoked a mal-
ison on the Mercer family that they should never have
a son to inherit the property—a prophecy which has certainly held good for several generations.

Another tradition connected with Aldie is that of a
famous witch, known as "Meg of Aldie," but of whose
history, whether real or mythical, almost nothing seems
to be preserved. She is said to have taken a great interest in a Laird of Aldie, who made an expedition to
the Holy Land with the special purpose of effecting in

addition the ascent of Mount Sinai. Some hazy memory
is perhaps here preserved of the Murrays of Tullibardine,
the ancient lords of Fossoway, having taken part in the
Crusades. Meg is said, according to some accounts, to
have accompanied her chief, but used her powers to
prevent the fulfilment of his vow as regarded the ascent
of the holy mount. Awaking one morning—so says the
tale—the Laird of Aldie found written on his arm :—

> " The Laird of Aldie you may be,
> But the top of Mount Sinai you'll never see. "

And so he never did, though he returned safe and sound
to his native land.

Aldie Castle is said to have been built in the sixteenth
century. If this date is correct, it probably refers to the
erection of the southern and more recent portion. It is
ascertained that in 1475 Isabella Wardlaw of Torrie, the
wife apparently of Laurence Mercer of Meikleour, and
assuredly the mother of Henry Mercer, was infeft in the
lands of " Estir-awdeis " and " Wester-awdeis," the lands
of Powmill and others. The common story is, that the
Aldie estate came into the possession of William Mercer
of Meikleour by his marriage with the heiress, the beautiful Aldia Murray, of the Tullibardine family, from
whom, moreover, it is said that the property received its
appellation. This is, however, a questionable assertion,
as it is much more likely that the name Aldie is of Celtic
origin. It has been derived by Colonel Robertson from
allt dubh (the dark stream)—a not unlikely origin, as the
Pow flows through the valley in front of the castle.

The following not very complimentary rhyme used to
be current regarding Aldie and its neighbourhood :—

> " Hard heads in Hardiston,
> Quakers in the Pow ;
> The braw Aldie lasses
> Canna spin their tow. "

At the east extremity of the castle slope is the old garden, now employed as a nursery of young trees. It contains two very old specimens of the oriental or real plane, which casts its bark every month. As is well known, what is ordinarily called in this country the plane is in reality the sycamore. From the woodland path which leads by the garden, the Cleish road may again be reached by proceeding north-east across the fields. Opposite the road by which we diverged to visit Aldie Castle, a path leads across the country in a northerly direction to the railway station at the Crook of Devon. Continuing about a mile and a half farther east on our original course, we see on our left the grounds of Tulliebole, and soon afterwards reach the eastern extremity of the parish of Fossoway, where it meets those of Cleish and Kinross. Here are the lands of Coldrain, belonging to the ancient barony of that name, formerly possessed, with the rest of Fossoway, by the progenitors of the Athole family. A little to the south of Wood of Coldrain farm is a square enclosure known as "Hall Yard," and extending to a little more than an imperial acre. It is surrounded by a ditch, and had contained at one time a castle, said traditionally to have been a hunting-seat of the Murrays.

Tullibardine, the ancient inheritance of the Murrays, from which the Athole family takes its secondary title, is situated in the parish of Blackford, on the north side of the Ochils; and the ruins of the castle which they inhabited are still to be seen in Tullibardine Moor. The lands and barony of Tullibardine, including Pitvar, Solsgirth, Blairingone, &c., seem to have been adjudged or apprised in 1545 from William Murray, and made over to Cardinal David Beaton of St Andrews. He had borrowed £2800 from the Cardinal, and had a right of reversion provided the money were paid within seven years. The Murrays were the leading family in this part of Scotland, and owned nearly the whole of the present parish of Fossoway. At Blairingone, on the left-hand side of the road in descending from that village to the Vicar's Bridge, they had a residence, of which till recently some faint traces still remained. Till 1873, moreover, the Dukes of Athole, their descendants, owned the farm of Dundrummie in this neighbourhood, along with the whole of the so-called Blairingone coal, which used to be worked to a great extent for the supply both of the adjoining country and the region of Strathearn, on the other side of the Ochils. They have, since the date last mentioned, ceased to hold any property in this district. A lintel-stone belonging to the old castle, and having a coat-of-arms sculptured upon it, was conveyed away at that time to Blair Atholl as a relic of the ancestral abode.

One other memory of the Athole family in Fossoway may be noticed. In going from Powmill by the road already mentioned as leading west from thence to Blairingone, the traveller, after proceeding about three-quarters of a mile, will see a pleasant shady road on his left, which will lead him in a south-westerly direction to an expanse of moorland interspersed with hillocks and scrub, and termed by the country-people "the Monk's Grove," which is, however, a corruption from "the Monk's Grave," a locality now obliterated and forgotten, but connected with a curious legend. In consequence of an act of sacrilege on the part of a chieftain of the Murrays in setting fire to a church in which a hostile clan had taken refuge, he had been compelled to make over the lands of Pethwer, or Pitfar, with others, to the monks of Culross. In after-times a dispute arose with this convent as to the boundary of the lands which they thus held. A meeting of the opposing parties took place, when one of the Culross ecclesiastics gave oath that he was at that moment standing on soil belonging to Culross Abbey. One of the Murrays, exasperated at what he considered to be perjury, struck down and slew the monk, on pulling off whose shoes they were found filled with earth from Culross. The fraudulent churchman was buried where he fell, and his grave was long shown as a memorial of the occurrence. A quarry which has been opened here has very probably effaced the burial-mound.

About half a mile due south from the Monk's Grave, on the slope of the rising ground, is the house of Pitfar, a modern mansion. Following the old road over the hill by Barnhill and Bankhead, we emerge at the house of Burnside (Alexander Macleod, Esq.), a little to the north-west of Saline village, on the old road leading from thence to Dollar. We are now again in the county of Fife, a rill which we crossed to the south of Pitfar separating the parish of Saline from that of Fossoway, and the county of Fife from that of Perth. At Solsgirth, in the south-west corner of the parish of Fossoway, where the latter abuts on Clackmannan, it is popularly said that you may stand with your right foot in Perthshire and your left in Fife, and then stooping down without shifting your position, you may rest both of your hands in the county of Clackmannan.

V.

FROM THE CAULDRON LINN TO THE FORTH.

The Vicar's Bridge—Lower course of the Devon—Sauchie Tower —Tullibody—Its church and other objects of interest—Farm of the " King o' the Muirs."

AT a little distance below the Cauldron Linn, about half-way between the Dollar and Rumbling Bridge stations, the Devon is crossed by a viaduct on the Alloa and Kinross railway. Here, too, it receives the West Gairney, a stream coming down from Kinross-shire, and known in the upper part of its course by the name of the Pow. Farther down still, about three-quarters of a mile above Dollar, it is crossed by the Vicar's Bridge, an ancient structure, originally erected by Thomas Forrest, the good Vicar of Dollar, but till within a comparatively recent period only a narrow bridge of nine feet in breadth, without any parapet; it was consequently impassable for vehicles. The more recent portion is on the west side, and here an inscription has been put up to the memory of the Vicar. The scenery around, though differing much from that at the Rumbling Bridge, is still very picturesque, and immediately above the bridge there is a good trouting-pool.

From the Rumbling to the Vicar's Bridge the course of the Devon has been through a deep, densely wooded ravine, but shortly after reaching the last-named point, the valley begins to widen out, and before reaching the vicinity of Tillicoultry, it is fringed by a broad belt of meadowland. This characteristic increases as it advances to the sea, and latterly the river makes its way through a dead level of carse-land.

Beyond Tillicoultry, and near the Devon Ironworks, on the right bank of the river, is the old ruin of Sauchie Tower, formerly the residence of the Shaws, the ancient proprietors of the Sauchie estate. This afterwards came into the possession of the Earl of Cathcart, and ultimately was acquired by the Earl of Mansfield, to whom it now belongs. The present mansion-house of the estate is called Shaw Park, and is picturesquely situated at the north-west extremity of Gartmorn dam, on an eminence covered with wood and commanding an extensive view. Sauchie is now a *quoad sacra* parish formed out of Clackmannan.

The long terrace that extends along the south bank of the Devon from the neighbourhood of the Rumbling Bridge almost to the mouth of the stream, by Powmill and Blairingone, comes to a termination at the ancient village of Tullibody, two miles to the north-west of Alloa. From this point a road leads almost due north, crossing the Devon by an ancient, high-arched bridge, and joining, a little to the east of Menstrie, the highway from Stirling to Dollar by the foot of the Ochils. Tullibody, from various reasons, is well deserving of attention. It formed originally a parish itself, and even claimed to be the mother church of Alloa, to which, notwithstanding a considerable amount of opposition, it was annexed by an ecclesiastical decree in the year 1600. Originally it belonged to the Abbey of Cambuskenneth.

Tullibody is rather an irregularly built straggling village, but it commands a fine view of the Ochils and the Devon valley. Robert Dick, the naturalist and baker of Thurso, whose biography has been written by Mr Smiles, was born at Tullibody in 1811, and passed here the years of his boyhood and youth. It is also notable in connection with the Abercromby family, who own a large amount of property in the parish, and take from it part of the title of their peerage. Tullibody House, the old mansion of the estate, stands close to the Forth, a little above Alloa. The celebrated Sir Ralph Abercromby, the hero of Alexandria, is sometimes stated to have been born there, but the more generally received account is that his birthplace was at another of the family seats at Menstrie. He was the eldest son of George Abercromby of Tullibody, who acquired also the property of Brucefield in Clackmannanshire, and retired thither after having made over the Tullibody estate to Sir Ralph. After the latter's death, a peerage was bestowed on his widow, and thus transmitted to his descendant, the present Lord Abercromby.

Tullibody is now a *quoad sacra* parish. The church, after long remaining a ruin, was converted into a mausoleum for the Abercromby family, and latterly, about half a century ago, was refitted as a place of worship. In the middle of the sixteenth century it had been subjected to peculiarly contumelious treatment at the hands of a French army which had come over to assist Mary of Guise in her struggles with the Reformers. They had retreated from the east of Fife, to which they had previously marched round by Stirling Bridge from Edinburgh and Linlithgow, and were now compelled to return on the same track by the arrival of a fleet of English vessels in the mouth of the Firth. Meantime, to cut off their retreat to the west, Kirkaldy of Grange had broken down the bridge over the Devon at Tullibody. The French arriving there and finding their passage interrupted, took off the roof from Tullibody church, and employed the beams in improvising a new bridge. Crossing the river by this means, they arrived at Stirling, and at last managed to reach Leith.

In 844 Tullibody is said to have been the scene of an engagement between Kenneth, the Scottish claimant to the throne, as representing his father Alpin, and Drust or Drest, the Pictish monarch by whom Alpin had been defeated and slain. It resulted in the entire discomfiture of Drust ; and the supremacy over Alban, or Scotland to the north of the Forth, was thus ensured for ever to the Scottish dynasty. The field of victory was long marked by a memorial stone, which more than half a century ago was removed, but its site is still pointed out, about fifty yards from the " Haer Stane." The last is a shapeless mass of basalt, of whose history nothing is known. It stands on the declivity of Baingle Brae, to the southwest of the village, and was formerly surrounded by a number of smaller stones, after the manner of the so-called Druidical circles.

At the north end of the church of Tullibody is a stone coffin, called the " Maiden's Stone," which is said to commemorate the faithlessness of a priest who had betrayed a young lady of good family in the neighbourhood. She died of a broken heart, and expressed as her last request a wish that her coffin should remain for ever at the church-door, as a warning and testimony against the treachery of man. The occurrence, the legend says, took place on the eve of the Reformation, and the guilty ecclesiastic, who had to save himself by flight, was the last priest who officiated at Tullibody.

To the east of the village is a large wood, known as Tullibody Wood, in which Montrose and his Highlanders encamped on their way to the field of Kilsyth. During the eventful year 1745, when the Highlanders were marching down on the low country and threatening Stirling, Ebenezer Erskine, one of the leaders of the Secession, held here his Sunday services. Just outside of it, at its north-east extremity, is the farm called the " King o' the Muirs," noted in connection with an alleged adventure of James V. It is said that this monarch,

having been belated when out hunting in the upper
barony of Alloa, and become separated from his attendants, sought shelter in a farmhouse, where he remained
for the night and received the utmost hospitality. In
special token of goodwill, his host desired his wife to
kill the hen that roosted next the cock, as being the fat-
test, and prepare it for his guest's supper. The king
was much gratified by all this kindness, but strictly preserved his *incognito*, and when he left next morning,
requested the farmer, a man of the name of Donaldson,
to call next day at Stirling Castle, and ask for the Good-
man of Ballengeich. Donaldson did so, and of course
was much astonished to find that he had been entertain-
ing the king. James presented him with the farm which
he cultivated—apparently a portion of the Crown lands
—though it afterwards came into the possession of the
Mar family. Whatever reliance may be placed on this
story, it is certain that it was occupied for generations
by a family of the name of Donaldson, who were, however, dispossessed by the Erskines about a hundred years
ago. It has been alleged, in excuse of this apparent
act of severity, that the Donaldson who was then tenant had become incorrigibly idle and negligent in the
management of his farm, as well as in the payment of
his rent, and that Mr Erskine,[1] after that his patience
had been tried beyond endurance, was at last obliged
with great reluctance to turn him out of his holding.
He retired to Alloa and died there, but retained to the
last the title of "king."

---

[1] There was no Earl of Mar at that time, as forfeiture of the
title had been incurred, though the estates had been bought back
and still remained in the family.

CONCLUSION.

CAMBUSKENNETH, THE ABBEY CRAIG, AND THE BRIDGE OF ALLAN.

CROSSING the Devon at Cambus, and proceeding along an open road through the level carse-ground, the traveller will arrive at the village of Craigmill, situated directly under the Abbey Craig, about four and a half miles from Alloa and two and a half from Stirling. It used to be noted in former days for the smuggling propensities of its inhabitants, but is now a very peaceful-looking, attractive little hamlet, after passing which, a road turning down to the left leads almost in a straight line through a tract of meadow-land to the site of the ancient Abbey of Cambuskenneth.

This venerable ruin, if ruin it can be called—seeing that with the exception of one massive tower, a pointed arch or doorway, and the walls of the *columbarium* or pigeon-house, there was till within the last twenty years nothing to be seen here but an expanse of rich greensward—exhibits, perhaps more than any other of the ancient Scottish abbeys, the most complete spectacle of grandeur effaced and buried. It stands on a level corner or projection of ground around which winds the Forth, a stream in this neighbourhood of so many turnings that a stranger feels thoroughly puzzled in endeavouring to unravel them, and is quite unable at a little distance to determine its line of course, or say whether the one solitary tower that presents itself to his view is situated on the left or right bank of the river. The position, though low and flat and suggestive of dampness, is nevertheless a very agreeable one; and the old predilections of the monks for sunny fertile places as admirably adapted for orchard and garden ground, are thoroughly conspicuous in the surroundings of Cambuskenneth Abbey. It adjoins a series of market-gardens and orchards which cover a loop of the Forth from east to west, and are still famous for their produce, more especially in the way of early summer fruit, such as gooseberries and strawberries. A straggling village is interspersed amid these, and the greater part of the territory forms part of the ancient Abbey enclosure, portions of the old walls of which are built into the cottages and garden dykes.

Cambuskenneth Abbey was founded by David I. in 1147, and was anciently called the Abbey of Stirling, from which it is only about half a mile to Cambuskenneth Ferry. This is the easiest way of reaching the place, as Causewayhead, at the south-west extremity of the Abbey Craig, is a mile due north from the ruins, and two miles from Stirling. The monks of Cambuskenneth were Augustine friars, who came from Artois in France. Several Scottish Parliaments were held within the walls of the Abbey, more especially one in 1326, not long before Robert Bruce's death, when the barons and clergy swore fealty to his son, Prince David, as heir-apparent to the throne. At the Reformation, the lands and buildings of the monastery came into the possession of Regent Mar, who, it is said, employed the stones of the latter in the erection of a structure on the Castle-hill of Stirling,

known as " Mar's Work," but of which nothing more
was ever executed than the east front, still existing as a
stately architectural fragment.   In the beginning of the
last century, the Abbey lands were purchased by the
trustees of Cowane's Hospital, Stirling, and still remain
in their possession.   In 1864 a series of excavations
were made, with the most important results, as nearly
the whole outline of the Abbey buildings, including the
remains of James III. and his queen, in front of the
high altar, were disclosed.

The existing remains of the Abbey, as now exposed,
consist of the foundations of a cruciform church, with
the high altar at the east end, in front of which stands a
tomb of modern erection, enclosed by a railing, in which
the bones of James III. and his queen have been reinterred.   The tomb was erected by the command and at
the expense of Queen Victoria, who is herself lineally
descended from James III., through the marriage of his
son with the daughter of Henry VII. of England.   A
thorn which grew near this spot, but has long since disappeared, used to be said traditionally to mark the site
of the royal burial-place.

The whole length of the space enclosed within the
foundations of the church amounts to 178 with a breadth
of 37 feet.   The north transept is very clearly defined
as a limb of the cross, and also the bases of the pillars
of the choir, with the lines of the north and south walls ;
but it does not seem possible to make out a south aisle,
though a north one can be traced.   The screen between
the nave and choir is also discernible, and a broad piece
of masonry, which may have been part of the foundations of a central tower.   The south transept of the choir
terminates in what appears to have been the chapter-
house, with the customary pillar in the centre which supported the roof.   The space occupied by the nave has

for a long period been partly formed into a small bury-ing-ground, which contains a fine pointed arch, in good preservation, that has evidently been the west doorway of the church. At the north-west corner of the church, but quite detached from it, stands the campanile or bell-tower—a substantial massive structure in the Early Eng-lish style, surmounted by a perpendicular battlement. It is entered on the south side by a doorway through a pointed arch, above which is a canopied niche, in which a figure of the Virgin, as patroness of the church, had probably rested. The tower is 70 feet in height, and has recently been repaired and restored, a process which in-cluded the filling in of the windows with glass, and the replacement of the roof of the second storey by a wooden floor. There are in all three storeys, and at the north-east corner there is a subsidiary tower, with a spiral stair-case. The basement storey is vaulted, with a hole in the centre of the groined roof through which the bell-ropes passed. The chamber on the first floor is lighted on each of the four sides by a lancet or Early English window; and a similar arrangement characterises the chamber above, except that the lancet-windows are double. A splendid view of the Ochils and windings of the Forth is commanded from the battlements, around the outside of which are some curious masks and figures. The cloister-court and conventual buildings had chiefly been on the east and south sides of the church, traces of all which are visible, including more especially the foundations of the refectory on the south side of the cloister-court. In the adjoining orchard is a place which used to be known by the appellation of "The Stairs," though nothing of the kind was manifest. On trenching the ground, however, there was disclosed a flight of steps, which in all likelihood had led to the cellars beneath the refectory. Various other remains are to be noticed in the expanse of greensward between the Abbey buildings and the river, and two walls still remain tolerably entire of a lofty building, which had evidently been the *columbarium* or pigeon-house.

The Abbey Craig, from which we diverged to visit Cambuskenneth, is a picturesque rock, forming a spur of the Ochils running from north to south through the grounds of Airthrey, and terminating in a rounded projection. Its sides are clothed with wood, mixed with rocky *débris*, and the southern extremity is almost precipitous, the hill here having an elevation of about 560 feet. Here, too, had been in former times an ancient vitrified fort, which has in great measure been obliterated in the course of the erection of the Wallace Monument, the lofty baronial tower, 220 feet in height, which has been built here in commemoration of the great national hero of Scotland. The foundation was laid in 1861, and the tower itself was designed by Mr Rocheid of Glasgow. It comprises three storeys or floors, surmounted by a crown like that of St Giles's Church in Edinburgh; and connected with the basement storey is a range of buildings, including the custodian's house, &c. It both forms a prominent object in the landscape, and commands a fine and far-extended prospect. Nearer at hand to the west it overlooks the plain of Stirling, where Wallace gained his important victory over the English under Surrey and Cressingham in 1297. The centre of battle was at Cornton, in the middle of the plain, a place which is traversed by the Scottish Central railway midway between Stirling and the Bridge of Allan. The wooden bridge over the Forth, which the English army attempted to cross, and sustained thereby such disaster, was situated at Kildean, about a mile above old Stirling Bridge, where some traces of the foundations are still visible.

Causewayhead, at the foot of the Abbey Craig, is two miles from Stirling, and the same distance from the Bridge of Allan, with both of which places there is a communication by tramcar. It derives its name from its being situated at the eastern extremity of the causeway which led to this point across the level ground from Stirling Bridge. It has increased greatly of late years since the opening of the Stirling and Dunfermline railway, and it contains an inn, besides a number of lodging-houses and some handsome villas. The highway from Stirling by the " hillfoots " to Kinross proceeds here over the rising ground to the right, in going from Causewayhead to the Bridge of Allan, and leads by the back of the Wallace Monument in a north-east direction towards Logie Kirk, where it turns due east, and continues almost in a straight line to Dollar. The grounds of Airthrey Castle (Lord Abercromby) adjoin it on the north, and extend in that direction between the Abbey Craig and the Ochils. They are very diversified and picturesque, and are open to the public every Thursday. The estate formerly belonged to Mr Haldane of Glen Eagles, who disposed of it early in the present century to the Abercromby family.

The road from Causewayhead to the Bridge of Allan is well sheltered from the north and east by the Ochils and the projection of the Abbey Craig, whilst it commands a fine view of the plain of Stirling and upper valley of the Forth, with the town and castle of Stirling on the slope or rising ground to the south-west. To the north-west appears the Bridge of Allan, now an imposing-looking town of considerable size, but which sixty years ago comprised little more than a few houses near the bridge over the Allan water, from which it receives its name. In 1796 the population of the Bridge of Allan included only twenty-eight families. It is three miles from Stirling, and has two good hotels (Philp's Royal and the Queen's), besides a large hydropathic establishment, which is extensively patronised.

From its sheltered position, the Bridge of Allan enjoys an extremely mild climate in winter and spring, and is therefore much frequented at these periods of the year. In the summer the climate is, as may be expected, apt to be close and enervating. The great foundation of its reputation was the discovery more than seventy years ago of a mineral spring in an old copper-mine, or rather of its properties, as it had been long known in the locality. The water is saline, anti-scorbutic, and aperient, and is raised from the original reservoir to the "Well-house" on Airthrey Hill, which is thronged, more especially in the morning, with crowds of visitors. Attached to the Well-house is a bowling-green, and also baths and billiard-rooms.

The Bridge of Allan abounds in beautiful walks in all directions in the immediate neighbourhood of the town, and there are also interesting excursions to be made to Dunmyat, to Sheriffmuir, and to Dunblane. The Allan, which comes down from the parish of Blackford, and forming the western boundary of the parish of Logie, joins the Forth near Stirling, discloses in this neighbourhood some charming rural scenes, which in the beginning of this century captivated the heart of Mat Lewis, the romance-writer, and called forth from his pen the well-known song of the "Banks of Allan Water." There is a very pleasant stroll of three miles through the Allan valley to Dunblane, which is well worthy of a visit, both on account of its venerable parish church, the ancient cathedral of the diocese, and also the quaint and primitive appearance of its streets. From Dunblane to the famous Roman camp at Ardoch is a distance of eight miles.

NCARDINE
Gallowridge
Blairhill
Insion
Bordie
Woodhead
Abbey
Blair Castle
Cas.
Torry
CULROSS
Torry Bay
Longannet
pt.
Preston I.
Light Ho.
R I V E R

MAP TO ACCOMPANY
"BETWEEN THE OCHILS
AND THE FORTH."
English Miles
FORTH
FIRTH OF FORTH
Charlestown
Limekilns
INVERKEITHING
North Queensferry
Inverkeithing Bay
St Margarets Hope
Rosyth Cas
Du Craig
Blackhall
Gellet
Pitreavie
Masterton
Middlebank
Balmule
Spencerfield
Donibristle
Donibristle B.
Dalgety Bay
Braefoot Bay
Braefoot Pt
St Colms Abbey
Inchcolm
Incholm
Dowling Pt
Cows & Calves
Inchmickery

cathedral of the diocese, and also the quaint and primitive appearance of its streets. From Dunblane to the famous Roman camp at Ardoch is a distance of eight miles.

INDEX.